RAVE REVIEWS FOR THE STARBRIDGE SERIES!

"This series offers well-told tales with a welcome note of realism about interspecies relationships . . . Recommended."
—Roland Green, *Booklist*

"This is the type of rousing adventure story which Heinlein made so popular a generation ago . . . Excellent."
—Andre Norton

"These novels emphasize relationships and challenge our understanding among intelligent races. The series also raises interesting moral and social questions."
—*Library Journal*

"This is space opera in the best tradition . . . just tremendous; I'm delighted to recommend it."
—Judith Tarr

"A. C. Crispin's publishers continue to shower glowing quotes on the covers of the StarBridge novels—and the novels continue to deserve them . . . So far, the series is batting a thousand!"
—*Dragon*

*Turn the page for more glowing quotes
for the StarBridge novels . . .*

STARBRIDGE
by A. C. Crispin

The first book in the series takes you to a distant asteroid, where StarBridge Academy begins its mission of extraterrestrial contact...

"A great success ... an adventure novel with some thought in it." —Vonda N. McIntyre, author of *Enterprise: The First Adventure*

"Crispin's aliens are a diverse and fascinating lot... She'll be the leading candidate for the title 'the Norton of the 1990s'!" —*Dragon*

★   ★   ★

STARBRIDGE: SILENT DANCES
by A. C. Crispin and Kathleen O'Malley

Deaf since birth, Tesa is the perfect ambassador to the alien Grus—whose sonic cries can shatter human ears...

"Plenty of action and drama ... *Silent Dances* entertains and does so while enlightening its readers about the cultural meaning of deafness." —*Gallaudet Today*

"Four stars ... *Silent Dances* shows the growth of a woman who finds her place in the future worlds." —*OtherRealms*

★   ★   ★

STARBRIDGE: SHADOW WORLD
by A. C. Crispin and Jannean Elliott

A young man learns the meaning of death—from a golden-eyed race of beings with tragically short life spans...

"A highly emotional and surprisingly successful story ... With its touches of humor, and an intriguing set of characters, the action-packed plot races along!" —*Locus*

"A vivid world ..." —*Knoxville News-Sentinel*

STARBRIDGE: SERPENT'S GIFT
by A. C. Crispin with Deborah A. Marshall

A young girl creates a mind-link with the StarBridge computer—and a series of deadly accidents threatens all life on the asteroid . . .

"This entertaining entry combines well-rounded, likeable characters; touches of romance; the strong but subtle theme of mutual cultural respect; and the quick pacing and technological tricks of the trade." —*Booklist*

"Fascinating . . . an excellent addition to any SF collection." —*Kliatt*

★　　★　　★

STARBRIDGE: SILENT SONGS
by A. C. Crispin and Kathleen O'Malley

Amphibious beings from a distant world land on the surface of the planet Trinity, threatening the native creatures—and the StarBridge ambassadors . . .

"Intelligently done . . . a good read and a great adventure with a wild mix of characters." —*Locus*

"Quarrels, jealously, pettiness, great heroic effort, respect for your fellow man, and a touch of love reflect the many layers of this well developed adventure tale . . . hard to put down." —*VOYA*

ANCESTOR'S WORLD

A NOVEL OF StarBridge

A. C. CRISPIN and T. JACKSON KING

ACE BOOKS, NEW YORK

For Paula, who understands

This book is an Ace original edition,
and has never been previously published.

ANCESTOR'S WORLD

An Ace Book / published by arrangement with
the authors

PRINTING HISTORY
Ace edition / July 1996

All rights reserved.
Copyright © 1996 by A.C. Crispin and T. Jackson King.
Cover art by Duane O. Myers.
Maps by T. Jackson King
This book may not be reproduced in whole or in part,
by mimeograph or any other means, without permission.
For information address: The Berkley Publishing Group,
200 Madison Avenue, New York, New York 10016.

The Putnam Berkley World Wide Web site address is
http://www.berkley.com

ISBN: 0-441-00351-6

ACE®
Ace Books are published by The Berkley Publishing Group,
200 Madison Avenue, New York, New York 10016.
ACE and the "A" design are trademarks
belonging to Charter Communications, Inc.

PRINTED IN THE UNITED STATES OF AMERICA

10 9 8 7 6 5 4 3 2 1

Acknowledgments

First, I would like to thank Ann Crispin for the opportunity to participate in a StarBridge adventure. Ann's suggestions and input helped shape this story in vital ways, especially with "her" character Mahree Burroughs. Also, I've loved every StarBridge story and I hope this one is a worthy addition to the grand string of adventures that have been enjoyed by readers young and old.

Information on "mud" chemicals and their function in drilling rigs was provided to me by my brother-in-law, Didier Vincent of Paris, France. He is a real mud engineer, having worked on rigs from Borneo to Nigeria to the North Sea. Another helper with details was Donna Logan, Reference Librarian for the Medford Branch Library.

As a professional archaeologist, I must thank those teachers who taught me well: my M.A. Committee Chairman, Dr. Clement Meighan—he sparked within me a love of ancient cultures and the puzzle-solving that has always been part of archaeology; Dr. Franklin Fenenga, who took me along on my first field dig in the plague-infested foothills of the Sierra Nevadas and who taught me how to play penny-ante poker while quite drunk; Dr. William Lipe, a fine archaeologist whose integrity and professionalism I came to respect and admire in the eight years I worked with him at the Dolores Archaeological Project in Colorado; and the Institute of Archaeology at UCLA, a place where my multidisciplinary interests were accepted and encouraged.

As a writer, I also owe many acknowledgments to authors past and present. Those who influenced me the most include Rudyard Kipling, Robert Heinlein, Poul Anderson, James White, Roger Zelazny, and Andre Norton. I could name more, but will leave it there.

Author's Note

A fine sourcebook on Etsane's homeland is *Ethiopia: A Country Study,* (Washington, DC: Library of Congress, 1993), edited by Thomas P. Ofcansky and LaVerle Berry. An excellent academic text on Dynastic Egypt is *A History Of Ancient Egypt* by Nicolas Grimal (Oxford, England: Blackwell Publishers, 1992.) Many books exist on the opening of Pharaoh Tutankhamun's tomb by Howard Carter, but the one that inspired me was *The Treasures of Tutankhamun* by I. E. S. Edwards (New York: The Viking Press, 1972). Readers interested in African culture and history may turn to *The African Experience* by Roland Oliver (New York: HarperCollins, 1991), a quality book full of wonder and tragedy.

My favorite ethnographic sourcebook for current day peoples is the *Atlas of Man,* edited by John Gaisford (London: Marshall Cavendish Books Limited, 1978). An older but still excellent textbook on basic anthropology is *Human Nature: An Introduction to Cultural Anthropology* by James F. Downs (New York: Glencoe Press, 1973). A fine overview of world archaeology can be found in the *Larousse Encyclopedia of Archaeology* (London: Hamlyn, 1972), edited by Gilbert Charles-Picard. Two fine works on the deciphering of ancient languages are *Breaking The Maya Code* by Michael D. Coe (New York: Thames and Hudson Inc., 1992) and *A Forest Of Kings* by Linda Schele and David Freidel (New York: Quill/ William Morrow, 1990). For those who want to know how rich and complex field archaeology can be, they can do no better than to read *Archaeology: Theories, Methods, and Practice* by Colin Renfrew and Paul Bahn (New York: Thames and Hudson Inc., 1991). Reading any of these works will quickly dispel the notion that "ancient astronauts" founded any of our great civilizations, when in fact our forebears were people of great knowledge, ability, and vision.

The details of earthfill dam construction were observed during the damming of the Dolores River Valley in Colorado, where I learned to respect the hard work, long hours, and professional knowledge exhibited by inspectors, excavators, grout pumpers, construction engineers, and honorable contractors. Not all dams are bad, and McPhee Dam now provides much needed water for drinking and growing crops.

Sadly, slavery still exists. The annual reports of the British group Anti-Slavery International document its presence in twenty-eight nations, including the variant forms of debt bondage, tenant serfdom, forced marriage, and the selling of children into hard labor or prostitution. Since 1839, Anti-Slavery International has educated about this abomination and lobbied for its complete eradication. Readers who wish to learn more or to support this long-established group may contact them at: Anti-Slavery International, The Stableyard, Broomgrove Road, London SW9 9TL, England.

Lastly, I commend to readers the study of anthropology, archaeology, linguistics, and ancient history—it is an adventure that can last a lifetime. You may find that studying the past is a wonderful way to value early accomplishments, while appreciating the present.

—T. Jackson King.

ANCESTOR'S WORLD

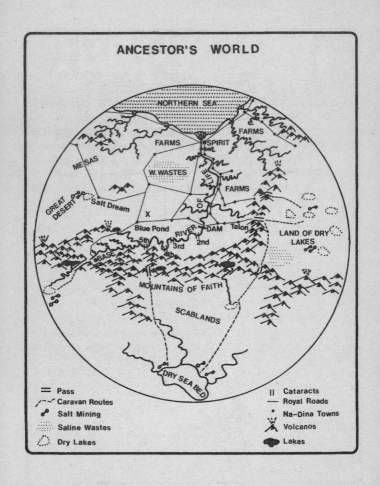

ANCESTOR'S WORLD

NORTHERN SEA

FARMS SPIRIT FARMS

MESAS

W. WASTES

FARMS

GREAT DESERT

Salt Dream

X

Blue Pond RIVER DAM Talon

5th 3rd 2nd

4th

BASE

LAND OF DRY LAKES

MOUNTAINS OF FAITH

SCABLANDS

DRY SEA BED

⚌ Pass	‖ Cataracts
–·– Caravan Routes	— Royal Roads
Salt Mining	• Na-Dina Towns
Saline Wastes	Volcanos
Dry Lakes	Lakes

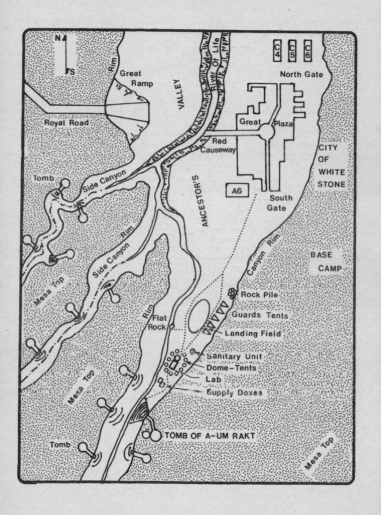

CHAPTER I

◆

The Gleam of Gold

Sweating nervously, Doctor Gordon Mitchell placed his chisel against the interstice of the tomb wall, wedging it carefully into the ancient mortar. He tapped once . . . twice. Then, satisfied that it was placed correctly, he drew back his arm and struck a ringing blow with his mallet.

Hard exercise in the still, hot air made him gasp for breath as he hammered, each blow carefully gauged. A wrong move might prove disastrous. This was a Royal Tomb of the First Dynasty of the Na-Dina aliens, and whatever secrets lay behind this wall had lain there for six thousand years. Was it possible the tomb was intact? He'd have that answer within the next few minutes. . . .

For six millennia an unbroken dynasty of Na-Dina Kings and Queens had ruled this planet they called *Halish meg a-tum*—Ancestor's World. The blue-scaled, reptilian aliens, who balanced upright on their tails like kangaroos, worshipped their ancestors as devoutly as they did their gods.

Ancestor's World perched dangerously on the edge of Sorrow Sector, and had been unknown to the Cooperative League of Systems until First Contact was made by the human-owned Nordlund Combine. When the reigning government made plans with Nordlund to industrialize Ancestor's

World as rapidly as possible, despite the loss of their most ancient ruins, the Traditionalist faction of the Na-Dina had sent out a cry for help to the CLS. The Traditionalist plea had been barely tolerated by the Modernist faction, who believed that rapid industrialization was their only route to respect among the star-spanning Known Worlds. There were fifteen CLS-member homeworlds, now, including Earth and the Simiu homeworld, Hurrreeah. Only homeworlds—as opposed to colonized planets—counted as "Known" Worlds, though CLS membership was extended to an entire species.

Gordon continued to hammer, ignoring the loud, excited breathing of his Simiu assistant, Khuharkk', who crouched four-footed beside him. Beside the alien an autocam hovered, silently recording, controlled by a gold sensor beneath the young Simiu's eye.

Khuharkk' was welcome company this far into the dusty blackness. They had excavated their way into a long tunnel that led in from the tomb's cliffside entrance. According to the paintings that lined the tunnel, this wall separated them from the burial chamber of A-Um Rakt, founding Deity-King of the Na-Dina dynasties. With the care of a diamond cutter, Gordon moved the chisel sideways along the line of white cement, extending his opening cut into the wall of stone blocks.

"Professor?" growled Khuharkk' in heavily accented English, edging closer as he spoke.

Gordon paused in mid-swing and sighed as the chisel head was suddenly eclipsed by a furred shadow. "Yes?"

"Should I fetch the autosifters?"

Mitchell shook his head. "This is delicate work. Best done by hand. And, Khuharkk' . . . you're blocking the light."

The young Simiu scuttled sideways with an embarrassed snort, and the baboonlike shadow that had blocked Gordon's view shifted, leaving the light cast by the hovering light-globe unobstructed.

"Thank you," Gordon said, shortly. "And about those autosifters . . . didn't Greyshine teach you the limitations of automatic diggers? Now stay quiet, and watch. You'll learn something."

"Yes, Professor," the Simiu muttered, sounding distressed.

Gordon experienced a flare of guilt. He hadn't always been this short-tempered. But much of his patience and good humor had disappeared after his divorce, after his wife, Jayna, had remarried the moment the ink was dry . . . after his daughters, Moira and Casey, had grown distant and gone off into space with their mother. His temper had worsened when he'd lost the academic roll of the dice and become a has-been to his professional colleagues. Just another washed-up field archaeologist . . .

"No!" he yelled, and slammed the mallet against the chisel. White dust flew as the line of cement cracked. The stone blocks loosened.

Nearly there . . . I'll show them. . . .

Tap tap. Tap tap again. Gordon paused, mallet poised, as the stone floor beneath his knees shivered like a giant animal ridding itself of a stinging insect.

Just another tremor . . . It had been nerve-wracking, at first, adjusting to the incessant seismic activity on this planet. Some days there were as many as thirty or forty discernible quakes, others "only" four or five. Gordon had had so much trouble sleeping during his first weeks here that he'd had to drink himself into a stupor to get any rest.

When the tremor stopped, he worked the chisel along a rectangular path, deftly cracking the cement. Soon he'd loosened a block of stone as wide as his shoulders. He could now push it inward, into the chamber, into a place where new air had not penetrated for millennia.

Gordon liked the Na-Dina, and admired their steadfast devotion to the past and their dead, though he found their bureaucracy as frustrating as he did any other. Na-Dina stood about two meters in height, and birthed their young in eggs. Their blue skin was adorned with painted ideoglyph designs denoting their parentage, social caste, and unbroken ancestral lineage. The aliens' devotion to their long-dead ancestors had drawn him here when the Traditionalists on the Council of Elders had petitioned the CLS for an archaeologist to help them preserve their past.

Gordon gestured to his assistant. "Anchor rope."

"Here, Professor." Khuharkk' handed him a rope with a suction device at one end. The Simiu hesitated, then said slowly, "Should I summon Beloran? He did say that if we found anything we were to call him immediately."

Mitchell scowled. "No, dammit, Beloran would come up with a dozen Na-Dina regulations and rites to follow. He wouldn't let us look inside for a week! He could be here if he wanted to be, but I'm not stopping work to go find him."

Carefully, Mitchell pressed the suction device against the brown block. Then he pushed at the stone, belaying its movement with the rope. It slid inward, then dropped down.

Musty air puffed against Gordon's face, its scent odorless. He gasped, heart slamming, nearly drunk on the old excitement. What lay within? In seconds, he would know. In moments, he could begin to solve the puzzle, bring to life a dead culture so that the past would live again.

"The torch," he said tightly. "Let's see what's inside."

"Here, Doctor Mitchell."

"Thanks."

Pressing his thumb against the torch's control pad, Gordon shone a beam of yellow light through the hole in the tomb wall and peered inside.

"Professor?"

Gordon couldn't believe his eyes. His skin chilled, and the hairs on his arms raised up. "Oh, my God!"

The human caught a whiff of the alien's musky, not unpleasant odor as the alien crowded closer. "What? What do you see?"

Gordon wanted to laugh ecstatically, but he controlled himself, because he had a feeling that if he didn't, he might weep instead. "Wonderful things," he said, thinking of another archaeologist long ago back on his home world. "Wonderful things, Khuharkk'."

Gold gleamed brightly inside the tomb. The sunlike sheen of *gold* lay everywhere. It covered the chamber's circular wall, where gold foil had been applied to the carved stone glyphs of First Dynasty Na-Dina, an undeciphered ideoglyph language. It shone from the ceiling, where blue paint and golden circles pictured the heavens above Ancestor's World. It sparkled on the floor, where funerary objects lay scattered, as if the honored attendants who'd served the First King had stepped away only for a moment. But what gleamed most brightly, most brilliantly, lay in the middle of the dark-shadowed chamber.

The sarcophagus of the King.

Shaped like the Royal Barge that even today sailed the muddy brown waters of the River of Life, the great river beside which Na-Dina civilization had grown up, the sarcophagus of King A-Um Rakt had been fashioned from *gold*. And not gold foil, either. *It must weigh hundreds of pounds,* Gordon thought. He mentally converted that to kilos, then stubbornly thought again of pounds, because he'd been born and raised in the Smoky Mountains of east Tennessee, where many humans still clung to old ways.

"By God, *now* they'll respect me," he growled in a voice almost as guttural and harsh as his assistant's. "I— *we* are going to be famous, Khuharkk'! As famous as Schliemann, Emerson, Alva, and Finder-of-Knowledge of the Heeyoon."

"May I see, Professor?" Khuharkk' was fairly quivering with eagerness.

Gordon smiled to himself, recalling the excitement of his own first dig, twenty-five years ago. He looked over his shoulder and into the violet eyes of his Simiu assistant. "Sure. Come. Come look at eternity!" He waved the alien youth forward.

What Khuharkk' saw made his neckfur stand on end, and his tufted tail rise up. Gordon also noticed how the Simiu's lips pulled back, revealing long, deadly canines. As the youth peered into the hole, his dark orange and red streaked bodyfur fluffed out even more, making him look much larger than he was. Finally, his assistant pulled back and turned to face him.

Khuharkk's eyes shone. "It . . . it's . . . oh, Professor! Wonderful! It's wonderful!"

"It sure the hell is," Mitchell agreed, grinning broadly. "Hey, Khuharkk', still think you want to be *just* an Interrelator for the CLS? You could go full time as an archaeologist after this dig!"

The Simiu sighed. "Maybe I will. That's what Professor Greyshine wants me to do."

Khuharkk' moved forward again, this time poking his muzzled face all the way through the hole, sneezing a little as the influx of fresh air into the ancient chamber brought with it some of the dust that hung in the tunnel. The alien's shoulders stiffened. "Professor? Move the torch to the right!"

Gordon did as requested, moving up closer to Khuharkk'. "What's the matter? Don't tell me it's been looted?"

"No!" Khuharkk' said, sounding incredulous. "Something else. Something I . . . I don't believe it! Look down . . . low on the floor, at the foot of the stone bier on which rests the sarcophagus." The Simiu backed out of the way.

Squeezing his eyes shut against the fall of mortar dust, Mitchell poked his head through the hole in the wall, squirmed to bring the hand torch inside, and swept its yellow beam downward. The better angle revealed something he hadn't seen when first he'd peered into the chamber. Something else besides gold gleamed inside, but it shone vibrant purple.

Shining like dark amethysts were an incised, jewel-studded sphere; a narrow, fluted drinking vessel; and a small, boxlike shrine. All three items lay on the floor at the foot of King A-Um Rakt's sarcophagus. They shone so brightly because they were made of purple metal, and because they did not belong here.

Dear God, they're Mizari artifacts!

Specifically, a Constellation Globe, a Sacred *Shrizzs* and a Star-Shrine lay at the foot of the alien being who, six thousand years ago, had begun the march of civilization for the Na-Dina people. But these objects had been made by reptilian, limbless Mizari, the founders of the Cooperative

League of Systems. The CLS was the alien-run league that humanity had received full membership in nearly three years ago.

The Lost Colony! How else could these things have been here for six thousand years?

Long ago, a group of ancient Mizari had left their homeworld, turned their starships toward the starry depths, and departed for worlds unknown to their current descendants. A year or so ago, the archaeological world had experienced a brief flurry when the eminent Heeyoon archaeologist Greyshine had reported a Star Shrine discovered at the Lamont Cliffs, near StarBridge Academy.

But that "find" had turned out to be a hoax, though it had, in its turn, led to a landmark discovery when the Ancient Dais was uncovered in an adjoining tunnel deep within the body of the little asteroid. Studies of what culture had created that artifact were still ongoing.

But *this* Star Shrine could not possibly have been planted. This tomb had lain undiscovered since it had been sealed millennia ago. Mitchell felt his head swim from more than the ancient air.

"They're Mizari, correct? Could they possibly be authentic?" growled Khuharkk' in awed tones.

"Hang on a second," Gordon muttered, scanning the remainder of the round-walled chamber. Pottery bowls, bronze vessels, sheaf-scrolls and daily life objects also lay on the floor. Finally, he forced himself to pull back and relinquish the sight.

When he faced Khuharkk', the Simiu's violet eyes shone as brightly as the artifacts. Gordon nodded. "Yes, Khuharkk'. From what I can tell without testing them, they're genuine Mizari relics. Must be from the Lost Colony. No other Mizari of that time traveled so far away from the Known Worlds. You know what this means, don't you?"

Khuharkk' fingered the pockets of his vest-jacket, hung about with small implements of their trade. "This means that the Mizari will support us in getting increased funding, right?"

Gordon nodded. "This is the find of the century, lad.

The Mizari Archaeological Society is going to shit bricks over this.''

Khuharkk's brow furrowed. "Shit . . . bricks?" he repeated slowly. "An idiom, sir?''

"Sorry, son.'' Mitchell found himself grinning wildly. "I meant that they're going to be very, very, VERY excited and really eager to help us out!''

He leaned back against the tunnel's cool stone wall, feeling like Heinrich Schliemann had when he unearthed the golden treasures of Mycenae. "Now we can get some large-scale *help*.''

"We certainly need it,'' Khuharkk' said somberly, staring at the hole in the wall.

"Damn right,'' Gordon said bitterly, recalling again their impossible task. This Royal Tomb, other side canyon tombs, the nearby City of White Stone, and thousands of other Na-Dina ruins would be flooded when the Nordlund Combine engineers finished building their dam. Bigger than Earth's Aswan High Dam, the giant rampart would block the River of Life, create a lake three hundred forty miles long by fifty miles wide, and inundate the upriver canyons.

The Modernist faction of the Na-Dina considered the loss of their ancient heritage a fair trade for the hydroelectric energy that would power new factories, mills, and cities. The Traditionalist faction had deplored this, but they weren't in power. All they'd been able to do was send out a request for an archaeologist to help. Gordon Mitchell had responded with a small field crew of two assistants and a pile of thirdhand survey and excavation equipment.

When he'd first reached Ancestor's World seven weeks ago, he'd hired twenty local laborers and set to work in Ancestor's Valley, where a score of dynasties had buried their Kings and Queens in tunnel-tombs cut into the canyon walls. It was a job to challenge even the resources of a great university—and all Gordon had was Khuharkk' and Sumiko Nobunaga, their Japanese Lab Chief. Plus the meddling claws of Beloran, the Na-Dina Liaison whose job it was to keep an eye on Gordon, his dig, and his discoveries.

Khuharkk' looked down the tunnel toward the distant

entrance, then back to Gordon, his expression worried. "Will we have enough *time* to dig everything before it's all flooded?"

"Time?" Gordon sighed and sifted ancient brown dust through his fingers. "No. Not to dig *everything*. But this discovery is bound to buy us extra time. We'll be able to properly excavate this chamber, and most likely the other tombs in the side canyons. With luck, we'll get through most of the City of White Stone."

"We'll need a specialist to analyze these Mizari relics."

"You're right. We're going to need a *lot* of specialists, in almost every field. But this"—he waved a callused, scarred hand at the opening in the tomb wall—"will bring them. Archaeologists can't resist the lure of an unplundered tomb."

As he finished speaking, he saw Khuharkk's ears prick up; then the sound of a distant footfall reached him, too.

Gordon gestured at the autocam, and the Simiu obediently turned it off with a wave of his hand.

"We'll also need time to negotiate the political minefields on this world," Mitchell said under his breath. "Nordlund won't take kindly to delays. This discovery is going to make Project Engineer Mohapatra very unhappy." He grinned unpleasantly. "I just wish I could see his face when he hears."

His display of teeth made Khuharkk's mane ruffle up; then the Simiu relaxed. "Doctor Mitchell, I just had an idea. Why don't I call Professor Greyshine at StarBridge? That way, even if Beloran ties us up in bureaucratic tangles, we'd still have the word out in the proper circles. Help would be standing by."

"Good idea." Gordon listened closely as the scrabbling footfall neared the dogleg angle in the tunnel, after which they'd be in sight of their visitor. They had only a few moments of privacy left. "Go ahead. Record a message and have Bill fly into Spirit and use the FTL transmitter at his embassy."

"I'm sure he'd be delighted to do it," Khuharkk' said. "He's been almost as interested in this dig as we are."

Bill Waterston was the CLS Interrelator assigned to Ancestor's World. Bill and Gordon had come in on the same ship together, and both of them had struggled ever since to deal with the Nordlund Combine, whose Project Engineer had arrived ahead of any CLS official. Gordon liked the earnest young man. Bill had been a big help in cutting through Na-Dina bureaucracy in the capital city of Spirit, and, when his schedule had permitted, he'd been quick to grab a spade and help out with the excavation.

Now the young Interrelator would have to deal with the cultural, historical, and political complications this discovery of alien artifacts was bound to generate for the intensely private, almost reclusive Na-Dina.

Khuharkk' nodded, a gesture he'd picked up from humans, as the footsteps rapidly approached. As Gordon had suspected, the newcomer was Beloran.

The Na-Dina stopped a few meters from them. Another tremor quivered the ground beneath him, and he steadied himself on his tail. The beam of the light-globe he was carrying swung a little, then steadied as the tremor eased away. Water sloshed in the canteen slung over his shoulder.

Blinking deep black eyes, Beloran looked beyond them at the holed-through tomb wall, then glared at Gordon. "You broke through," he said in sibilant High Na-Dina. Gordon heard the translation via his voder earcuff. "Why did you not call me? I should have been present."

Gordon stood up, brushed dust off his coveralls, and shrugged. "I tried to," he lied. "The com signal must have been blocked by the rock." Running his tongue over cracked lips, he stretched out a hand. "Hey, thanks for bringing water."

"Blocked?" Absently, the Na-Dina handed him the canteen, then squatted down to peer into the hole. The symbols painted on his left shoulder gleamed in the light from the globe.

The colorful glyphs denoted personal name, trade, parental status, job title and family clan, including whether the alien was related to the Royal House. Beloran wasn't. Maybe that's why he'd ended up in commerce, as a Merchant. Until recently, earning one's living by buying and selling was considered demeaning as a profession. But the First Contact had changed all that.

The shock of learning that aliens existed, and the necessity of finding a place for the Na-Dina people in a strange new universe, coupled with the practical necessity of finding goods to trade, had elevated the Merchant profession almost to the status of nobility.

Beloran let out a long hiss of mingled wonder and dismay. "It's *intact*!" he exclaimed a moment later. "The tomb of A-Um Rakt is intact!" On the alien's back, overlapping folds of scaly flesh quivered like jowls. His long tail thumped the dusty tunnel floor.

"Yes, it is," Khuharkk' said. "We are very fortunate!"

"Treasure . . ." Beloran added, as if he hadn't heard the Simiu. The Liaison sighed, sounding almost regretful. "This will delay the rising of the dam, will it not?"

"Possibly," Gordon said. Then he added, in a burst of honesty, "Probably. But, Beloran—look! That's your heritage, and it's wonderful! And also . . . there are *Mizari* artifacts there, at the foot of the sarcophagus. Your people may well have been the last species to have contact with the Lost Colony! That's a momentous discovery!"

"Mizari?" Beloran jerked his head out of the hole so fast that he banged it on the stone. The Liaison glared at them, obviously furious, his tail stiff with anger. "Are you saying that infidel outworlders were responsible for A-Um Rakt's glorious reign?"

"No!" Gordon protested. "Of course not! I'm saying that your God-King was so great that even aliens from another world wanted to pay homage to him, and left grave-gifts!"

"Ahhhh . . . Yesss . . . I can see that," Beloran said quietly, after a moment. "When you explain it that way, it makes sense."

The Na-Dina's tail relaxed visibly. "But, Doctor Mitchell, my job is to look out for the welfare of my people, and it is difficult to see how this discovery, marvelous as it is, will make up for the delay in the building of the dam that will bring us so many benefits." The Liaison straightened back up. He did not look Gordon straight in the eye, but that was not the Na-Dina way, so the archaeologist was not surprised. "However, I suppose congratulations are in order, Doctor Mitchell."

"Thank you, Beloran," Gordon said, matching the other's grave mien.

"Since you have already gone ahead and opened the wall, without my presence, I suppose the saying of the sacred words can be delayed a bit longer," Beloran said, his hissing voice punctuated with glottal clicks.

"Do your legends or records contain anything about the visit from the Mizari six thousand years ago?" Gordon asked eagerly. The Na-Dina were very protective of their records, and no outworlder had ever seen them.

The alien folded his blue-scaled forearms, mantislike, and bobbed his head to indicate a negative answer. "No. We have been unable to read the records from the time of A-Um Rakt. No one has been able to translate them. They are very different from both our modern tongue, and from Old High Na-Dina."

"Our new crew will almost certainly include an iconographer," Khuharkk' said eagerly. "Perhaps he or she will able to translate them, and that will be an even more momentous discovery than this tomb! Professor Greyshine always taught us that the value of golden treasure is finite, but the value of *knowledge* is incalculable."

"Indeed," Beloran said. His sharp white teeth gleamed in the light. "This"—he waved at the tomb wall—"must be reported to my superiors. I will depart at once for Spirit on my ground skimmer. The Ministry of Dynastic Affairs will be . . . most interested in what you have found. We will need time to consider what must be done."

Gordon glanced sideways at Khuharkk', and caught the Simiu youth's tiny assenting nod. They'd been right in their assessment of the Liaison's reaction to their discovery. Beloran was planning to tie them up in red tape. If the Liaison had his way, their progress in investigating the tomb would be slowed to a crawl.

Ostentatiously, Gordon unstoppered the canteen and gulped the cool water. "Much better," he said, wiping his mouth. "Here, Khuharkk', you'd better have some, too." He bent down to hand it to Khuharkk', keeping his body between the Simiu and the Na-Dina. "Find Bill," he whispered. "Tell him to get moving and contact Greyshine and the CLS."

The Simiu took the canteen, and took a long drink himself. As he handed it back to his boss, the youth nodded fractionally.

"Doctor Mitchell," Khuharkk' spoke up a moment later, "you were just about to tell me what equipment you wanted me to fetch. Should I bring the magnetometer and the portable sifter?"

Gordon nodded. "Yes, bring the banjo magnetometer, but we won't need the sifter for this work. Also bring the laser theodolite, and another autocam. While you're gone, I'll start photographing and recording the burial associations."

"Yes, Doctor Mitchell," Khuharkk' said, dropping from his squatting position to all fours—the preferred Simiu mode of fast locomotion. "I'll be back as soon as I can."

Gordon waved at his assistant, and the youth sprinted away. Golden dust hovered in the still air.

"I, too, must go," Beloran said. "If I leave now, perhaps I can reach Spirit before evening devotionals."

Gordon nodded. "Don't worry, Liaison, I have a lot of recording and mapping to do via remote-control autocams. If you return tomorrow, you can conduct your ceremonial rites then. I promise you that until you do, we will touch nothing in the tomb."

"Very well . . ." Beloran said grudgingly. "Though the word of an infidel will carry little weight, I am afraid, with my superiors. However, I will vouch for your honesty, Doctor Mitchell."

"Uh . . . thanks," Gordon said, feeling a pang when he remembered how he'd lied. But he truly didn't intend to touch anything—the work of recording everything in the chamber would take at least a couple of days. Certainly that would be plenty of time for Beloran to say his sacred words and conduct his religious rites.

Moments later, Mitchell was alone with his find. He dropped back to his knees and once again played the light over the inside of the chamber. For the first time, he looked closely at the wall glyphs and illustrations that covered the walls of the chamber.

This was a find greater than Carter's discovery of Tutankhamun's tomb. Greater than Alva's excavation of the Moche Royal Tombs of Sipan, in Peru. Greater even than Greyshine's discovery of the Ancient Dais. This discovery concerned the Mizari, powerful aliens who still lived, not peoples dead for half a million years.

I'm looking at my redemption, Gordon thought, feeling another fierce surge of triumph. It was an even headier draught than the Kentucky bourbon he had waiting for him in his tent. *Now, by God, they'll respect me. . . .*

"Bill!" Khuharkk' called, his voice a hoarse growl in the dry, baking air outside the archaeologist's camp. "Bill! I need to talk to you!"

Bill Waterston rose from a squatting position beside one of the Na-Dina diggers who'd been meticulously washing and sorting potsherds, and waved. He was a tall, lanky human, and from Khuharkk's point of view as homely as the rest of his species. He had a hairless white face, a squashed-in nose, ears that did not move, and a lean frame that lacked the muscles for tearing apart one's enemies in the Arena of Honor.

The Interrelator smiled as Khuharkk' loped up to him, careful to politely half cover his exposed teeth with one hand. "Hey, Khuharkk'! Where've you been? What's all the rush?"

The Simiu beckoned urgently, and the human moved over to join him, out of earshot of the workers. "Bill," Khuharkk' said, glancing around nervously, "we opened the tomb just now. It was intact!" Khuharkk' clasped both long arms across his chest, hugging himself with excitement. It was all he could do not to caper around like a child.

"Damn! Gordon didn't wait for me?" Bill scowled, his freckled features creasing, and shook his head. "He was supposed to wait for me and Beloran!"

"I know," Khuharkk' said, feeling torn between loyalty to a fellow StarBridge student and to his boss. "But, Bill, it's better that he *didn't* wait. You'll never guess what we found!"

Waterston's momentary irritation vanished in a wave of excitement. His green eyes gleamed. "Gold? Jewels? A mummy?"

Khuharkk' nodded. "All of that! But Bill . . . that's only a small part. There were Mizari artifacts there, at the foot of the sarcophagus! They've been there, undisturbed, for *six thousand years*. Think of what this means!"

Waterston's eyes widened incredulously. "Oh, my God . . . you mean the Lost Colony? That's the only thing it could be!"

Khuharkk' yipped a wordless assent.

Bill put a hand to his head. "Wow," he muttered. "I feel like I've had too much sun. What a discovery! Gordon must be beside himself!"

"Professor Mitchell says that now we'll be able to get in a decent team to excavate," Khuharkk' said, eying the arid landscape around them, bleak and formidable. "But only if we can get the word out to Professor Greyshine at StarBridge so he can help us find good people. I've recorded a message, Bill. Will you take it to Spirit and send it out for us, please?"

Khuharkk' held up the tiny data cassette. Waterston stared at him for a long moment, then frowned. "Khuharkk', my friend, I smell a rat. Why the secrecy?"

Deception never came easily to Simiu. The heavy crest of hair that ran up Khuharkk's neck and ended in a topknot between his ears drooped sadly. The youth sighed gustily. "Bill, you know as well as I do that if we don't get the word out quickly, before Beloran can get back to Spirit, the Traditionalists and the Modernists will spend weeks or months arguing about this discovery in their councils. They may forbid us to send a message at all!''

''Ohhhhhh . . .'' Bill shook his head ruefully. ''You're right, of course. But sending the message out without permission isn't exactly . . . ethical, my friend.''

Khuharkk' sat down on his haunches, lion-fashion, and ran a hand over his muzzle with its formidable fighting canines. ''The word will get out eventually; you know that. Nordlund will send the message if we pay them to do it. I could pilot a ship to Spirit and do it myself. But . . . so far . . . nobody has forbidden sending it, correct?''

''Yet,'' Bill added honestly. He hesitated, obviously thinking it over. ''Well, okay,'' he said finally. ''If I hustle, it'll be a done deed before Beloran is halfway to Spirit. Give it here.''

He held out his hand, and, solemnly, Khuharkk' dropped the tiny cassette into his callused palm. ''Thank you, Bill. I would prefer that the com operators at Nordlund not know about this yet.''

Waterston made a face at the mention of the giant mining combine. He beckoned to his friend, and Khuharkk' fell into step beside him as they headed for the landing field. ''No shit,'' he said sourly, carefully stowing the tiny message cassette in the front pocket of his coverall. ''Those Nordlund types are a real pain. I had a helluva go-round with the PE just yesterday.''

''You argued with Project Engineer Mohapatra?''

''I sure did,'' Bill said. ''Talk about smelling a rat, my friend . . . it stinks to high heaven up there.''

''They are doing something illegal?''

Bill hesitated. ''I've been doing a little quiet investigating, Khuharkk', and I found something that may mean trouble. Big trouble. When I get back from Spirit this evening, I'll tell you all about it, because I'd like your opinion on what, if anything, I should do.''

Khuharkk' nodded. ''Very well, Bill. I will be pleased to help. I met Project Engineer Mohapatra once . . . and he struck me as somewhat lacking in honor.''

''He's a sleazy devil, but a smart one,'' Bill admitted.

"He never misses a trick, and he knows everything that's going on. I wonder how he manages?"

"His pilots are in and out of camp almost every day with the jumpjet," Khuharkk' pointed out. "Since they offered to loan us one of theirs, and the dig could not afford one, we could not say no."

"Yeah. 'Beggars can't be choosers' is the human expression," Bill said.

Khuharkk' mentally translated the colloquialism into his own tongue, then filed it away in his mind.

Waterston smiled suddenly. Khuharkk', who'd had years of experience at reading human expressions, knew that smile had little to do with good feelings and a great deal to do with pure malicious joy. "Hey, I just thought . . . Mohapatra and his goons are going to shit when they find out about Gordon's find. This is bound to interfere with their dam-building schedule . . . and it couldn't happen to a nicer bunch."

"Doctor Mitchell and I already thought of that," Khuharkk' agreed. "That is another reason to keep the news from Nordlund as long as possible."

Bill squinted into the sun, shading his eyes. "Is the jumpjet there now? I want to get away from here before I run into Beloran. If he tells me not to send out any FTL announcement of this discovery, then I have to abide by his wishes." He frowned. "It's like a balancing act on a high wire, trying to act as an Interrelator on a world with two parties so diametrically opposed to each other as the Traditionalists and the Modernists."

"There's the jumpjet. It's just landing," Khuharkk' replied, shading his own eyes, then pointing at the landing field that lay on the far side of Base Camp. The long tube and wide wings of the jumpjet gleamed brightly in the late afternoon sunlight as it returned from the city carrying a load of artifacts and some very tired Na-Dina laborers. "It's bringing in the City of White Stone diggers," the Simiu added, identifying the figures coming down the ramp.

"Then I'd better get a move on," Bill said. Breaking

into a jog, he flapped a hand back at his friend. ''See you later, Khuharkk'!''

The Simiu waved good-bye. Although his people had never invented the concept of formal or informal farewells, Khuharkk', like any good StarBridge student, had learned to adapt to alien customs.

Pausing to sniff thirstily at the creek's water scent, Khuharkk' wished their communications weren't so poor. The government of Ancestor's World hadn't allowed the newcomers to install communications satellites in orbit. Nordlund had one FTL relay, and Bill's office in Spirit had another. Other than that, Ancestor's World was isolated from contact with the CLS.

The Simiu went down to the stream, a tiny tributary of the massive River of Life. Lowering his six-fingered hands into the cool water, he brought them up to his muzzle, sipped, and enjoyed the sheer pleasure of feeling the liquid sliding down his throat. Hurrreeah, the Simiu homeworld, was also a hot planet, but there, it was humid. Since coming to Ancestor's World, Khuharkk' had learned the real meaning of thirst.

He'd learned much in the past six weeks. This was an old, old world, with an ancient culture that did not adjust well to sudden disruptions. To avoid social turmoil, the Council of Elders had issued their decree: only the Nordlund construction crews would be allowed in, along with a small team of archaeologists and—this last grudgingly—a CLS Interrelator to assist with Na-Dina/alien interactions.

Swallowing one last cool mouthful, Khuharkk' turned back toward the camp. Honor demanded that he hurry, now that his mission to contact Bill was completed. Mentally listing the items he needed, he dropped to all fours and trotted up the bank.

Of course he was looking forward to helping Doctor Mitchell excavate the tomb—it was the chance of a lifetime. But, in another way, the whole idea made Khuharkk' uneasy. The Simiu had no concept of an afterlife, and the Na-Dina obsession with their dead ancestors and their ancient God-Kings and Queens was . . . unsettling.

Could the dead live on?

The Na-Dina certainly thought so. Many humans also believed in an afterlife. Who was right?

Khuharkk' didn't know. Here on Ancestor's World, belief in the afterlife, in the continuing existence of the Revered Ancestors, was the pivot on which the entire Na-Dina culture balanced.

In order to stay here and interact with the Na-Dina, he had to learn to respect and understand their beliefs. Could he? The Simiu did not adjust easily to other customs, other beliefs. . . .

Khuharkk' resolutely put disquieting philosophical questions out of his mind, and broke into a lope.

The ground quivered beneath his flying feet.

Bill Waterston slid into the pilot's seat of the jumpjet, checked the control panel instruments, and keyed on the external speaker.

"Clear away, everyone!" he announced to the nearby Na-Dina laborers. "Blast off in three minutes."

The outside pickups relayed grumbling as the laborers began moving out of range. They carried sacks of artifacts, environmental samples, survey and digging tools, and other archaeological arcana. Bill could see them moving past the viewport, carrying their sacks in talon-tipped, four-fingered hands. On the control panel, the auto-timer blinked its silent countdown.

Wonder how long ago Beloran left? Bill thought. The Na-Dina Liaison had his own private land skimmer, which had been furnished to him by the Nordlund Combine.

Bill patted his breast pocket, where Khuharkk's message resided. In a way, he felt a little guilty for agreeing to transmit it, when Beloran and some of the Modernists probably would object—on the other hand, the Traditionalist faction would applaud him for helping Mitchell to save their ancient heritage.

What would Mahree do? he wondered, thinking of the woman who was called "the first Interrelator." He'd been lucky enough to work with her as a mentor on his first assignment, and he was proud that she'd recommended him for this posting. Mahree Burroughs was a legend in the field of interstellar relations.

Even Mahree might find the Na-Dina a challenge, he decided, eyes on his gauges. *They hold out one hand in friendship, while despising those they meet as "infidels." They're rattled to discover they're not alone in the universe, and they wish they could be left alone, yet now they're rushing to embrace an alien technology far in advance of their own. A bundle of contradictions, that's the Na-Dina.*

The royal politics of Na-Dina society would have been a match for those of Imperial China during the Ming Dynasty, Bill thought grimly.

The jets blasted.

The jumpjet lifted straight up into the air, rising above the high walls of the canyon that sheltered Base Camp. It rose higher still, then angled the jet nozzles rearward and sped off to the northeast. Bill flew across the open desert, rather than along the twisting course of the River of Life. Its waters would eventually roll by the ancient metropolis of Spirit, capital city of the Na-Dina, in about fifteen hundred kilometers. This shortcut was indeed shorter—but boring. Below him the backcountry of Ancestor's World was a desolate vista of dry washes, sandstone mesas, and a few isolated settlements.

Well, there was a solution to his boredom problem. Bill turned on the jet's tail camera and aimed it southward, then watched the screen.

The Mountains of Faith stretched like a gray wall across the entire southern horizon. They were a white-capped rampart of raw granite rock, flaming volcanoes, and black thunderstorms that swept down over the Scablands of the backcountry. With the storms came lightning—incredible lightning. Bright yellow streaks of flame shot from heaven to earth, booming in one's ears like the kettle drum of doom. When he'd first come to Spirit, the lightning storms had scared him.

Then he'd felt his first earthquake.

Ancestor's World pursued an elliptical orbit around its older yellow star, an orbit that brought with it major climate shifts, dangerous electrical storms, and terrible earthquakes whenever the single moon pulled just right on the planet's tectonic plates. It got even worse when the sun and moon lined up. Then the entire planet vibrated. But the ancient Na-Dina people had persevered through their cycles of earthquakes, floods, death, and rebirth. Century after century, they rebuilt their cities of stone. They raised up monolithic temples dedicated to their Revered Ancestors. And they pursued a life of religious devotion mixed with fatalistic acceptance of their dangerous environment. Bill had to respect them.

The Interrelator swung the camera to the east, where a silver ribbon flowed along like an overfed snake. At least the seasonal flooding by the River of Life came just once a year, in the spring. But when it didn't flood, suffocating ash spewed out from volcanoes in the Mountains of Faith. And at camp, each night was stone cold once the sun went down. Not what you'd call paradise.

Bill shut off the camera and concentrated on his flying. He did hope the Na-Dina wouldn't sacrifice *all* their ancient heritage in the rush to modernize a society already well into its own Industrial Revolution. Hindsight, as they said, was twenty-twenty, and nothing could change the past. Ten months ago a Sorrow Sector privateer *had* landed, made an unauthorized First Contact, and traded for native arts, jewels, and gold nuggets. They'd left behind an FTL communicator, which the Na-Dina used to put out a call to anyone listening, inviting them to come and trade. The call had been answered by a geological survey team from the Nordlund Combine, a construction consortium with ties to Sorrow Sector.

The Na-Dina were within their rights to invite Nordlund to land and set up trade agreements—which Bill suspected had been the Combine's objective all along. The CLS had been left holding the bag of a botched First Contact, trying to help an alien people still in shock over learning that other peoples existed, while the Modernist faction pushed for rapid industrial development as the means of gaining independence from the CLS aliens.

Behind him, something scraped.

Bill turned in his pilot's seat and looked back at the interior of the jumpjet. *What was that?* The jet had been empty when he'd entered. The long tube of the jet had a simple layout: the pilot's cabin up front, the passenger cabin in the middle, and the sanitary unit at the far end. Below the central aisleway lay the cargo holds, but they had no access to the pressurized part of the jet.

Frowning, he touched on the autopilot, then released his seat straps and stood up. It was probably a sandrat that had sneaked aboard when the jet landed near the City of White Stone to pick up the laborers. Sandrats posed no threat to people, but they loved to gnaw on cables and wires.

The skittering scrape sounded again.

Bill stepped up to the bulkhead doorway and peered into the passenger area. A row of benches lined each side of the metal tube. At the far end, the sanitary unit door stood open, swinging drunkenly on its hinges. Unlatched. Maybe the rat was inside there? He started down the passage.

In the corner of his left eye, something moved. Something big that moved with blurring speed. Something that had been hiding behind the bulkhead wall separating the pilot's cabin from the passenger section.

Before he could duck, something hard struck his head. Even before the blinding pain hit, Bill heard the *crunch* of bone. Red agony billowed through him, engulfing him.

Bill Waterston tried to scream, but managed only a groan. Dimly, he was aware that he'd dropped to his knees, swaying.

"Nooo," he moaned despairingly. Then blackness replaced the blinding redness and he fell, smashing face first into the floor. His lips split open, blood flowed out to meet that coming from his head, and dull nothingness hovered close by.

Dad! he thought, then remembered his father had died years ago. Pain flared again as his broken nose filled with blood. Struggling weakly to breathe, he tried to turn over, to see who it was that was killing him. He had never hurt anyone. Who wanted him dead? But his strength faded away like the colors of sunset. Grief filled him . . . grief and regret.

His last thought was that he'd failed Mahree.

CHAPTER 2

◆

Salvage Archaeology

Deep in the bowels of the airless asteroid that was home to StarBridge Academy, Rob Gable sat alone in his office, head bowed, the backs of his hands pressed tightly to his closed eyes as he struggled to fight back tears. He didn't have time to cry. Later, perhaps, when the day's work was over, he could indulge himself and let his sadness overwhelm him, allow the emotional cleansing that weeping could bring. He was a psychologist and a medical doctor— he knew all about the damage repressed emotions could cause the human psyche.

But now was not the time to let his grief overwhelm him. He had things to do. Life went on. . . .

But not for Bill, his mind reminded him, bringing a fresh lump to his throat. *Bill's life is over. Why? Who could do such a thing?*

Waterston had been one of Rob's prize students, a young man who'd gone on beyond the role of student to assume that of a friend. Exceptionally able and mature for someone still in his early twenties, Bill had been part of the new wave of StarBridge-trained diplomats . . . one of the first to graduate and fulfill his destiny as an Interrelator. But now . . . years of study, all that work, all that dedication to the vision that StarBridge Academy existed to nurture . . . gone. Just . . . gone.

It's not fair. How could something like this happen? Rob wondered, aware that he'd asked this question many times over the years. The psychologist swallowed hard and ran a hand through his wavy hair—dark hair that was showing more than a hint of gray these days.

Clenching his jaw, Rob punched the FTL access code into the holo-tank, followed by Mahree's ID and the "override" code. Time to get things rolling. And it would help to talk with Mahree . . . though he hated to be the bearer of bad news. But if anyone could gain them the help they needed, the help Khuharkk's message had requested, it would be Mahree Burroughs, the CLS Ambassador-at-Large.

The holo-tank shimmered and then an image flickered into being. A woman sitting behind a desk in a room many light-years away looked up and smiled brightly, then stretched out a hand toward the screen. "Rob! How wonderful to see you! I'm glad you caught me. Half an hour from now, I'll be leaving to attend a trade conference."

Rob recognized Mahree's private office on Shassiszss Station, the enormous space station that orbited Shassiszss, the Mizari homeworld. Mahree, he was pleased to see, looked well. Becoming a mother had barely changed her slight figure, and, although she'd been a rather ordinary-looking girl, she'd matured into an attractive, even, at times, lovely woman. She wore no makeup, as usual, and was dressed in a businesslike navy outfit. Her long hair was braided and pinned up into a thick bun.

He smiled back. "Hi, honey. You're a sight for sore eyes."

They exchanged pleasantries for a minute or so; then Mahree's eyes sharpened. "Rob . . . you didn't just call to ask how Claire and I were doing, not at FTL rates, on an official channel. What's up?"

He checked the holo-tank's privacy light to be sure it was on, then began telling her about Khuharkk's call to Professor Greyshine, who had in turn called Rob. He described the magnitude of the discovery of the unplundered tomb of A-Um Rakt and the discovery of the Mizari relics the archaeologists had found inside it. Then, taking a deep breath, he added, "Honey, brace yourself. This last part is really bad news."

Her eyes widened. "What's happened?"

"Mahree, Bill Waterston has been murdered."

She put a hand to her mouth. "No! Oh, Rob! What? How?"

"I don't know. Khuharkk' didn't know. Bill left for the capital city of Spirit just after the discovery, planning to use the FTL transmitter there to report the news to the CLS Council. He never made it to his embassy. When three days passed and Bill still hadn't returned to camp, Mitchell dispatched a ground skimmer along his likely route." Rob paused a moment to steady himself. "They found . . . the body."

Mahree's face might·have been carved from stone. Her eyes gleamed with unshed tears, but her voice was steady. "How did he die?"

"His skull was crushed from a blow by some kind of blunt object. They found his body inside the jumpjet. There was no one around. No sign of another jet landing on the mesa top. No footsteps . . . nothing."

Mahree shook her head. "This is terrible. Who could have done such a thing?"

"I know how you feel," Rob said. His heart ached for her, as he sensed his own anguish mirrored in her voice, the taut lines of her body.

Slowly she settled back into her chair, her slim hands gripping the chair arms until he could see the bone-white of her knuckles beneath the skin. "He was a good one, Rob. The best Interrelator yet. I . . ." She paused, brushed at her eyes, then continued, her voice husky. "I don't envy you the call to his parents. I'll call later, on behalf of the CLS. Okay?"

Rob nodded. "His mother is a widow. I know Mrs. Waterston will appreciate hearing from you. She's a nice woman. Bill was . . . her only son."

Mahree winced. "Any idea who killed him, and why?"

Rob shook his head. "None. And the Na-Dina won't accept Irenic investigators for the case. They've appointed one of their own people to track down Bill's killer. I'll datafax you a copy of Khuharkk's message."

"Thanks," she said dully.

"Mahree . . ." Rob hesitated, but, knowing how limited her time was, plunged on. "Is it possible you can help Mitchell get some more people, better supplies, things like that? He's apparently made the find of the century out there."

She sighed, then nodded. "I think so. I'm certain that the Mizari Archaeological Society will be eager to finance the dig, at least. The transportation costs . . . well, I can call in a few favors. Esteemed Ssoriszs may want to finance a freighter for transport . . ."

She paused, eyes growing faraway, as she calculated.

"Great," Rob said. "I know Greyshine will be in touch with Esteemed Ssoriszs directly. He's so excited about this, I think he's going to go to Ancestor's World himself."

Mahree nodded. "Okay, let me get started on this. I'm going to have to handle much of this on the way to that conference on Arooouhl, but I'll cut my stay there from a week to a day. Just open the trade meetings and get them talking, then leave. Then a quick stopover back at Shas-siszss to pick up a very important passenger . . ." She gave him a wry glance. "Brace yourself, Rob."

Rob knew that look. "What are you cooking up now?"

"Get ready to have a new student at StarBridge."

"Who?"

"Claire."

"Wait a minute." Rob put up a hand. "Of course I'll be delighted to see her, but . . . why do I get the feeling I'm not going to be happy about whatever you're planning?"

"The CLS will need to send an interim Interrelator to fill Bill's job. I intend to go myself. Ancestor's World sounds like a really interesting place, and I've always been fascinated by archaeology. Claire can come stay with you for a couple of weeks."

Rob's mouth dropped open. "What? Why you?"

Her mouth tightened. "Bill was my friend. I intend to find out who killed him."

"Mahree!" Rob's cry of protest echoed in the confines of his office. "Bill was *murdered*. You're an Ambassador, not V. I. Warshawski!"

"V. I. *who*??"

Rob sighed. He was used to Mahree (and most other people) not getting his references to his beloved antique film collection. "Never mind. Mahree, this is the responsibility of the local police, not the interim Interrelator. You could be the next victim!"

"I'll work with the local police; don't worry. And I've been in enough tight situations that I know how to take care of myself." She leaned forward, intent. "Rob, don't bother arguing. I'm going because I owe it to Bill. I sent him to Ancestor's World, and he died there. I intend to find out what really happened."

Rob Gable mouthed a Mizari curse, one guaranteed to make one's scales fall off if repeated before the Star-Spirits. Mahree shook her head at him. "Cussing at me won't stop me."

He sighed. "When have I ever been able to tell you what to do? Please . . . Mahree, don't."

"Rob, I have to. I'm the Ambassador-at-Large, and Ancestor's World is high profile right now. Once Mitchell's discovery gets out, it's going to be even higher profile. The CLS needs somebody on the scene to help them evaluate what's going on—apart from Bill's death, I'd probably go there on a fact-finding mission anyway."

Rob shook his head, but there was nothing more to say. "Well, I'll love spending time with Claire, anyway. I just hope she'll be able to adjust well to other human students. She's never been around kids her own age, of her own species, before."

Mahree nodded. "That's true. We were planning to do this anyway in a year, remember. This will give us a chance to preview what it's going to be like."

Rob nodded. "Well, at least I'll get to spend time with

one member of my family.'' He heard the bitterness in his own voice, and saw Mahree's reaction; her eyes dropped, unable to meet his own.

"Rob, I'm really, really sorry I missed that family vacation we'd planned. Soon, we can do that. I promise. As soon as I get back from Ancestor's World . . .''

He gave her a quick, automatic smile. "Sure, honey. Have a safe trip, okay? Give Claire a kiss from me and tell her I can't wait to see her.''

She nodded wordlessly, her expression still troubled, and reached out to cut the connection.

Mahree's image vanished, leaving Rob Gable alone in his office. The psychologist sighed, sipped absently at his cold coffee, and ordered his computer to locate Bill Waterston's mother's com code . . .

On the home planet of the Heeyoon, Arooouhl, deep in the ruins of ancient Kal-Syr, Etsane Mwarka signaled her autocam to turn itself off and just *looked* for a moment at the beautiful paintings that covered an entire stone wall. The wall lay inside a hallway of the Great Palace at Kal-Syr, capital of the first Heeyoon city-state. The paintings did not look fifteen hundred years old.

"You're a beauty, aren't you?'' she whispered to the wall.

Yes, I am! the huge mural seemed to shout back at her.

Before her eyes marched long lines of the wolflike Heeyoon, their long gray muzzles opened wide as they howled forth their song of welcome. In a series of panel scenes, they welcomed the Heeyoon autarch Moonwise, first to unite the peoples of the Warm and the Cold Lands. As an Iconographer who spoke the Heeyoon language fluently it had been her job to document in color, black and white, and infrared photographs, and with pencil drawings, the ancient images, then classify and describe them.

She'd first seen pictures of this wall back home on Earth, at the University of Addis Ababa, where she'd been studying the history of her own people, the people of Ethiopia. Her father had been an eminent professor at the university, and he'd insisted upon having a scholar heir.

"Now, Etsane, I know you're tempted to go to Star-Bridge Academy and study xeno-archaeology," her father, Mefume, had said to her while she was still in high school. His dark brown eyes had flashed as he stood there with his hands clasped together, dressed in Amhara tribal dress. Her father was an old-fashioned man. "But, daughter, I want you to concentrate on studying the history of *our* people. We need young people to remember our glorious past."

"But, father!" Etsane had objected, arms crossed over her chest resentfully, "the history of the Amharas and ancient Aksum is *known*. If I become an historian, as you wish, I'll just be re-covering well-known ground! If I become a xeno-archaeologist, I'll get to study the ancient days of people totally different from us—people whose wonders are still waiting to be discovered!"

He'd blinked then, almost as if he were going to weep. He never did, never had in all the years when he'd raised her single-handedly, after her mother's death from the Hacking Cough. Instead, he'd just stood there in his book-lined study, surrounded by three-hundred-year-old carvings, paintings, and wooden busts that depicted her proud, hawk-nosed people, and waited for her to give in. She had, as she'd known she must. There was nothing she would not do for her beloved father.

"Oh, all right!" She'd even stamped her foot on the stone floor of the family farm, high up on the slopes of Mount Ras Deshen, in the highlands north of ancient Gonder. He'd smiled then.

"That's my girl!" Warm love had shone in his black face, a face still marked by the ritual scars he'd picked up during years spent among the Sidamo people of southern Ethiopia. "Now, about the specifics of your study, I'd like to suggest that you . . ."

Etsane blinked, coming back to the present, to a cold day in a cold stone hallway, standing before a painted wall that spoke to her as to few other Iconographers. Yes, she'd done as her father had wanted . . . studied the history of her people during her undergraduate years. But then, when she entered graduate school, she revolted, turning her back on Earth and the history of Ethiopia to do what she really wanted to do—study xeno-archaeology.

Her father had been very disappointed in her, and had told her so. For a few moments, she'd wavered, tempted to give in once again. Then she'd made herself stand firm. "I'm sorry, Dad," she'd said steadily. "I have to do what is right for me. This is right. Staying on Earth is wrong."

Her father had died during her first off-world assignment, when she'd interned with Professor Greyshine on a Mizari dig three years ago. Etsane had always wondered if he'd died of a broken heart, though she tried to tell herself that was silly.

As much as she loved her work, it was hard to shake off the disapproving shadow that was always with her. She was now twenty-three, and still the memory of her father's disappointed expression was enough to dull her enjoyment of even the most marvelous alien "find."

Now she stood before the wall, and whispered softly, "Father, I still remember. I haven't forgotten. I know what our people accomplished."

Hers were the Amhara people of Ethiopia, who traced their descent from Aksum's King Ezana, conqueror of ancient Meroe, to Yekuno Amlak, who restored the Solomonic kingship line to Christian Ethiopia, to Emperor Menelik the Second who defeated the Italians at Aduwa in 1896. Her father's family was of a Gonder noble house, while her mother came from a noble clan of the Tigrayan people, who shared with the Amharas their royal link to Roman-era Aksum. The book *Kibre Nigest* even said Ethiopia's kings descended from a son born to King Solomon and Sheba, Queen of South Arabia. Maybe so. Maybe not.

But she knew for a fact that her Nilotic-Semitic people had, for a time, ruled ancient Egypt. That was during the New Kingdom's Twenty-Fifth Dynasty. The Nubian kingdom of Kush had preserved classical Egyptian culture, and a black-skinned pharaoh had ruled the Kingdom of the Two Lands from his palace at Napata. But then the Assyrian interlopers arrived in 663 B.C. and drove out her people.

Later came the Ptolemaic Greeks and the Romans, but none
of them could match the spiritual devotion of the second
Kingdom of Kush, still in power above the Fifth Cataract
at Meroe. But finally, after Kush had passed into the nearby
kingdom of Aksum, which later turned Christian, the last
Temple of Isis had closed in the sixth century A.D.

Now all that remained of the greatness of ancient Kush,
Meroe, Aksum, and her royal Amhara forebears were
carved bas-relief walls, giant stone pyramids, memorial
stele and piles of iron-smelting debris. Plus the stubborn
faith of a people who'd long stood as a cultural bridge
between the peoples of the Mediterranean and Arabia, and
those of interior Africa.

But Etsane had left Earth, had made her own bridge to
the stars. Now she stood here, on Arooouhl, recording the
ancient images of an honored CLS race. She was doing
graduate work at the University of Kal-Syr. Perhaps her
iconographic decipherments of these images would add a
few lines of knowledge to the remarkable history of a proud
people. *Alien* people.

She signaled the autocam to "playback" so she could
check the images it had recorded, and saw herself move
across the tiny screen as she pointed out important features
of the mural.

She'd always been proudly tall, like most of the Amhara
people of Ethiopia, and her eyes were smoky black. She
was very dark, although her features were typical of her
people . . . thinner-lipped, with a high-bridged, Semitic
nose. Her hair, when she let it loose, was an unruly, wavy
black mane that reached nearly to her waist. When she'd
been in college, the boys had flocked to pursue her, though
some had been put off by her single-minded pursuit of her
studies.

Beside her feet, the combox beeped, shaking her out of
her musings. Grumbling at being disturbed, Etsane bent
down and signaled for her message.

The flat screen flickered, and an image took shape. It
was the face of Professor Greyshine, her former teacher and

mentor—and she could tell immediately that he was excited, wildly agitated.

"Attention, my former students, fellow colleagues, and esteemed researchers of the Mizari Archaeological Society. Doctor Gordon Mitchell has entered the burial tomb of the First King of the Na-Dina aliens on Ancestor's World, and discovered a fabulous golden sarcophagus nearly six thousand years old." The Heeyoon paused and his amber eyes stared intently, as if he spoke to her personally.

"This is just one of many ancient ruins that will soon be flooded by a dam now under construction. Time is critical. But most important of all, Doctor Mitchell reports the discovery of *Mizari* artifacts in direct association with the King's sarcophagus!"

What? Etsane wondered if this find had anything to do with the Mizari Lost Colony.

"The find is authentic," Greyshine said, calming a bit. "The tomb has been sealed for six thousand years. This is a call for help in carrying out emergency salvage archaeology operations. Mitchell's current team is very small, and lacks the equipment needed for a full-scale, multidisciplinary effort. He requests our assistance. I am leaving my own work at StarBridge Academy to help him, as is my mate Doctor Strongheart, who will conduct the Physical Sapientological Analysis of the burials. I'll head up the Settlement Pattern Analysis."

In the flat screen image, Greyshine looked down at a flimsy held in his paw-hands. "Mitchell also needs specialists in Faunal and Floral Analysis, Iconography, Paleoenvironmental Reconstruction, Lithics and Ceramics Analysis, and a Chronologist." The Heeyoon looked up, and his muzzle stretched wide in a grin she well remembered. "My colleagues, your assistance is needed. If you wish to help, please join us here at StarBridge Academy for transport to Ancestor's World. Mahree Burroughs has arranged for a freighter to transport us and our equipment. Thank you for your help."

Etsane rocked back on her heels, and considered Professor Greyshine's message. They needed an Iconographer.

Which made sense, based on what she'd heard about the Na-Dina culture. Sketchy reports from Mitchell's camp said the aliens lived beside an incredibly long river much like the Nile. They were agriculturalists of high sophistication. And they had built massive stone temples and burial chambers for thousands of years. Just like the ancient Egyptians.

Could this be her chance to show honor to her father's memory? Studying the Na-Dina might almost be like studying Egypt and Meroe. And with her knowledge of those cultures, she might have insights other Iconographers would lack . . . *Father, would this satisfy you?* she wondered.

She considered for several more minutes; then, smiling a faint, ironic smile, Etsane rose to her feet and slung the combox over her shoulder. She winked at the hovering autocam to follow her, and began walking down the echoing stone hallway.

Centuries ago, the Great Palace at Kal-Syr had stood all alone on a headland overlooking the blue waves of an inland sea. No longer. Now, it was an archaeological park surrounded by the capital city of the Heeyoon. The spaceport was only a half-hour away.

Etsane's long strides came faster and faster, until she was nearly running. She had to catch the next ship heading for StarBridge Academy!

Mahree Burroughs was the last person up the ramp leading to the freighter's cargo hold as the *Emerald Scales* prepared to leave Shassiszss Station for StarBridge, Ancestor's World, and points in between. Her running feet pattered nimbly up the ramp, but she was panting, more from the stress of hurrying than from the weight of the heavy duffel bag she carried over her shoulder.

Her daughter, Claire Burroughs-Gable, stood waiting for her just inside the corridor leading to the passenger quarters. Seeing her, Mahree smiled tentatively, wondering what kind of mood Claire was in; these days she changed her mood more often than her clothes.

The girl responded to her mother's smile with an impa-

tient "Come on!" wave. Mahree sighed, and the heavy
duffel bag seemed suddenly to double in weight as she
started toward the girl.

Claire resembled neither of her dark-haired, dark-eyed
parents—at fourteen, she was as tall as her mother, nearly
as tall as Rob, and fair-skinned, with reddish-gold hair and
changeable gray-green eyes.

At the moment she wore a greenish-gray jumpsuit that
clung to every line of her slight, newly developing figure,
and turned her eyes stormy gray. The girl's scowl and rigid
tension as Mahree approached spoke volumes. Claire had
never been separated from her mother for more than a few
weeks before this, and Mahree could tell she was uneasy
at the prospect.

"Mom, the Captain's been holding the ship for you for
the past half-hour!" she scolded. "C'mon, the CLS won't
fall apart just because you're gone for a few weeks!"

Mahree sighed. "I already contacted Captain Salzeess,
and he was able to alter the flight path. I apologized to him,
too. Let's go put my stuff away."

Claire gave her a sidelong glance, but said no more as
Mahree hoisted the duffel bag higher on her shoulder and
started off toward their cabin.

"Did you finish that essay assignment Esteemed Rissaszs
sent you last week?" she asked, fighting fire with fire. "Remember, you're going to be seeing her in just a little while,
and she's going to expect it to be done." The moment the
words were out of her mouth, Mahree regretted them. She'd
hoped that this trip to StarBridge could be spent regaining
some of the closeness she and Claire seemed to have lost
lately.

Coppery hair swung like a curtain as the girl shook her
head, her expression surly. "No. What difference does it
make? I won't be able to give it to her until we get to
StarBridge, and that'll be several days. I'll get it done,
Mom . . . c'mon, can't you get off my tail for two whole
minutes?"

Her daughter's insolent tone brought a wave of warmth
into Mahree's cheeks. She halted so abruptly the duffel slid

off her shoulder and thudded to the deck. She glared at her daughter, her temper rising. "Now just a minute, Claire. You have no call to speak to me like that. Esteemed Rissaszs told me that you're behind on several assignments. She said that—"

Claire folded both arms over her coveralls, and managed to look both tolerantly superior and sullen at the same time. "I *know* what she said. Just like I *know* you're not really mad about a stupid homework assignment. You're not mad, you're worried. You're thinking about—"

Mahree frowned at her daughter, then bent over to retrieve her duffel bag. "Stop it, Claire! I brought you up to be a *polite* telepath. You know better than to snoop like that! If they catch you doing that at StarBridge, you will be in really hot water!" Turning away without waiting for a reply, she strode off down the corridor.

Claire's footsteps sped up behind her as the girl worked to match Mahree's angry strides. "Mom! Wait up."

Realizing that her daughter was trying to be conciliatory, Mahree slowed down. "No wonder you can't keep up with your old mom; you're wearing your new shoes," she said, eying the spike-heeled, glittery sandals studded with Ri gems.

"I wanted Esteemed Ssoriszs to see them, since he gave them to me," Claire said, walking with great concentration on the high heels.

"Esteemed Ssoriszs has been in a generous mood lately," Mahree agreed. "If it hadn't been for him, we couldn't have gotten *Emerald Scales* to transport the expedition."

Funding *and* a transport. The Mizari, led by her old friend, had really come through, and quickly. Everyone was excited by the idea that *this* time there might be genuine clues as to where the ancient Mizari Lost Colony had gone.

"Let's compromise," Mahree said, returning to their original subject. "You can have the next hour or two to explore the ship, but as soon as we enter metaspace, you finish that assignment. Agreed?"

"I guess." Claire stopped before the door to their suite

and touched it open. Mahree followed her in, tossing her duffel on one of the narrow bunks. *Emerald Scales* was, after all, a freighter, and the ship boasted few luxuries.

"It'll sure be different, going to regular classes at the Academy," Claire said quietly. "After being tutored long-distance from StarBridge for so long."

"I think it will be good for you," Mahree said, speaking with a confidence she didn't entirely feel. "Your father and I have been planning for you to do this for a while. This new assignment just moves up the timetable a little, that's all."

Claire regarded her image in the reflective panel built into the wall. Mahree stared at her doubtfully. How would Claire react to being among so many other young people? Aliens she was used to; she'd grown up among them and spoke seven alien languages as fluently as she did her own tongue. But young people of her own species were as alien to her as a Mizari eggling would be to a child who'd grown up on Earth.

And there was no doubt that Claire was pretty. She'd attract quite a bit of attention at the Academy. Mahree sighed. Was Claire ready for this? Was she? Was *Rob*?

Boys. Dating. Sex—or, at least the potential for it. Mahree repressed a worried frown. The subject couldn't be avoided forever; sooner or later Claire would have to learn to live with her own species.

The CLS Ambassador-at-Large busied herself hanging up a few items of clothing from her duffel, then she wandered into the other room and sat down in one of the cushiony chairs, feeling it automatically adjust to her body contours. Kicking off her boots, she leaned back and crossed her legs, trying to relax. Claire followed her out of the bedroom and sat down on the small couch opposite her, her expression uneasy. "You're worried about me, aren't you, Mom? Worried that I'll get hurt by those other human kids? Especially the boys, right?"

Mahree fixed her with a stern look. "Have you been—"

"No, I'm not eavesdropping this time," Claire protested, flushing with indignation. "Anyone could tell you're wor-

ried; it wouldn't take a telepath. All moms worry about sex
and stuff. But I'll be okay. At least . . . I think I will.'' Her
voice, so sure at first, grew hesitant. ''Do you . . . do you
think the other kids will like me?''

''Of course they will, honey,'' Mahree said, smiling at
her daughter. ''What I'm worrying about is that you and
they have come from such different backgrounds, it may
be hard for you to adjust in the beginning, that's all. You
know what it's like, building cultural bridges between people, right?''

''Yeah,'' Claire agreed. ''It can be hard.''

''We'll talk about it during the trip. It'll help if you're
prepared. You might also want to study up a bit on Earth
and its colonies.''

''You mean study them like I would a new alien world
we were going to visit?''

''Exactly. In a way, their cultures are just as alien to you,
since you've never actually been to Terra, or Jolie, or any
of the other colonies. It can't hurt, right?''

''Okay, I will,'' Claire agreed. ''But, Mom . . . I'm not
the one you should be worrying about. *You're* the one who
might be in danger, right?''

''Danger? Me?'' Mahree shrugged. ''All alien worlds
have their own hazards, but—''

Claire shook her head, her expression grim. ''Damn it,
Mom, don't be so dense. Bill got killed there. Somebody
smashed his head in, right? What makes you think *you'll*
be safe?''

Ahhhh, yes. Blunt Claire. Mahree licked her lips, thought
of repeating the ''duty, honor, and CLS'' speech she'd
given Rob, then refrained as three bell-tones sounded from
the ceiling. ''We're undocking. On our way at last.''

Claire sat back on the couch, nodding slowly, her eyes
fixed on Mahree. ''I wish you weren't going. Mom . . . I'm
scared you won't come back.''

''Claire . . .'' Mahree hesitated. She'd been on the verge
of offering her daughter automatic words of reassurance,
adult words spoken to a scared child, but as she looked at

her daughter's expression, they died unspoken. Claire was too old for empty promises.

Instead she said, "Claire, there's no reason to believe that what happened to Bill had anything to do with his being the Interrelator on Ancestor's World. There are lots of other people there, and he might have made an enemy. As a matter of fact, the preliminary police report indicated that he'd been in some kind of argument with one of the Nordlund officials the day before he died."

"But you don't know anything for sure. What if someone just doesn't like having an Interrelator on Ancestor's World?"

"I've been in danger before, Claire," Mahree said, and as she spoke she had a sudden, vivid memory of the time they'd made the First Contact with the Simiu aboard the *Desirée*, long years ago. Those had been tense days, terrifying hours, especially when it seemed the Simiu would attack the ship, her Uncle Raoul would try to escape from Hurrreeah's space station, and war between the two species would prove inevitable.

But the war had been prevented. She, Rob, and their Simiu ally Dhurrrkk' had seen to that, escaping from the Simiu space station in a stolen ship and heading out blindly for Shassiszss to seek help from the CLS. They'd succeeded, Earth had joined the CLS, and she'd become the first person to ever be offered an individual membership in the Cooperative League of Systems.

Rob and Esteemed Ssoriszs had founded StarBridge eight years later. Mahree and Rob had lived together until the Academy was mostly completed; then their careers took them in opposite directions. If it hadn't been for Claire, born three years after the *Desirée*'s First Contact, when Mahree was twenty, they might have drifted apart. But their daughter had held them together, become the touchstone of their love. Mahree looked at Claire, noting the fear in her daughter's eyes, the concern for her safety, and had to blink back sudden tears.

"Honey, I'm going to be fine. Ancestor's World is pretty civilized. They were well into their Industrial Age when discovered, and they've got police. Unlike Bill, who spent part of his time in the Interrelator's Office in the capital city of Spirit, I'm going to be staying full time in the archaeologists' camp. I'll be surrounded by people all the time.''

Claire stared at her, unconvinced. Her daughter's lower lip trembled. Mahree sighed tiredly. Being a parent was like trying to communicate with aliens without knowing their language, tricky in the extreme.

Mahree realized that Claire had tapped into some of her own unconscious fears about this assignment she'd chosen to tackle on Ancestor's World. What if Bill Waterston's murder *wasn't* the result of a personal grudge? What if it was part of something more sinister, something connected with the nearby Sorrow Sector? Would she indeed be safe in the archaeologists' camp?

Rumor had it that the head of the dig, Mitchell, was an irascible man with a reputation for drinking hard, working himself and others hard, and not suffering fools gladly. The report she'd requisitioned on him had mentioned a messy divorce and numerous problems in dealing with his peers, especially in the past couple of years.

On the other hand, rumor was a notoriously unreliable thing. When Mahree considered the wild things she'd heard about herself over the years, she was inclined to give Mitchell the benefit of the doubt.

Her daughter's haunted expression brought her back to the moment at hand. Claire needed reassurance, truthful reassurance, not a sharing of worries. Mahree took a deep breath and gazed directly into the girl's gray-green eyes. ''Claire, I promise you. I'll be careful—and smart—wherever I go and whatever I do.''

Slowly, Claire nodded, but her eyes remained shadowed with uncertainty.

Mahree got up, swayed as the ship's grav fields chose that moment to adjust minutely, and walked over to sit beside Claire. Turning, she put her arms around her daughter's narrow shoulders. ''Honey, I love you, and I swear to you on my honor I'll do whatever I must to return to you. Okay?''

Claire nodded, her expression still somber, but Mahree could feel some of the tension go out of her. She rested her head against her mother's shoulder. "Mom, do you think Dad will be happy that we're all together again, even if it's only for a few days?"

Mahree gave her daughter a startled glance. "Of course he will! Why wouldn't he?"

The girl sighed. "When we're together, Dad wants it to last forever, Mom. He's sad when he thinks that it will only be for a few days or a few weeks."

Claire's statement hardly constituted a revelation to Mahree. She'd known for years that Rob wanted her to give up her position as CLS Ambassador-at-Large and settle down with him on StarBridge. He felt that Mahree could make an even better contribution as an instructor at the Academy than in her current work troubleshooting for the huge, interstellar confederation. After all, StarBridge was their best hope for a peaceful and prosperous Orion Arm.

Mahree could see Rob's point, and thought that he might even be correct, but the idea of staying permanently in one place was unthinkable. She'd roamed the stars for too long now. Alien contact and the delicate work of interspecies negotiation was in her blood, her greatest personal joy. Much as she loved Claire and Rob, even the prospect of being with them all the time couldn't compare with the sense of accomplishment she gained from her work. When Mahree was a young girl, just setting out aboard the *Desirée* on her way to Earth to attend college (a voyage that had never yet been completed), she'd wished fervently that she could be *special*. She didn't want a humdrum, ordinary life.

And, unlike most people, she'd achieved her dream— she *was* special. Her skills as a First Contact Specialist were legend; her rapport with aliens was a unique ability that had never been equaled.

But the undeniable fact that she was constantly disappointing those closest to her was painful. Last year, Rob had asked her to consider taking a year's sabbatical so they could have another child. He'd even offered to take a leave of absence from StarBridge and move anywhere she wanted for that year. Then, he'd promised, he'd raise the baby himself, on StarBridge, if she didn't want to stay in one place.

Mahree had been on the verge of agreeing to his proposition, but just then they'd gotten word of the Anuran invasion of Trinity. The invasion had had a major ripple effect in the CLS, as delegates argued vehemently over what to do about the new, aggressive amphibian species. And when that fracas had calmed down, there had been the faceoff between the Drnians and the Vardi over the Vardi embargo on Heeyoon fertilizers . . . and then there had been the clash between the Simiu and the Mizari over that newly discovered radonium asteroid . . . and then . . . and then . . .

Crisis and minicrisis, one after another. There was always an urgent problem to be solved, a potential problem to be averted. There was never enough time. Time . . .

Mahree felt a surge of old, familiar guilt threaten to overwhelm her.

For once, Claire remained unaware of her mother's distress. Mahree jerked back to the here and now, hearing the girl sigh loudly. "I sure hope so. It's been almost a year since I last saw Dad. Mom . . . do you think we can all visit the cabin on Shassiszss for a real family vacation after you get back from Ancestor's World?"

Mahree hugged her daughter closer, and settled deeper into the couch. Claire smiled and hugged her back. "Yes, I promise I'll make time for that family vacation after this is all over."

"Good!"

About them the freighter moved through the dark of space, rushing steadily toward the outskirts of Shassiszss' solar system, where they could enter metaspace without harm to the local star. Soon, Mahree thought, she'd have to go and appear at the Captain's Table, make polite conversation, thank Captain Salzeess for volunteering to help with the mission, meet the female Mizari Ceramicist, and then go over the list of archaeological experts to pick up at points between Shassiszss and StarBridge.

Emerald Scales wasn't a fast ship. They'd be nearly a week getting to StarBridge. Then a month's travel to reach distant Ancestor's World. Lying near the outer curve of the Orion Arm, the Na-Dina homeworld lay too close to the dusty gas clouds and veiled star clusters that made up Sorrow Sector. The notorious sector was the hiding place for criminals, outlaws, privateers, and miscreants from all the Fifteen Known Worlds. Ships were lost forever in its environs. The League Irenics had repeatedly tried to infiltrate the legendary criminal star-den, but none of their investigators had ever returned. . . .

Mahree shivered involuntarily, and Claire pulled back to gaze at her, her now-green eyes huge. "Don't be afraid, Mom. The League Irenics will keep you safe from Sorrow Sector."

Mahree smiled faintly. "Peeking again? Well, I forgive you. Did I ever tell you the story of how, just after you'd been born, we discovered you were telepathic?"

Her daughter blinked, then slowly shook her head, a soft smile escaping. "No. Never. Will you tell me again?"

Mahree Burroughs laughed, took her daughter's hand and squeezed it. Claire hadn't asked for her favorite story for nearly two years now. It made her feel close to tell it once more. "When you were very small . . ."

"How small, Mom?"

"Hardly as big as a minute," Mahree said, settling into the familiar litany.

"How big is a minute, Mom?"

Mahree made a space with her hands. "About *this* big . . ."

CHAPTER 3

♦

A New World

Etsane stood before the viewport in the Stellar Velocity vessel *Emerald Scales*, watching Ancestor's World revolve beneath her. They would be landing soon, but before she strapped in she wanted to see the planet from orbit.

Ancestor's World was a brown ball covered in reddish-brown traceries that resembled waterless riverbeds. The silvery sparkle of dry saline lakebeds spotted the planet. *So where's the water?* she wondered, and even as she thought it, they rounded the north pole and overflew the shallow Northern Sea. Instead of an icecap, Ancestor's World had a large sea filling its far north, one about the size of the Indian Ocean. The sea was fed by the muddy-brown waterway called the River of Life, which flowed northward in serpentine curves from the equatorial Mountains of Faith.

Etsane counted off the primary geographical features of the Na-Dina homeworld—one sea-ocean, one giant mountain range at the equator, and a dead seabed at the south pole. Then she spotted the angry blue-black of continent-wide storms, thunderstorms that flashed with yellow lightning, and recalled the turbulent weather Dr. Mitchell had mentioned. *Monster storms, earthquakes, and volcanoes,* she thought. *Nice place to visit, but do I really want to live here for a year or so?*

"Etsane, you're the luckiest of us all, I think," called Professor Greyshine. He and his mate, Doctor Strongheart, were curled nearby on Heeyoon cushioned benches.

"Oh? Why's that?" She touched on her voder earcuff, an automatic habit whenever she encountered aliens, even though she read and spoke Heeyoon fairly fluently. A month's practice conversing with Greyshine and Strongheart on the way here had certainly helped. Etsane smiled as she remembered one particular conversation. The elderly couple loved romantic poetry and had begged her to repeat the apocryphal story of how Solomon and Sheba had made love and founded the Royal House of Ethiopia.

"Professor, this is another piece in the puzzle of the Mizari Lost Colony," she pointed out. "Surely *you* are the most fortunate of us all?"

Etsane waved a hand, indicating the other members of the team who were also in the lounge. There was the sloth-like Shadgui Lithics Analyst, two humanoid Drnians, the Mizari Ceramicist, the Chhhh-kk-tu Paleoenvironmental specialist, and the Vardi Chronologist.

"He *is* fortunate," Strongheart agreed, nuzzling her mate fondly. "But, Etsane, he is talking about the painted pictures and bas-relief carvings that cover the walls of all the Na-Dina ruins. Even more than Kal-Syr, this must be a dream world for an Iconographer!"

"Oh, it is! It will be!" Etsane agreed excitedly.

The ever-changing view caught her attention, and she discovered that *Emerald Scales* had now entered the atmosphere and was descending to land. Below them, she could see the broad delta lands that lay at the mouth of the River of Life. So much like the Nile . . .

"Doctor Mitchell's preliminary report reminded me so much of ancient Egypt," she said, picking up the conversation where she'd left off. "I'll have to be careful not to let my own heritage influence me as I begin trying to decipher the ideoglyphs in the Royal Tomb of A-Um Rakt. Doctor Mitchell says he hasn't made any headway with them at all—they're very different from the hieroglyphs of Classical High Na-Dina.''

At that moment the soft ''prepare for landing'' chime sounded, and all of the passengers quickly strapped themselves into their seats. Etsane watched the freighter's flight upriver, eager to see the great city of Spirit and its new, makeshift spaceport. The capital of the Na-Dina lay a hundred kilometers above the densely populated delta farmlands, and its towering stone buildings soon caught her attention.

Etsane eyed the buildings, wondering if she could pick out different dynastic styles from this far away. Imagine flying like a bird over a city already ancient before Rome was founded!

Father, I wish you could see this, she thought wistfully. *You would have loved this, too . . .*

Beloran sat in the ground skimmer driven by Mitchell, the Sky Infidel who had caused him so many problems already and would, no doubt, cause him more in the future. Just ahead, the CLS transport was setting down at the spaceport field outside Spirit.

Just what we need, the Liaison thought sourly. *More Infidels.* Like the other aliens, these Infidels would also feel free to profane Mother Sky with their flying machines. Like Mitchell, they too would dig into Father Earth without reverence, without respect.

Beloran's tail kinked with resentment. *This is OUR world, not theirs!*

Schooling his ears and tail to calmness, he reminded himself that what his people needed, what he had bought them, was time. Time to industrialize *Halish meg a-tum.* Time to purchase or develop the technology that would make them the equals of these visitors from beyond Mother Sky. Time to grow strong, to arm themselves, so that the People would forever control their own destiny.

Beloran glanced sideways at the Infidel Mitchell, noting with distaste his flat features, his unmobile ears and lack of a tail. These humans had no feelings, no sensitivity, no reverence for history and tradition. They knew not the value of salt. They did not appreciate the value of water. They acted as if they had no fear of the future, and behaved casually with technology that seemed, to the Na-Dina, miraculous, even magical.

Infidel Mitchell glanced over at him. "This Mahree Burroughs who will be taking Bill's place knew him well," he said, expertly piloting the skimmer along the dusty road. "She was his mentor. He worked for her for a year before coming to Ancestor's World."

Beloran tensed at the mention of the young Sky Infidel who had met such an unpleasant fate. Finding the entire subject distasteful, he hastened to change it. "Did this female Infidel also attend the StarBridge school that drifts between the suns?"

Mitchell emitted a short, sharp sound that Beloran had learned betokened amusement. "No, Mahree Burroughs never *attended* StarBridge Academy. She was the inspiration for it. She helped set it up, and is widely known as the First Interrelator."

Beloran's ears fluttered with distress. If this female Infidel was famous, then the CLS no doubt valued her, as they had not, from all indications, valued Waterston. What effect might that have on the Na-Dina relations with the Sky Infidels? He must consider the implications carefully. . . .

"Here is the turnoff," the Liaison said, pointing with one talon.

"Yes, I see it." Mitchell turned the skimmer off the country road and headed for a gray metal building. The Infidels called it "the Skyport" and they had raised it in a single day, rather than the way a building should be raised, year by year, decade by decade. The Skyport was built of some hard alien substance, not of Father's gift, the native stone, as the Na-Dina built.

The new Infidels would be waiting in there until cleared by the Ministry of Commerce. Beloran noticed one of the Nordlund jumpjets also on the landing field. Being a Merchant, Beloran felt far more comfortable with the Nordlund

Infidels. Nordlund was here to make a profit, and profit was something Beloran understood.

And Nordlund was giving Ancestor's World something tangible. Nordlund knew how to build giant dams. They traded off-world wonders for Na-Dina goods. Their presence had given new status to the trade of Merchant.

The contracts Nordlund had signed with the Na-Dina promised enough hydroelectric power to double their world's energy production. That would make possible more factories, more mills. Soon the Na-Dina would be able to build all the wonders the Infidels used so casually, and then the People would have no more need for the off-worlders.

As the skimmer halted before the Skyport, Beloran sighed to himself. Time to school his manner, to pretend politeness to those who would rush into his world, overawe the rural people, and perhaps even challenge the power of the Royal House.

"We're here, though a bit late," said Mitchell. "If we hadn't had to stop for midday devotionals . . ."

Beloran thought back to that time by the side of the road, as he had prayed and meditated, with Mitchell's awkward accompaniment. The Liaison had enjoyed prolonging the rite, even as the archaeologist squirmed. . . .

Too bad Mitchell's entire archaeological camp could not disappear, like one of the remote Na-Dina villages found empty of inhabitants. The Disappearances had begun decades ago. Not everyone believed in them, but Beloran had seen one village for himself—echoing, deserted, desolate . . . as though the villagers had just . . . left.

As he moved to get out of the vehicle and follow Mitchell into the Skyport, Beloran repressed another sigh and steeled himself to meet this new wave of Infidel intruders.

Mahree Burroughs stood in the visitor hall of the Skyport, surrounded by milling archaeologists, piles of equipment and baggage. She sighed. There wasn't anyone, Na-Dina or human, here to meet them. Where the devil was Mitchell?

How the heck were they to find transport to Mitchell's

Base Camp? Surely the man had more sense than to expect them to land *Emerald Scales* downcountry, in a dangerous approach to a beaconless canyon?

Mahree realized uneasily that all of the archaeologists were regarding her expectantly. That was only fair, she thought grumpily—after all, *she* was the high-ranking CLS official. Trouble was, she didn't have the faintest idea of what to do.

She wiped sweat from her forehead, wishing she were wearing shorts and a sleeveless top rather than the black StarBridge jumpsuit with Interrelator insignia she'd put on that morning. Searching in her pockets, she ran fingers through her mane of waist-length hair, scooping it up into a ponytail so it was off her neck.

Just then, the double doors slammed open and in walked two people: a middle-aged human male, and a Na-Dina alien. Relieved, Mahree headed purposefully for them.

She was amused to note that Mitchell was dressed exactly like an archaeologist in one of Rob's antique films—rough khaki pants, leather boots, and a tan shirt with the sleeves rolled up. His muscular forearms were traced with scars and abrasions, old and new.

"Ambassador Burroughs?" the human called in a pleasant tenor, waving to her as he approached. "I'm Gordon Mitchell." He was tall and ruggedly good-looking, with a deep tan and brown hair streaked blond by the sun. His teeth flashed when he smiled.

"Mahree Burroughs," she said, striding up to meet him. She was too hot and sweaty to smile, but she nodded cordially as she held out her hand. Mitchell grasped hers in a rough-palmed grip. He smelled of new sweat and old dust. "And for the duration of this visit, Doctor Mitchell, my title is 'Interrelator.' "

Mahree slid a hand into her pocket and withdrew her CLS credentials, then handed them to the blue-scaled Na-Dina. While the alien glanced at them, she took another look at the archaeologist, and her eyes widened. Mitchell wore a *gun* belted to his waist. A pulse-gun!

Biting her lip, she forced herself to look away from the

weapon. She didn't want to create a scene in front of a Na-Dina official. Later, though, she'd have a LOT to say about that gun. Didn't the man have a grain of sense?

"Ambassador?" The Na-Dina was bowing to her, beady black eyes inspecting her one-piece StarBridge uniform; then the alien broke eye contact. "We apologize for our lateness. We were delayed in our arrival due to the midday obeisance." Mahree heard the alien's words in stereo—the translation to Mizari whispered by the voder earcuff she wore, and from her own knowledge of the Na-Dina hiss-click language. Alien languages were her speciality, and she'd gained a passable fluency on the trip out.

Mahree returned the Na-Dina's bow. "Esteemed Representative of the Royal House," she hiss-clicked, "I come bearing—"

"I'm not of the Royal House," the alien interrupted curtly. Nictitating membranes swept sideways over wet black eyes, and fan-shaped ears canted toward her. "I am Beloran, of the clan Flooding Waters, of the trade Merchant, Father of four eggs, and Liaison between the Sky Infidels and the Council of Elders." The alien looked behind her, then focused on her head, as if the bobbing tail of hair fascinated him.

"Forgive me if I misspoke," Mahree said hastily. "Your ways are new to me. I hope to learn them as quickly as I may, so that we may communicate effectively."

Beloran gave her another short, jerky bow, acknowledging her apology. "How shall we transport to Base Camp?" Mahree asked the liaison. "We have large amounts of equipment, as you can see."

"Yes, I see." Beloran didn't seem particularly pleased. "Your people are to stay here, load their belongings into the Nordlund jumpjet, and, as soon as the pilot is ready, you must all leave."

Mahree's eyes widened in surprise. "But I thought the Ministry of Justice was located in Spirit."

"It is," Beloran said. "However, the Council prefers that you Infidels refrain from entering our cities. The populace is still . . . unused to your strange forms. They might be distressed at seeing you.''

Mitchell frowned, then turned on the alien. "But, Beloran! Ambassador Burroughs has an appointment at the Ministry of Justice to discuss Bill's murder with Investigator Krillen.''

"That is not possible,'' Beloran said stiffly. "I cannot permit it.''

Mitchell opened his mouth to protest further, but was silenced by Mahree's quick "Let me handle this'' glance. She shook her head gently. "Liaison Beloran, much as I wish it were not the case, I must insist that I be allowed to keep my appointment at the Ministry of Justice. It has been nearly two months since Interrelator Waterston's murder, and I must report to his mother. In other words, I am under Temple Obligation.''

Beloran's fan-ears flattened, and his long tail lashed back and forward on the slick floor like an angry cat's. It took him a moment to control his anger, but finally, he bowed an apology. Then he reached under the leather strap that he wore like a sash over his scaled chest, dug out a ceramic token, and handed it to her. "Very well. If you must. And I insist that you ride with top closed and the windows of your vehicle darkened so as not to upset the populace. This seal will give you passage into the Temple of Administration, wherein the Ministry of Justice may be found.''

Mahree nodded. "Thank you, Liaison. Will you please tell the Nordlund pilot that I'm sorry for the inconvenience, and ask him or her to wait for our return?'' She gave Mitchell a quick glance. "I'm assuming you want to come along,'' she added.

The archaeologist nodded.

"I will instruct the pilot,'' Beloran said. "And the pilot is, undoubtedly, a male. On Ancestor's World, it is traditionally forbidden for the Na-Dina to fly through Mother Sky. But our church has issued a dispensation to the Infidels, providing only *males* pilot the Infidel ships.''

Mahree nodded. "Thank you for your instruction, Liaison. I will not forget.'' Quickly, she turned to her party and gave instructions for them to wait aboard the air-conditioned comfort of the Nordlund jumpjet. "I'll meet you back here in an hour or so," she said. "I have official business in Spirit."

Greyshine and Etsane nodded, promising to oversee the group so that things went smoothly. Mahree handed over her bags to the Ethiopian girl with a word of thanks.

Liaison Beloran, she noted, was already heading for the landing field, his long tail dragging behind him.

Mahree sighed. "Nice guy," she said to Mitchell. "Does he dislike all humans, or is it just me?"

"He's not crazy about any outworlders," Mitchell said. "Beloran is a cranky old cuss, but he's very conscientious. We've all gotten used to him being a stickler for the rules." He grinned wryly. "Bureaucrats . . . they're the same on all worlds, eh, Ambassador?"

"*I'm* a bureaucrat," Mahree reminded him, as they reached the double doors and stepped out into heat that felt like a blast furnace. The air seemed to suck every bit of moisture from her skin, mouth, and throat in a bare second. "And, speaking of following rules, Doctor Mitchell, aren't you aware that weapons are restricted on alien worlds by CLS regs?"

Mitchell opened the door of the small ground skimmer and waved her past him. His eyes narrowed, but his smile did not waver. "I suppose I should have taken it off before I came into town," he said, with a complete lack of regret. "But I'm so used to wearing it that I forget I have it on."

"Pulse-guns are dangerous weapons," Mahree said. "I must insist that you remove it, Doctor." She sat there, scowling and fuming, as the archaeologist walked around the skimmer and slid into the driver's seat.

"Pulse-guns are dangerous?" Mitchell started the skimmer and gave her a sardonic look. "Well, y'know what, Ambassador Burroughs? They aren't nearly as dangerous as the two blasters I keep in my footlocker at camp."

"Blasters?" Mahree was genuinely horrified. "What if one of the Na-Dina got hold of one? They could do terrible damage completely by accident!"

Mitchell slammed on the brake and turned to regard Mahree. All traces of laid-back good humor were gone, and the backwoods accent had completely vanished. "You listen to me, Ambassador. I have permits for these weapons. The CLS recognizes that the canyon country of Ancestor's World is full of dangerous predators—and there has been one murder already. This gun stays right here on my hip, and nothing you can say is going to change that. I keep my guns locked up when I'm not there. I've had guns since I was a boy in Tennessee, and I know how to handle them responsibly. Do we understand each other?''

Without waiting for her to answer, he turned away and the skimmer moved forward again.

Mahree was quiet for several minutes, thinking hard. She was going to have to work with this man for weeks, possibly a couple of months. Making him angry was counterproductive. She knew that possession of blasters was illegal even if he had permit for the pulse-guns. Still, if he kept them locked up . . . *You're supposed to be a diplomat,* she reminded herself, *but you've been acting like a priggish bureaucrat.* She wiped futilely at the sweat trickling down her face and into the neck of her jumpsuit.

"It's early summer," Mitchell said, with no trace of rancor in his voice. "Now you know why the Na-Dina evolved without sweat glands. And why they worship pools of cool water."

Okay, Mahree. Be diplomatic.

Mahree took a deep breath, then forced a smile. "How about we start over?" Holding out her hand, she added, "Hi. I'm Mahree Burroughs, who is usually nicer than this. Dying of heat exhaustion has made me grumpy, I'm afraid. I hope you've got something cool to drink."

The archaeologist nodded amiably, smiled, then reached over and shook her hand. "I'm Gordon Mitchell. Call me Gordon, please. And yes, I've got some iced tea stashed under that dashboard. Help yourself."

Mahree rescued the container from under the dash, swallowed some wonderfully cold tea, then watched as they headed for a distant stone-paved street. She could see clearly through the one-way polarization in the skimmer windows.

The streets of Spirit were crowded with Na-Dina steam buggies, animal-drawn-carts, and hundreds of Na-Dina on foot, their blue-scaled bodies a splash of bright color against the brown and green landscape. She pointed at the milling crowd. "Too bad the others can't see this. I feel like I've traveled back in time to ancient Cairo, or Baghdad."

"I know what you mean." Gordon waved ahead, gesturing at the dozen stone temples rising from the center of Spirit and the low blocks of residential neighborhoods that filled the irrigated valley. Ahead of them, in the center of the city, flat-topped stone pyramids rose for twenty stories about the rest of the city. "You know, Ms. Burroughs, Beloran doesn't express himself very politely, but he's right. Most of these people are still experiencing culture shock from learning they're not alone in the universe."

Mahree nodded. "Please. Call me Mahree. I know what you mean. It's too bad Sorrow Sector—and then Nordlund—got here first. A trained CLS team could have cushioned that shock for the Na-Dina."

She thought back to the briefing she'd given at Star-Bridge, based on information supplied by Mitchell, cribbed from Bill's notes on the Na-Dina. The notes had included a long list of interdicted technology, made up by the Traditionalists on the Council of Elders. Anti-grav, for example, was strictly forbidden. As were orbiting satellites. And the off-worlders were restricted to the site of Nordlund's dam and mountain mining sites, and Mitchell's archaeology digs.

"Do you understand why the Na-Dina are so resistant to off-world encounters?" Mahree asked. *She* knew, but wondered if Mitchell had read Bill's notes, or just collected them and sent them on. The man was obviously very busy with his dig, and being an alien contact specialist was *her* job, not his.

"Sort of," Gordon said. "They believe that they're holding Ancestor's World in trust for the Spirits of their dead

Ancestors. That those ancestors will hold them accountable for any profanation of the ancient traditions and rules.''

"Right," Mahree said approvingly. "It's hard for humans to imagine, a culture that stretches back for six thousand years that's remained almost the same from that time until the present."

"Except for their damned language," Mitchell said. "I sure hope Ms. Mwarka can decipher it. *I* haven't made a dent in it."

"Etsane struck me as very competent," Mahree said. "Professor Greyshine certainly thinks very highly of her." She took a deep breath. "How well did you know Bill, Gordon?"

"I didn't know him long, but we spent a lot of time together. He loved coming out to help on the dig. I liked him, he worked hard. . . ." His tanned features twisted in a sudden spasm, and he banged a fist against the dash. "Dammit . . . it just wasn't *fair*! I saw the body . . ." He swallowed hard, and Mahree realized he was shaking at the memory. "It was pretty bad," he finished softly.

"I'm sorry," she said. "I worked with him for a year or so, and I felt just terrible when I found out." She searched for a way to change what was obviously a very painful subject. "I see a light-pole over there. Streetlamps? I didn't realize the Na-Dina technology was that advanced."

Gordon nodded. "Think OldAm technology circa A.D. 1910. Electric lights. Dynamos. Telephones. Steampowered factories and ships. Marconi-style radios. And coal-fired steel foundries. Everything except free-flying balloons and Wright brothers-style aircraft. There are historical accounts that long ago, the Na-Dina males used to fly through Mother Sky on giant wings—hang gliders of some sort. But then the Royal House and the priests decided that was a profanation—and that ended flight on this world until we came here."

Mahree gazed in wonder as a large balloon lifted up from a flat platform atop one of the temples. A land-line held it tethered to the yellow sandstone pile, a building easily thirty stories tall, and one pockmarked with windows, balconies, and garden areas that splashed green across the great pile. "What's that building? The one with the balloon?"

Gordon squinted. "The Temple of Storms. Where the meteorologists hang out. Next to it is the Temple of the River, home base for some of the smartest hydrologists you're likely to find anywhere. On the far side is the Temple of Earth Quaking, where seismology studies dominate. Beyond them is the Temple of A-Um Rakt, where electricity and lightning are studied."

"And there?" she pointed.

"That's the Royal House, which we'll probably never get inside. Next to it is the Temple of Administration, site of all the government Ministries—and our destination."

As he finished speaking, Gordon halted the skimmer by the Temple entrance and parked it.

The two humans went into the building, after showing the seal Beloran had given them to the guard at the door.

Inside the temple it was mercifully cool. The ground floor's high ceiling was supported by massive pillars, all of it made of stone. As Mahree started across the polished surface, the floor trembled beneath her feet. She stopped dead, heart thudding, until the shaking and rumbling subsided. She glanced at Gordon. "Earthquake?"

He nodded. "Get used to it. Three, maybe four or more on an average day. Sometimes even more."

Mahree cast an apprehensive glance around her at the massive temple, picturing what would happen if those stone pillars fell. Guessing her thought, Mitchell grinned wryly. "Don't worry. The Na-Dina know all about baseplate isolation of structures. It takes a hell of a lot to knock down one of these temples."

"I hope so." As he indicated the way, Mahree started up the stairs.

Ten floors up, Gordon turned to the right, walked past several doorless entryways, and stopped before one. He pointed at the hieroglyphs carved into the stone lintel over the doorway. "Ministry of Justice, Division of Investigation. Krillen's office."

Mahree paused in the doorway. The office was lit with electric lights, and a cluster of crescent-shaped desks occupied the middle of the high-ceilinged room. Private offices lined the opposite wall. A squat, bright blue Na-Dina hurried toward them. "We seek Krillen, of the clan Moon Bright," Mahree hiss-clicked in High Na-Dina.

The official stopped dead, then bowed. "I am Makwen, of the clan Hard Clay, of the trade Ancestor's Law, Mother of six eggs, Prosecutor for this office. And you are?"

"I am Mahree Burroughs, of the clan Human, of the trade Interrelator, Mother of one egg," Mahree replied. "And this is Gordon Mitchell." She hesitated. Mitchell's file had mentioned an ex-wife and children, but she couldn't remember how many.

"Krillen of the Law is expecting you. Please follow me."

They followed Makwen across the room and down the line of offices. The Prosecutor stopped before a stone door. She pushed at the bottom half of the door and it swung inward, suspended by a shoulder-high beam that ran horizontally to either side of the entryway. *A giant cat door*, Mahree thought, amused, as she bent low and followed Gordon and the Na-Dina into the office.

Behind them, the weight-balanced door finished its rotation, slowing to a stop against wooden floor bumpers. Before them was a blue-scaled Na-Dina who wore a sash across his chest. Dozens of tiny gold chevrons studded the sash, and Mahree guessed that it denoted rank of some kind. The alien was squatting behind a stone desk cluttered with a pot, a bronze ruler, ink-bowl, writing styluses and a battery-driven Na-Dina clock. An open window loomed behind him. The Investigator looked up from reading a sheaf-scroll, and his clear eyelids blinked sideways. "Yes, Prosecutor Makwen?"

Bowing deeply, the Prosecutor introduced the newcomers. The humans bowed in turn. Mahree noted that Gordon introduced himself as: "Philosopher Mitchell, of the clan

Human, trade Archaeologist, and Father of two daughters.''

The Na-Dina Investigator bowed in his turn. ''And I am Krillen of the Law, Elder of the clan Moon Bright, Investigator of the Ministry of Justice, and Father of three children.''

They all stared at each other for a moment, then Krillen gestured to Makwen. ''You may return to your duties, Prosecutor.''

She scurried out the swinging cat door, and Mahree noticed that her long tail barely made it out of the way in time. She repressed a smile. *What an interesting species the Na-Dina are!* Glancing around the office, she saw that Gordon was leaning against a shelf stacked high with bronze measuring tools, a microscope, and other devices she didn't immediately recognize. Since there were no chairs for visitors—Na-Dina weren't configured to sit—she returned her attention to Krillen, who was studying both humans interestedly.

''Philosopher Mitchell, Interrelator Burroughs,'' the alien said after a moment. ''Please squat and share tea with me.''

Mahree hunkered down as well as she could, noting, with annoyance, that Gordon seemed able to squat and maintain that position effortlessly. *Too much desk work,* she thought, sipping the cool, bitter tea. It was so astringent it made her teeth ache, but she knew from her studies that humans could eat and drink most Na-Dina foods and beverages. This must be kalant-tea.

''Tell me, Interrelator Burroughs,'' Krillen said, his bright eyes fixed on her, ''do you demand the dead body of a now-living Na-Dina as reparation for the loss of your student?''

''*What?*'' Mahree choked on her tea, and her legs gave out. She sat down hard on the floor, sputtering. Gordon reached over and patted her back gently, steadying her.

Finally she was able to draw breath again, and began to apologize. ''Not necessary,'' Krillen said, waving a taloned hand dismissively. ''I should not have been so blunt, perhaps. It is plain that you still have much to learn of our ways, Interrelator.''

She drew a deep breath, suddenly aware of Mitchell's hand steadying her. She straightened up, and Gordon let her go. ''I certainly do, Investigator Krillen,'' she said. ''But I am a quick student. Do I understand you correctly? You would kill a Na-Dina citizen if I demanded blood reparation for Bill's death on your world?''

''Of course.'' Krillen reached out to the metal ruler lying on his desktop, tracing its markings with a sharp talon. ''Our most ancient Tradition calls for repayment in kind. A tail for a tail, a limb for a limb, an eye for an eye, a life for a life.''

Mahree shook her head. ''No, of course I don't demand that a Na-Dina be put to death. Besides, we don't even know that one of your people did the killing. It is just as likely that the murderer was a human.''

''It is far *more* likely,'' Krillen told her. ''Our Justice is harsh to some, but clear and swift, and our people respect our laws. We have very little theft, less assault, and perhaps ten murders a year.''

''For the entire planet?'' Mahree raised her eyebrows. Talk about civilized! Even the Mizari, who had been civilized space travelers since the time when humans were living in caves, had more crime than *that*. Though not much more. And their population was far higher, she reminded herself, especially considering all the Mizari colony worlds. . . .

Krillen nodded, human-style, something he must have picked up from Gordon during his initial visit to the Base Camp. ''Yes, for the whole world. Though many die each year from flood, earthquake, or storm. But that is the way of things.''

Krillen poured more tea into a cup and pushed it across his desk toward her. ''More tea?'' Mahree was fascinated to see him use his tail at the same time to curl around a bound scroll and place it into a floor slot. ''I have been studying the information on your species. This sweat-thing you do. It is not healthy. You must be careful to replenish your body's loss.''

She took the tea and sipped, grateful for the coolness. She was getting used to the taste.

"Here," Krillen said, watching her drink. "Have one of these, too." He offered her a large white pill.

Mahree took the pill, glanced covertly at Gordon, who nodded slightly. She popped it into her mouth. "Oh . . . salt!"

"Salt," Krillen agreed approvingly. "The Rock of Life. My readings indicate that humans waste both water and salt in their sweating."

"You are correct."

Gordon Mitchell took out a packet, removed a round pill, put it in his mouth, and chased it down with some of the bitter tea. "Krillen? Care to try some alien salt?"

Krillen looked to Gordon. "Free-will trade? No obligation? One of mine for one of yours?"

"Of course." As Mahree watched, Mitchell handed over one of his round pills, took back one of Krillen's oblong pills, and placed it in his packet.

Krillen popped the salt tablet in his mouth, and sat there for a minute, evidently savoring it as it dissolved.

Mahree smiled. "All part of Tradition," she guessed.

Gordon nodded. "The Na-Dina value Tradition, and have for six thousand recorded years, I've learned. They are not a people to take change casually."

She nodded. That jibed with her own studies of the culture. "Investigator Krillen, if your people value Tradition so much, why then have you invited so much change lately by selling your mineral rights to Nordlund in exchange for the massive changes they're making on the face of your planet? I mean, they're planning to *dam* the River of Life."

Krillen put down his teacup. "Ambassador Burroughs, when the first Sky Infidels came, they met a family clan of Merchants in the foothills of the Mountains of Faith. They traded for jewels, gold, and salt. The Merchants received back wondrous devices, and the Horn That Calls To The Stars. They presented the Horn to the Royal Family, who directed that the Horn be used to communicate with other worlds. The Elders among the Priesthood decided that it would please our Revered Ancestors to have strangers come and marvel at our world.''

Krillen picked up another scroll in the end of his tail, and filed it away. ''Nordlund came instead. And then the Modernists, the party in power, argued that the only way to gain respect from your CLS was to speed up our industrialization. Building more factories. Making more tools. There has even been talk that one day the Temple will permit the Na-Dina to pilot ships through the sky, the way our Ancestors were said to have done. The Priests have already created dispensations to allow Na-Dina to be passengers aboard the Infidel vehicles.''

Krillen paused, then looked over his shoulder as the afternoon sunlight flooded in through the open window. ''Ambassador, we must control our own destiny. We must not be the plaything of off-worlders. The Modernists rule the Royal House, as they do the other government Temples. I, however, am a Traditionalist. I fear the effects you Sky Infidels are having upon my world. I fear our heritage will be thrown away in the name of modernization.''

Mahree frowned. ''But Krillen, the CLS can interdict this world, can prevent ships from visiting without your permission. There is no need to sacrifice your heritage for . . . for—''

''Power? Technological marvels?'' Krillen said, his tone neutral. The alien gazed sadly at Mahree and shook his head. ''There is no way to step back from this precipice we face. There is no way to unlearn what we have learned so recently, O Mother of a daughter. Could you unbecome a Mother? Could the River of Life not flood each spring?''

Mahree glanced at Gordon Mitchell. ''When Nordlund finishes with it, the annual floods will probably cease, Investigator Krillen.''

The alien blinked at her, his consternation evident even to a human. ''If you are correct, Ambassador . . . my people must change their way of life even more than I realized.'' He made a little dismissive flick with the end of his tail.

"However, that is not my responsibility, thank the Revered Ancestors. But the murder of your student is. Shall we turn our attention to what I have discovered during my investigation?"

Mahree nodded. "If you please, Investigator."

"I have discovered very little that is definitive, Ambassador. The jumpjet was found south of the Western Wastes, atop a mesa far from any village, with only the human's body inside. Interrelator Waterston's skull was crushed— by a metal bar we found beside the body. There were no footprints outside, no signs of tracked or wheeled vehicles, nothing to prove that anyone but your student was inside the craft when it landed."

Mahree turned to Gordon. "You were there, correct?"

He nodded.

"Did Bill land the craft himself?"

Mitchell hesitated. "It's hard to say. We couldn't fix the time of death exactly, since several days had gone by. Dehydration . . . and . . . you know. Bill could have been killed while in flight, I suppose."

"Gordon, *how* did the jumpjet land? Was it set on automatic?"

The archaeologist shook his head slowly. "No. It was set on manual. The computer log showed that Bill set the ship on automatic, but that the landing was made manually." He shrugged. "I didn't do a complete check of the controls, I'm afraid. For one thing, we were all . . . well, kind of unhinged by what we found. And we knew we shouldn't disturb anything until the authorities could see it."

"The jumpjet landed in the middle of nowhere."

"Right."

Mahree turned back to Krillen. "Leaving no tracks or traces of how the killer either entered or left the ship."

"Correct, Ambassador."

"So we don't know whether Bill or his murderer landed the ship." She considered for a moment, then added, "Why would Bill land in the middle of nowhere?"

Gordon shook his head. "Maybe the murderer forced

him to land. If we knew whether Bill landed the ship or not, we could at least narrow it down that we're looking for a human.''

Mahree's eyebrows went up. ''Why?''

''Because, Ambassador, no Na-Dina may fly through Mother Sky,'' Krillen explained patiently. ''Special dispensation must be given for one of the People to even ride as a passenger on one of your craft. My people do not have the knowledge or the motivation to pilot your jumpjet. To do so would mean they had committed an unforgivable sin against Mother Sky.''

She frowned, chagrined. ''Oh, of course. Sorry, I'm not always this dense. It must be the heat.''

Krillen's tail lashed in anger. ''And this is not your profession, Ambassador, but it is *mine*, and I am angry that I have made so little progress toward solving this case!''

''Well, what about fingerprints?'' she asked. ''On the murder weapon?'' She glanced at Krillen. ''You know about fingerprints?''

''Yes, though we Na-Dina do not have them,'' he said, holding up his taloned hands to demonstrate. ''Our palms are scaled, and we do not sweat.'' His tail switched back and forth. ''To answer your question . . . no. No fingerprints.''

''Anywhere?''

''Except where one would expect to find them. On the controls of the jumpjet, yes. Professor Mitchell's, Interrelator Waterston's, as well as other human prints that I have yet to identify.''

''Most likely they belong to the Nordlund pilots,'' Gordon said.

''Wasn't there *any* clue?'' Mahree cried, frustrated.

''Just one,'' Krillen said, unblinking. ''I discovered several scale impressions in the pilot's seat cushion.''

''A Na-Dina was in the seat?''

''Axum,'' Gordon said heavily. ''Our crew boss. She frequently rode back and forth in the jumpjet when they were transporting the crew from dig sites. She admitted that she was fascinated by the jumpjet controls, and that several times she sat in the pilot's seat while the Nordlund pilot had the jet placed on automatic.'' Mitchell grimaced. ''Not that a Na-Dina can really sit very well. She sort of perched on her butt, using her tail to balance. Hence the scale impressions.''

''Are scale impressions like fingerprints?'' Mahree asked. ''Unique to a particular Na-Dina?''

''No,'' Krillen replied, as though he hadn't thought of such an idea before. ''Scale *patterns* are unique. But all scales are very much alike, depending on where on our bodies they come from.'' He opened his palm again to show her the tiny scales on his palm, then waved a hand at his chest, demonstrating the obvious difference in size.

Krillen's fan-ears pricked up. ''I photographed the mesa top. There is only the narrowest and most dangerous of animal tracks leading to the top. No way to take a skimmer up or down. No evidence of any other craft—even a village cart. The nearest village is fifty of your kilometers away, and the villagers have not seen a stranger in half a year.''

Mahree sipped more tea, frowning thoughtfully. ''I've read a lot of mysteries. They always say to focus on method, motive, and opportunity.''

Krillen hissed approvingly. ''Yes, we have a similar dictum. The method is obvious—bludgeoning to death. Who would have a motive?''

''Well, there was the argument Bill had with Project Engineer Mohapatra the day before he was killed,'' Gordon said. ''I told you about it, Investigator.''

''What was it about?'' Mahree asked.

''I'm not sure. Bill mentioned it to Khuharkk'. Said that something wasn't right about one of the Nordlund sites. But he was very vague. Told Khuharkk' he'd tell him when he returned from Spirit.'' Mitchell spread his hands in a final gesture.

Mahree eyed him. ''Something? What something?''

Gordon shrugged. ''No idea. I haven't been over to the Nordlund dam site for a while now. Last time I was there, everything seemed to be going along right on schedule.''

''Well, if Bill argued with Mohapatra, seems to me that

he could be a suspect," Mahree said. "Have you questioned him, Investigator?"

Krillen tapped his ruler on his desktop. "I tried to gain an appointment with him, but the Project Engineer has many allies within the Temple of Administration, the Temple of the River, and even on the Council of Elders. He did not respond to my request."

Mahree's mouth tightened. "Well, he'll talk to *me*. And to you. I'll see to it."

"Take it easy, Mahree," Gordon counseled. "One argument doesn't constitute a motive for murder! If I had a buck for every argument I've ever had, I wouldn't need the Mizari Archaeological Society to finance this dig. Besides, don't forget opportunity as well as motive. Project Engineer Mohapatra is so recognizable that I can't picture him sneaking aboard Bill's craft unnoticed. He probably has a simon-pure alibi that stretches clear back to Shassiszss!"

"Alibi?" Krillen asked.

Hastily, Mahree defined the alien word. "Well," she said after a moment, "who else might have had a motive?"

Gordon shrugged. Krillen's fan-ears twitched. "Young Waterston, from all accounts I have heard, was well liked and respected," the Na-Dina said. "However, it is possible that his murder was not done for personal reasons—rather, for ideological or profit motives. There are humans and Na-Dina who resent the presence of your CLS on my world."

"By humans you mean Nordlund, of course," Mahree said. "If it weren't for the CLS, they could do whatever they liked here, with no one to make them observe proper safety codes. By Na-Dina . . . you mean, one of the Traditionalist party? Someone who doesn't want change on Ancestor's World?"

Krillen turned the ruler over in his taloned hands. "Possibly. I believe we should forgo motive for the moment, and concentrate on opportunity. I have been intending to take more advanced equipment out to the murder site, for a lengthier examination. Would you be interested in joining me, Ambassador?"

Mahree nodded. "I was going to ask if I could go. I

brought along some forensic science equipment that might lend itself to a reexamination of the murder scene.''

Krillen's fan-ears perked up. "Equipment? What kind of equipment?''

"Infrared scanners. Biomolecule sensors. Gene-typing instruments.'' She was pleased to see that Krillen's eyes brightened as she named each item. "And a large-field microscope able to detect the smallest markings on that murder weapon. Interested?''

The Na-Dina stood up quickly, his long tail quivering. "Interested? Of course! When shall we make this journey?''

"As soon as we can arrange for transport,'' Mahree said. "Can I contact you from the Base Camp?''

"Yes, by relay to our communications radio in the Ministry,'' Krillen said. "We will speak soon, then.''

Mahree, recognizing the end of the discussion, nodded and scrambled to her feet. Gordon stood up from his squatting position with such boneless grace that she envied him as she tried not to rub her posterior, which had gone numb from sitting on the stone floor.

"Just let me get settled in at the Base Camp,'' Mahree said, as she and Gordon headed for the huge cat door, "and we'll make the trip right after that.''

"Very well,'' Krillen said. "I will accompany you back to where your vehicle awaits.''

Mahree ducked under the cat door, thinking of the heat outside, and wondering how long it would take to get back to the landing field and the air-conditioned jumpjet. . . .

Krillen of the Law walked beside the two aliens along the corridors of the Ministry, aware of covert glances from every doorway. Most Na-Dina had still not gotten a close look at one of the Sky Infidels.

The Investigator told himself the Ancestors would have been proud of how he had interacted with the Soft Faces. The male and female Infidels looked like unformed yolks spilled from the egg, so soft was their skin and so malleable were their faces. But despite their extreme ugliness, their spirits were recognizably those of civilized beings. They spoke the High Speech with respect, they offered the Rock of Life in return for hospitality. Krillen found himself respecting them, and was pleased that they appeared to have respect for him, for his position.

Gently, he smoothed his Sash of Rank. It was studded with tiny gold chevron pins, so many that they nearly covered its surface. They represented Cases Solved. One hundred and twelve, with one pin for each case. Years and years of devoted work. Few of his fellow Investigators reached a hundred before retiring to their home compound and luxuriating in their private ponds.

Krillen thought of the tools he used in his investigations, and wondered what it would be like to use tools invented by the Sky Infidels. Would such sophisticated technology eliminate the need for slow, painstaking, and relentless investigation? He had founded his life on such investigation, and he had never failed to solve a case.

But never before had he faced a challenge such as this. . . .

The trio reached the stairway and started down, with Krillen in the rear. The Na-Dina watched in fascination as the humans negotiated the steps designed for taloned Na-Dina feet with no sign of uncertainty or distress. "Most engaging!" he hissed softly.

The female Infidel, Mahree, paused and turned back to ask, "What's engaging?"

Krillen wasn't sure he should say, but falsehood was not in his nature. He found himself replying honestly. "The way you negotiate these stairs—even level surfaces! How in the name of the Revered Ancestors do you people manage to keep from falling over?"

Mahree's teeth showed suddenly, and she made a soft gurgling type sound. "You mean, how do we balance?" she asked.

"Yes," Krillen replied. "How can you possibly balance, with no tail?"

The male, Gordon, showed teeth also. "Krillen, we just

grew up walking without tails. I guess it's a case of learning to make do with what you've got.''

"Maybe we receive a dispensation from the forces of gravity," Mahree said, and Krillen could tell she was vastly amused—but not in a mean or hurtful way. "Actually, Krillen, you are not the first species to wonder why we don't fall flat on our faces."

They started down the stairs again, with Mitchell leading the way. His tall body moved so effortlessly, so fluidly, that Krillen wondered again about the ways of the universe. "When I'm drunk," Mitchell called back, "I do a good imitation of falling over."

"Drunk?" This was a word new to Krillen, a "made-word" recently adopted into their language since they'd lacked word-images for many of the customs practiced by the Sky Infidels. This word combination meant, literally, "salt hysteria."

"He means drunk from imbibing too much liquor," Mahree said, and Krillen thought he caught a faint edge of distaste in her voice. "An alkaloid-based liquid called ethanol, a chemical compound that disturbs human biochemistry, causing disorientation, and impairs the user's judgment. But it also produces a temporary state of euphoria, which is why *some* people are unwise enough to over-indulge in it."

"Ah, I understand you now," Krillen said. "We experience something similar when we eat too much of the Rock of Life. But that is rare. Only the rich can afford to indulge in such habits."

"Philosopher Mitchell," he added, as they reached the bottom of the stairway and started across the huge, columned hall, "when I was at your Base Camp before, when Interrelator Waterston had just been discovered, you would permit me only a brief glimpse of the tomb of A-Um Rakt. During my next visit, may I see the sarcophagus? Possibly touch it?"

"He didn't let you see it?" Mahree glanced quickly at Gordon. "That doesn't sound fair!"

"My record-keeping wasn't done," Mitchell said. "I'm

ANCESTOR'S WORLD

just doing things by the book, dammit! Howard Carter didn't enter Tutankhamun's tomb for weeks after his discovery. You have to measure everything, draw it, photograph it, make sure it's recorded down to the millimeter, Mahree.''

''Well, how is all of that progressing?'' she asked.

''Yesterday we removed the funerary offerings from the front half of the chamber.''

''What about the Mizari relics?''

''Still in situ.''

''I'm glad about that. I want to see them right away,'' she said.

Mitchell showed teeth again. ''Why am I not surprised?'' The human turned to Krillen as they all halted before the alien vehicle that hovered there on its fans, obediently awaiting the return of its driver. ''And, Investigator Krillen, I promise you that I will personally conduct you on an up-close tour of the tomb when you come out to the Base Camp. You can touch the sarcophagus . . . promise.''

Krillen bowed. ''May the Spirits of the Revered Ancestors smile upon us all, then, until we meet on that day,'' he said, returning to formality, and the High Speech. Then he relapsed into regular speech. ''Your vehicle . . . it travels quickly?''

Mahree nodded. ''Yes, it does.''

''Would you like a ride?'' Mitchell asked, waving a hand at the interior.

Such a simple offering to inspire such terror!

Krillen swayed, as if he had eaten too much Rock of Life, but recovered swiftly. He *was* curious, he found. ''Uh, yes. Thank you.'' Lifting his tail he climbed over the metal rim of the self-propelled craft, settled down in the rear storage box, and composed his soul for death. It was said by the priests at the Temple of A-Um Rakt that, each time one of The People took flight through Mother Sky, they risked death for such defiance of Ancestral wishes.

He knew better than that. He understood *radio*, when his rural cousins would have run from it. He even comprehended the round world, and the suns that lay beyond it, though that image felt like a nightmare. But he had grown up in a world where only The People, and the Revered Ancestors, roamed the land. No one else. And though his temple education whispered in his ear ''You are safe! Safe as a new-born scaly in the curl of his parents tails,'' Krillen found it hard to *believe*.

The skimmer vibrated, the fans howled loudly, and the craft . . . it lifted up into the air.

He flew.

Krillen, of the Clan Moon Bright, partook of the blessings reserved to the Ancestors.

CHAPTER 4

♦

Attack!

The jumpjet landed at Base Camp just before sunset, and Mahree waited until everyone had offloaded before she followed Gordon out of the passenger cabin. The archaeologist stopped at the top of the ramp and waved at the enclosing canyon walls. "Beautiful, isn't it?"

"Incredible," she whispered, seeing up close what she'd marveled at during the jumpjet's descent. She looked to her right, where the valley widened out. "Oh! Is that the City of White Stone?"

Gordon nodded. The evening breeze ruffled his sandy hair, and Mahree, who had changed during the trip into the shorts and sleeveless top she'd craved, felt a touch of coolness dispel the baking heat. "That's it. Six thousand years old, and parts of it look almost new. No one lives there now, though. It was King A-Um Rakt's capital."

"Have you excavated there?"

"We've barely touched it," Gordon admitted. "There's so much to do here that I wake up in the middle of the night worrying about how we'll even scratch the surface before this all floods."

"It's gorgeous," Mahree said, letting her gaze sweep over the outer wall of the city. Behind the wall rose flat-topped pyramid temples, similar to what she'd seen in Spirit. The high white wall enclosed the city, but in her mind's eye she saw what she knew from Mitchell's report lay there: massive temples, small, boxy homes, plazas, and open markets. A great stone causeway speared out from the western city gate, then marched down to the valley center, where it crumbled off into a deep arroyo. At the bottom of the arroyo ran the River of Life, its waters shallow this time of year. Mahree saw that a fallen pylon had gouged out part of the red stone causeway and thought of the earthquakes. She repressed a shiver. "I can almost hear the voices from the past, Gordon."

"I know. I hear them, too. Especially at night. You should see this place by moonlight. Talk about romantic . . ."

Mahree glanced at him quickly, then away again, as she fiddled with the strap of her duffel bag. How long had it been since she'd been anywhere or done anything that could be construed as romantic? Years, probably.

She drank in the dry air as another cooling breeze touched her face. They were surrounded by wild canyon country. Flat mesa tops towered high above their heads, reaching into the pale indigo sky. A volcano flamed in the western distance, and even where she stood on the elevated ramp, Mahree could feel the vibration of a microquake. It was as if this land, this world, was alive, stirring and rumbling like some great, immensely old animal.

"They were right to call it 'Ancestor's World,' " she whispered. "It even *smells* ancient."

He squinted at the setting sun as it lowered on the western horizon. "Hazy sky. Dust's thick in the air. We might get ashfall tonight."

Mahree had wondered about that when she sighted the distant volcano spewing forth its orange flames and black clouds. "Should I wear a filter-mask?"

"Not unless you have some sort of respiratory condition." Gordon leaned back against the ramp railing and folded his arms, regarding her intently. "It's pretty far away. The rainstorms wash most of the ash out of the air."

His eyes were light, hazel or blue-gray . . . Mahree couldn't tell for sure. She glanced away, breaking the eye contact, and pointed, almost at random, to a giant earthen ramp that lay downvalley, on the opposite side of the City of White Stone. "That rampway. What's it for?"

Gordon straightened up. "It's the access to the Royal Road. Starts up top on the mesa. Runs all the way back to Spirit."

Mahree's eyes widened in amazement. "But . . . but, how could the Na-Dina have known *where* to run the road? You told me on the trip down here that Spirit was founded three thousand years ago, and this is twice that old! Why build a road when—"

"When you don't know where you'll end up?" Mitchell grinned, then crossed deeply tanned arms over his sweat-darkened shirt. "The Na-Dina, or the People as they call themselves, have always trusted their fate to the dead Ancestors. Yes, the Royal Road was begun six thousand years ago, when Spirit didn't exist." He gestured at the arroyo. "As Na-Dina civilization expanded downriver, following the River of Life, so too did the Royal Roads reach out, arriving in the Delta millennia ago. Apparently one of the dead kings, the Revered Ancestors, told 'em to build a road into the wilderness, and by God they did. They had faith that it would go somewhere someday, so they built it. And eventually, it *did* go somewhere."

Mahree shivered, despite the baking heat that reflected back from the beige-banded canyon walls. This sense of the ages, of a history that stretched back into a misty past, was strange to her, alien in a way that the Na-Dina people themselves were not. She was used to aliens. But she wasn't used to six-thousand-year-old cities, or earthquakes, or volcanoes. . . .

She glanced at Gordon, who was staring north, where a mesa top glowed red-orange in the light of the setting sun. "Gordon . . . what made you choose archaeology—especially archaeology on alien worlds?"

He turned to look at her. "When I was a kid I read a lot of old books about exotic alien cities." A faint smile touched his mouth. "Some of 'em were by a guy named Burroughs. Any relation?"

Mahree smiled back. "No. But of course I read his books, too."

"Then you know what it was like, reading about places like Helium and Gathol. I used to lie in bed at night in the Tennessee mountains, imagining ancient cities on alien worlds. As I got older, I was drawn to studying the past. I wanted to understand how long-ago people made their choices. Whether they proved to be good choices or bad."

Mahree nodded encouragingly. "Historians always like to think that learning about the past will provide a key to understanding the present."

"As I studied history and archaeology back on Earth, I kept wondering about alien worlds. I wondered about *their* past. Whether it had anything to teach us. So in grad school, I concentrated on xeno-archaeology. Got my doctorate, and went out to dig." Gordon grinned self-deprecatingly. "But I never found any answers, I'm afraid. Just a helluva lot more questions."

Mahree felt the air still between them as the sun disappeared behind the mesa. She could feel the temperature drop immediately.

Gordon was looking at her, and suddenly the moment had grown far too personal. She cleared her throat. "So, how about a tour? Is that your Base Camp?" She pointed to a cluster of tents and buildings.

Mitchell nodded. "The dome is the Refectory, where we eat potluck style. Behind it is the Lab, where we analyze the artifacts, store them, and give thanks for the interior air-conditioning."

Mahree laughed softly. "I'll bet." The cool evening breeze brushed against her once more. "And the smaller domes encircling them?

"Dome-tents," Gordon replied. "Enough for private quarters, or double-up roomies, as people desire. Beyond them is our supply depot, and beyond that"—he pointed at a narrow sandstone canyon that led deep into the highlands—"is the Royal Tomb of A-Um Rakt, King of the

First Dynasty, founder of the City of White Stone. He's a personage revered by the Na-Dina as kind of a combination Galileo, Archimedes, and Quetzalcoatl.''

Mahree gazed at the purple-shadowed canyon. "Why so?"

Gordon shrugged. "He gave his people monumental architecture. He gave them agriculture. And he was the first Na-Dina King to prevent a civil war—as best we can tell from the records of later Dynasties." He sighed. "As Etsane may have told you, the records of the first seven Dynasties are written in ideoglyphs quite different from the hieroglyphs of Classical High Na-Dina. So we don't know what the first Na-Dina said about themselves. And the Revered Ancestors.''

Mahree noticed her compatriots had all moved into the silvery dome of the Refectory. "Is it dinnertime?"

Gordon nodded. "Probably. I usually eat in my tent, while I read the daily reports, but tonight is different. We got back here early, thanks to your ship's arriving a day ahead of schedule. Sumiko will probably scold me for bringing you all back before she had a chance to prepare a six-course Japanese dinner.''

"Sumiko Nobunaga? She's your Lab Chief, isn't she?"

He nodded, beckoning to Mahree to follow him, and started down the remainder of the ramp. "She keeps this operation on track."

Shouldering her duffel bag, Mahree followed. "Actually," Gordon added, "Sumiko organizes the data reporting. Axum runs the City of White Stone survey and excavations almost by herself."

"Axum?" Mahree felt her feet sink into the loose sand of the landing field. "Oh, yes, the crew boss."

Ahead of her, Gordon nodded quickly. "She supervises the best crew I've ever seen."

"Krillen seemed nice, and so have the others I've met." Mahree made a face. "Except for Beloran, of course."

"Sometimes he can be interesting to chat with," Gordon said. "We had a good discussion about the history of the Ninth Dynasty on the way over in the jumpjet. He's quite an expert on Na-Dina history, languages, and traditions.''

"Really? I wonder if he'd help advise Etsane about those ideoglyphs."

"Hard to say. Maybe if he was in a good mood." Gordon pointed at a prefab shed lying beside the trail. "Sanitary unit. Multispecies equipped. Big enough for four people at a time."

"Really?" she said, chuckling at the thought. "So you spent the Mizari Archaeological Society's first grant on a state-of-the-art toilet?"

Gordon glanced back at her, his eyebrows raised, as if he thought she faulted his judgment. "Well, this *is* the backcountry. Little luxuries help people endure the isolation."

"Hey, I'm all for it," Mahree hastened to add. "I've used enough exotic johns on different planets to be an expert, but that doesn't mean I *like* doing it."

The archaeologist shrugged, and resumed walking. "Actually, most of the money went into buying that monster of a warehouse for our Lab. I can sleep on a cot, but the artifacts and samples must be properly stored in a climate-controlled environment. Especially the perishable stuff."

"Perishable?"

"Burials."

"Oh." Mahree wondered at that, then remembered there were many more Royal Tombs lining the other side canyons that fingered out from this end of Ancestor's Valley. "Which tunnel-tomb is A-Um Rakt's?"

Gordon stopped just outside the circle of dome-tents. He pointed beyond the camp to an inclined rampway of stone and dirt that lay on the left side of the nearest canyon. "That one. The one with the biggest rampway. You can see five or six others beyond it. See the smaller ramps? The tombs are cut into the canyon walls, and the ramps provide access."

"Will you show us the Royal Tomb tonight?" Mahree hoped so, even though she felt worn out by the trip and the heat.

Gordon shook his head. "Not tonight. You and the other new folks need to get settled first, and the equipment inventoried and added to our stores, before we take that tour." Noting her disappointment, he added, "Cheer up. Schliemann searched for years before he found Troy. One more day won't spoil the experience. Believe me." He smiled reassuringly.

Mahree smiled back. "You're the boss, Gordon. And I can be patient. They train diplomats in that, too."

He chuckled. "After watching you with Beloran today, I can believe that!"

She glanced around at the stark countryside. "You said that you wore that pulse-gun because of predators. What kinds of predators?"

"There's one big bastard whose Na-Dina name translates to 'long-neck.' It's reptilian, but, like the Na-Dina, warm-blooded. Which makes it very, very fast."

Mahree took a firmer grip on her duffel. "What do they look like?"

"Long necks, armor-scales, teeth as long as your fingers. Think of a tiger-lizard combo. One of 'em attacked and killed one of the Na-Dina diggers the first week here."

"Don't you use repulsor wards?"

Gordon sighed. "Hey, give me credit for some common sense. Of *course* we have repulsor wards. But their ultrasonic wards don't seem to work on the larger life-forms hereabouts. Sumiko said something about reptilian hearing being lower than ours. If we went strictly by your book, more people would be dead."

Mahree felt uncomfortable, as if she'd spoiled the earlier mood of shared concern for Na-Dina history. "Sorry. I didn't know. You sure seem to have a thing about regulations and bureaucrats."

Gordon resumed walking. "Why not? Their regs, rules, and procedures are just like the crap I've put up with in academia. Hierarchies are not my favorite expression of human culture."

She had guessed that already. Would he lump her in with the worst of those bureaucrats? "Let me explain something

to you, Gordon. I'm not trying to be a prig. It's just that
I've seen, close up and personal, how incredibly destructive
the indiscriminate use of a weapon can be while trying to
establish good relations with aliens.''

He gave her a sharp look. "Mahree, I'm older than you.
I was an adult when the *Desirée* First Contact was made.
I remember it very well. You lost a crew member when
that guy Viorst went berserk and pulled a gun.''

"Jerry," she said, softly, with a flash of remembered
pain. "It was awful. Gordon . . . I'm not anti-weapon. I
learned to shoot on Jolie one summer when there was an
epidemic of neo-rabies among some of the small predators.''

He shrugged, but remained silent.

Mahree sighed and gave up, turning toward the Refectory
dome. "Is there something cold to drink in there?''

Gordon nodded, heading for a dome-tent on the edge of
camp. "Sure is. You go on. I'll be there in a few minutes.''

Mahree wondered at that, then chose politeness. "Of
course. See you soon.''

In the privacy of his tent, Gordon Mitchell sank down
onto his bunk, wiping his forehead in the heat. By morning,
the air in the tent would be chilly, but at the moment it was
still stuffy and hot. For a moment he considered turning on
his fan, but he wasn't planning on staying long enough.

Reaching under his cot, he pulled out a wooden toolbox.
Opening it, he grabbed the flask of Kentucky bourbon,
screwed off the top, put it to his lips, and swigged down a
long gulp.

Liquid fire ran down his throat, settling like a giant em-
ber in his belly. Warmth and numbness spread to all parts
of his body. He let out a long, gusty sigh as his muscles
relaxed.

I wonder if she'll try to confiscate my blasters, he
thought, eying the locked chest that held the two proscribed
weapons, then he shook his head. *No way,* he thought
sourly, remembering the long-neck crouched over the

blood-spattered corpse of the digger. He didn't want any more deaths.

Gordon sighed, eying the bottle, then decided against a second drink.

Not tonight.

Tonight he'd have people to talk to, other archaeologists. He wouldn't have to drink to relax and try to forget how lonely he was. He could talk to Greyshine, to Etsane, to the Mizari or the Chhhh-kk-tu. Maybe they'd have a game of poker or something.

Maybe he'd talk to Mahree again.

Or maybe not. . . .

She made him uneasy, and not just because she didn't approve of his weapons. He thought briefly about the picture she'd made, standing there in her sleeveless top and shorts, her long hair swinging in the night breeze. She was an attractive woman.

It had been a long, long time since he'd been attracted to any woman. Gordon frowned as he put the bottle away. Out here, in the remote backcountry, he couldn't afford to indulge in romantic fantasies. He was a grown man, a divorced man, the leader of this entire crew. He'd spent a long time building up walls, and he wasn't about to let them down for anyone.

Still, as he walked back to the Refectory, her image stayed before him, her dark hair and eyes, her smile . . .

Cursing softly under his breath, he tried to banish the image—only to find that he couldn't.

And *that* scared him.

Mahree dreamed of volcanoes spewing ash, rivers flooding, and a hot yellow sun that made her feel shriveled up like a prune, stripped of all fluids.

Investigator Krillen was in her dream, as was Beloran. And another shadowy figure, who at times looked like "the Mummy" in one of Rob's treasured antique films, and at times appeared like a robed and crowned Na-Dina.

She was walking through a canyon, and sometimes the

canyon became a tunnel. Sometimes she was herself, and sometimes she had talons and a tail.

It grew darker . . . darker . . .

Mahree realized she was in a tomb, and it was lit only by the setting sun, its yellow rays penetrating deep into the tomb. Red, green, and yellow images lined the walls of the tunnel, painted images of Na-Dina priestesses, Royal Ministers, and river barges that transported the King on his annual pilgrimage upriver, to the headwaters of the River of Life. They were bowing, and then she was kneeling, ready to pray for the annual flood—

—when suddenly, the tunnel floor beneath her feet rumbled sullenly, as if voices spoke to her from the wall paintings.

Earthquake?

Ka-blam!

Mahree jerked awake, blinking away the dream. What the—

Boom!

Explosions? She jumped to her feet, yanked her shorts on over the sleeveless leotard she slept in, and rushed barefoot out into the chill of night. "Gordon! Etsane!"

No reply, though sleepy voices shouted in alarm from nearby dome-tents. The moonlit night's chill stung her bare arms and legs.

Whap! A yellow flare dazzled her eyes.

She realized that the disturbance was up by the Royal Tomb. What was happening? It wasn't a storm; the night was clear.

"Gordon!" she yelled.

He rushed out of his dome-tent, clad only in shorts and boots, but there were two holster belts slung over his bare shoulder. "They must be trying to blow the armored door to get at the gold! Here!" Mitchell tossed her one of the belts.

Mahree caught it, then almost dropped it when she realized it was one of the highly illegal blasters. Just then, the whine of a pulse-gun broke the stillness. The blue energy bolt hummed past, so close she could smell it. The shot had come from the entrance to the Royal Tomb, just upstream from the Camp. "Gordon!" she yelled, half in appeal, half in protest as he raced past, heading directly for the site of the explosions.

"Protect the lab!" he shouted back. "Get Khuharkk' and Greyshine to set up a defensive perimeter with the repulsor wards!"

"Wait!" Mahree yelled. "Don't—" Her cry was cut off, and she fell flat as another pulse-bolt slashed randomly into camp, hitting the edge of Sumiko Nobunaga's dome-tent. The Japanese woman's cry of pain shocked her. Anger flared, and Mahree found herself on her hands and knees, scrabbling forward, after Gordon.

Moments later, she was running barefoot through the night, the heavy holster belt slung over her shoulder. Another pulse-bolt ripped through the night.

"I'm coming too!" she shouted at the figure she could barely see running through the moonlight.

"Head for the supply dump!" Mahree heard him yell.

She did, swerving to follow him as another pulse-bolt hit the canyon wall to her left, unleashing a shower of small rocks. Her feet stung, but Mahree ran silently, unwilling to give the unseen shooter the chance to aim at her voice. Behind her the camp erupted with Heeyoon snarls, Simiu growls, human screams and yells, plus the quick chatter of Drnian as people demanded to know what was happening.

She was panting as she reached the supply dump. "Gordon?" she whispered, halting. A hand clamped onto her arm, dragging her down, pulling her behind the metal boxes of the dump.

"Stay down!" he hissed.

Whap! A blue pulse-bolt passed just over her head, hitting the ground with a spurt of electrical flame.

They huddled together. Mahree's ears still rang from the explosions that had first awakened her. Her heart beat frantically, and for a second, she remembered Claire's worry.

"What's happening?" she whispered. "Who's doing this?"

"Smugglers, it's got to be. From Sorrow Sector, I'll bet," he hissed.

Of course, Mahree realized. *The treasure would draw them like flies.* Aloud she said, "We've got to get up there, stop them from getting into the Tomb!"

"Too dangerous," Gordon growled, breathing heavily. "They've got nightscopes. Infrared trackers. You're a glowing target whenever you leave shelter. So stay low!"

"And you?" She felt new anger at him for having the contraband blasters, furious anger at the unseen shooter, and sick worry for Sumiko and anyone else hurt by the random firing. "What are you going to do?"

"*You* lay down a series of quick blaster shots at the shooter's position." His shadowed form rose, crouching, preparing to spring forward. "I'll make a run for the canyon rockface, and try to flank him. It's in moon-shadow there and the rock is still warm with the heat of day. It'll mask my body heat. Ready?"

She thumbed off the safety on the blaster. "Ready," she whispered, sick with fear.

"Now!" he yelled, sprinting away.

Mahree stood up quickly and snapped off four blaster shots at the earth ramp that led up to the Royal Tomb's entrance. Four yellow beams slashed along the ramp-line, blinding her with their light. Something alien howled with pain. She had aimed where her memory said the dusty path ran, using the slant of the ramp as a guide.

Claws scrabbled behind her. She whirled, blaster ready, squinting as she tried to focus her dazzled eyes. "Halt!"

"It's me," snarled Professor Greyshine, his voice panting as the Heeyoon surged up beside her, moving on all fours. Another four-footed figure scampered after him, and her nose caught a familiar, musky scent. "And Khuharkk'."

"Honored MahreeBurroughs!" the Simiu growled in his own language, plainly shocked. "You are holding a *weapon*! How could you?"

Mahree's temper snapped, and she snarled back at him in perfect Simiu, "Do not presume to judge me, youngling!

It is not for youngsters to judge the honor of their elders!
Look to your own honor, O impudent one!''

Khuharkk' whined, then ducked his head. ''A thousand
pardons, Honored MahreeBurroughs.''

The memory of that agonized howl she'd heard was
haunting her. *Did I kill someone? Who? Oh, God!*

''What's happening back at camp?'' she whispered at
Greyshine, switching to Heeyoon. ''Is Sumiko all right?''

''For the moment,'' Greyshine replied. ''Strongheart got
Sumiko to safety in the Lab, along with the others. Etsane
is setting up repulsor-ward poles. What do we face here?''

She told them as much as she knew. ''Gordon should be
almost to the Tomb entrance by now. There's been no more
pulse-gun bolts. But I heard the sounds of several people
moving on the ramp slope, just before you arrived.''

''They're after the sarcophagus?'' Khuharkk' growled.

''And the Mizari relics,'' Greyshine said angrily. ''No!
They shall not have them! Khuharkk', come with me to the
creek. Gordon approaches on the left, the Ambassador
holds the center, and we will flank on the right, moving up
canyon. Come!''

''They've got nightscopes,'' Mahree warned.

''The water will cool our body heat,'' Greyshine promised. ''And we shall be cautious, and smell them before
they can see us.''

In seconds, they had vanished into the night.

Scrieee!

A yellow blaster beam reached out toward the creek,
striking rubble and sand. No one cried out. Mahree cursed
under her breath. That had come from a new position on
the ramp, from lower down. Gordon? Or someone else?
How many smugglers *were* there?

Voices cried out near the Tomb entrance. She recognized
a Heeyoon curse and a Drnian scream. Gordon was right,
she thought. Only Sorrow Sector could bring together so
many diverse species all bent on theft.

Human footsteps approached from the Camp. Mahree
dropped below the crate rim and looked back. The tall,
lanky form of Etsane Mwarka, blackness within blackness,

gestured at her. ''Where are they?'' she called softly, her deep voice filled with rage.

''Sumiko? How is she?''

''Wounded, but Strongheart says she'll be okay.'' Etsane joined her behind the pile of metal crates. On the ramp slope, the sound of a body falling shocked Mahree's ears. ''Where are the jackals who attacked us?''

Mahree levered herself into a crouch, peering over the pile of crates. ''Up there. On the ramp to the Tomb. But they've got infrared scopes, pulse-guns set for kill, and at least one blaster. Gordon is trying for the Tomb entrance. Khuharkk' and Greyshine are moving up the creek.''

''Good. We'll take the ramp!'' Etsane stood up and started around the pile of crates.

''Wait! You're unarmed!''

''I'm armed,'' Etsane said harshly. ''I've got the oldest and best weapon humans ever created. A sling. I used it to guard my father's goat herd from leopards.''

''You *what*?'' Mahree was incredulous.

''He was a an old-fashioned guy who believed in the traditional weapons, and taught me to use them.'' Etsane's teeth flashed white in her dark countenance. ''Trust me, I can handle myself. Come on, cover me!''

As Etsane darted away, Mahree stood up, assumed a wide-footed stance, and snapped off a couple of shots at the ramp, careful to close her eyes as she squeezed the trigger this time.

Scrieee! Scrieee! shrieked the coherent energy beams as they leaped out in an angry wash of pure energy.

Mahree began to run after Etsane as the young woman dived for cover behind a boulder lying near the bottom of the earth ramp. Her feet protested. ''Ow! Etsane, wait up! We can fight from here.''

Just as Mahree reached the boulder, a yellow blaster beam screamed over her head, hitting the metal crates of the supply dump. Boxes blew apart.

From the Tomb entrance at the top of the rampway, Gordon's voice rang out. ''Surrender!''

In the moonlight, Mahree could only make out the vague

shapes of two people struggling at the top of the ramp. Gordon and someone else. Etsane pointed suddenly at the rampway bottom. "There's the sniper. Get him!"

Mahree froze, her finger on the trigger. Could she really kill like this?

"Dammit!" Etsane was on her feet. Her sling whirled, then her shoulder snapped forward as she launched her missile. A human scream rang out. The Iconographer hissed with triumph.

"Gordon?" Mahree yelled. "You okay?"

"They're running!" he yelled back. "The gold's safe!"

"Let's go after them!" Etsane was panting and shaking with excitement. "We can't let them get away!"

"There are too many!" Mahree said, grabbing the young woman's arm. "Let them go. They didn't get what they came for."

The Ethiopian settled back on her heels, grumbling under her breath.

Suddenly, up canyon, on the opposite side of the creek, rocket engines flared redly and something that resembled a ship's lifeboat lifted out of the night shadows. It hovered close to the ground for a moment as a running figure reached it and jumped to make it onboard; then its belly jets flared blinding bright against the darkness. The roar of its takeoff filled the close-set canyon walls. Mahree and Etsane huddled together, hands clamped over their ears, as the thieves made their escape.

Seconds later, the ship was just a rapidly moving star in the night sky. Gordon called down to her, his voice overlaid with the tremor of pain. "Come on up, Mahree. The Tomb's safe. The smugglers are gone. And . . . and I need help."

Mahree got to her feet, wincing as a sharp stone stabbed her foot, then stumbled forward, forcing Etsane to walk, rather than run, up the night-darkened rampway. Before they could even start up it, Greyshine and Khuharkk' joined them from the creek, their fur dripping. Mahree felt a moment's pang for Khuharkk', knowing how Simiu hated to get wet.

"Honor was served!" growled Khuharkk' in a shaky

voice. "I fought one Simiu, and Greyshine knocked down a Drnian. They ran off when they lost their *weapons*."

Etsane grinned wildly. "I got one too! Filthy jackals . . . I *hate* tomb robbers!"

Mahree's shock at hearing that the smuggler Simiu had chosen to use weapons was only exceeded by her shock at Etsane's wild exultation at having caused bodily injury—perhaps even death. She took a deep breath as she holstered the blaster, trying to steady herself.

From the top of the rampway, she could hear someone—it must be Gordon—being wretchedly sick. "Gordon? You okay?"

Worriedly, she broke into a shaky run, ignoring the pain of sharp stones against her bare feet. Greyshine followed with the light-globe.

Gordon was sitting back on his heels, wiping his mouth, by the time Mahree reached him. There was a body lying near him, in the shadows.

Mahree looked down at it. "Is he—?"

Gordon nodded weakly. "Dead. Knocked my blaster out of my hand and was on me before I knew he was even there. We wrestled, and then I . . . I . . ."

As Greyshine arrived with the lamp, she could see—and wished she hadn't. The smuggler was a Heeyoon male. He lay on his back. There was no sign of a blaster wound, but the neck lolled at an unnatural angle. *Broken.*

"Gordon," she said quietly, "It was self-defense. There was nothing else you could have done."

"I know," he muttered. In the harsh light of the lamp, his face was gray beneath the tan.

Mahree took a deep breath—and promptly gagged. The dry night air was full of the smell of Gordon's vomit, and another, even stronger smell. Roasted meat, charred fur.

Clapping a hand over her mouth, she swallowed bile. "What happened?"

Mitchell gestured wearily at the armored door that had been placed over the opening to the tunnel. It sagged to one side, and there was a gaping hole where its locking mechanism had been. "They blasted the security door, which was the explosions we heard. But the Tomb chamber itself was protected by a stasis field, which delayed them long enough for me to get here. When the Heeyoon jumped me, the Simiu went in. He must've tried to short-circuit the time lock on the field . . .''

Mahree and Greyshine moved over to peer inside the door. When she saw what lay inside, in a charred puddle of fur, meat, and blood, Mahree staggered back, retching.

Etsane put a steadying arm around her shoulders as she heaved. Finally, wiping her streaming eyes, she straightened up.

In the hard-breathing silence afterward, Greyshine's calm, measured words sounded incredibly routine and ordinary. ''One of my people led them, I see. He carries the dye-mark of a Pack Leader. Khuharkk', please go and ask Strongheart to bring live flame. We must cremate the Pack Leader.''

''Yes, Professor,'' the Simiu youth rumbled softly. Mahree noticed blood streaking his coat, and realized that he'd been bitten on the shoulder—probably during his fight with the other Simiu. He turned and headed down the ramp, limping slightly.

Gordon looked over at Greyshine. ''Professor, I suggest cremating him where the smugglers' lifeboat took off. I don't think this fellow deserves to have his ashes mingled with royal dust.''

''Agreed,'' Greyshine said.

Etsane glanced briefly at the body of the Heeyoon smuggler, then eyed Gordon. ''Is the Tomb chamber safe? Did they damage anything?''

Gordon gave up on standing and slid down to sit on the stone sill of the Tomb entrance, his knees drawn up, his arms crossed over them, his whole posture one of exhaustion and recent nausea. ''No,'' he said wearily. ''They didn't get inside. Thank god.''

''I can't believe this happened,'' Mahree said, sitting down beside him. It felt heavenly to get her weight off her feet. ''One moment I was asleep, dreaming about the an-

cient Na-Dina, the next—'' She gestured weakly at the car-
nage around them.

"I'm glad you people came in a day early," Gordon
said. "If it hadn't been for you, Ambassador, and Etsane
and Greyshine . . . no way we could have fought them off."
He glanced at Etsane, seeming to focus on her for the first
time. "A sling!"

"She wounded one of the smugglers with it," Mahree
said. "I never saw anything like it."

Gordon gave the Ethiopian woman a weak grin. "Trust
an archaeologist to know how to use ancient weapons. I've
done some slinging myself. Took a course in ancient weapons and how to use 'em." He turned back to Mahree and
added, "And, Ambassador, you weren't kidding when you
said you can shoot. You wounded two of them on the
ramp."

Thank god I didn't kill anyone! was Mahree's first
thought; then, suddenly, she was fighting back tears and
shaking all over. Gordon reached out and took her hand,
while Etsane put an arm around her trembling shoulders.
"It's okay now. We're safe," the Ethiopian woman whispered.

After a moment Mahree regained control, and, looking
up, she saw the approaching figure of Doctor Strongheart.
The Heeyoon female carried two burning torches and her
med-kit.

It's over, Mahree thought. *Really over.* She looked at the
corpse of the dead Heeyoon, then closed her eyes, blocking
out the sight of the body, of the moon the Na-Dina called
"Mother's Daughter," and of Gordon's face peering at her.

"Mahree . . ." he whispered. "C'mon. Let's get you
back to your tent. You look like you've had enough."

"I have," she admitted. "Okay, just give me a hand.
I'll . . ."

With his help, she tried to get up, but subsided with a
cry of pain. "My feet!"

Strongheart was there, and she took in the situation at a
glance. "Ambassador, you're not walking anywhere tonight. Rest a moment, and we'll bring a lifter to get you

back down. Some of those cuts are serious," she said.

Mahree leaned back, and Gordon's arm came around her, supporting her. His body was blessedly warm. "Relax," he told her. "You heard the doctor."

For once, Mahree was glad to take orders.

Beloran stood at the edge of the dome-tents, watching the lights and voices move about on the Tomb rampway. He'd been awakened by the explosions, and had rushed to the Lab building, thinking something had blown up inside. Only when the blue bolts of sky-fire had come down from the rampway had he realized what was happening. By then, the Burroughs female was armed and fighting, while Mitchell had disappeared.

Too bad.

This raid by off-world smugglers would have been the perfect time for him to grab one of Mitchell's energy weapons and kill them both.

It would have easier and quicker than the steel bar he'd used to slay the Interrelator. And easily blamed on the smugglers.

Of course, it was frequently a mistake to act in haste. By the time he'd killed Waterston, Beloran had been planning the Interrelator's death for some time. The discovery of the off-worlder Mizari relics had just provided him with a catalyst, convincing the Liaison that it was time to act. And act he had, convinced that if he killed their Interrelator, the CLS would cease its meddling intervention in the affairs of *Halish meg a-tum.*

So he'd killed Waterston . . .

. . . and even more Infidels had come.

Turning away from the shouts and movements up on the rampway, Beloran shuffled away into the darkness, seeking the solitude of the City of White Stone. No one would go there tonight. No one would miss him in the confusion of the smuggler raid aftermath.

He needed silence, and solitude. Time to think, to plan. To consider all sides of the question. Should he kill this Burroughs female? The Infidel Mitchell had said that she was famous throughout the CLS worlds. If she died, would that serve as a warning to the CLS? Or a challenge?

Today the Infidels had talked with Krillen of clan Moon Bright. The Investigator had an impressive record. Beloran knew he had covered his trail thoroughly, perhaps perfectly . . . but still . . .

What if this Krillen became a danger? Perhaps he should consider eliminating him, too.

Would the death of Mahree Burroughs be the cause of further delay in the completion of the Great Dam? That was the last thing he wanted. But he sensed that she and Krillen would not rest until they discovered who had killed Waterston. And that kind of determination was a danger to him.

Beloran considered. If off-worlders died now, it must appear like an accident. A rockslide, perhaps. A flood death. A poisoning from strange food. Anything but an obvious murder, which had brought only more Infidels from the sky, and focused more unwelcome attention on his world. The Ancestors would not forgive him a second mistake.

The white walls of *Segor A-mun* rose up before him.

Beloran passed inside, therein to make penance for his arrogance.

CHAPTER 5

♦

The Royal Tomb

Just after lunch the next day, Etsane sat cross-legged on the floor of the metal-roofed Lab building. She wore only boots, shorts, and sleeveless blouse, in preparation for the heat outdoors. The Lab itself was cool, thanks to its climate-control unit. She watched as people wandered in and sat down on a crate or a chair. They'd been called there by Gordon Mitchell, their *astamari*, or Teacher, for a planning conference in the wake of the smuggler attack. Everyone was there, except Esteemed Lorezzzs, who had come down with a case of native "sand fever."

What would Mefume, her father, have thought of her behavior last night? Etsane could tell that she'd shocked Ambassador Burroughs with her actions. The Ethiopian woman grimaced. Well, so be it. She came from a people who fought to protect themselves, who shed the blood of those who would harm them.

One of the Drnian specialists, Natual, walked up and sat down beside her. Drnians were the most human-looking aliens she had ever met, though Natual couldn't pass for one of her people even in a very dim light. Still, he had two arms, two legs, and one head and wore clothing, even though his limbs were so thin they appeared almost stick-like.

Etsane had exchanged casual conversation with him aboard *Emerald Scales*, and recalled his cheerful, friendly nature.

As she hesitated, wondering whether to speak first, Natual blinked at her. He had huge, red eyes that had nictitating membranes, and no nose, only a depression where one would be on a human, with two small slits that were his nostrils. His flattened head bulged fore and aft, and was covered with hair that resembled coiled black wire. His tiny, round mouth wasn't capable of smiling, but his expression was affable as he asked, "Etsane, were you injured last night?"

"Not really," she said. "I scraped a knee, but that's nothing in comparison to what happened to Khuharkk' or Ambassador Burroughs—or Sumiko."

Natual nodded, for a moment seeming very human, despite his features and reddish skin.

"How about you?" she added.

Natual nodded, his species' sign of negation. "I slept deeply, as did Eloiss. We awoke after the battle had ended." The alien rubbed at his bulging forehead, the look in his large eyes calm and reflective.

"Eloiss?" Etsane remembered the Drnian female. "She's your mate?"

Natual made a low sound that she instinctively knew denoted amusement. "Nooo, she isn't. Just a fellow researcher. We Drnians don't necessarily associate sleeping companions with sexual partners, the way you humans do. What about you? Are you mated?"

The Ethiopian was taken aback at the question. If it had come from a human male, it might have meant he was interested in her romantically. Was it possible that Natual was coming on to her? Confused, she shook her head. "No, I'm not married," she said, then laughed self-consciously. "Except maybe to my work."

"What is your specialty?"

"I'm here to help with the iconography and linguistic

analysis decipherment of First Dynasty Na-Dina.''

"Ah, the Tomb walls with their undeciphered treasure of knowledge!" Natual said. "I wish you the best of fortune in your decipherment."

Etsane smiled at him, enjoying his company. *Well, why not?* she thought. "Thanks! What are you—"

She broke off as Gordon Mitchell, followed by Mahree Burroughs, Greyshine, and two Na-Dina, entered the room. Obviously, the meeting was beginning.

Mitchell rapped a trowel against the tabletop, and all conversation ceased. "Your attention, please." The archaeologist spoke English. His voice echoed through the cavernous hall, accompanied by tiny whispers as voders translated his words into each listener's own language.

Silence fell. Etsane glanced around and caught the quick smile of Sumiko Nobunaga, the Lab Chief and Khuharkk's Star Bridge pair partner. Then the young woman winced when the Shadgui named Hrashoi accidentally bumped her bandaged arm. Beyond them, a score of Na-Dina squatted off to one side, forming a double line of blue-scaled, long-tailed people. She'd met their crew chief, a female named Axum, last night.

Mahree Burroughs spoke first. "Friends, colleagues, I am quite concerned by last night's attack. Preliminary investigation indicates artifact smugglers had hoped to steal the sarcophagus, the grave goods, and the Mizari relics from King A-Um Rakt's tomb. Since they struck on the last day before *Emerald Scales* was due to arrive—and, of course, our ship reached Ancestor's World early—it is possible that they've been monitoring some of our transmissions. Luckily, they failed. But we suspect major Sorrow Sector involvement."

The Ambassador paused, crossing her arms over her formal black StarBridge uniform. "We are going to notify the CLS, of course, and ask that the League Irenics increase patrols and surveillance in this sector. But we all know how big space is, and thus how daunting a task that is."

She gazed intently out at the group. "We're also informing the Na-Dina Council of Elders. Investigator Krillen flew into camp this morning to confer with us about security measures. With all of this in mind, Doctor Mitchell and I feel that it is only fair that we offer any who wish the opportunity to leave this camp. You volunteered to help excavate the find of the century—*not* to be targets of armed smugglers. Anyone who wishes to leave may go back to Spirit and take a cabin aboard *Emerald Scales* until we can arrange for transport back to Shassiszss. Is there anyone who wishes to leave?''

Off to the side by the Lab Chief's enclosed office, the Vardi alien who'd offered to be the project Chronologist shuffled forward. Etsane watched as the two-meter-tall alien, who resembled a purple-green stalk of broccoli, fluttered its mid-body tendrils, releasing a peppery scent. Her voder translated the alien's scent-language.

"This one, the heat oppresses," the Vardi "said," the mechanical voice translation flat and emotionless on her voder. "This one, violence abhors. Return to Spirit, depart the planet, this one desires."

Mahree did not seem surprised. "Of course, Honored One. Our Liaison, Beloran of the clan Flooding Waters, is leaving shortly to consult with the Council of Elders. He used the camp radio and called for a Nordlund jumpjet to come back here. You may return with him."

The Vardi fluttered its tendril-leaves. An astringent mint smell tickled Etsane's nose. "This one, your offer accepts."

"And now I'd like to introduce Investigator Krillen of the Law," Mahree continued.

The Na-Dina walked up to stand beside her, and spoke to the assembly. "Helpers to the spirits of the Ancestors, we regret that your introduction to our world was so unpleasant. This morning, Liaison Beloran and I conferred as to how best to protect you while you carry out your task of helping our people to preserve our ancient heritage. We have decided to request that a unit of the Queen's Own Guard be deployed here for the duration of the dig."

Dr. Mitchell smiled. "Great!"

Etsane felt relief. Guarding the many Royal Tombs that

had been cut into the canyon walls of Ancestor's Valley
was a job for professionals, not for a mixed bag of alien
archaeologists and researchers.

She knew a little about the Queen's Guard from studying
Na-Dina culture and history on the trip here. The Guard
Sisters were unbred females who'd pledged themselves to
the service of Be-Oun, Queen of the Forty-Sixth Dynasty,
and a power in the land equal to that of her husband, the
King.

As Krillen stepped back, Doctor Mitchell took his place.
"Investigator Krillen and Liaison Beloran, we all thank
you. And now, I'd like to formally welcome all of you who
responded so promptly to my request for help. I guarantee
we'll keep you busy!"

Chuckles and sounds of amusement rippled around the
room, and everyone relaxed a bit. "However, it will be a
week or more before the Guard steam barge can make its
way upriver to our camp. Until then, we must post a nightly
watch." Mitchell glanced around the room, fixing on the
Na-Dina crew boss. "Axum, would your diggers be willing
to help with guard duty?"

The Na-Dina bowed. "It is the duty of the living to preserve the sleep of the Revered Ancestors. Set your watch
schedule, Philosopher Mitchell. We will serve."

Mitchell smiled and nodded. "We thank you, Axum."
He looked over the assembly. "Questions, comments?"

Their Mizari Ceramicist lifted her triangular head, her
myriad tentacles waving, and Mitchell nodded at her. "Yes,
Esteemed Lorezzzs?"

"A suggestion, Doctor Mitchell." The Mizari looked
around the room, her emerald green eyes unblinking. "The
sadness of last night may perhaps be relieved by the joy of
seeing the Star Shrine, safe and secure in the Tomb of the
Esteemed A-Um Rakt. Is a visit possible?" The intricate
pattern of amber and silver scales on Lorezzzs' back shimmered as her coils shifted. "There is much work to be done,
but surely, we may show respect to the King of the First
Dynasty of the Na-Dina?"

Yes! Etsane looked eagerly to Mahree and *astamari*

Mitchell. She hadn't been inside the tunnel-tomb yet, and
holo-vids just weren't the same. Beside her, Natual gestured
excitedly.

Mitchell looked to Etsane's former teacher. "Professor
Greyshine. Is the rampway clear? The tunnel . . . empty of
impediments?"

The elderly Heeyoon grinned, red tongue lolling, reminding Etsane of a dog she'd had when she was a girl.
"It's clear. And I must admit, I too am excited by the
prospect of visiting a six-thousand-year-old god-king."

Beside Greyshine, Etsane saw Khuharkk' shiver slightly,
and wondered if the Simiu was suffering from the wounds
inflicted by the smuggler. But the rest of the group was
plainly eager. Ttalatha ch'aakki, the Chhhh-kk-tu, chittered
as she groomed her creamy fur. Eloiss's and Natual's eyes
shone bright red. Even Hrashoi, the sloth-and-toad Shadgui
symbiont who rarely showed any emotion, rose up to his
full two-meter height. Axum and her cadre of Na-Dina diggers banged their digging tools against the Lab floor, raising a din that forced Teacher Mitchell to raise his arms.

"All right! Time for a tour of the Tomb!"

Khuharkk' brought up the rear as Doctor Mitchell led the
way up the ramp to the Tomb entrance. After all, he'd
already seen the treasures close up. He felt depressed and
shamed by the events of last night—not personally, for he
had fought well, acquiring two impressive Honor Scars—
but ashamed for the people of his own world, Hurrreeah.

To think that not just one, but *two* of his people had
carried and used *weapons*! The knowledge made him feel
sick. How could they have degraded themselves so? Honor
demanded that he, Khuharkk', third son of Nearkk' of clan
Red Claw, attempt to redress the Honor debt the smugglers
had incurred from their attack on the Na-Dina world and
treasures.

But how?

Ignoring the pain and stiffness in his shoulder, Khuharkk' strode on, wondering how he could cleanse the
Honor of his people. Yes, he could work hard at preserving

the heritage of the Na-Dina. He would take guard duty after working hard all day cataloging the artifacts. He would be tireless in his devotion to helping Dr. Mitchell.

Would that be enough? Khuharkk' realized, not for the first time, that he did not understand the Na-Dina the way he should. He knew that they took their debts seriously. In that way, they were like his own people. But, while he knew *facts* about the Na-Dina, he did not understand their mind-set. For someone ostensibly studying to become an Interrelator, that was not a good thing.

In a world where Honor lay in the devotion shown to dead ancestors, he felt adrift, uneasy. He neither believed in an afterlife, nor understood how anyone else could. Yet that belief lay at the core of Na-Dina culture, custom, and history. He recalled hearing Honored MahreeBurroughs address his class one time, talking about how each Interrelator had to become a living bridge of understanding between two cultures.

He should become such a bridge. Honor demanded that he do so, to do his best work here on Ancestor's World. But the Na-Dina's dreams were not his dreams, their path to Honor was not his path.

What could he *do*?

The black-skinned female human with the long wavy mane noticed that he'd lagged behind, and slowed her own pace so she walked with him, shoulder to shoulder. Khuharkk' gave her a grateful glance.

She had fought fiercely last night, impressing even him. Though she used a sling to throw a stone, rather than grapple and bite in the Simiu way, still she had used her own muscles, her own strength, to strike down her enemy.

Khuharkk' liked humans, unlike some of his people. Three years ago, he'd entered into a close relationship with the human child, Honored HeatherFarley. In the Simiu way, he'd become her Uncle. He missed Heather, and wrote to her frequently, looking forward during each mail call for her responses.

Perhaps Etsane was lonely, too, and would value his

friendship, as Bil! had. Khuharkk' found himself hoping that was so. . . .

Etsane's excitement rose with every step she took as they entered the tunnel leading to the Tomb. Beside her, Khuharkk' paced, silent and brooding. For a moment, the Ethiopian woman wondered whether the Simiu was in pain, and thought about asking him; then they encountered the first of the paintings.

"Ohhhhh," she heard Sumiko murmur. Etsane couldn't even manage that. She just stared, wide-eyed.

The rich mineral pigments of red ocher, yellow calcite, copper green, and limestone white filled a long series of panels that lined both sides of the tunnel. Illuminated now by a string of electric lights hanging from the plain stone ceiling, they gleamed with color nearly as fresh as on the day they had been painted.

They're gorgeous! Etsane thought, with mingled awe and delight.

The first panel showed the creation of Ancestor's World, a vortex of lightning, earth, salt, and water that coagulated into the landscape she had seen from orbit. A blue-scaled kangaroolike deity stretched her long tail around the globe, as if protecting it. The second panel showed a mighty King riding the River of Life on a golden barge, his scales inlaid with silver, gold, and jewels, one talon-hand clasping a long pole similar to those used by nearby servants, who poled the barge over the blue waters. The King's other hand held a pile of salt cakes, as if he was making an offering to some deity.

Etsane caught her breath when she saw the third panel. This one, easily ten meters long, depicted a snake-headed Na-Dina who directed hundreds of other Na-Dina in the construction of the City of White Stone. Beyond the city, workers were building a great stone pond. The last section showed the end of the causeway (intact, of course, in the painting) that led from the city down to the River of Life. Giant reed-ships were being launched, their white lateen sails billowing in an invisible breeze.

This painting's immense scale reminded her of Old
Kingdom Egypt, where the Pharaohs of Upper and Lower
Egypt wore the white cone and red crown of the Two Lands
to show they were born to godliness. They had no doubt
of their divine right to rule heaven and earth.

And here at the upper end of the River of Life, just below
the snow-capped peaks of the Mountains of Faith, the First
Dynasty King of the Na-Dina had likewise taken hold of
his people with one mighty taloned hand and propelled
them down through the ages, through forty-six dynasties in
an unbroken line of succession. His vision had built the
City of White Stone. His vision had caused the great Temples to be built. And his vision, even as he died, had been
the spark that caused this Valley of Tombs to be built.
Surely A-Um Rakt had been a *negusa negast*, a King of
Kings.

The last panel began at the bend in the tunnel, and
stretched ahead thirty meters to where it ended just outside
the Tomb of A-Um Rakt. This painting showed images of
Na-Dina priestesses, Royal Ministers, and river barges as
they transported the Great King on his annual pilgrimage
upriver, to the headwaters of the River of Life, there to
pray for the annual flood. This King was snake-headed,
though behind him stood a smaller King and Queen who
bore blue-scaled Na-Dina heads. Etsane wrenched her eyes
from the end of the panel, only to join in the assembled
gasp as Teacher Mitchell turned on the lights in the Tomb.

"Gold!" Natual gasped. "Gold everywhere you look!"

"The Star Shrine! The Sacred Shrizzs!" hissed Lorezzzs,
her tail twitching just like a Na-Dina's.

Etsane's height allowed her to see clearly into the chamber that had been walled off six thousand years ago. The
Tomb's main chamber was round and dome-roofed. On the
ceiling, blue paint and golden circles pictured the heavens
above Ancestor's World. Below the dome stood a solid
block of red porphyry, serving as the bier on which rested
the intricately tooled sarcophagus of the King. Made from
solid gold, the coffin of King A-Um Rakt had been shaped

like the Royal Barge that even today sailed the muddy-brown waters of the River of Life.

Etsane stood on tiptoe, craning her neck, not wanting to miss anything.

The top of the barge showed the outline of a Na-Dina, with short arms crossed over a scaled chest, and taloned hands clasping the pole rod and a brick of salt, while the long tail curled around his feet in a maternal pattern that intrigued Etsane. The head, though . . . that was snakelike, a near copy of the Esteemed Lorezzzs' own ancient visage. To the right she caught sight of a side room, its piled-up grave goods untouched and unrecorded. The Teacher had named it the Treasury. She looked back to the main chamber.

Standing beside the bier, Mitchell caught her eyes. "Etsane, do you think you can decipher *those* glyphs?" he said, gesturing over his shoulder at the walls of the Tomb.

On the curving chamber wall, sheets of gold leaf had been hammered over carved stone ideoglyphs from the ancient First Dynasty language. Row after row ran around the Tomb, telling a story unknown.

The Ethiopian took a deep breath, feeling exultation surge up in her. *This is what I was born to do,* she thought. "I'll try . . ." she began, then stopped herself. "Yes! I *will* learn what the glyphs say! I promise on my honor as an Amharan!"

Gordon Mitchell smiled. Standing beside him, Mahree too looked pleased. The rest of the crowd moved into the chamber, stepping over the remains of the sealing wall. All but Khuharkk', in a gesture of utmost respect, with palm up, fingers curled inward.

"You pledge your Honor to your duty. I honor you for that, O human of black stone. If there is any way that I may help you achieve your promise, I will."

Touched by his words and gesture, Etsane held out her own hand, placing her fingers into his leathery palm. "Thank you, Honored Khuharkk'," she said, wishing she could speak his language. "I will let you know if there is anything you can do."

"Etsane!" Gordon Mitchell called out. "Come see the Star Shrine up close!"

"I'm coming!" she said. "I can't wait!"

She wriggled her way through the crowd, going to her knees so she could see the roped-off part of the Tomb, the area not yet recorded and cleared.

The Shrine resembled a box-house made from purple metal, with tiny doors at the front, star patterns carved on the peaked roof, and who knew what else inside. Beside it lay one of the sacred Mizari drinking vessels, and a globe incised with star patterns picked out in brilliant jewels against the dark amethyst background.

In the shadows at the back of the room rested ceramic pots, bronze cooking vats, and a table frame whose wooden members sagged drunkenly, held together only by hammered gold sheeting.

Warm wet breath puffed against her ear. "Female descendant of a Royal House," hissed Lorezzzs, "do you not feel at home here?"

Etsane shivered, and blinked back tears. She felt privileged to be here, to be within touching distance of these ancient marvels. She looked up, seeing Ttalatha, Sumiko, Natual, Eloiss, Hrashoi, her two Heeyoon mentors, Khuharkk', Axum the crew boss, Mahree, Doctor Mitchell, and the Na-Dina detective Krillen all watching her. She felt a special kinship with these people, who were going to work together to uncover the secrets of the past. "Oh, Lorezzzs," she whispered, "I *do* feel as if I've come home!"

For a moment her father's face flashed before her eyes, proud and austere, every bit as royal-seeming as the image of A-Um Rakt. She wished with all of her being that he could see what she was seeing, could be with her this day. . . .

CHAPTER 6

♦

The Angry Planet

The next day, Mahree and Krillen prepared for the trip to the remote rural site where Bill had been murdered. They loaded Beloran's skimmer with her sensor equipment, food and water, and camping gear. Gordon insisted that Mahree take one of his pulse-guns in case they ran into smugglers, and she reluctantly agreed.

When they were ready to go, they waved good-bye to Gordon, Etsane, Beloran, and Greyshine, who had come to see them off, and climbed into the skimmer. They took their places in the cockpit with Mahree in the pilot's "seat." Beloran had modified the skimmer for his purposes, removing the top and the human pilot's seat and substituting a backless bench that would accommodate a being with a tail. Mahree found she could manage, though it was uncomfortable.

Krillen squatted to her right, his long tail extending back into the interior compartment. Turning the vehicle on, she felt it surge, levitating on its cushion of fan-forced air. She glanced at her passenger. "You're remarkably calm, considering a female is piloting this skimmer."

Krillen's fan-ears flickered. Nervously, she thought. "Guiding a ground skimmer does not . . . really count as a violation of Tradition. You never raise the craft above head-height. It is flying through Mother Sky that is sacrilege.''

Mahree called up a simple map on the craft's cartometer, satellite imagery being forbidden here. The Royal Road that began west of the city led northeast to the distant farming village of Blue Pond, and the mesa top where Bill had been found lay just beyond.

Mahree glanced in that direction, where blue-black thunder clouds hovered over a northerly arm of the Mountains of Faith. Would those clouds ease this dry heat? Since the craft had no top, the sun beat down mercilessly. She pressed the yoke, and the craft began to move. ''Whatever you say, Krillen.''

The Na-Dina tugged at the sash on his chest with one talon-hand. ''I can see that you are skeptical of our ways, that you do not understand. It begins with Father Earth and Mother Sky. And the Law of the Ancestors.''

''*Mother* Sky?'' Mahree prodded him, wanting to learn more and to practice her High Na-Dina speech. ''On Earth, most cultures consider Sky a male symbol. How do Na-Dina see things?''

Krillen's ears flickered quickly, then flared, the body-sign of amusement. ''It is not a question of how we *see* things. It is a matter of Law laid down millennia ago by the Ancestors. We follow their rules. When we do, we prosper. When we don't, we suffer.''

Mahree turned her attention back to the stone-paved Royal Road. Though built in the First Dynasty six millennia ago, the wide road had been kept free of blowing sand and even lava flows ever since. Crews of Na-Dina workers labored mightily to maintain it. Such devotion! ''What does the Law say about the work roles of males and females?''

Krillen sighed, a mannerism Na-Dina shared with humans. ''You are just like most females. Curious, curious, curious. Without their curiosity, we would not have discovered electricity.''

She found the Investigator's bland, elliptical manner both frustrating and a challenge. ''Is electricity the domain of females, then? Lightning *does* come from Mother Sky.'' Mahree glanced his way.

The Na-Dina fluttered his ears. A laugh. ''What curious

logic you off-worlders pursue. No. Actually, the Domain of Mother Sky is reserved to service by males, while the Domain of Father Earth is served by females. It's all very simple.''

"Simple?"

Krillen glanced at her, his beady black eyes opaque. "This is going to be a long trip, isn't it?"

She laughed and focused back on the Royal Road. "Perhaps, but I meant no disrespect to your customs. We can discuss other matters, if you like.'' Mahree pointed at the deep washes lying ahead. "Geology, for example. I studied up on it during the trip here. Aren't those deep washes indicative of transform faults?''

Krillen looked left at the volcanic cones of the mountain spur that bounded them on the west. "I believe so. I remember my uncle's sister saying something about how much work it was to maintain road crews out here. To fix quake damage. And clean up after lava flows.''

Mahree studied the landscape, and her little map. "This whole area looks like what we call a rift valley, where adjacent tectonic plates are pushed apart by deep, upwelling magma.'' She grinned at the alien. "See? I uphold the female responsibility to serve Father Earth.''

"No doubt you think of our customs as laughable. But you must understand, if we are to proceed.'' The alien swished his scaly tail, disturbing the tarp-covered supplies in the rear. "This Case involves a human male, doing what males usually do. Tempting the anger of Mother Sky by flying through her. It is said that in the Beginning Mother Sky surrounded the world with her tail, in the embrace of a mother. Father Earth supports and feeds his people, just as a father nurses the new-hatched offspring. So Earth is our Father. Since each gender knows best the needs of the other, why, females work for Father Earth. They are the best miners, engineers, stone cutters, architects, dambuilders, farmers, and military guards to be found. Why else do you think Axum hired an all-female dig crew?''

Mahree had been unaware until that moment that Gordon's dig crew was all female. Did he know? Grinning to herself, she asked "And the males? What are they best at?"

The alien sat back from the dashboard, his attention now focused on the thunderstorm clouds sweeping down from the mountain spur. "Weather forecasting, for one thing. But it does not take a male to see what those clouds threaten. Make for high ground. Quickly!"

Mahree swung the skimmer off the Royal Road, climbing out of the deep wash they'd been in. In moments they reached a rock-strewn ridge that offered a wonderful view of the River of Life to the east. She shut off the fans and they settled to the ground. Suddenly the hair on her neck rose up, her ponytail frizzled, and her bare arms felt the caress of static electric charges. The Na-Dina pushed open the door and began to clamber out. "Krillen, wait. We're safe here."

"But metal draws Sky's Touch."

Mahree shook her head. "The rubber skirt on the bottom of the skimmer insulates us from contact with the ground."

Yellow lightning flashed to the left, bright as the blaster shots the other night. Moments later, thunder boomed with such a *crack!* that her whole body vibrated. "Seven seconds. It's ten kilometers away." Mahree looked at Krillen, who had flattened against the skimmer floor like a trapped mouse. Lightning flashed again, closer this time. The thunder boom rattled the tarp-covered equipment in the back.

The rain fell, like a waterfall, drenching her to the skin. In seconds the floor of the skimmer was awash in pounding rainwater. Below them, in the formerly dry wash, Mahree saw a wall of brown wetness surging their way, quickly reaching nearly to the crest of her ridgeline.

Krillen swung his snout her way, his eyes filled with fatalism. "The Mother comes in Her anger. It must be that She is displeased by the Sky Infidels who scarred her face when they came for the Tomb treasures."

Lightning exploded a hundred meters from them, burning a black scar on the ridgeline. "She comes for us!"

Mahree slid over and leaned out into the deluge, reaching for the door handle. Cold rain doused her as she pulled the door shut with a thump. "That felt good." She licked at a droplet running down her face, then chuckled. Krillen sat up, his ears starting to relax.

Ka-boooom!

The biggest strike yet rocked the skimmer, splitting open a nearby boulder. Krillen cringed, eyes wide. "She comes for us!"

Mahree blinked, hardly believing what she was seeing. "It's . . . ball lightning!" Translucent bluish spheres of co-agulated lightning-charge danced in the rainy air like sun-spot mirages. Coming toward them, toward the metal of the skimmer.

"Aiiee!"

"Krillen, relax. We're in no danger. Look, the rain is stopping." The blue spheres, closer now and not veiled by rain, were very insubstantial-looking, and, as she watched, they faded away into little sparkles.

The sky began to lighten. Mother Sky had spared them her Touch.

Krillen told himself it was illogical to believe the female alien was an emissary from Mother Sky. He was temple-educated, father of three grown offspring, and an Elder of his clan. He knew better than to believe the old superstitions. Still . . . *someone* had intervened with the Mother, stopping the storm like that. Perhaps she knew of an ancient custom of the Law that his people had forgotten. Over forty-six dynasties, not all is remembered. Witness the loss of understanding of the ideoglyphs of the First Dynasty.

He considered her bravery, her strength in the face of certain destruction. The best soldiers, the bravest fighters, were always females, but somehow, this was different. It *must* be that she was an Ancestral Ghost, traveling among them in this odd disguise.

When the skimmer regained the Royal Road and they'd driven for a time, she turned to him and met his eyes. "Krillen? Are you all right? You haven't said a word since the storm ended. Did I do something wrong?"

"You can do no error, I think." He watched her stare at him, noting for the hundredth time the strange eye-blinks.

Mother's Eye came out from behind the clouds, and golden warmth poured over them. "You were correct to insist we stay inside."

"Theory. Only theory. Rubber is a good insulator. But I've never seen ball lightning before. It's very rare where I come from."

"Here it is common." Krillen continued to gaze at her, wondering why she seemed uncomfortable. He watched as she looked up at Mother's Eye, squinting so her forehead skin crinkled together like the soft shell of a new-birthed egg. Then she went back to piloting the skimmer, a tension in her facial muscles that Krillen didn't recognize. His eyes didn't waver.

Yes, the Minister of Justice had been correct when she warned him that the Sky Infidels had no appreciation of the fragility of life, or the permanence of death. Perhaps that explained the bravery. And the cavalier attitude toward the elements. This female never offered water to Father Earth, never tossed salt to Mother Sky. The sunlight glistened on her eyes, brightening the dark irises to a rich umber.

"Krillen, is something bothering you? You're looking at me very strangely."

Mother! He must have violated some social taboo of her people. He took his eyes off her face and instead focused them lower, at the two mounds on her chest. Suddenly, she brought the craft to a halt and turned to face him. "Krillen, please. Why are you staring at me? Did I do something wrong?"

She glanced down at herself, following the direction of his fixed gaze. "Uh . . . I . . . We humans call them breasts. They come two to a woman, and are one of our secondary sexual characteristics. They generate a liquid with which we feed our newborn. What has gotten into you?"

Krillen bowed apologetically. "My deepest apologies, Ambassador. I was not looking at your . . . breasts. Among the Na-Dina we show gratitude and respect by staring . . . by giving our complete attention . . . in the name of the Revered Ancestors, I meant no disrespect."

The female was staring at him now, but he could tell it

was not a compliment. Krillen hurried to add, "You have mistaken my intention, but perhaps it was . . . fortuitous. I'm afraid I was on the verge of making a great blunder."

"How?"

Krillen lifted his left arm. "See the nipple? When my wife gave birth to the eggs of our triad, her Birth Scent aroused my milk glands. By the time each egg hatched, I could hardly walk down the street without leaving behind a trail. Males of the People feed milk to newborn scalies. It is the prime duty of fathers. Just as Father Earth nurtures the plants grown by our females." He lowered his arm, covering the shrunken armpit gland. "Your breasts show that you are definitely not an Ancestral Ghost."

She stared at him for a moment, then suddenly smiled. He could tell she was amused, but attempting, out of politeness, not to show it. "Oh. That's good . . . I guess."

Mahree stayed quiet for a long time, her attention fixed on the Royal Road. In these parts, it was straight as a pole, going up and down ridges, crossing ravines on stone bridges, and in general giving no quarter to the undulating landscape. At this speed, they should reach their destination before nightfall.

When the sun had begun to dip, she glanced his way. "Krillen, do you miss your wife? Your family? Being away for several days must be hard."

His chest squeezed tight. The image of his wife Nalado filled his mind's eye, reminding him of what he had sacrificed too often, all for the row of gold chevrons that adorned his Sash of Rank. He sighed. "Yes, I miss her. To accompany you, I had to miss our twentieth Pond Anniversary. But she understands. She was an architect, before retiring early to raise our offspring."

"Careers can be like that." She blinked, but kept staring at him. A compliment? "I miss my daughter Claire. She's staying with her father, Rob, on a distant asteroid we call StarBridge."

"The place where Interrelator Waterston studied?"

"Yes. It is a place of study and training, much like your Temples. Young people come there to learn the languages of other peoples, to learn how to be good diplomats, and a few even learn how to touch mind-to-mind, though that is very rare among humans.''

Krillen gave silent thanks for that blessing to Mother Sky. At least his thoughts would be known only to Her. "You . . . you are not a mind-toucher, are you?''

She laughed softly. "Noooo. But my daughter is. It makes a parent's life hard.''

Ahhh. Something they shared in common. "A parent's life is always hard. You know too much and have so little time in which to share it with your offspring, before they grow up and think they know as much as you.''

Mahree glanced quickly at him, then back to the road. "Quite so. What is that?''

He scanned the mountainous horizon. A volcano had erupted not long ago, and now a thin sheet of fast-moving lava was coming toward them faster than a person could run. "Father's Anger." The ember-red lava under the crusting surface stretched as far as he could see. "There are many volcanoes in this region. The crews must work constantly to keep the roads clear.''

He peered at the lava flow, calculating from long experience of living on this dangerous world. "The front edge is wide here, but Sand Lake is just ahead. If we can make it there, we should be safe.''

"Hang on!" Mahree bent forward. The skimmer flew ever faster.

Krillen hung on, his talons digging into the dashboard.

Just as they came in sight of the far edge of the molten flow, the skimmer shuddered and bucked. "What's wrong?" he cried.

Mahree fought the steering yoke. "I . . . don't . . . Power! We're losing battery power.''

The skimmer slowed more. Krillen wondered if Father Earth was upset by the finding of the Royal Tomb. Elsewise, why would he send his Anger after them?

As the two occupants of the skimmer stared at each other in horror, the air cushion died and the craft settled to the stone-paved road with a crunch.

Krillen glanced back at the approaching lava flow. There was a good chance it would reach them. It might not engulf them, since it was thin—but the heat would surely kill them. "What's happened?"

Mahree grimaced. "Something's wrong with the batteries." She swung around and scrambled back to the rear of the skimmer. Wondering whether they should try to make a run for it, Krillen followed. Mahree pulled at the engine access plate. "Ouch!" she cried. "It's boiling hot. And it's stuck! Help me!"

Krillen caught the edge of the darkened metal plate with his finger talons. He pulled hard. With a groan, the plate opened. Noxious fumes spewed out.

"Ooof!" cried Mahree, turning her head from the terrible smell.

Krillen held his breath and looked into the interior of the engine compartment. Two blackened boxes that were obviously electric batteries smoked with white fumes. "They are dead." He looked upslope. The orange-red lava surged and buckled toward them like molten fire.

Mahree looked up. "Damn it!" She clenched her jaw, her eyes wild with fear and frustration, then she reached under the storage tarp and pulled out a piece of alien equipment. "Krillen! Disconnect the cables from the dead batteries. I'm going to try and jump-start the skimmer! Watch out for the acid!"

Why defy Father's Anger? But perhaps Sky Infidels did not know how futile this was. He did as directed, even though the half-melted casings leaked acid onto his hands. His scales repelled it, but the pain was strong.

Mahree pulled two long wires from the back of her alien box. She twisted them onto the thicker cables that had been connected to the ruined batteries. Then she pushed past him, reaching for the yoke. "Hold the box! Keep the cables from separating!"

Krillen did that. A hissing sound made him look up.

Father's Anger roared toward them, red and orange and angry. Its fury bubbled high, as if . . .

Wheee-rup!

He felt the craft lift up on fan-blown air. "You did it!"

"Grab something!" cried Mahree.

Krillen wrapped his tail around the door handle, and prayed to Mother Sky that he, a poor Investigator tossed into the clutch of off-worlders who did not know how to show proper devotion to her, might yet survive. Survive to teach them the ways of the People. Survive to see Nalado once more. Survive to . . .

"We're going to clear it!" yelled Mahree.

"We are?" Krillen blinked, looking up. The lava flowed with a crinkling, sticky sound. The heated air pushed forward by its rapid approach dried his eyes and buffeted his face. It felt like Mother's Eye had come down to Father Earth. To slow the pace of Father's Anger?

"Yes!" she yelled joyously as they sped beyond the northern edge of the flow.

Behind them, molten rock roared across the stone pavement of the Royal Road. Ahead of them shimmered the blue waters of Sand Lake. His heart thumped in his chest, his tail dropped limply to the floorboards, and Krillen, of the clan Moon Bright, knew that Mother Sky had other plans for his future. "Thank the Ancestors!"

Mahree slowed the headlong rush of the skimmer, looking over her shoulder at the alien box he held in his acid-burned hands. "Oh, Krillen! You're injured."

He flared his ears. "Better than being roasted to death." He blinked at her. "May I put down this device?"

She nodded. "Yeah. Just . . . just wedge the replacement battery into place. Use my duffel bag. Don't let the wires come apart."

Krillen did as directed, then rejoined her on the front bench seat. The rush of hot afternoon air across his face felt . . . delicious. "It's not often one escapes Father's Anger. We seem to be blessed by the Ancestors."

Mahree frowned, then glanced at him. "Maybe. But those batteries shouldn't have melted down like that. The overheating sensors built into the batteries were disconnected. And someone must have put the wrong kind of electrolyte into the batteries."

Krillen didn't like what he was hearing. "You mean . . . the battery failure was *intentional*? We were supposed to be stranded out here?"

Mahree nodded. "Or worse. The fumes could have poisoned us, or they could easily have ignited . . ."

His ears drooped. Who among the people at Base Camp wanted them dead? "This could only have been done recently. By someone who knows about alien transports. Who? One of your new scientists?"

She wiped sweat from her forehead. He noticed that her hand was trembling. "I doubt it. But that leaves only Gordon and Khuharkk' and Sumiko and—"

"Axum and her diggers," Krillen said harshly. "They are very familiar with your devices. They even ride aboard the jumpjet when going to the City of White Stone."

Mahree looked at him, curious. "Why would a Na-Dina want to kill us? Or Bill, for that matter?" She frowned. "But none of them can pilot a jumpjet, can they? Hey!" She pounded her fist against the dashboard. "The Nordlund pilot who brought us from the spaceport—he left before the smuggler raid. So maybe—"

"*He* sabotaged the batteries?" Krillen said. "Perhaps. If Bill was dead before the jumpjet landed, then only someone with pilot knowledge could have been the murderer."

Her jaw muscles clenched. "I can't *forget* that, Krillen. Is that what you think? That he was already dead when the ship landed?"

"I have no evidence to suggest that. I am hoping that your alien machines will give us some. But my instincts . . . after twenty years at my job . . . my instincts tell me that Bill was dead before the ship landed."

Mahree gripped the steering yoke tightly. "God, I don't like this. It means someone in camp tried to kill us. And it would have looked like an accident, if it had succeeded. We face a deadly foe."

Krillen nodded slowly. "Perhaps several foes. We must think well, and carefully. Yes?"

His colleague grimaced, showing many teeth. "Yes. But that's something I'm good at. Especially when I'm angry."

* * *

That night Mahree was brought to a simple, two-story stone building to be introduced to the Matron in Charge of Blue Pond, the small farming village that lay at the nexus of the Royal Road and several feeder routes. As they entered, the Na-Dina female came around from behind her low work counter, joining them in the spacious foyer. She was slightly smaller than Krillen, and the scales of her fan-ears had faded to a silvery blue. The Matron, Coreen, listened sympathetically as Krillen described their escape from the lava flow.

All Mahree wanted to do was take a bath, wash her hair, and sleep on something that didn't tremble underfoot. As if on cue, the stone floor under her boots rumbled to a series of microquakes.

"You were lucky," Coreen said sympathetically. "You could have joined the list of Disappearances."

"Disappearances?" Mahree said, putting down her overnight bag. "What are they?"

Krillen looked embarrassed. "A rural fable," he muttered.

Matron Coreen lifted her tail. "Not to those who live outside your cities, Investigator. I myself saw an empty village on a trip beyond Salt Dream. It was unsettling."

Mahree could see how people might disappear on a planet where lava flows and earthquakes struck without warning. "Krillen, what about the Royal Road? It's blocked now."

Krillen seemed to welcome the change of subject. "That it is." The Investigator glanced briefly at Coreen. "Matron, tens of kilometers of the Royal Road are buried under the new flow. Have you been expecting such an eruption?" He looked down at the stone floor.

"No." The Matron stared at Krillen. "The snores of Father Earth *have* been louder of late. And they do not match the decennial Pond cycle common for these parts."

Mahree wondered at that. "Pond cycle? What's that?"

The Matron eyed her politely. "For two millennia, Blue Pond has been famous for its earthquake forecasting, based on observations of ripple patterns in the village's Royal Pond.'' She shook a claw at the floor. "The ways of Father Earth are familiar to us. And the Temple of Earth Quaking often sends acolytes to study with us. My own daughter follows now in the family tradition.'' She looked up, again fixing her attention on Krillen.

The Investigator shuffled nervously. "Uh, your clan is blessed by your family's devotion, I am sure."

Strange. Mahree wondered why the Matron stared at Krillen, while the alien kept his gaze downcast. As if embarrassed. Or nervous about something. But no, his ears perked skyward, showing an emotion she hadn't seen before. "Krillen, perhaps we should go to our rooms? I need to find some soap and then take a bath."

Both Na-Dina looked sharply at her, then cast their gazes downward. Mahree got the clear impression that she'd just stuck her foot in her mouth. After years of dealing with alien customs, it wouldn't be the first time she'd made some kind of gaffe without intending to.

After a short, loaded silence, Krillen asked, "Matron in Charge, is your . . . is your cleansing pond available for nonfamily use?''

"It is." The Matron eyed Mahree. "Daughter of Sky, my name is Coreen, of the clan Farms Well, of the Trade Father Snoring, and I am Mother of two eggs. My cleansing pond is located in the courtyard behind the kitchen. You may use it tonight."

Tension sang between the two aliens, and Mahree hadn't the slightest idea of what she'd said to set it off. Too tired to worry more, she touched her forehead in the greeting custom of the Na-Dina. "Mother Coreen, I am honored by your sharing." The female's fan-ears twitched. "Uh, I am Mahree, of the clan Human, of the Trade Interrelator, and Mother of one daughter," Mahree said softly. "My family gives you thanks."

"Your thanks are accepted." The tension eased. The Matron offered them each a ceramic token, inlaid with a cloisonne glass pattern. "Your room ownership tokens. No one will disturb you so long as these hang from the pivot-bar. Do you require a meal?''

"No," said Krillen. "We brought our own food. Thank you for asking."

Coreen shuffled back behind her counter, tail lifting. "As you wish. You are both welcome to join the break of our morning fast, at first light of Mother's Eye."

Mahree shouldered her duffel bag, wondered if her equipment would be safe in the skimmer, then recalled the Na-Dina penalty for theft—amputation of one or both hands. She shuddered, and followed after Krillen as he shuffled up the stone steps to the second floor, his tail slithering through a rut cut deep into the edge of each step.

"Uh, Krillen," she said after they had passed out of earshot of Coreen. "What did I say wrong back there?"

Krillen continued climbing but slowed. "We Na-Dina can speak bluntly. I will oblige you. Bathing is often a sexual activity among us, and your juxtaposition of my name with your desire to bathe could be construed to mean that . . . you wished to share sex with me." Mahree opened her mouth, but found nothing to say. "Of course, I know better from observing your species' toiletry rituals at Base Camp. Matron Coreen does not."

Mahree felt her face grow warm. *Good grief! That's a new one!* "Oh, Krillen, I'm sorry if I embarrassed you."

"No offense taken." The alien stepped out of the stairwell into the stone hallway of the upper floor, his supply bag in one talon-hand, the room token in the other. He pointed with his tail. "That is your room, on the left. Mine is here. Do you wish to be awakened for morning devotions?"

She was still trying to recover her aplomb. *Morning devotions? Oh, yes.* "Uh, yes, please. I would be honored to share in your devotions. Thank you for inviting me."

Krillen pushed open the cat door of his room and laid down his supply bag inside. Looking over his shoulder, he stared at her. "You're quite welcome. I hope you enjoy your bath and your night's rest."

"Just one more thing, Krillen. I noticed Coreen staring

at you intently, but you kept your gaze downcast. Does this mean she is . . . appreciative of you, for some reason?''

Krillen blinked rapidly, then sighed. ''Serves me right, daring to be blunt. Some kinds of gazing are, well, different . . . Coreen's mate has joined the Ancestors, yet she is still lively, even at her age. She was inviting me to share a soak in her pond, then her bedchamber tonight. I declined.''

Krillen turned to go into his room.

''Oh,'' Mahree murmured. *God, it's been a long day . . .*

Minutes later, Mahree stood at the edge of the stone-lined pond in the rear courtyard. Alone under the stars of early evening, she shucked off her shorts, panties, and blouse, then climbed into the shallow waters. The water was sleepy-warm, heated by the light of Mother's Eye during the day. Easing down with her back resting against the rough warm stone rim of the pond, she stretched out her legs and decided to soak first.

It was luxury. Pure, sensuous luxury.

Her pores opened up. The soles of her feet softened. The salty sweat floated away. And when she sank under the water to soak her hair, coming up for air with a shout, she felt indeed as if she had experienced something sexual.

The stars above spoke to her. Rob was out there, somewhere amid those stars. Awake? Asleep? Asleep and dreaming of her?

Mahree refused to continue that line of thought; it would just make her even lonelier and more depressed. She swam a few short laps and got out.

She slipped on her clothes, then padded back to her room, ducking under the cat door. *I'm so tired, I'm not even hungry.* She was, however, thirsty, and had a long, cool, refreshing drink from her canteen.

Then, pulling a faded old sleep-shirt over her head, she walked over to the padded, circular bed platform. Lying down, she tossed and turned, experimenting with positions. Na-Dina beds were too small for humans, even for a woman of medium height. She wondered for a moment whether Gordon Mitchell had ever had to try sleeping on a Na-Dina bed. He was a big man. . . .

After a few minutes, her body relaxed and her eyelids grew heavy . . . so heavy.

And there was somebody with her, in the darkness. Mahree felt her arms tingle as he stroked them sensuously. His hands traced the contours of her shoulders, trailed along her neck, then moved downward, covering her breasts.

It had been such a long time since she'd made love . . . Mahree, half realizing she was dreaming, reached up to draw his face down to hers, wanting his kisses, wanting *him.*

His features hovered before her, dreamlike, indistinct. "Rob?" she tried to say, but of course she was dreaming and could make no sound.

And then the shifting image coalesced, sharpening, becoming, for a moment, only too clear.

Gordon Mitchell.

Mahree gasped, and awoke. *No,* she thought. *No, I won't. I can't.* Shaken, she lay there, making herself relax, muscle by muscle. *It was only a dream,* she repeated to herself, reassuring herself. *You can't control dreams. They're not real. Nothing happened. I didn't DO anything. Relax . . . relax . . .*

But it was a long, long time before she was able to sleep again. . . .

CHAPTER 7

◆

The Locked Room

The next morning, as the golden gleam of Mother's Eye cleared the eastern horizon, Krillen watched Mahree of the clan Human offer water to Father Earth and salt to Mother Sky. Kneeling on the sandy ground of the rear courtyard like he and Coreen, she seemed unusually subdued. Perhaps the lava flow of yesterday still worried her.

Mahree looked to him. "Krillen, did I do that properly?"

"Very properly." He glanced briefly to Coreen, who sat on his right; then Krillen looked away and bowed low to Mother's Eye. "Mother Sky, we your Children honor you. Give us another day in which to honor the Ancestors, and we promise to show true devotion." He slapped his tail hard against the ground, as did Coreen.

Mahree quickly slapped her palms against the wet sand. Then she spoke. "We are finished?"

"Yes." Krillen stood up and brushed wet sand from his knees. He winced. His hands! They still pained him despite Coreen's healing salve. "Now to our travels. If we leave immediately, we should reach the mesa top before Mother's Eye scalds our feet."

Mahree stood up too. "Thanks to the replacement batteries the Matron gave us and my tinkering with the recharger, we'll get there." His colleague brushed sand from her bare knees. She was dressed as she had been yesterday, though the blouse was of a different color. Her supply bag lay behind her, like his. She bowed to Coreen. "Matron Coreen, thank you for your hospitality. Thank you also for inviting me to your morning devotions."

The Matron smiled with her ears, clearly pleased by the alien female's piety. "It was a minor sharing. My home is your home, my water your water, my . . . salt, your salt."

She was honoring the Ambassador with the offer of salt? Krillen was both amazed and pleased. Mahree, seeming to understand the importance of her words, bowed deeply.

They left Blue Pond in a glow of good humor. So good he hardly noticed how they flew above the ground, through the unsupported air, until they were nearly at the mesa.

The skimmer slowed as they approached the desolate pile of brown rock. Mahree looked at him. "Is there a way up to the top?"

Krillen pointed to the southern edge of the flat-topped mesa. "That way. A rockfall ages ago created a ramp of boulders. Sand has blown over it, filling in the crevices. I was able to walk down it when last I was here. It should do."

"Thanks." Mahree aimed the skimmer and sped them that way, unmindful of the pebbles that flew to the touch of her air fans.

When they reached the top of the mesa, there was the jumpjet, just as it was when Krillen had last seen it.

"I'm surprised Nordlund didn't insist on retrieving it," Mahree said.

"They could not. By my order, it has been left undisturbed," Krillen said. "One of the primary rules is not to disturb the scene of the crime until the investigator has discovered everything he or she can about it."

"But Bill was killed so long ago."

"Long?" Just when he was beginning to think he understood these Humans. "Two months is not a long time. Some cases I have solved took ten years to close."

Mahree kept her eyes fixed on the rock-strewn ground,

guiding them safely around several large boulders. Krillen let out his breath. "Well," she murmured, "now I understand why Gordon was anxious for me to come out here. The sooner we check this out, the sooner he gets back his camp jumpjet."

Ahhh. She was concerned over obligations owed to the Philosopher. "Don't worry. The Nordlund Combine has always diverted a jumpjet to Base Camp, whenever requested."

"Like the one that brought us down from the spaceport? It came again to pick up Beloran and the Vardi." Mahree stopped the skimmer not far from the jumpjet's ramp. "That's very cooperative of them."

"Of course they are cooperative." Krillen waited until the skimmer touched earth, then got out. He reached for his supply bag. "We have great mineral riches in the Mountains of Faith, and the Council has given them exclusive exploitation rights—for off-world trade, that is. Still, our Finders of Fact know the Law well, and made sure a reversion clause was included in the original contract. Nordlund is thus attentive to our requests."

Mahree chuckled. "I'll bet. Though it seems the Project Engineer has reason to resent our presence." Standing by the rear of the skimmer, she pulled the weather tarp off her equipment and waved at it. "I'll bet this stuff is something not even Nordlund possesses!"

Krillen stared at the off-world devices. "What are they?"

Pointing, she explained. "An autocam. Controlled by this gold bead I put just under my eye. See? I wink, it records. I look to one side or another, the camera tracks the same way. I move, it follows after me. With this we can record everything in the jumpjet so we can look at it any time we want to."

She pointed at another device. "That's a portable scanner, tunable from infrared all the way up to ultraviolet. It radiates light, like Mother's Eye, and can reveal residual impressions, leftover heat, wear patterns, stuff like that. And this"—she pointed again—"is the autosampler. It bags up, seals, and records crime scene evidence from the microscopic up to palm-size. I borrowed it from Gordon. This is a standard archaeological field tool."

"Yes indeed," Krillen said, marveling at the off-world technology. No wonder the Modernists were so determined to have it all for their own!

"And, in the best Sherlock Holmes tradition . . ." Mahree grabbed a metal band adorned with a stem, at the end of which gleamed a glass tube. She put it on her head and pulled the band down until it covered her forehead. Then she moved the glass tube in front of her left eye. She smiled at him. "It's a large-field microscope. It enlarges anything I look at, by powers of ten controlled by my blinking, and the number of lenses that cycle in or out of the tube."

Krillen looked down at his supply bag. Into it he'd stuffed his bronze writing slate, a blank sheaf-scroll, ink and stylus, evidence bags, measuring tape, photo-prints of the crime scene he'd taken right after the body was found, a collapsible telescope for distance viewing, a large battery-light—the latest invention of forensic science, able to il-luminate the evening without shedding torch fragments on the crime scene—and glass plates for the mounting of blood and tissue samples. Krillen sighed at the unspoken comparison.

Mahree was quick to sense his mood. "Look, I apologize if I'm showing off too much. This is my first chance to try out this stuff. And . . . I really want to find Bill's murderer. But, Krillen, you're the one with the gold chevrons, you're the one who is the expert detective. Not me."

Krillen's tail twitched with emotion. He was touched by her words, and the faith she expressed in his abilities. He glanced over to the west, where an isolated range of moun-tains rose up out of the mesa lands and the town of Salt Dream held onto a precarious existence at the edge of the Great Desert. The horizon was clear of clouds. He turned back to Mahree. "Very well, then, let us begin."

He waved at the mesa top around them, then up at the open door of the jumpjet. "The first thing you should know is that no rains have fallen since the murder. Nor have any sandstorms visited. The season is too early. And we are beyond the reach of Father's Anger, so the Ash of Sorrow has not fallen here in a long time. Thus, the ground is as it was when your colleague died.''

Shouldering his supply bag, Krillen took out his sunshade, clipped it to his forehead scales, and noticed immediately the easing of light reflection off the sand. ''Now, if you will follow after me, I will retrace my steps up to the jet's stair-ramp, enter the craft, and then proceed to the pilot cabin.''

''After you,'' Mahree said quietly.

Krillen found his old track pattern, where he'd paced over his own footprints time and again during his first examination of the crime scene. A Prime Principle of Case Solving is to minimize the Investigator's disturbance of the crime scene. He was pleased to note that Mahree was careful to follow his footsteps exactly.

Single file, they walked up the ramp and into the stifling hot interior of the jumpjet. Krillen blinked, adjusted his pupils to accept light from the shadows, and then pointed for her benefit. ''To the right is the sanitary unit. Its door was unlatched and open when I entered. We stand in the central aisleway. And to our left is the pilot cabin.'' Picking up his feet, Krillen headed that way, hugging the left-hand side of the aisle.

She gasped. ''Is that Bill's blood there on the floor?''

It had dried to a rusty brown in the ensuing two months. He fanned his ears affirmatively. ''Correct. There was also brain matter leakage. Tissue and blood samples were taken.'' Her silence puzzled him. ''And there, to the right, is the metal bar used to crush his skull. See?''

Walking slowly, Mahree came closer. Krillen swung his tail to the left, giving her room to walk. The autocam floated over her right shoulder. She blinked her right eye twice, presumably turning it on. Her face was paler than he recalled. Perhaps her sweating, with its loss of fluids and salt, was weakening her. ''Do you feel able to continue? Do you need salt? Water?''

''Noooo.'' Mahree choked, then swallowed hard. She patted the autosampler hanging from her waist-belt, but absentmindedly, as if she did not intend to use it. Then she unclipped the scanner from her belt and aimed the device at the metal bar, using her pocketknife to turn it over so the device could record every bit of its surface.

The tubular steel bar itself was very ordinary. Many were used in construction platforms at the dam site, or elevated recording perches at the City of White Stone. "Does your device show anything unusual?"

Mahree clipped the tool back on her belt, then shook her head. "Hard to say. There are whorl patterns on the bar that could be wear marks. Or they could just be differences in tempering of the metal. I'll have to show these scannings to the Metallurgist when I get back to Base Camp. You say you found no fingerprints on the bar?"

"None."

"Do you mind if I step closer and examine it with my large-field monocular?"

"Go ahead. But be careful not to step in the dust film that lies underneath the bench seats. There could be residual footprints under there."

"Of course." Moving carefully, Mahree stepped to the right, stood on the aisle-facing bench seat where it ran along the outer hull of the jumpjet, and bent forward. Blinking with her left eye even as the autocam hovered over her right shoulder, buzzing to itself, she stared intently at the bar on the floor, again using her knife to roll it over.

Moments later she looked up, rubbed at her neck, then pointed at the bar. "You're right. No fingerprints at all." She glanced up at him. "Now that we've examined it, will you be taking it back to Spirit?"

Krillen fanned his ears affirmatively. "Yes, now that you have seen the murder site."

"Okay." She stepped down off the bench, again watching where she put her feet. "Now I want to see the pilot cabin."

"You may enter yourself. I've been inside." Krillen peered at the control panel, clearly visible even though the pilot and copilot seats were hidden by the partition walls on either side of the aisleway. "Please record everything inside, including the boot scuff-marks near the entry. Do not forget the settings of the instruments.''

Mahree nodded. ''Of course.'' She moved carefully and lightly, walking along the bench seat cushions rather than touching the metal floor. The autocam followed her like an obedient servant. She peered around the partition wall and then went in, carefully, turning her head to record everything. ''Okay, it's all recorded,'' she said after a moment. ''If I put on gloves, may I touch the controls? There are some things they can tell me.''

''You may,'' Krillen said. The Na-Dina watched intently as she bent over the pilot's console, unwilling to sit in the seat.

After several minutes of fiddling with the controls, she looked back up. ''Okay, this is interesting. This ship was almost certainly landed by Bill's killer, not Bill himself.''

''How can you tell?''

''I compared the chronolog in the ship's computer to the piloting log in the nav-computer. The chronolog says that thirty-two minutes into the flight, Bill put the ship on automatic. At that time, he was heading directly for Spirit. But then, within five minutes, the ship's controls were changed to manual, and course changes were entered to bring the ship over this mesa, where it was landed manually.''

Krillen was thinking fast. ''You are reasoning that Bill's murderer hid aboard the ship, lured Bill back to his death, then came up here and assumed manual control of the ship to bring it here to land on the mesa top?''

''Yes,'' Mahree said. ''I'd guess that's exactly what happened. There's no reason that Bill would have corrected course to head for this mesa. And if he was forced to land the ship here, why take him back there''—she gestured to the front of the craft—''to kill him, when the murderer could have killed him here in the pilot's seat?''

''I agree with your reasoning,'' Krillen said. ''Besides, from the way the body was lying, and the angle the blows were struck from, I would say that the murderer struck from behind, in a surprise attack.''

He pointed at the controls. "What else do those instruments tell you?"

"Not much," she said. "But hang on a second." She bent over the pilot's seat, examining it with her magnifying lenses. "Well, you're right. Those impressions are definitely caused by a Na-Dina's scales. I wonder just how long before Bill was killed that Axum was perched in this seat. Maybe we should talk to her and to the Nordlund pilots."

"We will," Krillen promised.

"I wonder," she said, staring around her at the cabin, "if the artifact smugglers might be responsible."

"But what would they have to gain?"

She shrugged. "I don't know."

Krillen gazed again at the seat, at the soft material that Philosopher Mitchell had told him would mold itself to the body contours of the pilot. "Please record the seat in close-up detail," he said, and, when she was done, he spent several more minutes measuring it minutely from every angle.

"Perhaps," he said thoughtfully, "Axum learned to pilot from observation. Na-Dina are not stupid. Beloran drives the skimmer we are riding in today."

"But I thought that for a Na-Dina to pilot a ship through Mother Sky would be sacrilege!"

"Yes indeed. But someone who could commit murder might not balk at being cast out from Mother Sky and rejected by Father Earth, knowing his or her soul must walk forever apart from the Revered Ancestors and their glory."

She watched him measure, then said quietly, "This isn't an easy case, is it?"

Krillen glanced over his shoulder at her. "No case is ever easy. Some are just less hard than others." He reached into his supply bag and brought out his silver-nitrite camera. Checking that the film pack was inserted, he motioned at her. "Do you mind? I would like to take my own final photographs of the murder weapon, that corner, and the pilot cabin before we leave."

"Of course," she said, wiping sweat from her brow. "But if you don't mind, I'm going to wait outside. I'm getting dizzy from the heat."

"Surely." Krillen said, busy with his camera. When he'd finished taking his shots, he stowed the metal bar in a specimen bag, then stood surveying the scene, comparing it to the pictures he'd taken last time of the angle of the body. Yes, he'd been right. The killer had hidden in the sanitary unit, crept forward, then attacked Waterston from behind.

"Krillen!" Mahree called, her voice urgent. "Would you come out here, please? I have something to show you."

He turned, made his way out of the craft, and stepped out onto the top of the ramp. Mahree was bent over, her face held close to the outer hull. Over her right shoulder, the autocam buzzed. And her left eye monocular lenses shifted in and out of the field of focus like sandrats feasting on a corpse. "What is it?"

Mahree stood back and pointed at the shiny hull that looked like silver, but was really a metal called aluminum. "See that?"

"I do." The metal was known to the Temple of the River, and to the expert miners who used hydro-sluices to excavate the bauxite from which it was made. "The metal is called aluminum. So?"

"Not what I meant." She looked his way. "Krillen, there are minute *scratches* on the metal. They look like claw marks to me. Would you take a look?"

When she stepped back, hanging onto the railing that enclosed the top of the ramp, he stepped forward. Pulling out his hand magnifier, Krillen chose the twenty-power lens, flicked it into place, and peered through it at the metal.

"Yes! There are four scrapes there. Three in a row, then one set off to the side." He stood back, staring at her. "You realize what that pattern matches?"

Mahree nodded. "The three fingers and thumb of a Na-Dina hand. Human fingernails are too soft to scar aluminum. But your fingers are tipped by talons."

How could this have happened? Krillen considered. He supposed that one of the laborers could have unintentionally scratched the ship's hull . . . stumbled and caught her balance, for example. "This could be accidental, perhaps," he said.

"Or it could mean that a Na-Dina killed Bill, while someone else piloted the ship," Mahree said.

"Or that our killer is indeed a Na-Dina who has chosen to damn him or herself by learning to pilot your sky traveling vessels." Krillen considered. "We must definitely talk with Axum when we return." The Investigator sighed. Truly, the Fourth Postulate of Justice was ever-present— "Even the unthinkable must be considered when solving a case."

Mahree looked back at the nearly invisible scrape marks on the hull. "Krillen, isn't it proper to ask *why* those marks are there? Scrapes on the door latch would be expected, as the dig crew entered and exited the jet. But these scrapes here, they're five handspans *away* from the door latch. Right near—" She paused, touched briefly the metal railing she leaned against, then backed away from it hurriedly. "The railing! Someone could stand on it, perhaps as they climbed onto the jet's roof. What do you think?"

Krillen felt warm excitement. Combining the knowledge base of his alien colleague with his own knowledge of crime and his world was indeed an improvement. While a novice in Revelation, she knew how to think. "I think you should turn your monocular on the hull above those scrapes and see what you see."

She did so. A second set of scrape marks was found a short arm's reach above. Then a third, up near the crest of the hull. Mahree teetered on the stair railing, with her boots perched on the rail, one hand braced against the hull, and the other hand fluttering in the air. Incredible. Human balance without the aid of a tail was truly magical, Krillen mused.

"Steady me," she called out. "I'm going to climb up to the top of the jet's hull."

Krillen thumped his tail in appreciation of her daring. "Go ahead," he said, climbing onto the railing himself so he could steady her as she crawled up.

With his help, she scrambled up the slick surface, slipping a bit, but her boot soles were made of material that clung, and she found purchase.

"Wow," he heard her say nervously. "It's pretty high up here. Ten meters or so off the ground. Hope I don't fall."

Krillen hoped so, too. He had no idea how to pilot the skimmer.

"Now let's see . . ." She crawled about on the top. "Yes! There's a pattern here, but the scrapes are farther apart than the first set."

"Our foot talons tend to spread over time," he said, stepping back a little so he could see the roofline. "The older we get, the wider they spread."

"Like footprints?" Mahree called down.

Krillen recalled the sight of her naked feet yesterday, when she'd removed her boots after the thunderstorm and drained the footgear. "Yes."

Mahree nodded, then moved forward slowly, her monocular clicking as multiple lenses moved into place. "Left. Right. Left. Right. About a one-meter stride."

Hmmm. "That would be equal to the stride of a middle-aged Na-Dina, of either sex."

Mahree crawled farther along the silvery hull, ending up at the part that covered the pilot cabin. She looked to the right and the left, then down again, then—moving slowly—she stood up. The afternoon breeze fluffed out her long hair and whipped at her loose blouse. Her voice was borne to him on the hot wind. "Krillen, the scrape marks end here. As if . . . as if whoever climbed up here just stepped off into the air."

"Come down," he called. "Let us inspect the perimeter of the mesa for tracks."

They walked it together, slowly, "reading" each bit of ground. Nothing. Then they spent a long time examining the far side of the jumpjet for some signs of tracks, tail rubbings, any indication that the Na-Dina had climbed onto the roof, jumped, and landed.

Again, nothing.

Who could survive such a fall, and walk away? Without leaving tracks?

Krillen shook his head. How did this all fit together? He

couldn't imagine. This case would require more thinking, much more consideration on his part. He would have to go over everything again. And again. Until he figured it out.

He was Krillen of the Law, and he had never failed to solve a case. And he wasn't going to fail this time, either.

CHAPTER 8

♦

The Unexpected

A week after the smuggler raid, Etsane sat at her desk inside the Lab, staring glumly at photo-strips of the Royal Tomb ideoglyphs. How would she *ever* decipher the First Dynasty inscriptions?

She had already applied Kerry-Howard's Method for classifying the attributes of the persons, ideas and institutions in the tunnel panels. That was simple iconography.

She'd also compared the two versions of Na-Dina hieroglyphs with the ideoglyphs found in the Tomb, using stepwise and empty-set analysis. There had been a partial overlap in pictogram and phoneme matching, but the order of phrasing, the way the ideoglyphs began and ended a phrase, and the homophone variation rules still escaped her. She was left with a few translated words and a cryptic phrase—tantalizing bits, but . . .

"You look like you need a break."

Mahree Burroughs stood beside Etsane's desk, a recording slate in one hand, her expression sympathetic. The younger woman sat back, rubbing her stiff neck. "I guess I could." She shoved the seemingly untranslatable glyphs toward the middle of her desk.

"Here," Mahree said, putting a glass down on the table, "have some iced tea."

"Thanks, I need it," Etsane said. "You got back the day before yesterday, didn't you? I haven't had a chance to ask you how it went."

"Interesting," Mahree said, pulling up a chair. "Gave me a chance to see what life is like for the Na-Dina who live in the rural areas. We also nearly got fried by a lava flow."

"What?" Etsane stared at her new friend in horror.

Briefly, Mahree explained about the sabotaged batteries that had so nearly proved disastrous for herself and Krillen. "All in all, it was a narrow squeak," she finished.

"I'll say! Who do you think might have done it?"

"I don't know. Krillen wanted to question Axum, and I was present when he did. I felt sorry for her. She was so distressed to realize she might be under suspicion, and insisted she'd never done anything with the intention of harming another person. I believed her."

"But she admitted to sitting in the pilot's seat aboard the jumpjet."

"Yes, though she acted really ashamed of herself, because it verged on being blasphemous for her to have that kind of interest in flying through Mother Sky." The older woman glanced over at the pile of Etsane's work.

"So, how are you coming? Gordon is pinning all of his hopes on your being able to translate the ancient Na-Dina glyphs."

"I know," Etsane moaned. "Every time I think about that, I get the shakes. Mahree . . . I'm not getting anywhere. Do you have any linguistics training?"

"Yes, of course," Mahree said. "I've studied languages practically all my life. Is there something I could do to help you out?"

"I don't know. Do you know any ancient forms of Mizari? I keep thinking that some of these glyphs have a resemblance to Mizari—but maybe I'm just imagining that, because of the artifacts that were found in the tomb. Can you take a look at all of this and tell me if *you* see any similarity?''

"Yes, I know several forms of ancient Mizari. And sure, I'll take a look." Mahree picked through the pile of jumbled strip-sheets, her expression thoughtful. "Are these the glyphs that are causing you so much trouble?" She shuffled them around on the broad desk. Her eyes narrowed. "Etsane . . . there really *is* some similarity between Mizari Four and these ideoglyphs from the Royal Tomb!"

"*Really?*" Etsane moved her strips so that they flowed in a left-to-right manner, the way Na-Dina script was written.

Mahree peered closely at the work. "Let's see—you're dealing with a round wall adorned with seven strips of ideoglyphs measuring twenty meters from the right side of the tunnel entry around to the left, with one strip stacked atop the other." She moved the strips into the proper configuration.

"Yes," Etsane agreed, helping her. "The strips start at the floor and go up to where the ceiling arches into the domed skyscape. So the writing—and reading—convention had several options. Right to left. Bottom to top. Top to bottom. And the left to right I've assumed, provisionally, of course, starting with the bottom row of ideogylphs."

Now Mahree pointed to Glyph Twenty-One, a series of curlicues, dots, and a triangular face that had perplexed Etsane to distraction. She looked up as Mahree fiddled with the strip, smoothing it out. "You really think these are related to the ancient Mizari language?"

"I'm sure of it." The diplomat pointed at other strip-rows of ideoglyphs, tapping her finger at five different phrases. "Look at this, and there, there, then this one and this. Those are Mizari Four phoneme-glyphs. Corrupted, of course. But definitely Mizari—or at least what the Mizari used around six thousand years ago."

Etsane looked across the lab to where the Esteemed Lorezzzs lay coiled before a row of ceramic vessels brought in from the Royal Tomb. "We need another expert in this language. Lorezzzs is the representative of the Mizari Archaeological Society. Perhaps she—?''

Mahree shook her head. "Very few Mizari have made a study of Mizari Four. *I* have—with the help of the Esteemed Ssoriszss.'' She scooted her chair around so she was sitting beside Etsane as the Ethiopian woman peered at the strip-sheets. "But it's mainly a hobby. Something to do in between extended diplomatic meetings.''

Mahree finished speaking with a smile, and gave Etsane a look of frank curiosity. "You know, you're pretty young to be so experienced at all of this. How did you get into it?''

The younger woman blinked, then marked the ideoglyphs that Mahree had identified as Mizari Four. "Iconography was my first love. That's what got me my Heeyoon scholarship to study the paintings at Kal-Syr. Then postgraduate study of cross-cultural sapientology and multispecies linguistics at the university on Arooouhl. I've been working now for almost two years.''

Mahree sat back from the photo-cluttered desk, seeming surprised. "You made it into postgraduate studies early.''

Trying to shake her long-standing feelings of being out of place with the habits and expectations of other people, she wet her lips and said quietly, "Well, I earned my *Lycée Supérieur* at seventeen with a thesis on the temple art of New Kingdom Egypt.'' She remembered it all too well. "At twenty, I left for Kal-Syr.''

Mahree spoke softly, as if she had noticed the pain in Etsane's last statement. "You must be very special to have accomplished so much at such a young age.''

Etsane sat back in her chair, both pleased and embarrassed at the praise. Pulling at one of her braids, she shrugged. "My father began teaching me when I was four. He was a Professor Emeritus at the University of Addis Ababa, and taught me several languages—Gi'iz, Tigrayan, Oromo, Sidamo, and English. When mother died early, he and I—were alone together.'' She blinked her stinging eyes rapidly. "He set high standards. I always met them . . . until he decided that I should stay on Earth and become a professor like he was. I had decided I wanted to be a xeno-archaeologist. Soon after, I left Earth on scholarship to study on Arooouhl. It was the only time I ever disappointed him, he said.''

The Ethiopian took a deep, ragged breath from remembered pain. ''He died soon after.''

Mahree placed a palm on Etsane's arm to still the nervous fingering of the braid. Her eyes held only understanding. ''My dear, sometimes the hardest burdens are not what others demand of us, but what we give ourselves. Trying to please a memory . . .'' Mahree's expression turned distant, as if recalling something from her own life. ''Memories should console, not enslave.'' Then the diplomat focused back on Etsane, smiling gently. ''About this series of Mizari Four glyphs, have you considered . . .''

Etsane listened as Mahree made a suggestion for the linguistic comparison of Mizari Four with Temple and High Na-Dina, cross-linked to the Tomb ideoglyphs. It was a good idea, a pathway of multivariate factoring that she suspected even Professor Greyshine, her old mentor, would be hard-pressed to pull off.

She realized that her work here on Ancestor's World was truly one way she could honor and fulfill her obligation to her dead father. The thought warmed her. But as exciting as a possible breakthrough was, Etsane was surprised to realize she was just as excited by finding, in Mahree Burroughs, a friend.

Khuharkk' followed Professor Greyshine as the elderly Heeyoon walked up to the South Gate of the City of White Stone. He watched as Greyshine lifted his handheld record-slate, pointed the device's top edge at the curving arch that framed the gate, and activated the slate's graphics recording capability. The device, featuring drawings, photograph tracking, artifact location recording, and coding of artifact collection bags, never left the professor's hands when awake and stayed close by him even when he slept. Khuharkk' pulled his own slate from his neck and sat on his haunches while checking the readouts.

Greyshine's ears swiveled in the Simiu's direction. "Khuharkk', where's the robot flyer? Is the radar probe ready?"

Accustomed to the professor's constant worry over every detail, Khuharkk' replied, "The flyer is involved with a plant inventory transect for Doctor Ttalatha along the up-river canyon rims. She requested its use today so she could build a present-day baseline for her paleoenvironmental studies."

The Heeyoon stopped recording the gate arch and lowered his slate. He fixed amber eyes on Khuharkk'. "Well, we'll need it soon. Right now, I'd like that radar probe to run a series of ground transects between here and the Red Causeway."

"Yes, Professor." Khuharkk's job, as Camp Technologist, was to maintain all the analytical equipment needed for their work. Adjusting the software of the ground-penetrating radar probe required continuous input, which was why he spent half of each day following the chairman of his senior pair project.

As the professor moved on, Khuharkk' followed him through the open sandy area lying between the city's high stone walls and Outlier Building A-Six. Greyshine stopped just as they reached the western corner of the city wall and pointed toward the half-ruined causeway that led up from the River Gate.

"There! Set the radar probe to run linear transects between here and the near wall of the Red Causeway," Greyshine said. "I want to see if, as with ancient Egypt, the Na-Dina buried any Royal Barges next to the causeway's wharf."

Khuharkk' doubted that, but loaded the required parameters into the radar probe and watched it float off to begin its run. "It's started, Professor. When it's done, I'll dump the subground images into—"

"My slate!" Greyshine barked sharply, then lowered his long ears as if realizing how peremptory he'd been lately. "I'm sorry, my friend. I didn't mean to be so abrupt. It's just—the job here is daunting! The lake will flood this ruin in only three years. We need the resources of six universities!"

Yes, the Royal Tomb would be flooded in three years, Khuharkk' thought glumly. It felt more like a scant three weeks.

Greyshine lowered his slate from its recording of the River Gate's two pylons. "The earthfill dam will be completed in one year," he grumbled, almost to himself. "The diversion lake already there will start to back up and begin filling the five hundred and sixty kilometers of river canyon lying between us." The Heeyoon sighed wearily. "So many *other* ruins will be flooded long before this one. Flooded and lost forever."

Khuharkk's heart sank at the bitter reminder.

Greyshine nodded, still speaking more to himself than to his assistant. "According to Doctor Gordon, there are thirty-four temple cities, three island ossuaries, and at least two hundred forty farming villages lying *downstream* of the dam site, between it and the capital, Spirit. They're currently populated and will not be flooded. But how many temple cities, burial caves, tunnel-tombs, and abandoned farm villages do you think the Na-Dina accumulated from the dam site up to *here*, to the City of White Stone?"

Khuharkk' looked away, feeling Greyshine's frustration keenly. "I have no idea."

"Neither do I," Greyshine remarked, his tone almost affable. "Nor do the modern Na-Dina, despite the valiant efforts of the Temple of Records historians. The population centers have moved, over the millennia, farther and farther downriver." The Heeyoon waved across the wide valley, toward the Great Ramp that rose toward the canyon rim and the mouth of the Royal Road. "The upper reaches of the River of Life, and from the First Cataract to the Fifth Cataract, have been unpopulated for over a thousand years. We have so much to learn and so little time to learn it in."

The Simiu struggled for optimism. "At least with the robot flyer we can—"

"We can reduce the workload of fifty years to a decade or so," the Heeyoon interrupted. "Thanks to the equipment donated by the Mizari Archaeological Society that Ambassador Burroughs brought in.''

Khuharkk' watched the radar probe complete its third subground sounding transect. "But we don't have a decade, Professor. We only have three years."

"I know," the Heeyoon grumbled. "We'll make do with what we have. If the Revered Ancestors are willing, I will, by the time of the weekly research conference, present Doctor Mitchell with a preliminary inventory of all sites recordable from aerial surveying. That should give us a rough inventory of sites, all the way from simple hunter-gatherer camps of twenty thousand years ago, to modern-day salt evaporation ponds."

Khuharkk' looked upcanyon. "By means of the robot flyer?"

"Yes."

He began to appreciate his own critical role of Technologist in this giant, multidisciplinary effort. Without his labor-saving and remote-sensing equipment, they had no hope of even completing the aerial inventory, let alone doing major excavations at more than this single ruin.

The Heeyoon moved away, heading toward the slanting ramp of the Causeway. "So, let us do what we can in the time we have. I need to make a graphical record of the North Gate, measure the relationship of the northerly outliner buildings C-Four, C-Five, and C-Six to the city's north wall proper, and have your robot flyer do an ultraviolet scan of the entire valley floor around the city. All before nightfall."

Once more, the Simiu followed the Heeyoon, while checking his own slate to confirm that the rest of the remote-sensing equipment either stored at the Lab, or out on field assignment, was still in prime working order. "Professor, do you think we can get more funding from the CLS?"

"I doubt it." Greyshine slung his slate from his neck and began climbing hand over foot up the tumbled rocks of the causeway scar. "The CLS gave Doctor Mitchell an initial grant last year, when the Traditionalist faction of the

Na-Dina Council of Elders requested assistance in making an archaeological survey, inventory, and test excavation of this valley. With the finding of the sarcophagus and the Mizari relics, that assistance was increased tenfold.'' Greyshine's bushy tail swung rapidly as the elderly archaeologist balanced atop a boulder. ''But there are other planets where crops have failed, where natural disasters exceed resources, and they too call for help.'' The Heeyoon reached the top of the Red Causeway and paused, breathing deeply.

Khuharkk' followed, moving rapidly over the rocky core of the Causeway. Reaching the top, he joined the Professor. ''Is there any chance the Na-Dina Council of Elders might delay completion of the dam?''

Greyshine laughed harshly. ''Unlikely. The Modernist faction of the Council is already worried that finding the Royal Tomb will be a hindrance to their industrialization plans. Nordlund follows a tight timeline. Archaeologists must fit into the narrow crevice between alien wishes and commercial plans.''

Khuharkk' told himself that they were doing the best they could, but it did no good. During his next guard watch, he knew full well the night would be crowded with images of long-dead cities being drowned under muddy water. And there was nothing he could do to prevent the loss to the ages.

That same night, Etsane took her first turn at guard watch. She shared the long midnight stretch with Khuharkk', who also walked back and forth along the canyon rim overlooking Base Camp, the Landing Field and, in the downstream distance, the City of White Stone. The City glowed in the bright light of Mother's Daughter, newly risen over the southern horizon. That glowing ball, twice the size of Earth's Moon, was an odd contrast to the ruddy glow of erupting volcanoes that fringed the southeastern part of the horizon where the Mountains of Faith rose like a hellish wall.

Thanks to the elevation of the canyon rim, Etsane could

see the gleaming surface of the River of Life as it snaked easterly through the enclosing horseshoe of the mountains. The side canyons were deep here, back-cut long ago by the river. While there were places where arable bottomland had formed in a dead arm of the river, high canyon walls contained the waters until after the First Cataract, where the land opened out into a wide valley. At that point the river turned north and continued flowing through densely populated farmlands until it reached the delta, where it fingered out into a dozen rivulets that emptied into the Northern Sea.

Etsane sighed. Imagining what she could not see might interfere with what she must watch for. Lowering the scanner eyeshade, she blinked, adjusting her eyes to the pale green of the nightscope. Then she fingered the com unit clipped to her waist and spoke into a collar pickup. "Scanner check, Khuharkk'. You show clear? No predators? No smugglers?"

"I show clear," he said in a growly voice. "Scanner shows no other life-forms. Out."

She double-tapped the com unit control pad. "Out."

The silence of the night puzzled her. Etsane turned and walked downriver along the canyon rim, away from Khuharkk', who would now turn and walk upriver. In the highlands of her homeland, she'd always heard the rasp of crickets, the rustle of marmots, and the howl of a rare lion. After centuries of deforestation in the ancient mountain uplands that overlooked the Horn of Africa, her land had mostly recovered from the Great Devastation of three centuries before. There were half as many people in Africa as when man had first walked on the Moon, but at least now they no longer died from malaria, AIDS, Ebola Fever, famine, and the other catastrophes that had once accompanied the war, poverty, neglect, and greed of those centuries.

Dismissing the past, Etsane listened intently. Where *were* the local equivalents of those night animals?

The Ethiopian woman blinked the eyeshade nightscope off starlight magnification, blinked over to infrared, and searched for the body-heat signatures of small creatures. Turning away from the valley bottom—where the cluster of dome-tents glowed pale red and the metal Lab building lying at the ring's center glowed dark crimson—she scanned the ground lying to the east.

Like a wrinkled apron, it rose up to meet one arm of the Mountains of Faith, while in the south a similar rise turned into foothills, then high peaks. A high mountain lake lay in that direction, as did a rocky pass that connected with the southern hemisphere of Ancestor's World.

Suddenly something small, red, and swift moved across Etsane's field of vision.

Walking toward it, Etsane wondered if it were reptilian, insectivore, or something else. Most of the reptilian life here seemed immune to the ultrasonics of the repulsors. Furtively, she reached behind to the small of her back, and felt the outline of the pulse gun Dr. Mitchell had insisted she wear. Khuharkk' knew she'd have her sling, but he didn't know she had the high-powered pulse gun, while he, of course, was weaponless—if a mature Simiu could ever be said to be weaponless, naturally armed as they were with formidable teeth and claws.

She knew most Simiu abhorred the human tendency to find the answers to difficult questions in weapon-fire, and Etsane cared for Khuharkk' enough to respect that. However, guard watch was dangerous; that's why they maintained it so rigorously. The smugglers were armed and wouldn't hesitate to kill. And while most of the large predators were rarely encountered, they maintained the watch because they could not risk an unexpected attack. The pulse gun was a last resort. Khuharkk' did not even know she had it. If the watch was quiet, he would never need to.

By the time she drew near enough to identify the small, rustling animal, its little red tail had already disappeared. Swinging her head from side to side, Etsane searched for other life signs. Then she stopped. She listened hard, straining for every vibration. The smugglers could move silently, she knew. A chill ran up her spine. Was something there, or were her nerves finally failing?

Then she saw it. Looming as large as a Terran Siberian tiger, one of the massive beasts they called the long-necks moved gracefully along the rolling rise of land that lay to the south of her, perhaps a kilometer away. As she watched in silence, not even daring to breathe, the creature stopped. The breeze shifted, swirling around Etsane and carrying her scent downwind. She swallowed. She was alien to this world. Surely, the leggy, powerful predator would have no interest in her foreign scent and would go its own way. The huge, indistinct red image of the warm-blooded reptile shifted position, its angular, carnivore's head moving from side to side as if tasting the air. Tasting her scent.

As if it suddenly spied her, it turned its entire body to face Etsane's much smaller one across the expanse of ridge. She froze, praying that it needed motion to detect her actual presence. Her hand crept to her com unit slowly. The massive animal reared back on its hind legs, its head swiveling. *It will go its own way now,* Etsane willed it. Then it dropped to all fours and moved purposefully toward her.

"Khuharkk'!" Cursing, she slapped the com unit control pad on. "Khuharkk'! Predator alert! A long-neck's coming for me, fast. Range—" Her voice cracked as she read off the integers glowing at the top of her eyeshade. "Range is one thousand meters and closing. Estimated speed, thirty klicks an hour. Mass, about two hundred kilos."

"Etsane!" The alarm was clear in his voice. "Retreat! Something that large will not be deterred by the repulsors."

"I know!" Her mouth suddenly dry, Etsane felt the weapon-belt at her waist. Repulsor ward on the left, her sling with bag of rocks on the right. Her hunting knife was strapped to her thigh. And, strapped to the small of her back, was the pulse-gun that *astamari* Mitchell had insisted she carry. Out of respect for Khuharkk', she had worn it concealed beneath her loose blouse.

Etsane felt the impulse to draw it and shoot the beast down. But then she envisioned Khuharkk's disgust if she resorted to a *weapon*, and suddenly it seemed as severe and unforgiving as her father's. Surely she didn't have to kill the creature with a *weapon*!

The Simiu had told her to retreat. That made sense. But when she forced herself to turn away from the vision of the

advancing predator to get her bearings, she found that behind her, the canyon rim dropped off in a vertical fall of
more than fifty meters. She did not trust herself to find the
place where a rockfall had piled up in a makeshift ramp.
Retreat suddenly seemed far more dangerous that the approaching animal.

"Khuharkk'! There isn't enough room. I'm backed
against the canyon rim!"

"I'm almost there!"

Self-consciously she touched the pulse-gun, then pulled
her hand away. How angry would he be? He'd despise her
for violating his taboo. Etsane glanced upcanyon. The Simiu's bright scarlet form sped along at an amazing pace, as
he ran on all fours. Looking from one glowing image to
the other, she realized with sick certainty that the night
creature would reach her first. What would her father tell
her to do?

"*Remember the leopard!*" a voice whispered.

Yes! Shaken from her paralyzed stance, Etsane pulled
her sling out, felt in her bag for a large piece of hard quartz,
loaded it into the sling, then put two more thumb-sized
rocks in her mouth, where they would be ready for reload-
ing. It *was* a weapon, and with luck a hard shot to the head
would drive the creature away, sparing its life—and hers.

The night of the smuggler raid, Khuharkk' had not objected to her use of her sling. Stretching her arm out to the
right, she made the meter-long projectile weapon whistle in
the night air. Then, in one fluid motion, Etsane let loose
one string while snapping forward with all the strength she
had.

The predator howled and spun around as the stone hit its
mark hard.

Now it would flee, and they would be safe! Her exhila-
ration lasted only seconds—almost immediately, the now-
furious animal gathered itself and broke into a fast lope.

She did not stop to think about the danger an injured
creature posed. Quickly she spit out the second rock, slung
it, and tossed. Before it could hit its target she had reloaded
a third stone, slung it, and then shouted when she struck

her target twice at over a hundred meters distance. The massive animal yowled, but kept on coming.

"*Etsane!*" Khuharkk' called, nearly running full tilt into her.

"I hit it three times, but it keeps coming!" she said, in frustrated disbelief.

"I can see it in the moonlight! It's too big to be brought down by stones. We must retreat now!"

Her feet felt rooted onto the ridge. It was irrational, she knew, but she was convinced that if they turned their backs now, the beast would be on them before they could make it over the canyon rim.

Use the pulse-gun, her inner voice warned. Glancing at Khuharkk''s nearness, she could not make herself do it. She was so mixed up with fear, adrenaline, and the need to react she didn't know what to do.

"Try the repulsor ward," Khuharkk' barked, to her amazement. "It will not affect the animal, but you can disorient it by firing at the ground in front of it."

Yes! the woman thought, pulling out the ward. She twisted the power knob to "full" and fired at the ground in front of the rapidly closing creature.

Blue light flared, blinding her. She cursed silently, realizing their night vision was now compromised. Blinking to clear her eyes, she strained to hear the running scrabble of the clawed beast.

Etsane heard it. Still advancing. She fired at the ground again and again, trying to create a safe fire-zone around them, hoping the animal would get tired of having stones and dust hurled at its face. Dimly she could see it evading the blasts, dodging around them. The ward slowed it, but did not stop its steady approach.

She felt Khuharkk's warm palm press against her arm. "I have already called for help," the Simiu's rumbling voice told her. "I can only hope to slow its advance until they arrive. You must find your way down the slope while I fight it."

While he fights it? Without even thinking, she grabbed a

handful of his mane in her fist. "You can't fight that thing, Khuharkk'! You'll be killed!"

And in the eerie glow of her augmented night vision, she saw the odd burgundy gleam of his eyes as they stared at her, saying so much clearly than his words ever could—*I am a Simiu. My death will be rich with Honor, for I will have saved my friend.* Then he turned without looking back, and launched himself toward the enraged, wounded reptile.

"No! *NO!*" she screamed at his retreating back. There was no time for thinking now. Khuharkk' reared up toward the animal even as it spun to meet him, their challenging screams matching each other's ferocity.

"*NONONONO!*" she shouted, her voice as loud in her ears as their enraged roars. The pulse-gun was in her hand without her even being aware that she'd reached for it. She aimed the weapon cleanly over the Simiu's head and struck the rearing Long-Neck between its heavily ridged eyes.

It bellowed, flinging its head back as Khuharkk' sank his teeth and claws into its snaky throat. Etsane fired again, hitting it below the jaw where the beam could pass through to the brain. The heavy creature crashed heavily to the ground, Khuharkk' clinging grimly to it. It was dying now, its reactions automatic. A powerful arm swung heavily against the Simiu, claws gouging a trail over Khuharkk''s arm and shoulder, but still he clung to the animal through its death spasms.

"Khuharkk', no! Let go!" Etsane yelled, firing again at the head. Like the mindless shark that could kill even when it was dying, the monster rolled, pinning Khuharkk' beneath its bulk, then rolled again with the Simiu atop it.

I need a clean shot to the base of the skull to sever the spine, Etsane realized, then ran around behind the flopping creature. Forgetting all her fears for her own well-being, she drew too close, and the flailing foreleg of the paddling creature scraped the bare skin of her forearm. She ignored the stinging pain to locate the one spot—

—and, with great deliberation, she fired squarely where the spine met the skull.

With a last, great sigh, the beast stilled and collapsed into a lifeless heap.

Only then did Khuharkk' lift his bloodied head and meet her gaze—as she stood facing him, the hated weapon firmly in hand.

"I couldn't let you die," she blurted. "Not to save my life. If I'd kept my head, reacted faster, maybe I could've gotten away and you wouldn't have done this. I couldn't let you die because of me. I'm so sorry about the weapon—"

He was beside her now, the smell of the alien animal's blood fresh on his fur. "You had this all along?" he rumbled, indicating the pulse-gun.

She was trembling, shaking from head to foot as the adrenaline rush left her drained. "I didn't want to use it. I know it offends your culture. But I couldn't let you die!"

Gently, he patted her arm. "You hid this from me out of respect for my Honor. Allowed me to battle the creature. Etsane, you could've been killed yourself, all to spare my feelings."

She blinked, realized he was—chuckling?

"Young human, do you know how long I have worked with your people? I understand your culture and respect it; I have for a long time. I know that it is different from my own. That you would endanger yourself so greatly to honor my culture—it has been a long time since any human has honored me so. I thank you. And I thank you for saving both our lives."

So surprised was she at his reaction, she felt the last vestiges of her strength fail, and she grabbed at his right shoulder to steady her shaky legs. His fur was wet. She blinked. Her own arm gleamed moistly. She lifted the eye-shade and stared. In the white moonlight, their blood ran red.

She could hear voices chattering over the com unit, hear scrambling up the slope as help arrived.

"Our injuries are minor, but they will scar," he commented, sounding oddly smug. "We'll have a good story to tell, won't we, Etsane?" He sounded winded, as if the mad tackle of the creature had taken everything he could give. "Etsane, you fought with great Honor."

"Even—even with a weapon?" she said dazedly, hardly believing his acceptance.

"You saved my life."

"You were willing to sacrifice yourself to save mine."

Khuharkk' gripped her shoulder. "We share more now than just professional honor. We share an Honor Bond."

"That's great." Etsane felt dizzy again, and weaved as she stood in the cold night air. "What is it?"

Khuharkk" laughed weakly. "It's what Simiu warriors share when they've faced down death together. Come now. The others are here to help us. We will not last much longer on our feet."

And as the first rescuers approached them with med-kits, weapons and stretchers in hand, the two warriors sank to their haunches in the sand, leaning against one other to keep from collapsing as bonelessly as their enemy had.

Even as Doctor Strongheart hurried to them, Khuharkk' assured her, "If we lean on each other, then neither can fall."

Closing her eyes in weariness, relief, and intense gratitude, she let the warmth of his body sustain her as she realized how very right he was.

CHAPTER 9

♦

Trap

The next afternoon Etsane was busy at her desk in the Lab, puzzling once again over the ancient Na-Dina language, when Sumiko came out of her office, stood by the Lab's front entrance, and glanced at her watch. "Time for the big show," she called to Etsane. "We've got a front-row seat for the second coming of A-Um Rakt."

"What?" Etsane had been concentrating deeply, and it took her a moment to catch up. Then her brain clicked into gear. "You mean they're bringing the sarcophagus down to put it in the Security Chamber? Here? *Now?*"

The woman nodded. "Yes. I just got the message. They're up there attaching the a-grav units right now! Very shortly the Golden Barge of A-Um Rakt will float out of his Tomb, down the ramp, and over to our little establishment. Accompanied by the crown jewels, of course."

"Including the Mizari relics?"

"Naturally."

Etsane noticed that the Japanese woman's statement had caused a stir among the other researchers. Ttalatha looked up from her computer screen, her masked snout wrinkling excitedly. She began grooming herself, trailing retractable claws through her short, creamy fur. Beside her, Hrashoi the Shadgui shook its slothlike shoulders, the Gui toad part of the symbiont visible as a flash of red hiding among the long black fur of the Shad's thick neck. The Gui's saucer-wide eyes stared at the front entry, seeing for its sightless host. Natual waved at her from his station beside Eloiss, the female Drnian who did the floral analysis of materials brought in by the Na-Dina dig crew.

Etsane looked back to the waiting Lab Chief, who wore a white lab coat over her shorts and blouse. "Sumiko, can you see what's going on over one of the remotes?"

"Sure can. Want a blow-by-blow description?" the Lab Chief called, as she stared at the screen of the holo-vid unit in her office.

An affirmative cheer went up. "Okay, then," Sumiko said cheerfully, "here goes! They're starting down the rampway. Doctor Mitchell is running around the a-grav unit, clucking like a mother hen checking her eggs."

The audience chuckled appreciatively.

"Dr. Strongheart is bringing up the rear, both paws on the back of the barge, keeping it perfectly level. Khuharkk' is handling the a-grav controls. Professor Greyshine is dancing around, alternating between two and four feet, waving for the Na-Dina dig crew to get out of the way. Esteemed Lorezzzs is actually slithering along *underneath* the barge. I sure hope that a-grav unit doesn't hiccup! Then there's Ambassador Mahree, who is trying to keep everyone calm."

Another chuckle arose from the assembled researchers.

"And, don't let me forget. Axum is there, overseeing the workers, trying to keep them out of Greyshine's way as they make obeisance to the King's sarcophagus. And of course there's Beloran, who is walking along, swishing his tail and wearing a snotty expression—so what's new?"

Laughter rewarded her sallies, and she grinned unabashed.

"And . . . they've reached the bottom of the ramp safely, and they're heading straight for us! Okay, so where's the applause for my stellar announcing skills?"

Etsane clapped wildly. Natual did likewise. Eloiss copied

him hesitantly. The Shadgui watched. But Doctor Ttalatha jumped up and down like a youngster.

"Coming through!" Gordon Mitchell bellowed moments later from outside the door that Sumiko held open.

Sumiko grinned excitedly as the barge "sailed" past her.

The golden sarcophagus was easily three meters long, a meter wide, and it came to a halt hovering about one meter above the Lab's stone floor. Mahree, Khuharkk', Greyshine, and Axum crowded in after the dust-covered figure of Doctor Mitchell. He looked at Sumiko, his face lighting up with a big grin. "Once we close the door of the vault, I'm going to be able to get my first decent night's sleep since we found this thing. Is everything ready in the Security Chamber?"

"Yes, Gordon," Sumiko said, rushing to the front of the line. She reached out to touch the hand-tooled gold of the barge, her fingers trailing reverently over red and yellow cloisonne glass inlays, silver plaques, bronze bosses, and the slim snake-head of A-Um Rakt. "Ohhh! I couldn't resist."

Beloran entered the Lab, his fan-ears laid back with displeasure and anxiety, his tail twitching. "Female Philosopher, please show us the way to the Chamber."

The Lab Chief recaptured her usual cool poise. "Of course, Liaison. It's right back here, behind the artifact shelving."

Etsane watched the bustling entourage trail along after the floating a-grav unit and its unique cargo. Going around the Secondary Receiving Tables, the group walked down the far sidewall of the Lab, passing out of sight behind long rows of artifact shelving.

At the rear of the building lay the climate-controlled room for perishables, where organics were kept, taking up one-half of the rear portion. The other half was the vaultlike room dubbed the Secure Storage Chamber, or SSC.

Doctor Mitchell had ordered the door to the SSC when he'd first found the tomb of A-Um Rakt two months ago. The heavy steel door had been forged by the Na-Dina to Mitchell's specifications, and had been completed and flown in via jumpjet the day before yesterday.

The time lock that would ensure the security of the SSC was one of Professor Greyshine's contributions. The door had been made to fit around it, and yesterday, Doctor Mitchell and Khuharkk' had spent hours welding it into place and hanging the door.

Now, Doctor Strongheart could more easily do her tissue sampling and genetic analysis of the King's remains inside the Lab, while the Na-Dina Council of Elders—and fussy Beloran—would feel much more reassured knowing the Tomb treasures were protected by a steel door and a time lock.

The SSC was also fitted with an emergency radio transmitter that could be used to call as far as Spirit in case of another smuggler attack.

Natual came over to her after the raucous, order-giving retinue had passed out of view. The alien's dark brown skin looked warm and smooth where not covered by his loose tunic and short, knickerlike pants. His red eyes gazed down at her appreciatively. Etsane knew by now that Natual was interested in her, and that he was interested in being more than just a friend. She wasn't sure how she felt about that.

Natual was nice, and they got along well, and enjoyed their time together. But . . . he wasn't *human*. Etsane had heard of aliens and humans having relationships, though it was comparatively rare. Sometimes love happened between people of different species. And, from what little she knew of Drnian physiology, it might be possible for a human and a Drnian to mate.

Once or twice she'd found herself thinking along those lines and her mind had just *shut down*. She just wasn't ready to consider anything so major as the idea of having a romantic relationship with an alien.

But Natual obviously didn't share her misgivings. Etsane knew he liked her; he made that flatteringly obvious. As she gazed up at him, wondering what to say, he held out a large glass of water still cold from the Lab Chief's refrigerator. "Are you thirsty?"

Etsane realized she was, and the thoughtfulness of the

gesture touched her. "I sure am. Thank you so much." She took a long drink as Natual moved to perch on the edge of her desk.

"You are very welcome," he said. His black wiry hair shone in the bright light of the Lab, and his small, round mouth tried to curve upward. He'd evidently been practicing trying to smile in the human manner. "I wonder whether you would like to come over to my tent tonight. For dinner, which I will be pleased to make for us. It's much better than Refectory food."

His red eyes held hers compellingly. "We could discuss the reactions of our respective species to death and near-death experiences. You had what Doctor Mitchell referred to as 'a close call' last night."

"Yes, I did," Etsane admitted. "When I saw how *big* that long-neck was, it was pretty scary." She hesitated, but then thought, *Hey, even if Natual isn't human, he's still a gentleman. It's not like he wouldn't accept no for an answer. Just eating dinner with him doesn't commit me to anything.* So, aloud, she said, "Sure, Natual. I'd love to try some of your cooking. What time?"

Natual bobbed his head, obviously pleased. "About an hour after sunset?"

"That's fine," Etsane said. "I'll be there."

Mahree stood at the back of the room, craning her neck and standing on tiptoe, trying to see the treasures of A Um Rakt. But she was not a tall woman, and there were too many people in the way. The crowd was too thick for her to edge closer to the sarcophagus. The gold gleamed with a lustrous sheen under the lights of the room, and she found herself longing to touch it and the other beautiful things she could see. What would it be like, she wondered, to touch something that was six thousand years old?

She turned her head, found Doctor Strongheart standing beside her. "I'd really like a private tour," she said to the Heeyoon. "Maybe I should ask Gordon to give me one tonight, after dinner."

"Why don't you?" Strongheart said. "I'm sure he'd be

pleased to show off his finds.'' The physician showed her teeth in a wolfish grin. ''Not to mention that he'd then have you all to himself, Mahree. I sense that he would not be averse to that idea.''

Mahree found herself blushing hotly, and for a moment she remembered her dream at Blue Pond. ''Strongheart, you're as hopeless as your mate, trying to play matchmaker with every human that comes along.''

''What is wrong with a bit of romance?'' the doctor asked, feigning innocence, widening her golden eyes. ''Here we are in a remote location, far from civilization. Rob Gable is far away, and Gordon Mitchell is here. Among my people, such liaisons are not unknown, and the same is true of your people. I know, for I have watched Robert Gable's films many times at the Academy. I saw *Casablanca* several times.''

Feeling a pang at the mention of her lover and the father of her child, Mahree just shook her head. It wasn't that she'd never known any man but Rob over the years . . . sure she had, from time to time. Short-term flings while spending six months or more away from Rob were something that she'd indulged in a few times. She suspected that Rob had done the same, over the years. He and Janet Rodriguez, for example . . .

But they'd made it an unspoken policy never to ask and never to confess their extra-relationship involvements. It made things easier that way.

And it was true that Rob Gable was the only man she'd ever loved.

''I don't think I should bother Gordon with a request for a private viewing,'' she told Strongheart. ''He's so busy these days, he barely has a moment to himself.''

The Heeyoon cocked her ears sympathetically, but said no more.

''I'm getting claustrophobic from the crowd,'' Mahree muttered, edging back from the press of scaled, furred, and human bodies. ''I'm going to take a shower before dinner.''

''I will see you later,'' Strongheart said.

*   *   *

Later that same night, Beloran stood in the dark shadows cast by the Lab and watched as the Burroughs female left the Refectory, heading for her dome-tent. Dinner had run late, due to the excitement caused by the removal of the treasures, and it was only a few hours until midnight.

Beloran blinked, watching the human's quick, purposeful strides as she reached her dome-tent and went inside. Good . . . very good. Now she would find the message he had left, laboriously copying it from words that Infidel Mitchell had used in his written reports. Nobody suspected that he, Beloran, could both read and understand (though not speak) the main human language, but he had had months to learn it, and, once he had realized that the humans were his primary enemies, he had applied himself to studying it assiduously. After all, he was a scholar in addition to being a Merchant.

The message had been simple—block letters printed on a sheet of datafax flimsy, saying, "Meet me in the lab before midnight and I will give you that private tour." Beloran had not attempted to reproduce Infidel Mitchell's signature, but had just scrawled a capital "G" at the bottom of the message.

He'd been standing right behind the human and the Infidel Heeyoon when they'd had their talk, and his fan-ears had swiveled to catch every word—just as they had caught Infidel Mitchell's "private" command to Khuharkk' on the day he'd finally had the pleasure of killing Waterston.

When Beloran had heard the Infidel woman talking about wanting a private tour of the King's treasures, he'd known it was time to arrange another "accident." The first one had failed—though, from what he'd heard from the gossip around camp, not by much. Infidel Burroughs and Krillen of the Law had nearly been caught by a lava flow when the batteries he'd sabotaged had failed, stranding them in his skimmer.

Beloran hadn't even figured he'd be lucky enough to have them fail during a lava flow. He'd just hoped they'd die far enough from civilization that the weak Infidel female would have succumbed to the heat from Mother's

Eye. But Krillen, it seemed, had managed to save them.

The Liaison silently cursed the Investigator. He was a traitor to all of *Halish meg a-tum*!

The human female walked into her dome-tent, switched on the light, moved about for a few minutes, then came back out. Standing in the yellow rectangle cast by her tent light, she looked toward the Lab. Beloran held still, nearly certain the Infidel did not possess the Na-Dina ability to adjust her sight to draw in more light. In the dark shadows cast by the low-hanging Mother's Daughter, his blue scales should be invisible.

Infidel Burroughs stepped away from her dome-tent. She followed the trail around the Refectory, along the far side of the Lab building, then entered by the side door next to Mitchell's office. Pressing his ear against the still-warm metal of the building, Beloran heard her footsteps turn toward the far end of the building, and then proceed on, in the direction of the SSC.

Good . . . good!

No one else was inside the Lab. No one would be likely to visit until morning. And the vault door operated on a time lock. Once closed, it would not open until morning. Beloran knew the code to open the door, and had made sure that it was already open, standing slightly ajar. The Infidel female would think that Infidel Mitchell awaited her.

He would not have dared to be so bold in his trap if Infidel Mitchell had not been so arrogant as to open the time lock within full view of the assembled research crew, plus the diggers. Mitchell was not expecting trouble from within the camp—his only precautions were directed toward preserving the treasure from the smugglers.

Beloran heard her steps slow and halt as she neared the partly open door to the SSC. Slowly, making not a sound, he crept around the building and waited, poised, by the side door. She was there, before the vault.

Yes, he told her silently. *Go in. Go in and die, despoiler of my world. . . .*

As Beloran watched, the Burroughs female poked her head around the vault door. "Gordon?" he heard her call.

Then . . . it was going to work! She was stepping inside!

Beloran threw himself forward with the speed of a hunting long-neck. Through the Lab he raced, tail up, light-footed, quick. In a second he was at the door, both taloned hands outstretched. They met steel, and with his entire weight behind his hands, the heavy door swung closed with a crash.

Yes!

Quickly, Beloran altered the setting on the time lock, spinning the timing dial randomly and then setting it with a final click. From within he could hear muffled shouts and thumps as Infidel Burroughs beat on the steel door.

The Liaison headed back out of the lab almost as fast as he'd come in. Now he would go to her dome-tent, and, if she had left it there, he would find and destroy the message flimsy.

Then . . . then he would wait. He would not be able to rest until he was sure she was dead. He would watch the lab, and count the minutes. When he was sure she would never trouble him again, then he would seek his own sleeping place.

In a way, Beloran thought, it was ironically fitting. The off-worlder female would suffocate in the vault, accompanied to her death by the body of the First Dynasty King. Perhaps A-Um Rakt would bless Beloran for his piety in bringing him a grave offering after so long in his tomb. Perhaps the favor of this Revered Ancestor would help to offset the sacrilege that he, Beloran, had committed when he'd flown the alien ship through Mother Sky.

Beloran scurried through the camp, moving through the shadows with practiced ease. . . .

"Gordon?" Mahree stepped inside the steel vault of the Secure Storage Chamber, and was momentarily distracted by the glory of the golden sarcophagus of King A-Um Rakt. Was he hiding behind it, planning to jump out and scare her, or do something equally idiotic?

No, Gordon wouldn't do that.

Mahree hesitated for a second, then decided she didn't like this, not at all.

She turned around, heading back for the half-open door.

Wham!

Before her eyes, the vault door crashed shut.

Her mouth dropped open; then her heart slammed in fear.

Oh, shit!

Silence.

Not even the sound of footsteps outside penetrated the thick metal of the vault door. Maybe it was some kind of mistake?

She rushed over to the door, pushed on it, then cried out and pounded with her fists. "Hey! I'm in here! Let me out!"

Her only answer was the *snick* as the sealing bolts slid into place.

Oh, God.

She gasped for breath, her chest tight, and thought of how Gordon had told her that the chamber was sealed—no ventilation shafts, no vents, nothing. Panic nibbled along the edge of her mind.

"No!" she told herself firmly; then she turned and inspected the vault chamber by the glow of its ceiling lights. No shadows here. No darkness. Just her, the shining gold casket of the King, and . . . the radio!

"Yes!" she yelled with relief, rushing to the far side of the vault and throwing open the metal casing.

Inside lay broken plastic, smashed chips, a deformed battery.

Turning around, Mahree pressed her back against the cold metal wall of the vault and sank slowly to the floor. Wrapping her arms around her knees, she hugged herself tight.

She was alone.

Obviously, the message from Gordon had been faked. Someone had planned this trap as a way to get rid of her. Someone wanted her dead.

How much time did she have before all the air in the sealed vault was gone? Hours . . . probably. Until morning?

Doubtful. All too soon . . . she'd know for sure . . .

Panic surged up again, and this time, it won. Surrounded by four metric tons of titanium-steel, Mahree Burroughs began to weep. She cried softly, knowing this was the end—and that she'd broken her promise to her daughter to stay safe and return to her.

"Claire . . . oh, Claire. I'm so sorry."

Up on the canyon rim, Khuharkk' paused in his night guard duty. His scanner eyeshade had been set to infrared, the better to detect the presence of new Long-Necks.

His companion over on the other ridge tonight was Axum, head of the digging crew. She was armed with one of Doctor Mitchell's pulse-guns, and Khuharkk' was under strict orders from the boss that if he detected any sign of a Long-Neck, he was to call Axum immediately, and let her deal with it with her weapon.

The thought of doing so disgusted him—but orders were orders, and Khuharkk' had to admit that he didn't think he could bring down an adult Long-Neck by himself. They were just too big and too fast.

Khuharkk' had volunteered to take the first guard shift tonight, because he could tell that Doctor Mitchell needed the extra rest. The human had been working himself constantly, and he wasn't a young man.

Besides, he'd welcomed this chance for an outing in the cool night air. He peered around him, searching through his eyeshade for any other moving thing. Though Axum held the upstream end of the canyon rim, he had not seen her blood-red scanner image since they'd split apart upon arriving atop the mesa. No doubt she hunted the night like a Na-Dina, using her sense of smell to warn her of a Long-Neck's approach. Simiu could smell well too, but she was sensible enough—or corrupted enough, his brothers would say—to accept technological help in defense of others.

Red light flashed.

A blob of something glowed down in the Camp. A fairly large blob that seemed to have just exited from the dark red oblong of the Lab. He'd thought everyone was asleep long ago. Who could that be? Someone who needed the sanitary unit at this hour?

Khuharkk' blinked, enlarging the remote sensing image. The blob tripled in size on his scanner eyeshade, and grew in detail.

The Simiu knew instantly that the blob was a Na-Dina.

The heat signature of a Na-Dina was distinct from that of a human, or that of any of the other aliens in Camp. For one thing, their body mass was one-third larger than humans. For another, the red blob showed a curlicue streak that had to be the long tail of a Na-Dina. Khuharkk' watched the blob, waiting to see it go into the sanitary unit, but instead it just stayed in one place, outside the Lab.

Why?

The ground of the mesa rumbled under his feet as a distant volcano belched, and microquakes added in their multipart harmony. Were the Revered Ancestors trying to give him some kind of answer?

Khuharkk' watched, and, eventually, the blob disappeared among the string of round dome-tent blobs, going into one of them. It could have been any of the individual tents, or even one of the barracks tents of the dig crew. It was impossible to tell because residual heat still glowed from the tent fabrics, veiling fine detail.

Growling low in his throat, Khuharkk' decided to check in with Axum, ask her opinion on whether they should rouse Dr. Mitchell to report this. "Axum," he said, triggering the intercom unit. "Axum, come in."

The speaker button in his ear remained silent. Where was she? It was possible that she was out of line-of-sight comunit contact, hidden perhaps below a rolling foothill. Perhaps she had retired into an arroyo to attend a call of nature.

Khuharkk' watched for several minutes more, trying Axum at intervals, before he decided just to forget the Na-Dina wandering around the camp. Probably one of the workers had indigestion and had gone out for a walk before retiring.

He decided to continue his patrol. Time enough in the morning to mention what he'd seen to Doctor Mitchell. His assignment, after all, was to watch the surrounding mesa top for any sign of an approaching predator—or a smuggler. The comings and goings of the people in the camp were not his concern.

Khuharkk' walked away, scanning for any sign of predators.

Hours had passed, and Mahree Burroughs knew her time was truly running out. The air in the vault was growing bad, so bad she was beginning to gasp. Her head pounded, and she was sweating.

Her mind whirled as she reviewed her predicament for the thousandth time. How to get out? She had no weapon. She had no plasma-torch. She had nothing, nothing that would punch through four metric tons of metal. And with the radio dead, and the vault door time-locked from the outside, nothing short of an earthquake would crack open her prison.

In a way, it was almost funny. Like one of those bad romance novels where the heroine, who was always as dumb as a box of rocks, got herself shut up in the tomb with the mummy.

Except that she wasn't in a tomb. She was in a place that was a lot more secure, and far more airtight.

She lay down on the floor, hoping to conserve her air by not expending energy. It was all she could do.

But she knew already it wouldn't be enough.

Soon she would find out what lay on the other side of life. Mahree thought of Rob and Claire, her parents, her uncle Raoul, her friends. Was there an afterlife? Would she see them again?

Soon enough, she'd know. . . .

On his return swing past the camp from the interior of the mesa, Khuharkk' stopped again at the canyon rim. He'd been unable to raise Axum for all this time, and he was getting very worried. She'd been out of contact for several hours. What if she was injured somewhere? Perhaps she'd fallen down a night-shadowed crevice. The patrol rules were for them to operate as a pair, in regular contact. Like he'd done the other night, with Etsane. That contact had saved her life.

Khuharkk' double-tapped the com unit hanging from his neck. It was Doctor Strongheart's turn to be Security Chief tonight. The frequency band changed. "Doctor Strongheart?"

The radio buzzed as lightning crackled on the western horizon, then cleared. "Wha—who's calling?"

He smiled at the sleepy sound in the elderly Heeyoon's voice. "Sorry to disturb you. Khuharkk' here. Axum has disappeared from com unit contact."

"Blast!" Strongheart sounded irritated. "How long without contact?"

Khuharkk' glanced at the chrono on his night visor. "Three hours. Maybe a little more."

"What!" The Heeyoon now sounded fully awake. "You should have called me earlier. Any sign of predators?"

He paused. Should he mention the Na-Dina heat signature down in the Camp? "No. Not up here."

"What about anywhere else? Don't make me drag this out of you!" Strongheart snarled. "Give me a complete report!"

Khuharkk's tufted tail raised straight up, as if in salute to a Clan Leader. "I have not seen Crew Boss Axum since we arrived on patrol duty," he began. "She went south, upstream, along the canyon rim. I went north, then came back, then inland, and now I am returned to the canyon rim." He paused. "Earlier, I saw the heat signature of a Na-Dina loitering outside the Lab. After several minutes, it disappeared into one of the tents. That is all."

"All!" Strongheart sounded both distracted and upset. "Could this heat sign have been Axum?"

He thought of how she'd appeared when first they'd gone on patrol. "It is possible."

The com unit radio held silent a moment. Then it rasped. "Return to Base Camp. Immediately. I'm going over to the Lab to check on the SSC. Strongheart out."

"Out." Khuharkk' tapped off the com unit, turned, and ran for the rockpile and the way down.

Now he was really worried.

When Strongheart's call came in, Gordon was enjoying his first night of sound, peaceful sleep in weeks. He was, however, one of those individuals who can pass from sleep into complete alertness in a matter of seconds. "Mitchell here," he snapped, hitting the "send" button on the intercom.

"This is Strongheart. Meet me at the Lab. Now!"

Yanking on his shorts, he shoved his feet into his boots, and ran out into the night. The Lab was ablaze with lights. He opened the door, wishing he'd come armed, and called out, "Strongheart?"

"Back here!"

The SSC? Gordon felt cold sweat break out on the back of his neck. Had someone made another attempt to steal the golden sarcophagus? "Coming!"

He ran down between the rows of metal shelving on which rested thousands of artifacts and field samples, reached the end, and turned right. Strongheart stood in front of the time-locked vault door, her gray tail fluffed out, her paw-hands resting on the steel of the door, her entire manner one of intense concentration. Her medical kit rested at her feet.

"What?"

"Shut up." The alien female closed her amber eyes, then laid her head against the thick vault door. One ear pressed against the metal.

Gordon looked at his watch. It was long after midnight. What in the name of the Revered Ancestors was going on?

"Strongheart, what in hell is going *on*?"

She snarled at him, then stood back. "The time lock has been reset. The digital readout is different from how I left it, just before we went to dinner. And there is a scent trail that leads up to here, then stops."

Gordon swallowed hard. "Lots of us went in there today."

Strongheart stepped back and went down on all fours. She paced slowly back and forth, her nose almost brushing the floor. "This trail is fresh. I scent two trails. One human. One Na-Dina."

"Human!

Amber eyes stared at him. "Female."

"Mahree!" He raced forward, banging against the metal.

"That won't do any good," Strongheart said gruffly. She rose up to her usual two-footed stance and blinked at the digital time lock readout. "I've tried to cycle it back. To undo the new time lock. It won't recycle and open. Someone has reset it, and then randomized the algorithm."

Cold chills raced down his back. "Mahree's inside! I know it."

Strongheart eyed him. "Or Etsane. Or Sumiko. Whoever is in there will not last much longer. The vault is airtight. She's suffocating, Gordon."

"No!" He turned, raced back to his tent, unlocked his chest, and grabbed his blaster. On his way back to the lab, he stopped and checked Mahree's tent. The light was on, but it was empty. Just as he'd expected. Obviously, the unknown killer had tried again. *But you won't succeed*, Gordon promised silently, as he ran back to the vault.

When he reached the SSC, the archaeologist stood panting, steadying himself until he could aim safely with the blaster. "Stand back, Doc. Don't look."

The Heeyoon stepped back and closed her eyes. "This will ruin the door, you know . . ."

"Do you think I care about that?" he cried in anguish, imagining what was going on inside. He assumed the correct firing stance, feet apart and balanced, then aimed the blaster, steadying it by bracing his wrist with his other hand. He'd have to fire in short bursts and check his progress, or there was a chance he'd burn right through and vaporize the treasures—or Mahree—inside.

Breathing slowly and lightly, Gordon Mitchell leveled the blaster, closed his eyes, and pulled the trigger. He heard the *scree* of the beam and the hiss of vaporized metal. Gordon counted slowly to three, released the trigger, and squinted at the smoking, red-hot hole he'd bored in the vault door around the time lock. *Nearly halfway through . . .*

Hurry, hurry! his mind screamed, but he forced himself to stay calm as he triggered the weapon again.

This time he kept his left eye closed, and squinted with the right as the beam erupted. Despite the sunlike glare, he kept the narrow beam pointed at the center of the lock.

Scriiiiieeeeee!

The fumes from the vaporizing metal made him want to gag. The whole area around the lock glowed red-hot, yellow, then edged up toward white . . .

Suddenly there was no metal left—Gordon's finger seemed to recognize that even before his eye did. Hastily, he stopped firing, praying that Mahree wasn't pressed up against the glowing door.

Laying down the blaster, he opened both eyes. His right eye was filled with yellow dazzle, but he could still see through the one he'd kept closed. Gordon sprang forward, snatching up a pry bar from a nearby lab table. Thrusting the bar into the hole he'd made in the steel, he pulled, feeling the bar sink deep into the still-molten metal of the door. The locking mechanism, made of tougher plas-steel, was still partly intact, but the door around the lock was gone. He yanked the entire locking mechanism free, and it crashed to the floor.

The door swung open.

As the fresh air rushed into the smoke-filled vault, he heard someone coughing inside, and felt relief so strong that he nearly staggered. "Mahree!"

The smoke was so thick that he nearly tripped over her before he saw her. She was not burned, thank all the stars in the heavens. Gordon bent down, slid his hands beneath her knees and her back, and scooped her up. He was so charged with adrenaline that she seemed nearly weightless as he carried her out into the clean, fresh air.

She was coughing weakly, trying between spasms to say something—his name? "Easy, honey," he said tenderly. "Take it easy. You're safe."

Suddenly Strongheart was there before him. ''Lay her down here.''

Obediently, Gordon laid Mahree's body down on the top of the lab table she'd cleared off. He hesitated, still holding her hand. *If she had died* . . . he thought, and realized he was shaking at the thought.

''Mahree . . .'' he whispered, again, and a moment later, he felt her fingers squeeze his tightly.

''Gordon!'' Strongheart showed formidable teeth. ''She needs oxygen! Now out of my way!''

Still saying a prayer of thanksgiving, Gordon Mitchell stood aside, and let the doctor minister to her patient.

CHAPTER 10
♦
Big Job, Big Hopes

Two days after the attack on Mahree, Gordon sat at the head of the Lab conference table and tried to dismiss his worries for her safety. At least she'd agreed to wear a pulse-gun while in camp, and to go nowhere alone.

He'd been stumped at first as to how to explain the wrecked door in the SSC, but had finally come up with a story about a lone smuggler who'd managed to creep into camp undetected, but who'd been scared away when the heat sensors in the lab had been activated by his blaster fire.

Mitchell and Khuharkk' had rigged a replacement door that would serve until a new one could arrive from Spirit, and he'd arranged to stand guard in shifts.

Gordon scowled as other researchers came in and headed for their seats. It was time for the weekly conference, and the long table filled rapidly. More people lined the walls, as the murmurs of conversation and the chatter of competing voders filled the air with a dozen languages. It was too early in the morning for people to be this awake.

"Good morning, *astamari*," said Etsane as she passed, one of the last to take her seat.

"Morning." He was pleased to see the Ethiopian woman

looking recovered from the animal attack of three days ago.

"Here's your coffee, Boss." Sumiko stood nearby, offering him a mug of steaming black brew.

"That sure smells good, Sumiko. Thanks." He took the coffee, then grinned. "You're promoted."

Sumiko looked dubious, then headed for her seat. "Only if that means I get a raise. I *already* run this place."

Khuharkk' came in and sat next to Etsane, hunching his shoulders so the bright red scars of his two Honor Fights were visible. The sight seemed to unsettle Sumiko.

Well, at least she'd sent word to everyone that today was The Day. Not for ogling A-Um Rakt's Royal Barge, or even the Mizari relics that were driving his Ceramicist nuts. This was the day to hear Greyshine's aerial survey report, and to get a handle on just what kind of insane job they faced. The robot flyer had finished its survey of the river canyon from the dam site up to Ancestor's Valley, and now they would all learn the specifics.

Gordon noticed Mahree staring at the double squad of rifle-armed Na-Dina who lined the Lab's side wall, and at their female leader, who shared a seat of honor at their table.

"Ambassador," Gordon said as he rose to make the introduction, "I'd like to introduce you to Pokeel, Chief Marshal of the Queen's Own Guard." He indicated the Na-Dina who wore a red-dyed Sash of Rank. She also wore a quite effective repeating rifle slung across her back. "Her unit of forty Guards arrived late last night on the supply steambarge."

Mahree looked relieved. "That's reassuring. After the smuggler raid and that animal attack on Etsane, we can use the help of professionals." She stood, faced the Na-Dina alien, touched her brow briefly, and bowed. "Pokeel, I am Mahree of the clan Human, of the Trade Interrelator, Mother of one daughter, and I welcome you to our camp. May your salt always be pure and your water always fresh."

The Na-Dina Marshal rose from her resting squat. Her

fan-ears fluttered in a complicated manner Gordon had yet to decipher. "Mother Who Turns Anger Into Happiness, the honor is mine. I am Pokeel of the clan Sharp Teeth, of the Trade Fighter, Mother of four eggs, and Marshal of the Guard." The alien female clasped both talon-hands over her sash-hung chest, bowed back to Mahree, and then thumped her long tail. Nearby, Axum also thumped her tail, as did the females of her crew.

Mahree seemed to understand the tail-thump. When both had reseated themselves, Gordon looked back to Axum. She'd explained her patrol absence the other night by saying she had been tracking a Long-Neck to make sure it was not headed for the camp, and had accidentally turned off her com unit during her scrambles through the brush.

Had she been the Na-Dina heat-blob that had been abroad in the camp that night? Khuharkk' had thought otherwise, saying the intruder had been larger than the middle-aged female. Axum was invaluable in running the White City dig crew. Gordon prayed that she wasn't the killer.

Putting down his coffee, the archaeologist looked around the table, catching everyone's attention. "Before we hear Professor Greyshine's report on the aerial survey, perhaps Axum can fill us in on the other Na-Dina who arrived on the same barge with Marshal Pokeel. Axum?"

The Crew Boss stood from her resting squat. She touched her forehead briefly, then flared her silver-tipped ears in what he'd learned was the Na-Dina version of a smile. "Esteemed colleagues, I have good news. While the Liaison has always done his best to assist our operations"—she paused, flicking a glance toward Beloran, sitting on Gordon's left—"still, we have faced too much digging for too few people. I sent a message to my clan requesting assistance. Clan Digs Well has sent us an additional *one hundred* diggers. Thus, we will be able to excavate at multiple sites, not just the City of White Stone."

"Wonderful!" Khuharkk' barked his approval. "Now we might stand a chance of accomplishing our work!"

"Excellent," Strongheart agreed, sounding relieved. "I was told there would be a Na-Dina doctor among them."

Axum lifted her tail. "True. A Doctor of Life from the Temple of Medicine volunteered to serve our people. He is even now setting up a dispensary at the Marshal's camp, which lies next to the jumpjet landing field." The Crew Boss turned to Gordon, her small, black eyes staring into his. He saw no deception there. "While I was sharing morning devotions with the Doctor, he told me that the Temple of Records has dispatched two Philosopher-Historians to assist in our work."

"They did?" Gordon felt a happy surprise. He'd been bothered by the indifference of the urban Na-Dina to the impending loss of a large part of their ancient heritage. Now it seemed as if the Traditionalists on the Council of Elders had prevailed over the Modernists and sent him some help. Just as Axum had, without his requesting it, brought in more diggers. "That's wonderful, Axum. When will they enter Base Camp?"

She glanced at the wall clock. "By midday. They must make devotions to Father Earth and Mother Sky. Fortunately, they are a female and male pair, so we should be covered." She squatted back down.

Beloran hiss-laughed, as did Marshal Pokeel. Mahree smiled knowingly, as if she too understood the reference.

He noticed Greyshine's bushy gray tail wagging so fast it was almost a blur. Definitely anxious. He grinned. "Professor, it's your turn. Please give us your report."

Greyshine's look brightened. "Thank you!" The Heeyoon pointed his record slate at a wall-screen. Light flared and a flat image of Ancestor's Valley, taken from an altitude of three hundred meters, filled the wide space. "Honored colleagues and guests—our task is immense. This is our present research focus. But it is only a minor part of the total task."

The Heeyoon thumbed the slate and a new image came up, this time showing a color-coded geographic map of the river canyon, running from the dam site up to the City of White Stone. "The distance from here to the dam, along the River of Life, is five hundred sixty kilometers, with a river elevation drop of one hundred forty meters. The canyon walls vary in height from fifty to one hundred eighty meters, rising downstream. There are thirty-eight side canyons.'' Greyshine paused as people finally came to understand the size of the area to be flooded. ''The width of the main canyon varies from three to twenty-five kilometers. Total ground surface to be flooded is five thousand, one hundred, and twenty-four square kilometers.''

Around the table people reacted with amazement. Gordon had known the figures, but still felt shocked. Mahree caught his eye, offering her sympathy. He nodded grimly, then looked back to the Heeyoon.

Greyshine continued. ''The lake will flood the place we now sit to a depth of twenty meters. At the dam itself, the depth will be one hundred sixty meters.'' Greyshine flicked through a series of color graphics that illustrated his point. ''The water mass impounded behind the dam will—when the lake has filled—amount to nearly one hundred and sixty *billion* cubic meters.'' The conference room grew still with shock.

Beloran whispered, ''That is a great deal of hydroelectric power, yes?''

Gordon set his jaw. ''Yes, it is. But there's a lot of research yet to be done.''

The Liaison's eyes darkened, as if he would argue. Gordon looked away, focusing on the wall-screen.

Greyshine switched to another overhead graphic, this one showing the dam site itself, the planned powerhouse, and a double spiderweb of lines that took off to the east and west of the dam. ''You are all aware this dam is being built to provide thousands of megawatts of hydroelectric power for Na-Dina industrialization. What some may not know is that the lake will *also* feed an extensive network of irrigation canals that will be built as Phase Two of this project. The Na-Dina hope to expand farmlands lying to the east and west of the dam site, thus increasing food supplies.''

Gordon looked around the conference table. His Star-Bridge students Khuharkk' and Sumiko seemed stunned by the scale of the construction project. So did Etsane, judging by her sour grimace. The Na-Dina present at the conference table were not surprised, as best he could tell, though they did seem a bit unnerved by the graphic images. Well, they *were* taken from high in Mother Sky. Mahree had explained to him just how sensitive a subject that was with the Na-Dina.

Gordon waved at Greyshine, who was flipping through more drawings and photographs. "The Na-Dina have made a choice for water storage, power generation, and industrialization. We must now deal with the consequences of those decisions." He paused. "How *many* sites are there?"

Greyshine sat down on his cushion. "In raw numbers, four thousand, one hundred two sites, ranging from overnight cooking pits of Na-Dina hunter-gatherers—dated at nineteen thousand years ago—to twelve temple cities of the Eighth, Twelfth, Sixteenth, and Thirty-Second Dynasties."

Around him, reactions ranged from numbed shock to visible outrage. Gordon sighed, rubbed fingers through his hair, then smiled weakly. He looked around the long table, eying the somber faces. "Before the scope of the task overwhelms us, let's remember that this *is* the find of the century! We can do a decent sampling of sites before the flooding. We *can* excavate a number of the temple cities, plus the tombs here in Ancestor's Valley, and make a major contribution to Na-Dina history."

Gordon pointed at Greyshine. "Professor, if I know you, you've already stratified the entire river canyon into sampling strata, cross-linked it with Ttalatha's vegetation and soil mapping, and ranked the sites in each stratum in order of research importance. You've probably even made the time to do a randomized selection within each research category—a classic stratified random sample. Correct?"

Greyshine looked up from his record slate, his wolfish ears perking up. Lifting the slate, the Heeyoon pointed it at the wall-screen. "You are correct." A new aerial graphic appeared. "This is an orthographic, elevation-corrected map of the entire river and canyon system, with all sites marked on it. Red squares are temple cities, red dots are abandoned farming villages, blue triangles are water control or shipping sites, purple dots denote burial sites, green shading indicates salt-killed farm fields, yellow shading indicates bottom lands or flat benches, like the one the city rests on. Over here the open triangles, crosses, squares and lines indicate prehistoric sites, locales belonging to the ancient forerunners of the Na-Dina dynasties.''

The expressions of Beloran, Axum, and Pokeel ranged from frustration to puzzlement.

Greyshine noticed. ''In salvage archaeology, we are required to study not *only* monumental cities and great tombs, but also the most humble of sites.'' He waved at the screen. ''Family homes, hunting camps, even the stone debris left behind when a few ancient hunters sharpened their spearheads before going off to hunt. We cannot just ignore older sites solely because they are less spectacular than the Royal Tomb of A-Um Rakt. Do you understand?''

Gordon had been watching Beloran during his colleague's explanation. The Modernist seemed highly disturbed. His tail twitched. ''Professor Greyshine, diverting effort to study these scratchings in the sand will reduce the labor time available for studying the temple cities.'' Beloran looked to Gordon. ''Philosopher, I protest this diversion of scarce resources.''

Gordon addressed the entire group. ''Our primary effort will go to the temple cities, the many Royal Tombs from the various dynasties, and to studying the period of Na-Dina history covered by written records. The last six thousand years.'' He clenched his jaw, then forced himself to relax as he faced the Liaison. ''But this river valley was home to other cultures, other Na-Dina, long before the First Dynasty was founded. We will do them the same honor as we do to A-Um Rakt.''

The alien's tail rose. ''But it will take longer—''

''Beloran!'' Axum slapped her tail against the floor. ''I have cousins who serve the Temple of the River. They may be hydrologists, irrigators, and construction engineers, but the women of the Temple understand the need to show *proper* devotion to Father Earth.'' Her eyes moved from Beloran to Pokeel and back to the irritated Liaison. Axum's hiss-clicking rose in timbre. ''*We* of the clan Digs Well will work furiously. We will make daily devotions to Father Earth, but we will *not* abandon the study of our Ancestors to favor today's People—those impatient to catch up with the technology of the Sky Infidels.''

Beloran lowered to a dark-eyed squat. "My piety is unimpeachable," he muttered.

A long silence ruled the conference table.

Gordon noticed Mahree trying to get his attention. "Ambassador? You would like to comment?"

"Yes, I would." Mahree stood and bowed once to each Na-Dina, ending up with Beloran. The alien's ears flattened, as if Mahree's attention was not something he welcomed. "Esteemed Liaison, I will be returning to Spirit shortly, to consult with Krillen of the Law, to check with our freighter captain, and to give a full report to the Council of Elders on the smuggler attack." She paused. Gordon wondered why Mahree's statement seemed to make the Liaison even more nervous.

"But I will add to my Council report the immensity of the task faced by Gordon's people. I will be fair, but"— Beloran's ears lowered even more—"but in a matter of ethics, Doctor Mitchell must follow his professional standards. And if we are to honor the Revered Ancestors by studying their remains and their ruins, isn't it best to discover the *entire* picture?" Mahree paused as Pokeel and Axum fluttered their ears in emphatic agreement. "After all, we would not want to arouse Father's Anger by showing poor devotion to those who sleep within his chambers."

Beloran sank into a low, low squat. "I do not wish to be the cause of impiety to Father Earth."

Gordon grinned. Mahree had turned her sojourn with Krillen into a telling argument with the officious Beloran. Like Maoist-era China with its disastrous Great Leap Forward program, the urban Na-Dina who belonged to the Modernist faction believed themselves infallible, their decisions without error.

He nodded at Mahree as she sat down. "Excellent point, Ambassador. Uh, could you put in a request to Krillen for the release of our camp jumpjet? It's still out at the mesa, under his Evidence Hold.''

"Of course. But could you come with me and make the request yourself? Nordlund is diverting a jumpjet to take me to Spirit. It'll be here at midday." She faced him squarely, barely showing a hint of a wry smile. "Interested?''

Gordon was definitely interested, though the idea of spending hours alone with Mahree aroused conflicting feelings in him. On one hand he desired nothing more than time to be with her, to talk to her, to learn to know her better. On the other . . . he knew that with every day that passed, he was getting in deeper. His profound attraction to her scared him, even as it excited him.

Now he met her eyes for a moment, then looked away. "Sure," he said. "Sounds like a good plan. Let's finish this conference, and we'll talk later." He turned back to Greyshine. "Professor, what's your plan for dig crews?''

The Heeyoon resumed his presentation. On the screen, a section of the orthographic map enlarged. "The initial work of two crews will include one temple city, four farming villages, thirteen prehistoric base camps, a Royal Granary, the commoner burial grounds located near the Third Cataract, and whatever else they find.''

Gordon rubbed his chin. "And the other four crews?''

Greyshine flipped through a series of enlargements. "Axum's crew stays here at the City of White Stone to cover the Highland Canyon stratum. A second crew will work the Upper Canyon Stratum downstream, a third the Lower Canyon area just upriver from the dam, and a fourth will handle the Mid-Lower Canyon area." The Heeyoon settled back onto his cushion.

Across the table, Natual raised a hand. "Professor, do you have any estimates on the *amount* of faunal remains we can expect to receive?''

"How many?" Greyshine seemed almost weary. "In Earth's past, a group similar to ours spent eight years excavating the ruins of Anasazi Indians at the Dolores River Valley, in the state of Colorado, in OldAm. That group found about fourteen hundred sites in a large valley also set to be flooded by a dam.'' The Heeyoon's expression showed open sympathy. ''In eight years they dug one hundred sixty sites and recovered four million artifacts, ranging from a Great Kiva down to stone chips left over from tool-sharpening. You ask how many faunal remains?'' The Heeyoon's amber eyes looked to Gordon, then back to Natual. ''Prepare for a half million.''

''A half *million*?'' Natual fell back into his chair.

Gordon understood the younger alien's dismay. The Drnian had never before dealt with a project of this size.

The Esteemed Lorezzzs, their Project Ceramicist, lifted her triangular head. ''Professor, your estimate for ceramics?''

''Two million, from whole pots to shards.''

And so it went, from specialty to specialty.

As Gordon sat back in his chair, Mahree caught his eye. She shook her head slowly, her expression supportive. He appreciated her understanding. He suspected her work with the interstellar diplomatic corps of the CLS was the closest approximation to the research program he was responsible for.

He found himself looking forward to being alone with her. Was there any chance she felt the same way? All he could do was hope that she did. . . .

On board the rising Nordlund jumpjet, Mahree watched as Gordon stored his overnight bag behind the seat that faced hers. She wondered when he'd notice the great view visible through the side window.

She'd been a bit surprised to find that the jet diverted by Nordlund was the one dedicated to the Project Engineer, who'd refitted the craft with pale brown carpets, overstuffed recliner seats, two couches, a wet bar, an in-flight kitchen, a tub bath, and even a bedroom at the rear of the craft. It was one more sign of the massive financial investment Nordlund had made on Ancestor's World. Why? Why invest so much money up front? The drill-mining sites in the

Mountains of Faith would not yield commercial quantities of ore for another year or more. If then.

Up front, the Nordlund pilot pushed aside the drape blocking her view of the pilot cabin. He offered Mahree his best professional smile. "Ambassador Burroughs," he called. "Would you and Doctor Mitchell mind if I took the long way to Spirit? Along the river?"

The pilot's smooth manner and calm air of authority might go over well with the Project Engineer, but she found it irritating. Mahree looked to her guest, who watched her as attentively as any Na-Dina. "Gordon?"

He turned in his seat to glance back at the pilot. "Captain McAllister, is it?" The man nodded rather patronizingly. Gordon smiled tightly. "That sounds fine with me, Captain. Guess you'd like to show off the dam site, huh?"

"Yes." Captain McAllister's deep-tanned face tensed, but the smile held. "It's a perfect opportunity to get an aerial overview of the diversion dam, the main axis trench excavation, and the diversion tunnel. They're making the river diversion today." The pilot showed perfect teeth. "We could see a real gusher as the river changes course."

Gordon looked back to her, his eyebrows lifting. "Mahree?"

After Professor Greyshine's sobering report, she had all too good an idea of what the Nordlund engineers and earth-movers were doing to the River of Life. But she was obligated to learn their side of the situation. She nodded. "Sure. It's not every day you see a three-kilometer-wide river shoved off its course and forced through a tunnel."

Captain McAllister's smile wavered. "But, ma'am, that's the only way we can excavate down to bedrock. So we can get the best footing for the earthfill of the dam."

Gordon turned back to the pilot. "Captain, please *do* take the long way to Spirit. The river route. Why don't you call us on the intercom when we arrive at the dam?"

McAllister nodded and vanished without another word.

Gordon turned around in his seat, touched the recliner arm-control, and lifted his eyebrows again. "Do you mind if I rest my boots on the lounge table?"

Mahree felt bemused. "Gordon, if there's one thing I've noticed since coming to camp, you *always* put your boots atop any place you wish. Of course. Go ahead." She smiled to convince him she was only teasing.

He returned the smile. Then he put his boots on the table between them, his manner that of a small boy getting away with something. "Thanks. I think best when my boots are propped up on something."

She grew serious. "No, I must thank you. And this is the first chance I've gotten. For saving my life in the vault. *Thank* you."

"Hey . . ." His eyes met hers. Their gazes locked and held. "Any time. I've never gotten the chance to save a fair lady before." He gave her a boyish, lopsided grin that made her heart turn over. "Though it *was* a shame to ruin that time lock."

Mahree felt herself blushing, as she realized he meant what he said. For a moment she thought he might lean across the table and touch her—and she wanted him to, she discovered, frightened by the strength of her own reaction.

But he didn't.

Instead he looked away, out the window. "Fantastic view, isn't it?"

She eyed his boots, resting atop the small wooden table. Her gaze ran up his long legs to his narrow hips, then to his khaki-shirted chest. A dark tan showed at his neck and on his arms, where he'd rolled up his sleeves. His squarish face had been freshly shaved. And his sun-streaked hair lay in fresh-combed sandy curls. But the squint lines around his light eyes seemed tense. As if he were aware of her examination.

"There you go, changing the subject," she teased, realizing that she was flirting—and that she was enjoying it. She hadn't felt so *alive* in years. "What were you really going to say?"

His cheeks hollowed a bit, then he faced her, and it was obvious that he was *not* having fun. She sensed pain, and confusion. "Mahree . . . I'm starting to feel that . . .

maybe . . .'' He floundered for a second, then rallied. ''That you're a very special woman. To me.''

She found that she couldn't think of anything to say to that. As she mulled over possible replies, Gordon looked up, his manner veiled once more. ''Did you ever wonder why Nordlund is investing so damned much venture capital in such a longshot contract?''

Mahree licked her lips. ''I *was* wondering. This jumpjet is rather luxurious.''

He scowled, then glanced aside, staring darkly out the window. ''Yeah. But these appointments are petty funding to Nordlund. The big money is three years' worth of construction crew salaries, several freighter fulls of earthmoving equipment, at least three full-size drill-mining rigs, and prefab accommodations for over six hundred alien and human workers.'' Gordon looked back to her, his manner professional. ''Ambassador, no company invests that kind of venture capital without some damned good reason. And Nordlund ain't in the trade of 'lift up our poor brethren on far stars.' ''

''I agree.''

He inspected her now, looking from her boots up her bare legs to her shorts, her belt holster with pulse-gun snugged into it, then on up to her lime-green blouse, her neck—her eyes.

She blinked. ''So. What riches abound on this planet? Other than arky ruins?''

Gordon grinned sardonically. ''You're right. This *is* a gold mine for my career. But even I'm small chips to Nordblund.'' His mood sobered. ''They've got enough money to buy lots of help. Including local help. What do *you* think? Did Axum shut you in the vault?''

She broke eye contact to look out the window. Long kilometers below, the cobalt River of Life undulated over sand bars, around sandstone cliffs and over rapids, tracing a series of S-curves east to the horizon. It was midday, and Ancestor's World shone like a brass lamp, the only green lying in narrow strips along the river course.

Mahree turned back to Gordon. ''I *should* suspect her,

after what happened. After all, she's a Na-Dina, and Krillen and I found evidence that a Na-Dina was aboard Bill's jet, during—and *after*—it landed.''

With each word, his face grew more grim.

''And a Na-Dina closed the vault door on me the other night. So''—she looked down at his scuffed boots—''tell me why I *shouldn't* suspect Axum.''

The boots did not move. Finally, he sighed. ''I like her. I trust her. She's never betrayed me, or done anything other than what I asked.''

Mahree looked up, seeing new pain in his hazel eyes. ''That's all? Her story about following the Long-Neck; that doesn't sound weak to you?''

Gordon crossed rough-knuckled hands over his waist, covering the turquoise belt buckle he wore. He lifted sandy eyebrows. ''Sounds dumb, doesn't it? Yeah, she could have doubled back on Khuharkk', climbed down to the Camp, locked you in, and gone back up to the mesa. I don't believe she did. Otherwise, why call for digging help from her Clan? Why would she take my side against Beloran?'' He lifted his hands, laced his fingers together, and rested his chin on them, staring curiously at her. ''I just trust her. Do you?''

Mahree sighed her relief. ''Yes, I do. I wondered if I was crazy to do it, after all that's happened. If so, I'm glad I'm not the only one.''

''You aren't. But, Mahree . . . I wish to hell so many people didn't have reason to want you—and the CLS oversight that you represent—out of the way.'' Gordon counted on his fingers. ''First there's Nordlund. Then there are the Modernists, especially Beloran. Then there are the smugglers. You have too many enemies, my dear.''

She heard the endearment, and wondered if he'd meant it, or if it was just a figure of speech. ''Gordon, besides helping with my report to the Council of Elders, I could use your assistance another way.''

''Oh? How?'' He watched her very directly.

Facing him steadily, she said, ''The jumpjet out at the murder site. I'm sure we can get it released, after I talk to

Krillen, but I also want to borrow the ship's shuttle from the S.V. *Emerald Scales*. I don't want to offend the Na-Dina by flying it myself, so . . . would you be my shuttle pilot?''

He relaxed. "Of course. That will give us two long-range transports at Base Camp, including one that can make orbit." Gordon paused. "You're concerned the smugglers might return?''

She nodded, noting that it was nice to work with someone as sharp as this man.

Gordon nodded back, then changed the subject back to more personal matters. "Mahree . . . would you show me that holo of your daughter? I think I'm the only one in camp who hasn't seen it.''

He had two daughters of his own; she'd read that in the job file on the way out from StarBridge. And though they were grown, he must miss them as she missed Claire. Mahree dug through her bag and found the holo-cube. In it, her tall, slim, chestnut-haired daughter looked up with oh-too-serious blue eyes. "This is Claire.'' Mahree handed him the cube.

Gordon took it, his scarred fingers cradling the image. "She's beautiful. And smart-looking. Takes after her mother.'' He handed the cube back.

Mahree felt . . . warm. She realized she was blushing again. Putting the cube on the table between them, she pointed at his hands. "Lots of scars. How did they happen?''

Gordon leaned forward, chuckling as he lifted one hand and inspected it. "Trowel-sharpening scars. Archaeologists religiously sharpen the edges of their trowels. Makes for a clean scrape in an excavation unit, so you don't smudge the soil layers in the profile.'' He blinked owlishly. "Twenty-five years of trowel scars.'' He lowered his hand.

She took a chance. "Could I see pictures of your daughters?''

His jaw clenched. Then he smiled, though she saw the pain behind it. "Sure.'' Reaching into his overnight bag, he turned back, holding two color flats preserved in clear plastic.

Mahree took the flat image pictures. One showed a young woman perhaps eighteen, with red hair and green eyes. The background of the picture resembled a college dorm room.

Gordon spoke quietly. "That's Moira. She's the oldest. Eighteen. The other one is Casey. She's fifteen."

Mahree looked carefully at the second girl. She had red hair too, teeth that were a bit oversized, and a freckled grin that reminded her of Gordon in his unguarded moments. She wore a uniform. She handed the plates back. "They're beautiful young women."

Gordon took the photo plates from her and put them back into his bag. "Those photos are three years old. I haven't seen them since their mother took them off to some family business on Nishto, in the Apis System. That was right after the divorce." He faced her again.

She hated seeing the pain in his eyes. "Gordon, I'm sorry." Mahree reached out and touched his hand.

He watched her small, smooth hand that so sharply contrasted with his own gnarly one. The moment grew intense—too much so. Gordon stirred, removing his hand gently. "You know, I'll bet Project Engineer Mohapatra has got a private stash of decent liquor somewhere in here. Think I'll help myself."

He busied himself for a moment, then returned with two glasses.

Mahree raised her glass in a toast. "Let's give 'em hell, Gordon."

He grinned suddenly. "I'll drink to that." He clinked his glass against hers, then drained half of the potent golden-brown brew.

Mahree sipped the fiery liquid, savoring its smoky flavor, then placed the glass on the table. "I'll drink to anyone who saves my life." She heard the ice settle in her glass. "And I think you're pretty special, too."

The moment was interrupted by Captain McAllister's voice coming over the intercom. "We're coming up on the dam site now. If you'll look out your window, I'll explain what you're seeing.''

Mahree sat back in her chair, both irritated and amused, as Gordon's boots returned to the table, carefully avoiding her still-full glass. "Proceed, Captain." She met Gordon's gaze once again. A different look shone there now. A look of patience.

Together, they marveled at the River of Life, and how its curving course could match their own lives.

CHAPTER 11
◆
Smuggler's Luck

Mahree sat on the hard floor of Krillen's office and watched as the Investigator poured cold tea for her, for Gordon, and for Prosecutor Makwen, who'd been invited to sit in on their meeting. The afternoon heat was stifling, and the coolness of the office felt like a dash of mint.

Gordon noticed her glance and gave her a warm smile. Mahree returned it, sensing again that tenderness, that caring that she wasn't sure how to deal with—it both excited her and made her nervous. By now she could no longer pretend she wasn't attracted to him. She was. And yet . . . she was only here on Ancestor's World for a few weeks— perhaps a month or two at the most.

Did she want to start anything under those circumstances?

Especially since she knew, instinctively, that any relationship with Gordon Mitchell would be far more than just a casual fling between two lonely humans far from home.

"So," Krillen said, after taking a sip of tea, "tell me, please, all about this second attempt on the life of Ambassador Burroughs."

Mahree opened her mouth to do so, then closed it, and gestured at Gordon. "You go ahead," she said. "I still can't talk about it without getting the shakes."

Mitchell nodded, and proceeded to fill the Investigator in on what had happened the other night.

Krillen and Makwen both listened intently. "And you say a Na-Dina was wandering around the Camp?" the Prosecutor said, when Gordon was finished. "Was the Simiu sure of his identification?"

"Yes, he was."

"And where was Axum all this time?" Krillen asked.

"She told us that she'd picked up on the trail of a Long-Neck, and followed it, to make sure it wasn't trying to get near the camp. She'd accidentally shut off her com unit, so she couldn't hear Khuharkk' calling her."

Krillen fixed Gordon with an intent gaze. "And, Philosopher Mitchell, do you believe her?"

Gordon took a deep breath. "Krillen . . . I do. I'm not sure why, exactly, except that my instincts tell me that Axum was telling the truth. Dammit, I *like* her. She's worked hard for me. She's dedicated to what we're doing. I can't believe she'd try to hurt one of us."

The Investigator listened carefully, then turned to Mahree. "And what about you, Ambassador? You who have had dealings with so many species other than your own. Were you present when Philosopher Mitchell spoke with Axum?"

"Yes, I was," Mahree said. "And, Krillen, I believed her, too. Axum seemed genuinely horrified to realize how close I came to death, and even more horrified that one of her own people might have been involved."

Krillen picked up his bronze ruler and sat turning it over in his taloned hands as he thought. "It is true that any evidence against a Na-Dina in this instance is purely circumstantial. The would-be murderer may *not* have had anything to do with the heat sign the Simiu saw on his night-visor."

"That's true enough," Gordon said.

"What of the faked message Mahree found in her tent?"

"It was gone when we looked for it," Mahree said. "Not surprising, I guess."

"And who besides Doctor Strongheart might have over-heard your conversation about asking Philosopher Mitchell for a private tour of the treasures?"

"The SSC was so crowded we could barely move," Mahree said. "It could have been literally anyone."

Makwen fixed them all with a level stare. "I believe it is time for Investigator Krillen to interrogate Liaison Beloran," she said.

"He will be insulted," Krillen said, obviously not relishing the idea. "And he has powerful allies in the ruling party. Allies that go as high as the Royal Family, Makwen."

"This would not be the first time a highly ranked official has been involved in a crime," Makwen pointed out.

"True," Krillen admitted, with an audible sigh. "I have been reaching the same conclusion, Prosecutor. I am not looking forward to that interview, however. I had hoped to finish all of my review of the evidence before tackling the Liaison." The Investigator held up a taloned finger. "As I see it, there are still three possibilities. One: someone from offworld, but unrelated to your Base Camp, killed Bill Waterston and tried to kill the Ambassador, after failing in an attempt to kill both the Ambassador and myself."

"Unrelated to the Base Camp . . ." Gordon considered for a moment. "You mean from Nordlund."

"Or the smugglers," Mahree added.

"Correct." Krillen held up another talon. "Two: the murderer is actually two people working in concert. One from Base Camp, the other an off-worlder from outside."

"And three?" Makwen asked.

"Three is that one person, working from Base Camp, is responsible for everything that has happened. Most likely a Na-Dina, either Axum or Beloran."

"Krillen, have you found anything in your forensic analysis from the information we collected?" Mahree asked.

"I have made progress," Krillen said. "The analysis of the murder weapon makes me tend toward possibility two or three."

Mitchell leaned forward. "What did you find?"

"With the help of the off-world magnifiers, I was able to study the steel bar very closely. The stress marks on it were illuminating. Then I made some tests, using some of the Nordlund pilots who had flown into Spirit this past week, as volunteers. The pressure-grip of a human compared to one of the People is different. The kilograms per square centimeter of force that can be exerted by humans is less than that exerted by the People."

"So the whorl patterns showed that a Na-Dina had gripped the bar to do the killing?" Mitchell asked excitedly.

"Almost certainly."

"Beloran," Gordon said. "It's got to be Beloran."

"Gordon, you're jumping to conclusions," Mahree said. "Just because he's a cranky old cuss doesn't mean he's guilty. There's not one shred of evidence that isn't circumstantial to link him to either crime."

Krillen gazed at her, fluttering his fan-ears approvingly. "Very good, my colleague," he said. "You have learned well."

"But a Na-Dina killed Bill!" Mitchell made a frustrated gesture. "You just said so!"

"Correct," Makwen said. "But, Philosopher Mitchell, you are on a world full of *millions* of Na-Dina. The People work at Nordlund as well as your Base Camp. Personally, I favor the number two choice—that a Na-Dina, working with an off-worlder, committed the crimes. How else would the Na-Dina have been able to land the ship, unless a human or other alien pilot was also aboard?"

"Have you interviewed every off-world pilot, Krillen?" Mahree asked.

"Yes. The chief suspect at this time is one Mario Gonzales Ortega. His regular jumpjet run is to a drilling rig camp in the Mountains of Faith, near the Lake of Stars. On the day of Interrelator Waterston's death, he was logged in as making a run to the Base Camp. He was also the pilot who brought me to Base Camp the day after the smuggler raid."

"So he could have sabotaged the batteries!"

"Perhaps," Krillen agreed. "It is certainly possible.

Some of my inquiries about Infidel Ortega have been interesting. He is apparently constantly short of funds. He engages in what you off-worlders call 'games of chance.' ''

"So that's a motive," Mahree said. "Money. If we consider that a Na-Dina could have been paying him."

"Yes, that is a motive. But what, my friends, could be the motive for our unknown Na-Dina killer?"

Mahree and Gordon looked at each other and shrugged.

"Can you think of anything, Investigator?" Gordon asked after a moment.

Krillen shrugged with his tail. "Possibly. I have been tracking reports of unusual activities all along the River of Life, and your smuggler raid is by no means the first time someone has looted, or attempted to loot, one of our ancient tombs. The villages report that looting has increased dramatically since the off-worlders came to Ancestor's World—but that it has been going on for a long time."

"That makes sense," Gordon said. "There's a big market for illegal antiquities." He thought for a moment. "Maybe that so-called 'First Contact' months ago *wasn't* the first. Maybe Sorrow Sector made earlier contacts long ago, and kept them very, very secret. This could have been going on for decades."

"For decades!" Mahree felt sudden surprise, then told herself it fit in with the likelihood of a Sorrow Sector smuggler as one of the plotters. If artifact-looting had been confined to the hinterlands of Ancestor's World, so as to avoid official Na-Dina attention, that would explain how the smugglers had known *where* to raid. The murderer in their midst explained how they'd known *when* to attempt the raid at Base Camp.

"I hate looters!" Gordon said angrily. "They're always there, and we archaeologists are always just a half-step ahead of them—*if* we're lucky."

"Have you ever caught any Na-Dina looting the tombs of the Revered Ancestors?" Mahree asked.

"Yes," Krillen said grimly. "And when we do, our penalties are very, very harsh. So looting is rare, among our people. But, of late, there has been a tremendous upsurge in their activity.''

"Catching the thieves is very hard," Makwen said. "They strike, and then are gone quickly. Almost like the Disappearances.''

Gordon looked at Makwen, his expression puzzled. "Disappearances? What disappearances?''

Krillen's ears fluttered, as though the Investigator was embarrassed. "They are widely believed to be a rural fable.''

"Not so!" Makwen protested, flaring her ears. "They are real!''

"Tell us about them," Mahree said quietly. "Please?''

Krillen sipped his tea, then cleared his throat. "From time to time we receive reports from the backcountry of individuals, a caravan group, sometimes even a small village, suddenly disappearing—just vanishing with no trace." The Investigator put down his cup. "The Ministry of Justice investigated the first few reports very thoroughly, some forty years ago. Nothing was found, except an empty village or inn, always in a very remote area.''

"Well, *why*?" Mahree asked. "What happened to them?''

The alien blinked. "You must realize that our world is very changeable. Floods. Thunderstorms. The Ash of Sorrow. Whole villages are sometimes wiped out by these events, or by the jolt of Father's Snoring when it quakes enough to bring down even a Temple. That is enough to account for the Disappearances.''

"I do not believe that," Makwen insisted stubbornly. "I am from the backcountry, and I *saw* a village not far from my own where there had been a Disappearance. Food was left on the tables, partially eaten. Yet there had been no earthquake, no flood, no ashfall. But every person—male, female and small scaly—in Talon village was *gone*. We never saw them again.''

Gordon looked to Krillen. "Disease? Plague? Investigator, could they explain what she describes?''

"No," Krillen said bluntly. "But the occurrences are

few in number. They are greatly outnumbered by the natural loss of life caused by flood, earth quaking, storm or
volcanic eruption.''

Mahree glanced at her wristwatch. It was time to leave
for her report to the Council of Elders. "Investigator, we
must leave for our appointment with the Council," she said.
"But it occurs to me that now would be a good time for
us to take that trip to visit the Nordlund sites and talk to
Project Engineer Mohapatra. I'll arrange for a jumpjet to
come and get you tomorrow or the day after. Will that be
satisfactory?''

Krillen hesitated. "We have nowhere near the evidence
to link any Nordlund employee to these deaths," he said
finally.

"Yes," Gordon said, "But, Krillen, don't forget that Bill
was talking about finding some evidence of wrongdoing,
and then he died. Do you think that's pure coincidence?''

"Possibly," Krillen said. "However, I agree that a discussion with the Project Engineer and a tour of the Nordlund sites is in order. I will be ready when your jumpjet
arrives.''

Gordon nodded. "And we can regain the use of our
jumpjet out on the mesa, Investigator?''

"Certainly," Krillen said. "I will put through the pa-
perwork today. You may take your shuttle out to the site
and retrieve it immediately.''

"Great. We really need it. Thanks, Krillen.''

This time, the Investigator did not accompany them as
they left the office and walked the corridors of the Ministry
of Justice. "We've given him a lot to think about," Mahree
said to Gordon as their footsteps resounded on the stone
steps.

"And vice versa," the archaeologist agreed.

Ninety minutes later, Gordon sat in the shadows of the
meeting chamber of the Council of Elders, high on the uppermost floor of the Temple of Administration. He listened
as Mahree presented her report to the sixteen Na-Dina elders, who squatted in a circle. They rested on the brown

stone floor of the dome-roofed chamber, a pile of salt tablets lying in front of each elder. The white pile was flanked on the right by a pot of tea, on the left by a pitcher of water. And in the center of the circle, clean brown sand filled a sunken pool area. The sand showed dark stains from water devotions, tossed salt lay atop it, and stuck into the sand was something he'd never before seen. Effigy sticks carved from red porphyry, in the shape of a Na-Dina. Each one represented a clan of the Na-Dina.

He mentally counted them. Sixty-two!

The effigy sticks crowded the middle of the sand disk, their beautifully carved faces flickering with shadows cast by wall sconces that illuminated the chamber. This was a very, very old part of the Temple, easily a thousand years in age, and polychrome paintings covered the wall behind him. The chamber was almost unique—a round sand disk occupied the room's center, with a ring of Elders encircling it, while behind them curved the walls of this circular room. Most Na-Dina structures were rectangular, square, or triangular in geometry, except for the tombs of the Royal House and those of some commoners. Clearly, this was a room dedicated to the Ancestors, not to the living.

Mahree had been talking now for almost forty-five minutes, giving a full report on the CLS support to Gordon's dig, the work begun by the new researchers, the smuggler raid, and the investigation into Bill's murder. She had *not* mentioned, however, the attempts on her own and Krillen's life. Now she was attempting to caution the Na-Dina about their dealings with Nordlund, and the dangers of too-rapid industrialization.

The representative of the Temple of the River tossed a salt tablet into the sand pit, interrupting Mahree. By protocol, she had to squat and listen. Which she did.

"Interrelator," hiss-clicked the rather young female Elder. "We have heard all these arguments about too-fast industrialization and the damage to our culture from your predecessor, Interrelator Waterston." Mahree showed respect by staring directly at the speaker, a member of the Modernist faction on the Council. "What would you have us do? Would you sell us uranium reactors, so as to generate power from the Wailing of the Ancestors?'' she asked, using a new Na-Dina term for nuclear fission.

What? Gordon felt shock. He hadn't realized the Council's technical advisors had picked up the basics of nucleonics. From their dealings with Nordlund?

Mahree seemed equally surprised. She stood to reply. ''Elder Renzees, we prefer not to do so. They are an old technology, and the waste products they create are deadly.''

The Temple representative flared her solid blue ears in a strange gesture. ''Then will you sell us fusion reactors? I hear that the power which fuels Mother's Eye is the greatest in all Creation.''

Gordon could tell that, despite her fifteen years of interstellar diplomacy, the Na-Dina's bluntness had rattled Mahree. ''I'm sorry, no,'' she said. ''The Cooperative League of Systems has a rule that prohibits the transfer of such advanced technology to worlds where it has not been developed by the native species. Such power is—''

''Best *kept* from people whom you treat as new-hatched from the egg,'' interrupted the representative from the Temple of A-Um Rakt, a younger male who also belonged to the Modernist faction. The alien tossed a salt tablet into the sand pit, then flared his ears at the speaker he'd interrupted.

Mahree bowed to the Na-Dina woman who'd first asked about alternative power sources. ''Your pardon, Elder Renzees, but in this matter I am not a free agent. I must follow the rules of my Council of Elders, just as your people must heed your decisions.''

Looking to the male who'd interrupted her, Mahree slapped the black fabric of her blouse. ''Elder Sashoon, we of the CLS have high *respect* for the Royal House, the Ancestors, and all the people of Ancestor's World. That is why we have spent scarce funds to support Doctor Mitchell's study of Ancestor's Valley, and the Tomb of A-Um Rakt.''

She paused, glanced back at Gordon, then continued. ''I wish there were another way, but we of the CLS have found that things usually work best when a world makes its own decisions and choices. Whether in technology development or in cultural change.''

Another Na-Dina tossed a tablet onto the sand disk, this one a female showing the silvery-blue ears of advanced old age. ''Interrelator, it is because some of us agree with that statement that we have supported *others* on this Council''—her ears flared at the two Modernist members—''who dcsircd to build thc Grcat Dam at thc First Cataract. We sorrow over the loss of Ancestral remains, but the rise and fall of the River of Life is a constant. Some ancient places have always been lost to Father's Anger or Mother's Tears. At least this loss is in service to the People, for new farmlands and the energy to power factories that will . . . make us and your CLS more equal.''

Gordon blinked, surprised to hear such a statement from Elder Salween of the Temple of Earth Quaking. The elderly Seismologist was the leader of the Traditionalist faction, a firm backer of his efforts, and someone who never spoke in haste. Mahree looked troubled, then bowed to Salween. ''Elder Salween, I too wish there were some other way. But think! You are a great people, with six millennia of reflection. Surely, in all that time, you have learned the value of a slow and measured approach to making major decisions. True?''

A different Elder, the representative of the King and the Royal House, tossed out his own salt. ''Interrelator, that is indeed our practice, and so it has been from the time of the First Dynasty. But.'' The alien, a middle-aged male whom Gordon had been told was often the swing vote in the Council, flared his ears at Mahree, then offset that gesture with a direct stare. ''But never before have Infidels descended from Mother Sky. Never before have the People considered such a marvel. And never before have we had to weigh in the balance the entire future of the People. If we do not progress, and quickly, our heritage might be lost anyway. Through the influence of the New Marvel, you offworlders. Is that not true, Philosopher Mitchell?''

Mahree sat down, then looked back at him. ''Gordon?''

Damn. He'd been squatting behind her, trying to avoid

notice. Gordon stood and bowed low to the representative
of the Royal House. "Elder Hakeem, it is true that, in
Earth's history, when one culture met another, the result
was often great damage to the weaker of the two.

He thought of the European colonists who'd come to
OldAm and Polynesia, of the Muslim culture in North Africa after the fall of Rome, and of Imperial China invading
early Korea. However, the CLS is not Earth. Their peoples
have histories both similar to, and different from, my own
Earth. Most importantly, the CLS has a group of Sky-flying
Marshals, the League Irenics, who can usually prevent
unauthorized visits to a world that is in *protected status*.
The Council could choose to make Ancestor's World such
a planet."

Silence fell in the Council chamber.

Gordon squatted back down, hoping he'd helped Mahree.
But when the female Elder representing the Queen's Household tossed her own salt into the sand pit, he was thrown
for a loss. That Elder, though a Traditionalist whose ears
were just starting to show silver, had never before spoken
during his prior meetings with the Council.

Mahree rose and bowed. "Elder Alasoo? You have a
question?" She then squatted back down.

"No," the alien said bluntly, then looked around the
circle. "Some observations and a statement. I observe that
despite this offer of help from your Irenics, an off-world
craft attacked the Royal Tomb of the First Dynasty and
attempted to steal our Ancestor's remains. That is sacrilege." The other Elders, of both factions, fanned their ears
and thumped their tails, loudly agreeing. "I observe that
only off-worlder weapons, and your bravery, drove them
from our sacred soil. I further observe—"

"But, Elder Alasoo," Mahree broke in hotly, "the Tomb
is now protected by forty Sisters of the Queen's Own
Guard, armed with rifles and—"

Realizing that she'd interrupted the representative of the
Queen's Household, Mahree squatted abjectly. "My apologies, Elder." She tossed two salt tablets into the sand pit.

Alasoo sighed. "Accepted. You are young still, you believe strongly, and you mean us well. We all understand that.'' Gordon leaned closer to Mahree's hunched-over back, as anxious as she to learn where the Elder was heading. ''But facts are facts. Power is power. And one thing the Royal House has learned through the ages is to never rely on the promises of strangers when matters of state are at risk.'' The female looked at Mahree, her manner direct and firm. ''Your CLS may, or may not, be able to do all that you say. But we live here. We hold this world in trust for the Revered Ancestors. It is our *duty* to strengthen and *defend* our world!''

Alasoo's statement echoed off the chamber's dome.

Elder Sashoon tossed salt onto the sand pit. The young Modernist stood up, his tail lifted, his ears flaring. ''Elder Alasoo, *our* devotion to Mother Sky is boundless. I am pleased to advise you that the Temple of A-Um Rakt, always known for inventiveness in Weather Cannons and Rain Rockets, has developed a long-range cannon. The barrel is rifled, it is quite portable, and the shell it fires can reach far into Mother Sky.''

Everyone, including the humans, crouched in stunned silence. ''With this weapon, the Queen's Own Guard can defend the Sky over all our Royal Tombs. And . . . one of our Senior Electricians tells me that it may soon be possible to throw artificial balls of Mother's Touch at any Sky Infidel!''

Gordon's heart sank. Had the Na-Dina developed some kind of pulse-gun? Or cannon? God, he hoped not. But the males who ran the Temple of A-Um Rakt had the benefit of six millennia of weapons design. And the female Honorary Members of the Temple—who followed in the steps of the Sister who had invented the electric battery centuries ago—seemed to have forged an unholy alliance with this world's munitions manufacturers. Mahree looked over her shoulder at Gordon, her face drawn, her dark eyes troubled. The last thing they needed on Ancestor's World was an arms race!

''What?'' An elderly male surged to his taloned feet.

Gordon recognized him as the representative for the Temple of Storms, a member of the Traditionalist faction. The alien hurriedly threw out salt. "Why were we not informed of this desecration of Mother Sky? It is bad enough that Sky Infidels *fly* through her. For the People to throw back Mother's Touch at her, that is . . . that is—"

"Blasphemy," said Elder Salween, tossing in her own pill. "Council Elders! This new munitions effort is separate from the dam project, and the report of our two guests. Let us reserve further discussion until they are finished. Does any one have other questions for them?"

One more did. The representative of the Temple of Records tossed her pill and looked at Gordon. "Philosopher Mitchell, have your experts made any progress in deciphering the ideoglyphs inside the Royal Tomb? The loss of records from the first seven dynasties is a pain still felt by us."

Mahree sat with her legs crossed, her head downcast. He could tell she was depressed by the apparent allying of the two factions, and the possibility that the Na-Dina were considering trying to shoot CLS craft out of Mother Sky.

Gordon stood, then nodded to the elderly female who'd been a key supporter of his dig. "Elder Talteen, yes, we have made some progress." Around the chamber circle, fan-ears perked to attention.

"What progress?" hissed Salween, breaking protocol.

Gordon knew why they were so eager. The Interregnum of civil disorder between the Seventh and Eight Dynasties was the sole break in civil control by the Royal House. Worse than any subsequent civil war, the Interregnum had resulted in the sacking of whole cities, the loss of most records from that period and, by the time the Eighth Dynasty reasserted Royal rule, the hieroglyphic language had shifted into the two present-day versions of ancient Temple Na-Dina, and recent High Na-Dina.

Gordon bowed to the Temple of Records female. "Elder Talteen, I'm pleased to announce that thanks to the efforts of Etsane Mwarka, our team Iconographer, and with the help of Professor Greyshine and Interrelator Burroughs, we

have established the presence in First Dynasty Na-Dina of
ideoglyphs drawn from Mizari Four. A language spoken by
the oldest members of the CLS."

That did it. The assembled Elders broke protocol in a
riot of hissing, salt tossing forgotten. He didn't blame them.
The discovery of Mizari relics in the Tomb had suggested
the presence of off-worlders on the planet long ago, at the
start of their own history. Now, the Mizari Four ideoglyphs
proved that off-worlder influence was greater than a brief
stopover. It takes time to influence a language. And the
Elders were clearly upset by the apparent influence on the
start of their civilization.

Gordon tossed salt into the sand. Then water. When he
tossed the water bowl into the pit, where it broke loudly,
people finally shut up.

"Elder Talteen, we are still in the earliest stages of linguistic analysis of this new discovery. We are far from even
a partial translation of the Tomb inscriptions. But we have
made a breakthrough, thanks to the help of the new researchers from the CLS."

Mahree glanced at him, her expression pleased and
thankful. Then she turned around and tossed salt. She stood.
"Elders of the Council, be assured that I, Doctor Mitchell,
and all his team are exerting our best efforts to *honor* your
Ancestors by rescuing their remains, and their knowledge,
from destruction by the new lake. We will keep you informed as new progress is made."

The Temple of Records Elder stared at Mahree. "You
have made an old woman's final years her best years." The
stare stretched longer than any Gordon recalled seeing
among the Na-Dina. "I am pleased we sent two Philosopher-Historians to you, to participate in this great wonder."
The female bowed low to Mahree, to Gordon, and then
squatted down.

Elder Salween stood up. "I see no other questions." She
looked to Mahree, dipping her head politely. "You and
Philosopher Gordon are excused. Thank you for a . . . most
interesting report."

Mahree nodded back. "It has been an honor, Elder."

But in Gordon's ears, her words rang hollowly in the stillness.

Mahree sat in the pilot cabin of the shuttle she'd borrowed from *Emerald Scales*, watching through the thick quartz nose-windows as the camp's jumpjet lifted off the mesa top. Under autopilot control, the jet rose vertically, rotated, and flew off to the southwest, aiming for Base Camp and the landing field beacon. Gordon sat to her left, in the pilot's seat. Touching the control panel deftly, he brought online the shuttle's a-grav hover-and-lift engines, taking them up to a thousand meters elevation.

"Watch this," he said, grinning boyishly at her. He slapped *On* the main fusion drive. A string of lights flashed amber-red on the panel as the MHD units pumped fuel through the sun-hot center of the craft's plasma bottle. The shuttle spat out a flaming tail of stripped hydrogen and oxygen ions.

As they surged forward, Mahree felt the sudden weight of their racing start for just a moment, until the inertial damping field came on. She tugged at the straps holding her against the copilot's seat, then glanced his way. "Gordon, did you put some bourbon in our fuel tanks?"

He laughed, a warm easy laugh that had come more often of late. "Nope, just reliving my youth. When I was in grad school in Tennessee, I used to fly cargo SSTO's down to Brazil during winter vacation." He guided the craft, tipping the nose up and letting the shuttle climb rapidly.

"Flying those crates paid for my tuition, and taught me how to compute a suborbital parabolic in my head. One hour to anywhere on Earth. That was the motto of those rigs. Two hundred fifty years old, some of 'em were, but they were tough babies."

Mahree noticed how the night sky, full of stars and the white disk of Mother's Daughter rising over the southern horizon, had now darkened. She pointed it out. "Gordon, we're already in the mesosphere. Why the high altitude? In straight-line flight we'd be at the camp in ten minutes. Or less."

He nodded casually, even as the slant of the shuttle steepened. "Yeah, I know. I thought you might enjoy taking the long way home, and seeing the stars up close."

She saw his hopeful smile, and smiled back. What the heck. They'd both been working such long hours, it was fun to have a break. "Sounds perfect."

Gordon grinned mischievously. "Want to get a close look at the equatorial volcanoes?"

Mahree was tempted, but such joyriding was a violation, in spirit at least, of the CLS promise to the Council to keep off-worlder flights through Mother Sky to the minimum needed for their work. "No, thanks, Gordon. The stars are clear enough from here."

She leaned back, seeing the glory of those stellar pinpoints as the sky turned almost black overhead. They were in the purple-black ionosphere, where the auroras played and temperatures dropped precipitously.

"Hey!" Gordon jerked forward. A yellow light had begun blinking on the control panel. "Mahree, that sensor is picking up Type Three neutrino emissions. From a fusion ship drive. Does *Emerald Scales* have a second shuttle?"

She shivered, as if cold water had been poured down her neck. Leaning forward, she scanned the strip of over-the-horizon sensor readouts. "No, it doesn't. Does Nordlund have a shuttle?"

"Nope." Gordon's right hand moved the manual yoke forward. The shuttle's nose lowered and they began to curve around the planet in a suborbital arc. "Mahree, who the *hell* is running a transport-sized ship drive? And on the far side of Ancestor's World at that!"

She looked at him, feeling her heart race. "The smugglers?"

"Damn it!" Gordon's jaw muscles tightened visibly. "Why didn't *Emerald Scales* pick this up earlier?"

Mahree wondered about that, then remembered the relative positions of the Mizari freighter, their shuttle, and this alien intruder. "Solar masking, Gordon! Mother's Eye puts out one hell of a lot of neutrinos, like all stars. Even though neutrinos penetrate solid matter easily, we wouldn't pick up a drive plant emission from the *dayside*. Think of an ancient fighter plane hiding in the glare of the sun.'' She paused, thinking it through. ''*Unless* the transport was flying off to one side of a line connecting Ancestor's World and Mother's Eye. At a right angle to that line. Then it would flare against empty space, making it stand out to our sensors.''

Gordon nodded slowly. ''Got it. Makes sense. And the only reason *we* picked it up is because we're at high altitude, gallivanting about on the nightside of Ancestor's World.'' He touched on a sensor screen. ''The emission source is moving, going in for a landing on dayside. I'm going to follow them, see where they land. Maybe we can stop them, or at least get Krillen to alert local authorities.''

''But what if they spot us?''

''We can avoid that, if we fly low enough. I'm going to full manual, so I can bypass the fail-safes.''

Gordon pushed the yoke forward even more. Attitude jets flared at their nose, and under their belly. The view in the nose-windows changed radically. Suddenly, Mahree was staring straight down at the wrinkled brown surface of Ancestor's World. She clutched her seat with both hands and swallowed.

As Gordon steepened their dive even more, Mahree's stomach lurched as the inertial damping field again lagged behind Gordon's abrupt flight changes.

''Are you sure you know what you're doing?'' she gasped, as the ground rushed up at them dizzyingly.

He grinned at her, his eyes—*They're blue-gray*, she noted with part of her mind—twinkling. ''Sure. Trust me.''

They fell . . .

CHAPTER 12

◆

The Raid

Gordon watched the hull temperature readouts, gauging how far he could stress the titanium-beryllium hull of the shuttle. It was a damned fine craft, Mizari-built, and he had no doubt it would hold up. But if he wanted secrecy, he couldn't afford to look like a streaking meteor to someone on the ground. He called to Mahree. "Would you handle the emission tracking? I've got to pay attention to my hypersonic flight envelope."

"Right," Mahree said, reaching out to the sensor strip. She tapped in a series of commands.

He concentrated on their plummeting dive down into dense atmosphere. "Passing through the mesopause, coming up on the stratosphere."

"Tracking. Neutrino sensor is now showing all three types of neutrinos—muonic, electronic, and tauic. The target is dumping large amounts of muonic neutrinos."

Gordon tried to remember his college nucleosynthesis classes, couldn't, and chose not to worry about it. "What does that mean?"

His partner moved to touch another part of the panel, a data bank of ship types. "It means they're showing the drive emission signature typical of a C-Class transport."

The ship was about the size of *Emerald Scales*, then. With long-range metaspace reach, as well as the ability to make planetfall. Mahree frowned thoughtfully. "The neutrino mix in the drive emissions says transport, and the weakness of the electronic neutrinos suggests to me this is an *old* ship."

Gordon moved the flight yoke carefully, adding a slight curve to their dive. "That *big*? I'd have expected a smaller ship. Hell, the most valuable artifacts don't really mass that much."

"A good point." Mahree tapped the data bank again. "Why the hell are the smugglers running something this big and this slow? It doesn't make sense."

"I don't know either," Gordon said. "We're passing over the Great Desert, heading for dayside. Now in the troposphere." He jiggled the yoke more firmly, and with his other hand tapped in a drive command. "Slowing to supersonic. I'm extruding my flight control surfaces." From the rear of the shuttle came a grinding rumble as stubby delta wings and a bobbed tail pushed out from the basic wedge-shape of the craft.

Mahree lifted a hand as sunrise glared suddenly through their nose-windows. "Ouch." She lowered her hand when the automatic polarization darkened the window. Then she looked his way. "Gordon, they're slowing to land. About nine hundred klicks ahead. Is there anything in that region?"

He thought a moment, recalling the basic geography of Ancestor's World. "That's on the opposite side of the planet from Base Camp. It's a highland plateau area, inhabited mostly by remote farming villages. They get enough rain from the Mountains of Faith to farm, even without irrigation or river diversion. But it's really isolated."

Gordon leveled the shuttle's flight track into a straight-line one. The craft rattled badly as they curved out of their precipitous fall; then the vibration bled off. "In the troposphere now, moving at Mach Three. ETA about ten minutes."

He glanced down at their travel bags. "Open up my bag, Mahree. I packed the pulse-guns, just in case we ran into trouble from your admirer. I have a feeling we might need them."

She nodded, though he could tell she wasn't happy. "And now, hold on to your seat, Mahree. We're about to practice some close-terrain following. That ship must have radar and, though the ashfalls we're now flying through will screen us some, I prefer to drop into the radar clutter of the local mountains."

"Drop?" Mahree winced. "Ohhhh, Gordon. Not again!"

Mahree gulped as Gordon shed more altitude, sending them into a corkscrew flight line that needled through a narrow canyon. He jinked to the right around a red-glowing volcano, then flew them down the middle of a long rift valley bordered on both sides by snow-capped peaks. The transport had set down, her sensors said, about two hundred klicks ahead and to the southwest of their current flight track. She touched on a new screen. According to the orbital map made by *Scales*, Gordon's plateau resembled a fissured tongue that struck north from the equatorial mountains. The ancient flood-basalt flow had long since been carved up by earthquakes, shear zones, strike-slip faults, and the watery erosion of time.

Krillen had told her that the reach of the Forty-Sixth Dynasty extended even this far, but the visits of Guard Marshals and their units did not make up for the fact there was no river barge access to this place, unlike the opposite hemisphere. Although the Royal Roads *did* connect this part of the planet to Spirit, and ships crossed the Northern Sea. Radio might make a difference, but the thunderstorms still played havoc with their own long-distance connection to *Scales*, let alone the Na-Dina's more primitive, low-powered version of radio.

Shaking her head, Mahree focused on the sunlit landscape of a new part of Ancestor's World. It was a rugged, weather-slashed place, where the green of a forest or a meadow field flashed briefly, then was lost to black lava flows, red erosion channels, and sandy pockets that lay in wind-shadow.

Gordon pointed at a high-walled mountain pass. "That's our gateway to the plateau. Hang on."

"Hanging on," she gulped. The shuttle tilted over onto its side, flashed out of the rift valley and into the pass, then leveled out as Gordon pushed them down, down to within a hundred meters of the flashing red, green, and black landscape.

She gulped and nearly choked. "Gordon. I think I'm going to be sick."

He looked at her with concern. "Sorry. I'll take it easier."

Mahree swallowed, then breathed deeply as Gordon slowed the headlong rush of the shuttle. She checked the sensor strip. "They're just ahead, behind that ridgeline on the horizon. There's a"—she looked over and checked the orbital map again—"a bowl-valley beyond it, grassy it looks like, but without any local habitation. The valley is cut off from the rest of the plateau by steep erosion-cut canyons."

Gordon looked at her, his expression somber. "Sounds like a perfect smuggler base to me." He turned back to his piloting. "I'm taking us on a-grav up to that ridgeline, then I'm going to set down just below its crest. There are scanner eyeshades in my bag. We can check this out from a distance, without walking up to their front door. Okay?"

"That's a plan," Mahree said, thankful for anything that took her mind off her stomach. She twisted in her seat, reached back, and pulled over Gordon's bag. She pulled out the two pulse-guns and their holster-belts, next the scanner shades, and finally a water bottle for each of them. She'd learned early in her stay here to never go anywhere on Ancestor's World without water and salt pills.

Etsane sat at the edge of the camp creek, her bare feet dangling in the cool water, her dinner plate lying to one side. Instead of eating with the rest of the specialists at the camp Refectory, where the others had given up waiting for the return of *astamari* Mitchell and Mahree, she'd chosen to eat out under the night stars.

It was a beautiful evening, with the white light of Mother's Daughter casting a silvery sheen over water, rocks, and the curving sandstone walls of the canyon. This place, lying next to a large flat rock that Sumiko often used for sunbathing, was one of her favorite places at camp.

She found herself thinking of Natual. The meal he'd prepared for her the night after the animal attack had been piquant, tasty, and served with a flare that made her give serious thought to Natual the person. He'd proved an interesting, enjoyable companion, encouraging her to talk, and listening to her intently as she'd told him about her life in the Ethiopian Highlands, of her family homestead above Gonder, and how much she wanted to live up to her father's memory.

In his turn, Natual had told her about his own people, commenting that Drnian death beliefs included a belief in ghosts. Spirits of the departed could choose to linger after the funeral rites, if they thought a relative needed help or a task had been left undone. Shyly, Etsane had confessed that at times, she'd thought she'd sensed her father's spirit hovering near her.

When they'd parted for the evening, they'd shared a hug, but Natual hadn't tried to push it beyond that. Etsane had gone back to her tent, smiling, and proceeded to read up on Drnian biology.

Boots scraped in the dark behind her, coming from the direction of the landing field. Etsane turned to look at the newcomer. As if her thoughts had conjured him up, she saw Natual coming toward her.

"Care for company?"

"Sure," she replied. "Come sit down."

Etsane smiled at him as he sat down beside her. "Hello." Pulling her feet from the water, she sat cross-legged, feeling the breeze drying them.

"Did you enjoy your dinner?"

Etsane laughed. "Not nearly as much as I enjoyed the

one you made for me. You're a good cook, Natual.''

He shifted closer to her, until his bare shoulder nearly brushed hers. ''I'm pleased. Your happiness is important to me.''

''I'm really glad we've become friends,'' she said. ''Your happiness is important to me, too.''

He gazed at her intently. ''Friends . . . yes, we value friendship, Etsane. But . . . is it *only* friends? Could it ever be more?''

She took a deep breath and slid her feet into her boots, concentrating on lacing them up while she struggled to find an answer. He kept silent, and she knew his eyes had not left her. Finally, she looked up. ''I don't know, Natual. Maybe. That's an honest answer. It would take . . . time. And patience. This is all very new to me.''

He nodded. ''I know. It is new to me, too. But I know that I want to try to see if our friendship could grow into something more.'' Natual tried his smile on her again. He was getting better at moving his mouth into an upward curve. ''Did you know that we Drnians are a patient people?''

Reaching toward her, he held out his hand. Slowly, hesitantly, Etsane placed her fingers into his, noticing how different his body temperature was from her own. He was warmer, his skin textured differently from human skin.

She smiled at him. ''Patience is a virtue on my planet,'' she said softly.

As they reached the ridgeline crest, Gordon motioned to Mahree to drop to the ground. She did so. Together they adjusted their scanner eyeshades, setting them to telescopic, and then spied on the long tube of the smuggler transport. He noticed the ship had landed beside a group of corrals, but there was no livestock nearby. Just a stone building that resembled a herder's hut, though it was big enough for six people.

As they watched, the ship's cargo hatch opened and an offloading ramp extruded. Four coveralled crew members marched out, each armed with repulsor wards, and took up positions on either side of the ramp. Where the ramp met the grassy floor of the valley, one of the corrals stood with its gate open. Figures moved inside the shadowy cargo hold.

"Gordon?" Mahree said, sounding puzzled. "If these are smugglers, where are the ruins?"

He sweated in the midday sun, feeling it strange to so suddenly jump from the middle of the night at the mesa, to midday here on the opposite side of the world. "I know. It's weird. Almost as if this place is—"

"Gordon!"

The pain in Mahree's voice matched that in his heart. "Oh, God," he said. "No, not that. I thought we were rid of that."

"*Slaves!*" she cried out, then lowered her voice as she pointed to the line of captives being herded out of the hold and down the ramp. "Oh, God! Several Heeyoons, a Vardi, a dozen Drnians, a Shadgui, some Elspind, a dozen Na-Dina, three humans, and—"

"No Simiu," Gordon whispered. "They're too aggressive to make good slaves. No Apis. No one that can fly." He watched the ugly scene, feeling nauseated. "Look at the way they're moving. What's the matter with them?"

"Bastards!" Mahree reached out, gripping his arm. Her nails dug painfully into his skin. "They've drugged them! To make them more controllable. And when they try to wander off, they get the rods. Those must be stun-prods, not repulsors. Look at the way that woman went into con vulsions!"

"I see." Gordon wanted to turn away . . . but instead he watched as over sixty intelligent people from half a dozen species were roughly shoved, prodded, and herded into the first corral.

He squinted at the slaver crew. They appeared to be two Heeyoons, a Drnian, and a heavyset human male. Suddenly a fifth slaver appeared in the cargo lock, standing as if overseeing the operation.

Gordon peered at the alien, who was still standing in the shadows. He—or she, or it, it was impossible to tell—appeared to be directing the operation. "Who the hell is that guy?" he muttered.

"Gordon, that's an *Anuran* down there, standing in the cargo lock," Mahree whispered.

Mitchell had heard of the warlike race of slave-owning amphibians when they'd invaded Trinity a year or so ago. He'd thought the Anuran worlds were under interdiction by the CLS. At least one of the amphibian people appeared to have escaped that fate.

Mahree flipped up the eyeshade with her other hand and looked at him. "Think he's the leader?"

"He could be. But he could also just be the trademaster. Look down at the first corral and tell me—what is the common denominator among all those captives?"

He felt her trembling beside him, and took her hand, squeezing her fingers, as much for his comfort as hers. "They're all in pain," she whispered, in response to his question. "They're all captives. And they're all going to a living hell if we don't *do* something to stop this!"

He shook his head at her warningly. "Shhhhhh!"

The fury in her eyes eased. "I'll be quieter," she mumbled.

Gordon touched her face gently. "Hey. Please don't hurt so much. I . . . it hurts me to see you like this."

She blinked, and tears slid down her face. "Slavery. Never again, Gordon. *Never again.* We wiped it out in Mali, in Sudan, in Arabia and in South Asia by 2020. The CLS makes sure it doesn't reoccur on their worlds." She rubbed her hands against her eyes, then looked to him. "So how do we stop this?"

Gordon looked away, his own vision blurred. He nodded down at the corral, now full with offloaded captives. "What I meant by common denominator is that all those folks belong to species with outposts in this part of space. Near Sorrow Sector. There's no one from Trinity here, nor any oceanic or flyer types. No one with special environmental needs."

He took a deep breath. "Mahree, slaves are taken for *work*. For hard labor. For doing things that are cheap to do even with robot factories. And for . . . other things. More *personal* services.''

"No!" she protested, not missing his meaning. "We can't let them get away. They don't look like they're getting ready to go anytime soon. Maybe we can get help, rescue them!"

Something else had just occurred to Gordon Mitchell. He stared at Mahree as a light dawned inside his brain. "Mahree, what if the artifact smuggling is incidental to the presence of slavers here on Ancestor's World? What if . . . what if this explains the Disappearances?" She gasped. "Sorrow Sector landed here, just as they may have done at other remote outposts or frontier worlds, to grab slaves. At first. Then they heard rumors about the ruins and, as a sideline, the ship's crew does a little looting of artifacts.''

Her face was tense, pale, beneath the tan. "You're probably right, but, so? What does that mean to us?"

Gordon licked his lips. "It means this is part of a long-organized operation. They stop here to sort their captives. See how they're moving a few into other corrals now? Maybe for pickup by another transport, one that goes on into Sorrow Sector. Or maybe they've already done a Disappearance raid elsewhere on Ancestor's World, and are stopping here to process their wares.''

"Wares!" She looked as though she might be sick, but managed to control herself. "We have to *do* something, Gordon.''

"I agree. But they're too well armed for us to take them by ourselves. See those blasters they're wearing?"

Mahree trembled next to him, her body touching his. "I see. But we *must* stop this!"

"You're right." Swallowing thickly, he looked to her. "Mahree, take the shuttle back to camp, ask Pokeel to come here with some of her people, along with any researchers who volunteer to fight, and return to me. Then we'll free the captives.''

Mahree faced him, her eyes dry, her expression grim. "No. *You* go back to camp and do that. You're a better pilot than I am. You know where your two blasters are stored, I don't. You're the organizer around here, I'm not. And''—she turned her gaze back to the abomination below—''I'm the Interrelator for this world. The Na-Dina are my responsibility. This must be stopped now, and I will *not* leave these Na-Dina, or the others, to an uncertain fate.''

''I don't want to leave you, Mahree.'' Fear swept over him. Fear that she would be hurt. Fear that she might be captured by the slavers.

Fear that he would lose her, as he'd lost everyone else he'd ever cared about.

Gordon realized he was gripping her shoulder tightly. She smiled at him, a brave, heartbreaking smile, and in that moment, he realized that he loved her.

''Mahree . . .'' he whispered hoarsely.

She nodded at him, as though she understood. ''Gordon, there will be time for us later. I promise.'' He lifted his hand from her. ''But now, we must use our brains. I'm the one who speaks six alien languages. I'm the one with a responsibility to the CLS. And I'm armed with a pulse-gun. Go now.'' The expression in her dark eyes made his heart lurch. ''But hurry back to me.''

Gordon nodded. ''All right. You win. I'll be back in an hour, okay? While I'm gone, you stay safe, understand? Swear to me on Claire's life that you won't do anything brave or foolhardy. You'll just watch, okay?''

She nodded. ''I swear it on Claire's life, Gordon. Hurry!''

Gordon Mitchell slithered back until he was safely out of sight, then got up and ran for the shuttle.

The trail to the creek dipped as the ground changed from sandy to gravelly, and Khuharkk' dropped to all fours to negotiate it more easily. He broke into a lope, knowing from the scent she'd left on the trail that his friend Etsane was just ahead.

Moments later, he caught sight of her, sitting by the flat rock. She was not alone. The Drnian male, Natual, was sitting next to her. They were holding hands.

Khuharkk' reared back on his haunches to consider the implications of this, and decided that the best thing he could do was to leave before they saw him.

He turned to do so, but was halted a second later by Etsane's voice. "Khuharkk'! We're down here! Come on!"

The Simiu ambled down the trail until he reached the couple. He couldn't help noticing that, while Etsane seemed genuinely glad to see him, Natual didn't.

"I am sorry if I disturbed you," he began. "But I—" He broke off, ears pricking up. "Someone is approaching at a high-speed trajectory," he said, his Simiu pilot training coming to the fore.

Etsane jumped to her feet, looking around wildly. "Smugglers?"

"It is not the camp jumpjet," Khuharkk' said. "That landed an hour ago. Possibly it is the shuttle Honored MahreeBurroughs mentioned bringing back to camp. But why the excessive speed?"

Now they were all on their feet, staring. They could make out the lights of the approaching vehicle now. There was no doubt that it was coming in very, very fast. The retro-blast it made boomed in their ears, making them all flinch. "Something is wrong," Khuharkk' said. "I am heading for the landing field."

"Me, too," Etsane said.

Natual did not bother to reply, simply broke into a surprisingly fast run.

They were all panting by the time they reached the field. Khuharkk' could see the shuttle's door was already open, and the ramp was moving out.

Etsane drew even with him, then pointed. "Look! It's Doctor Mitchell, there in the passenger section airlock."

Khuharkk' narrowed his pupils against the strobing glare of the shuttle's running lights. "Doctor Mitchell?" he yelled. "Is there a problem? Where's Honored Mahree?"

Mitchell jumped to the ground, not waiting for the loading ramp to finish extruding. The man ran toward them. "Damn! It's good to see you three here. You can save me some time. I need help."

Mitchell skidded to a stop in a spray of gravel. Khuharkk' thumped his chest. "By my Honor Scars, I will help however I can. What do you need?"

"Combat," the archaeologist said bluntly to them. "Mahree and I tracked a smuggler transport coming in for a landing on the dayside of Ancestor's World. Thought it was just coming in to loot some tomb. It wasn't." He tried to catch his breath. "They're *slavers*! They brought in a group of sixty slaves, from half a dozen species. Mahree is still there, keeping watch in case they try to leave before we get back. I'm here to get Pokeel's help. There are a dozen or more Na-Dina in the group."

Khuharkk' felt dark fury. What an insult to this world! What a wound to the heritage of the Na-Dina! Thanks to language lessons from Axum, he had grown to respect her people, even to understand somewhat their way of Honor and their devotion to dead Ancestors. He snarled out his offer. "I will return to fight and free these captives! Take me!"

Mitchell looked away from Etsane, whose face had grown hard and stiff. The older man nodded abruptly. "Your Honor Challenge on behalf of the Na-Dina is accepted." Their leader looked back to Etsane and Natual. "You two don't have to come. This is all-volunteer. But anyone who comes must carry a weapon. Except for Khuharkk', of course."

Etsane was already nodding. "Count me in! I'll get my sling!"

Natual raised a thin arm. "Me. Count me in. I may be a researcher, but I know when it is time to fight for what is right." The Drnian mimed aiming. "I know how to handle a pulse-gun."

"Good." Mitchell unbuckled his holstered gun and handed it to Natual. "Take this one. I'll get my two blasters from inside the Lab." The man pointed at Khuharkk'. "My Simiu friend, you go wake up Chief Marshal Pokeel—assuming my retro-blast hasn't already done the job! Ask her to bring ten of her people."

"Why so few?" Etsane asked.

"Because we've got to save room for sixty passengers. It'll be damned tight." He made shooing motions. "Now get going! Run! We've got ten minutes!"

By the time they all gathered back at the ship, they had more than enough volunteers. Gordon weeded them out, making sure he took only those who were best armed, and the most experienced.

As he was sending them up the ramp into the ship, someone tugged on his sleeve. Mitchell whirled to find Axum there. "Doctor Mitchell! I found something!"

His temper flared. "Axum, now is *not* the time for archaeological dis—"

Axum flared her ears in the sign Mahree had said meant contrition. "Doctor, what we found today was *not* old, but new. You must see it for yourself. I . . . I believe it relates to Bill's murder."

Gordon paused for a half-second, staring at her. "All right," he said. "Keep this to yourself. I'll see it tomorrow, I promise. In the meantime—Axum, I'm trusting you with the safety of the camp. Don't fail me, okay?"

She drew herself up. "I will not, Doctor Mitchell. You have my word."

"Good."

Etsane sat in the front section of the shuttle, just behind the open pilot cabin, and struggled for control. *Slavery.* The very word made her go cold with anger. She rubbed her bare arms briskly, trying to restore circulation. Then she checked her supply of quartz stones, and the suppleness and readiness of her sling.

Ready, yes. She was ready.

Her mind kept presenting her with instances out of her world's past, in which people with skin the color of her own had been victimized in just that way. And the slave-traders had not just been whites. No, they had included people from rival tribes who'd ruthlessly captured their neighbors and *sold* them like cattle. The same had happened in Arabia and South India.

She licked dry lips. *Slavery. How can it be happening again?*

Across the aisle, Doctor Strongheart looked her way. "Etsane, this must be painful for you." The female Heeyoon's gaze carried deep sympathy. Of course, Etsane thought. Greyshine and his mate, alone among the aliens in camp, had probably done extensive reading about Earth's bloody history.

Marshal Pokeel's Guards were checking their rifles, their bandoleers of ammunition, and the hand-to-hand knives they wore strapped to their waists.

A number of the researchers had chosen to come along, including little cream-colored Ttalatha, who was sitting between the Heeyoons and the Na-Dina warriors. The Paleoenvironmental specialist was staring down at the pulse-gun she held in her six-fingered, claw-tipped hands.

Gordon's voice echoed back from the pilot's compartment over the intercom. "Chief Marshal, do you have suggestions on how we should carry out this raid?"

"You have described to me the layout of this slave camp, Philosopher Mitchell," she replied. "But seeing it firsthand is essential to planning any small-unit action."

"Here." Mitchell touched the middle of the control panel, lighting up a holo-tank lying between their seats. "Marshal, if you will examine this screen, I'll give you an aerial view of the layout."

Moments later, Pokeel looked up, her long snout showing sharp white teeth. "The plateau is isolated, and that valley is grassy, with much open ground. Not good. I will have to consider this."

Etsane gulped and clutched her sling so tightly her hands hurt.

Gordon went to a-grav support when they got within fifty kilometers of the slaver camp. Besides being less noisy than the main drive, the a-gravs allowed them to hover. And he could use the attitude-control chemical jets when they needed to maneuver to a final landing. Until then, they coasted in on widespread delta wings, holding altitude two hundred meters below the ridgeline that encircled the high-land plateau. Moving the yoke carefully, his feet pressing the aileron pedals delicately, Gordon added down-flaps as they came up on the ridgeline. He landed a few hundred feet from where he'd left Mahree.

"We're landing," he said tersely over the intercom to the passenger compartment. "No one leaves until I do. Keep the chatter low, and no one fires on anything without an order."

The shuttle grounded on the rock bench where he'd landed the first time. Glancing through the nose-window, he searched for the black of Mahree's StarBridge uniform, but did not see it. Damn! He turned to the Na-Dina Guard leader. "Pokeel, I suggest we share command on attack *planning*, since I'm familiar with our weapons. But you should be in full command on the ground. This is your land, your people are captive, and frankly, I've never led a raiding party." He got up.

Pokeel hissed her approval, then followed him out into the aisleway. "A good recommendation. I accept." Flaring her ears, she addressed her soldiers. "Sisters, heads low. Tails flat to the ground. Maqueen, you stay behind to guard our transport. Bites-Hard, you are second in command to me. Now move!"

The ten Na-Dina rose up, rifles held in their talon-hands. The Camp volunteers also stood, their expressions determined but worried. Gordon didn't blame them. He was scared, too.

He checked to make sure his blaster was secure in his holster, then led the way down the loading ramp. At the bottom, he stared out to where she'd been.

She was gone.

Where are you, Mahree?

Mahree crawled out from under the boulder where she'd hidden when two smugglers had walked by on a patrol of the perimeter. She stood up cautiously and waved at Gordon, saw his expression change from anxious worry to joy.

Oh, God, she thought, *what are we going to do? I think I'm falling in love with him! But I can't be!*

He hurried up to her, followed closely by Pokeel, nine of her Guards, and six volunteers from Camp, including Etsane and Khuharkk', who ran together. They were screened from direct sight of the hut by scrubby brush, but still they hunkered down and spoke in whispers. "You moved. Why?"

Quickly, she explained. "But I don't think they have posted guards on the perimeter," she added. "They just did that one sweep."

"Here, put this on," Gordon said, holding out the second blaster. Mahree hesitated, then quickly complied, turning her pulse-gun over to him. Quickly, he handed it to Greyshine.

Mahree looked at Pokeel. "Chief Marshal, the four pulse-guns are flexible weapons, from stun to disrupt, which kills. Our two blasters are like the light of Mother's Eye. Nothing will stop them. They can even penetrate the hull of the transport out there."

She paused and wet her lips, then gratefully took a swallow from a canteen Gordon offered her. They were all huddled around her, the hot sun of midday reflecting off metal, fur, and scales. "If possible, I favor stunning the smugglers. Unless they use deadly force."

Gordon frowned. "Mahree, they're carrying *only* blasters. That's deadly force anytime one fires."

Pokeel's ears flared questioningly. "Range. What's the range of your weapons?"

Gordon spoke first. "A kilometer for blasters. Three hundred meters for pulse-guns. Both make a noise when fired."

The Na-Dina Chief Marshal nodded, then pointed at the scanner eyeshade hanging around Mahree's neck. "Is that a far-viewer? Like our hand scopes?"

"It is," Mahree said, removing the eyeshade and holding it out. "Would you like to use it to scout the slaver camp?"

"Yes," Pokeel said, taking the eyeshade and arranging it on her domed head with little difficulty. "This works by blink-control?"

Mahree shook her head admiringly. The Na-Dina Marshal had clearly been watching her and the other CLS volunteers when they used the devices during ruin surveys. "It does. Enlarges or decreases by powers of ten. Range displays across the top of the shade."

"Good," Pokeel said. "Please wait for a brief span while I survey our target."

They waited respectfully until the Na-Dina Marshal reappeared.

"Philosopher, Ambassador, there is a standard small-unit tactic for this situation. It is called Flank, Decoy, and Attack. I recommend we use it now."

Mahree looked at her. "Please explain. And tell us where and how you want the camp volunteers deployed."

Pokeel nodded, a human mannerism she'd quickly adopted. "Very well. Bites-Hard, you will take one other Sister, circle around this crestline, and approach from the opposite side of this valley. You will be unarmed." The other Na-Dina flattened her ears, but did not protest. "The two Sisters will approach the encampment, behaving as if they are herders in search of lost *nokseem*."

Bites-Hard fluttered her ears in the Na-Dina sign of acquiescence and comprehension.

"Your appearance will draw the Sky Infidels out of their sky vehicle and the stone house, and around to the far side of the Sky craft. Most or all of the Infidels will then be looking away from this side of the valley. We shall attack from this direction, when the maximum diversionary effect is achieved. Understood?"

"Yes, Marshal!" Bites-Hard said, and, as they watched, she beckoned to another Sister. The two left their weapons and slipped away into the brush to begin their circle of the little valley. The Marshal turned back to Mahree and the archaeologists.

"Ambassador, your people will take the left flank, with you and Philosopher Gordon staying close enough to me for voder communication. I suspect radio com unit broadcasts could be detected by these Sky Infidels. Correct?"

Gordon nodded swiftly. "Correct. Radio silence." He turned to pass the word back.

Mahree watched as Pokeel waited until Gordon finished; then the Na-Dina pointed at the crestline. "My Sisters and I, we will form a skirmish line on the right flank. Half will stay there to cover us as we run downslope to the corrals. The rest of us will run like Long-Necks and hope to reach the captives before the slavers on the far side of the transport become aware of our approach."

Mahree's heart beat fast. The plan made sense, but it also depended on luck, timing, and the expectation that the slavers would not kill the two Guard Sisters on sight, but let them approach. She accepted a replacement scanner eyeshade from Gordon, whose grim expression matched her feelings. She followed after Pokeel as the Marshal led them, with everyone crouching, up to the crestline of the ridge.

Overhead, Mother's Eye beat down, baking the rocky ground with a dry heat that drove moisture from her neck, made her bound-up hair itch, and sapped her energy levels. She took another drink of water and washed down a salt pill, and noticed many of the others doing the same thing.

Etsane and Khuharkk', she observed, were sticking close together as they prepared for the raid. Gordon moved into place beside her, blaster in hand, his expression grim and determined.

She gave him a glance, reached out to squeeze his hand briefly, and whispered, "Stay safe, Gordon."

He nodded. "You too, Mahree."

Together, they endured the waiting.

Etsane crouched behind the crestline, waiting for the two Na-Dina Guard Sisters to come over the far ridge and head down to the valley bottom, there to decoy the slavers. To her left, Khuharkk' crouched on all fours, his long-muscled arms flexing, his lips pulled back to display sharp canines, his manner very feral, very deadly, and very honorable. He met her gaze, his violet-hued eyes bright with something alien.

"May we both achieve Honor," he growled.

"Yes," Etsane said. "May we both fight well."

The Simiu turned his gaze back to watching the poor captives huddled below in the corrals. She did the same. It was horrible to watch them suffer from the sun and the heat. Mahree had said they'd been given water only once since landing, and most seemed half crazed with thirst. Two Heeyoon wandered up to the edge of their corral, motioning to one guard for water. The guard instead reached out and touched them with his stun-prod, sending the gray-furred beings reeling back to fall on the dusty ground of the corral. They lay there in the merciless glare from Mother's Eye, twitching feebly from the effects of the stun. The other slaves stared at them, drugged into indifference.

"The Guard Sisters approach," Khuharkk' said softly.

Etsane lowered her scanner eyeshade, blinked to telescopic, and watched as the two soldiers ambled down the far slope, their blue-scaled tails dragging listlessly, as if they'd been out hunting for lost herds the entire morning.

Etsane stretched and flexed her muscles, getting ready to run. She'd done track in school, and, though not of Olympic quality, she'd always been the fastest in any competition.

Reaching down, she took three quartz stones from her bag, loaded one into her sling, and held the other two in reserve in her left hand. "Khuharkk'," she whispered, "do you think there's a pilot inside the transport? I see four guards on the ground, and the Anuran amphibian inside the cargo lock. Look! They've spotted the Sisters!"

"I see!" Khuharkk's hackles rose up in a ruff of thick orange fur. "And yes, there is likely a pilot on standby, in the transport. I would order such a thing if I were in charge of a Fight Group."

Etsane watched as three of the four ground guards moved away from the corrals, circling around the gray tube of the transport, and headed out to meet the two Na-Dina. A new movement showed in the cargo hold lock. "Look! The Anuran is coming out, too."

Khuharkk' was panting with eagerness. "Just a little far-

ther,'' he urged the slavers. ''Go. Go around the ship's tail
end. Go!''

Etsane scanned the ground between her and the nearest
corral. The distance was a long five hundred meters. The
ground was mostly open and grassy, with only a small boulder scattered here and there. Most boulders were tiny, not
big enough to hide behind. A very few were person-sized.
One of that size lay on the far side of the valley, close to
the approaching Na-Dina Guard Sisters.

Almost ready . . . any moment now . . .

She tensed, waiting for *astamari* Mitchell to give the
word to rush.

She and Khuharkk' were stationed at the outer edge of
the left flank. If they moved ahead of the rest of the group,
they would not interfere with anyone's aim. They were both
fast, she knew. If only they could be quick enough to stop
the remaining guard from turning on the rescuers and slaves
with his blaster!

Etsane thought of her father, of his carved wooden staff,
of the tribal scars on his cheeks, and of how he had been
a fierce believer in freedom for all. *Father, help me to free
these people*, she prayed silently.

Suddenly the order came. ''Go!''

Springing to her feet, Etsane raced like the wind.

Khuharkk' bounded down the grassy slope and surged
forward on all fours, glorying in the challenge he faced.
Here was an Honor Challenge that would bring Honor to
his entire clan!

Etsane raced along beside him, her two feet flashing as
her long bare legs propelled her forward, nearly matching
his own four-footed gallop. He admired her for her speed;
few humans could run with a Simiu the way she was doing.

Ahead of them, a few of the captives were staring at
them, a slow, reluctant hope dawning on their faces.

He angled his forward rush so as to keep the bulk of the
stone hut between him and the single guard, a Drnian,
whose back now faced them. Briefly, he felt relief that the
sole guard on this side of the transport was not one of the

two Heeyoon or the heavyset human. Both species had excellent hearing, and they would have heard them earlier than the Drnian.

Off to his right, the other rescuers hurtled down the slope. Professor Greyshine and Doctor Strongheart were in the lead a bit, despite their age. Heeyoon could run almost as fast as Simiu. And, truth to be told, they had the lungs for long-distance running, which he did not. Natual ran respectably, though he did no better than the talon-footed Na-Dina. They bounded along like the Earth kangaroos he'd seen in a wildlife holo, but the aliens battled more wind resistance than he or others who ran close to the ground. Ttalatha ch'aakki was a masked blur of cream and chocolate fur, her narrow tail stretched out straight behind her. Mahree and Doctor Mitchell held the center of their line, doing well for humans of their age, but still more than a hundred meters behind him and Etsane.

She was running easily, twirling her sling as she readied it for her toss. Though it was a *weapon*, Khuharkk' had grown to admire her skill with it.

Khuharkk' fixed his attention on the stone hut, alert for the sudden emergence of an unseen smuggler. If anyone was unlucky enough to emerge from that doorway, he was *ready*.

Etsane kept her eyes on the back of the Drnian guard, who held a blaster in one hand, a stun-prod in the other. The male stood halfway between the stone hut and the front end of the transport, behind which moved the three other guards and the Anuran overseer, who were still walking out to confront the Guard Sisters.

She fixed her eyes on the middle of the guard's back. Her readings about Drnian physiology had told her that Natual's people had a spinal cord that was very similar to human anatomy. A direct hit at the base of the neck or the spine—depending on how her target was standing—should prove incapacitating.

She revved the sling to high spin. She and Khuharkk' were now more than halfway to the corrals and the guard, approaching at a slant from the left side. The others were now far behind.

Eying the distance left, she decided she was close enough to make her first shot. A little under two hundred meters . . . at that distance, she seldom missed.

Aiming with her shoulder, she spun, and snap-tossed.

Khuharkk', seeing her throw, angled toward the hut. Still running, Etsane reloaded her sling, spun the stone, and threw again just as the first stone hit the Drnian guard right in the middle of his back.

His blaster fell to the ground, but, as he doubled over and fell to his knees, he managed to hang onto his stun-prod.

"The hut!" Khuharkk' shouted. "Someone's inside!"

Etsane's second stone hit the left shoulder of the Drnian, causing him to drop the stun-prod. The alien's big red eyes stared at them in shock. His mouth opened—he was going to warn the others! Quick as thought, Etsane spun her third stone, snapped it forward, and watched with satisfaction as it hit the Drnian's bulging forehead. "Yes!" she breathed to herself as the guard toppled over bonelessly.

Motion blurred on her left.

A tall, skinny human rushed out of the stone hut with a blaster belt in hand, at first running toward the fallen guard, then turning when he heard their pounding footfalls. He wore only shorts, as if he'd been asleep. With fear-widened eyes, he struggled to loose the blaster from the holster. Khuharkk' hit him in a deadly parody of a football tackle. They rolled over and over, and she could hear nothing except his screams and the Simiu's growls.

Etsane swerved toward the corrals, where a dozen captives were aware enough to have struggled to their feet. Three humans, two men and a woman, gathered up the few rocks lying in the front corral. Nearby, the two Heeyoon captives who'd been hit with the stun-prod did the same. Other captives were alerting their fellows to the rescue, cautioning quiet. She waved at them, her hands motioning them to lie flat.

"Down!" she hissed as she skidded up to the nearest

corral. "Get *down*," she said in Mizari, hoping some of them knew the language. "There's going to be shooting!"

One of the men, a young man in his twenties who showed a red welt across one cheek, Asian eyes, and grim anger, nodded at her. "Right!" He turned from collecting rocks to urging and gesturing the captives to lie flat.

Etsane rounded the corral grouping, coming to a stop by the front corral entrance. After collecting the unconscious Drnian guard's blaster, she climbed over the metal gate and crouched behind its open framework, determined to keep the slavers from harming her charges. Behind her pounded the footfalls of Mahree, Doctor Mitchell, Greyshine, Strongheart, Pokeel, Natual, Ttalatha and the other Na-Dina, closing rapidly.

Scrieee!

Etsane flinched as a blaster fired on the far side of the slaver transport. Oh, no! Had Bites-Hard been shot?

"Dishonorable coward!" yelled Khuharkk' as the skinny human spun away from the Simiu's claws and teeth, leaving behind trails of red blood and the blaster belt. The wounded guard headed for the rampway leading up to the open lock of the cargo hold.

Etsane reloaded her sling, thought of knocking him out, then let him escape as the two Heeyoon crew-guards rounded the nose of the transport, double streaks of gray fur as they ran toward Khuharkk'. She turned to aim her sling at them, but one of her comrades fired a pulse-gun, its blue bolt of electrical fire passing over the corrals to hit the nearer Heeyoon, who fell unconscious. The other Heeyoon moved toward Etsane, one paw-hand drawing his blaster.

It never even occurred to her to use the blaster—instead her reaction was automatic, just as it had been back in the hills above Gonder. Snap! Her stone hurtled toward him, but the alien, warned, had a Heeyoon's quick reflexes, and he managed to dodge her throw.

He aimed his blaster at Etsane, who froze. "Now you die!" he snarled in his own language, which, unfortunately, she understood all too well.

Blap!

Without warning, he staggered backward, blood spouting from his chest as one of the Na-Dina Guards scored a mortal hit. Etsane looked back the way she'd come, unable to see her savior. But she did see the others running up to the back corral and spreading out to defend the captives. Mahree, Teacher Mitchell, and Pokeel were a tight threesome.

"Look out!" cried one of the human women behind her. Etsane whirled, saw where the woman was pointing.

The Anuran overseer and the remaining Drnian guard ran around the tail of the transport, only to be confronted by Khuharkk' and a mass of Na-Dina Guards kneeling on the ground, rifles at the ready. The other human slaver guard, a bearded man, suddenly darted into view. "I'll cover you!" he shouted.

The Anuran and the Drnian lowered their blasters and bolted for the loading ramp. The human glared wildly at the slaves, and then, deliberately, aimed his blaster at the terrified people huddled on the ground.

Scrieee!

The man uttered a high-pitched shriek that was cut short, and suddenly half his body was no longer there. Etsane gasped in horror as the remaining half crumpled and fell.

She fought back nausea.

Blap, blap, blap! That was the rifle fire from the Sisters. Their bullets kicked up dirt just behind the fleeing Anuran and the female Drnian guard, who angled to keep the front corral between them and the rescuers as they ran toward the transport's ramp.

The Drnian male whom Etsane had downed suddenly appeared, running behind them.

A well-placed Na-Dina bullet dropped him in his tracks.

The Anuran and the Drnian had made it—zigging and weaving, they'd reached the rampway and dashed up it, just as two pulse-gun shots ricocheted off the hull of the ship.

Suddenly a high-pitched hum sounded as the unseen pilot switched on his main drive.

Mahree ran up, her blaster raised to cover the open lock. "You hurt?" she yelled at Etsane.

"No!" Etsane watched as Mahree just stood by the corral gate, not firing. "Shoot the ship! Keep it from taking off!"

"No!" Mahree kept her blaster aimed, but did not fire. "Let them escape. If they're cornered, they'll use their blasters. Or worse."

As Etsane watched, trembling with rage and hatred, the gray tube of the transport shuddered, then rose on its a-gravs, its main drive tubes glowing as the pilot prepared to push the craft away from the grassy valley.

With a rush, the ship was gone, nothing but a shrinking dot in the pale sky of Ancestor's World.

Etsane felt her legs go weak. She looked up as Mahree unlatched the corral gate and came up to her. "They *deserved* to die," Etsane said bitterly. "You should have fired that blaster at the ship. You could have disabled them, so we could have gone in after them."

Mahree looked upset by her words. "Etsane . . . if we'd disabled the ship, they could have fired their main drives here on the ground and vaporized all of us! Did you think of that?"

Etsane felt her mouth drop open in horror as she pictured what could have happened. No, she hadn't thought of that. "You're right," she whispered to Mahree. "Oh, God, you're right."

"Actually, it was Gordon who warned me," Mahree said, smiling at the archaeologist as he came over to see how they were. "I wouldn't have thought of it, but he did."

Etsane gazed at Mitchell. "You were wise, *astamari*."

Later, she sat in the shade of the stone house, exhausted, sick and trembling with reaction, and watched the mopping-up operation by the Guard Sisters. Pokeel whistle-clicked rapid-fire orders, setting up a defensive line around the stone hut and corrals, just in case the slavers tried to return with reinforcements. Doctor Mitchell went up to the ridge to move the shuttle down, so they could bring the freed slaves aboard.

Doctor Strongheart and one of Pokeel's field medics treated the wounded, including the groggy Heeyoon prisoner. Bites-Hard, it turned out, had been badly burned when the Anuran had fired his blaster at her, just as she ducked behind a boulder for cover. No one was sure whether she would survive. Etsane fervently hoped so. She was still amazed by the Guard Sister's courage at walking right into the slaver camp.

One of the captives, the Vardi, had perished from heat prostration. But sixty-one of the captives had survived, with only minor injuries.

Natual, Ttalatha, Professor Greyshine, and Mahree were ministering to the captives, comforting them, offering water and salt tablets, and helping them realize that they were finally free after their ordeal.

Khuharkk' came over to sit down beside Etsane. The Simiu's feet and hands were scraped raw from the run over the rocky ground. Violet-hued eyes inspected her. "You earned great Honor today, Etsane."

She laid her head back against the door post and fought back hysterical tears. "I don't feel very well, Khuharkk'." She mustered a quivery laugh. "I've got the shakes so bad that I can't even stand up."

"Battle is never easy," he said, "and the aftermath is often even worse than the actual event."

"No kidding," she said. "But, Khuharkk' . . . you fought well, also. You earned great honor."

It helped to remember that he was her friend, and someone she could lean on, as she had the other night.

"We earned Honor together," he said solemnly. "I would like to share our Honor always. If you agree, I would consider us Honor-Bound from this day on."

"What does that mean?" she asked. "Tell me, so I'll understand what an honor I'm being given."

"It means that from now on, your Honor is my Honor, and my honor is yours. We will fight for each other when necessary, and be friends until we are no more. Together or apart, we will always have this bond of shared honor."

Etsane nodded. "I understand. And I accept. Nothing would please me more. I will be honored to become Honor-Bound with you, Khuharkk'!"

Joy filled his eyes, and he put out his hand, gripped hers tightly. "This gives me great happiness, as well as Honor, Etsane."

They sat there together, and Etsane realized she was no longer trembling.

When the shuttle carrying the rescuers landed at Base Camp, Mahree let the others exit first. Only then did she step out onto the top of the stair ramp. She looked up, unbelieving, at the bright stars of night and the white glow of Mother's Daughter low on the western horizon. There was still an hour to go before sunrise, despite the extra time spent in shuttling the captives to Spirit and transferring them onto the *Emerald Scales* with the assistance of Captain Salzeess. When they were finally safe, she'd sent off a call for help to the CLS Irenics, and, finally, met with Krillen to turn over the Heeyoon prisoner and explain what had happened.

Had it only been eighteen hours or so ago that she and Gordon had spoken to the Council of Elders? Incredible. It felt like eighteen days. She was beyond exhaustion, beyond mere weariness, running as she was on adrenaline, coffee, and a warm feeling in her heart as she recalled the joy in the faces of the people they'd freed.

Gordon followed her out onto the top of the ramp, then waved at the retreating figures of Pokeel, the Guard Sisters, Greyshine, and all the others. "A good night's work, Ambassador. We have some brave friends, don't we?"

She nodded, sharing his exultation at their victory. "Yes, they're the best. They risked their lives for others, and, thank God, we won!"

He put his arm around her waist. "I'm too wound up to go to sleep. How about a swim in the creek? Flat Rock will be deserted at this time of day—or should I say night?"

Mahree hesitated. Instinctively, she knew that if she went with him now, their relationship would change forever. Did she want that?

He was gazing down at her, his expression suddenly anxious. She could feel how much he wanted to be with her, and discovered that she felt the same. "Okay," she said.

Together, they walked through the last of the moonlight toward the swimming hole favored by most of the camp. The night was unusually warm for Ancestor's World, as though the spirits of the Revered Ancestors were smiling upon them, pleased with their night's labors.

When they reached Flat Rock, Gordon was already unbuttoning his shirt. He tossed it aside, and then, unselfconsciously, kicked off his boots and unfastened his belt buckle. Struck by a sudden attack of shyness, Mahree primly turned her back, and heard him laugh.

"Last one in is a rotten egg!" he said, and then came the sound of a great splash.

She turned back to find him treading water in the deepest of the pools, obviously waiting for her to do the same. For a moment she considered jumping in with her clothes on, but, dammit, she was an adult, she *knew* where this was going, and getting her clothes soaked wouldn't stop it. Nor, she discovered, did she want to.

But she did step behind a huge boulder to shuck off her clothes, then she ran full tilt toward the pool and jumped.

It was cold, and she came up gasping, feeling it wash away all the weariness, all the stress of the day. The cleansing touch of the water was like a benediction. She tossed her mane of hair back over her shoulder, realizing she was grinning crazily. "Whooooo!"

She swam a few strokes, until her feet hit the sandy creek bottom. Then she lifted her feet and floated, gazing up at the stars. They were still bright, but Mother's Daughter was far down, and the faintest of glows was brightening in the east.

A hand touched her shoulder, and she floundered to her feet, finding herself facing Gordon. The expression on his face was intent, yet oddly serene. His body shone wet in the moonlight, the hair on his chest dark against the lighter skin. He stood there, not attempting to touch her further, only letting his hand rest on her shoulder.

Her nipples tightened painfully. "Gordon . . ."

"I want you," he whispered. "I care about you so much

... Mahree ... I thought I couldn't feel this way anymore. I haven't loved anyone in so long ..."

She swallowed, knowing how much that admission must have cost him. Then, slowly, she raised her hand and touched his chest, let her fingers sift through the wet hair. Rob's chest was nearly hairless, and for a moment, she felt a wave of guilt at what she was about to do.

Then he pulled her to him, not gently, and kissed her, and she forgot everything else except how much she wanted him, too ...

They made love on Flat Rock, shivering in the night air, warming each other with the heat of their joined bodies.

Their first time was urgent, their mutual arousal too great to allow them to prolong their pleasure.

But then, as Mother's Eye crept over the eastern horizon, turning Ancestor's World and Flat Rock shades of pale crimson and rose, they made love again, slowly this time, sensuously ... each delaying their release until they could hold back no more. ...

And afterward ...

I love him, Mahree realized, as she lay snuggled against his shoulder while he slept. She watched Mother's Eye ascend, and felt as though she were being torn in two. *May the Revered Ancestors help me ... may they help us both. ...*

CHAPTER 13

♦

The Chambers of
Father Earth

Early in the afternoon of the same day, Krillen of the Law
arrived at Base Camp aboard the jumpjet that Khuharkk'
had piloted through Mother Sky. The Investigator was
slowly losing his fear of hurtling through thin air, and he
wondered whether that constituted blasphemy.

His friend Mahree had relayed a call to him via Nordlund's com unit when she'd awakened mid-morning. She'd
told him that Khuharkk' was on his way to Spirit to bring
Krillen out to the Base Camp immediately. Axum, she'd
said, had something important to show all of them.

The moment he saw Philosopher Mitchell and Ambassador Burroughs, Krillen sensed that something had
changed between them. They did not touch, but the look
on their soft faces reminded him of when he had been
newly wed.

After they exchanged greetings, Krillen asked, "So what
has Axum found, Doctor Mitchell?"

"We'll show you." Together, Krillen, Gordon, and Mahree headed out of camp, down toward the landing field.
"Axum was using some of our off-world equipment to scan

for buried artifacts when she came across this," the archaeologist said, stopping beside a place where the sandy earth was newly turned.

"We didn't disturb it," Mahree was quick to add, as Gordon produced a shovel. "We just covered it up again and called you. I'm sure this must be connected with Bill's murder, though I can't imagine *how* yet."

Krillen watched as Gordon Mitchell carefully dug into the ground, moving the soil spadeful by careful spadeful. The Investigator moved forward as he saw the edge of something white that appeared to be fabric. "What can it be?" he asked.

"Wait," said Mahree. "You'll see."

Krillen stared, fascinated, as Mitchell uncovered a bundled pile of hollow metal and wood tubes and struts, and many meters of cloth. The cloth shone dully in the light of Mother's Eye, and he realized it had been treated to make it watertight. He looked at it, totally at a loss to explain what the thing could be, when suddenly, he realized what it was. "A glider!"

"Right," Gordon said. "We call them paragliders or parasails back where I come from. I used to fly one, years ago. But this one was never made on Earth. It was made here, Krillen. By a Na-Dina."

Krillen was down on his knees by this time, poking carefully at the broken glider. It had obviously been buried in haste, its struts and supports snapped so it could fit into the smallest space possible. "There are legends of the days when my people flew through Mother Sky in these," he said. "But then the Temple declared it sacrilege, and no more were built."

"The fact that Axum found this and told me about it exonerates her from suspicion, in my book," Gordon said. "She'd have no reason to show it to me unless she was innocent."

Krillen was forced to agree.

"Who among the Na-Dina would know how to build one of these, Krillen?" Mahree asked.

The Investigator blinked at her. "Only someone who was

familiar with old records," he said slowly. "Familiar with traditions from long ago. A scholar."

All of them looked at each other, and a name hung in the air, unspoken.

Beloran.

"Has anyone seen him lately?" Gordon asked.

"I haven't," Mahree said. "But he's been keeping pretty much to himself since Marshal Pokeel arrived."

"My friends," Krillen said, levering himself back up, "we must not race ahead of ourselves. If Liaison Beloran built and flew this glider, and then thought better of it and buried it here, that is suspicious, yes, but it does not prove anything beyond the fact that he was guilty of sacrilege against Mother Sky."

"But this glider . . . I'm sure it ties in with Bill's death!" Mahree insisted. "Why else would he hide it like this?"

"We cannot be sure that the Liaison built it," Krillen reminded her. "Although he must be questioned about this discovery. If I do not like his answers—and I suspect that I will not—then I will take him into custody."

"Do you think he might be working with Ortega?" Mahree asked. Then she looked at the timepiece on her wrist and cursed softly. "Damnation, I forgot! We have an appointment with Project Engineer Mohapatra today! The raid drove it clear out of my mind!"

Krillen looked once more at the broken glider. "Bury it again, please," he said to Gordon. "I must think about this. I believe it is indeed time to speak with both Infidel Ortega and Project Engineer Mohapatra."

"We're leaving right away," Mahree said. "The jumpjet should be here to fetch us any minute."

Beloran stood behind the Refectory wall and watched as the Nordlund craft lifted into the blue sky of midday, a silvery tube balancing on a yellow-orange belly flame. Inside it were Infidel Burroughs and Krillen of the Law. He'd listened to them speaking to the Nordlund pilot, expressing their wish to speak with Infidel Ortega as well as Project Engineer Mohapatra.

Well, they would still be able to see the Project Engineer. Mario Gonzales Ortega was a different matter.

The Liaison wondered what the three had been doing out at the landing field. Was it possible they suspected him of something? He'd hidden his tracks so carefully . . .

He needed to think of new ways to arrange an accident for the Burroughs Infidel—and for Krillen of the Law. Moving around the Base Camp unhindered was far more difficult since Marshal Pokeel had arrived with her troops.

No longer could the Liaison move through the night unseen. The Sisters saw through shadows as well as he. And the off-worlders now wore scanner eyeshades at night.

Not to mention the deadly pulse-guns always worn by Burroughs and her new mate, Mitchell. *May the Revered Ancestors curse any spawn that they might have* . . . Beloran thought, feeling frustrated rage trying to break free within him.

With an effort he fought it back down, though it was growing harder to keep his anger bottled up. Beloran looked down, sighed, then headed off for the tombs, where he kept watch over the doings of the black-skinned Infidel female, the one called Etsane. She was trying to translate the ancient glyphs, and Beloran feared that she might actually succeed—and what she might discover if she did.

It was bad enough that the Sky Infidels had come to his world, shaking the self-confidence of even their greatest scientists. Now the Infidels were causing the People to doubt their ancient history, their heritage. They were out to prove that all the Na-Dina glory had come from the visit of the snakelike Sky Infidels they called Mizari.

Beloran knew better. Like everyone, the Infidels were motivated by profit. They sought to influence his world, to control, to take economic advantage. Already, the Guard Sisters clicked excitedly over the long-viewing eyeshades given them by the Burroughs female. For all their noble, altruistic words, the Soft Faces would take control of his world. Take control as the People slept in the embrace of their Ponds, ignorant of the danger.

The People *must* become as powerful as the Sky Infidels.

They must fly once more through Mother Sky, as the ancient records said they had done. The need to control their own world had been shown by the astounding presence of slave-raiders on the far side of *Halish meg a-tum*. That had shocked even the Traditionalists on the Council. Beloran stopped on the sandy path, thinking about that.

Perhaps the Council would listen closer when he and his Modernist allies warned of the flood of Soft Faces that were sure to come, when the diggers of the past found definitive proof of a connection with the Mizari snake-people. What did it matter if Sky Infidels had visited before? They had left, and the People had flourished for six millennia, proud of their Royal House, proud of their devotion to Father Earth and Mother Sky, and in control of their destiny.

But now the Infidel called Etsane threatened to uncover the language of the ancients. That threatened the People with an even greater disaster than that already caused by the finding of Mizari relics beside the Barge of King A-Um Rakt. Infidel Etsane bore watching.

Perhaps more . . .

Mahree enjoyed the lush comfort of the Project Engineer's personal jumpjet. Too bad the blond hunk Captain McAllister was piloting again. The man's admiring glances at her figure were so blatant as to be insulting.

Mahree looked at Krillen as the alien squatted on the carpeted floor, the recliner seat pushed back so he could enjoy the trip Na-Dina style. The set of his fan-ears showed a mix of concern for her and distraction.

"Well?" she said in High Na-Dina, prodding at him. "Where is this drill-site we're going to see?"

Krillen curled his long tail around taloned feet, a fastidious gesture. "Not far from Base Camp, actually. About two hundred kilometers to the southwest, and deep within the Mountains of Faith. The drilling crew is doing mineral extraction not far from the Lake of Stars."

Mahree smiled to herself. "How did it get that name? The lake, I mean?"

Krillen's ears lost their distracted appearance. "The water is so pure the bottom of the lake can be seen clearly, despite its great depth. There are white calcite deposits on the bottom which resemble the stars at night, resting in the dark embrace of Mother Sky."

"What a beautiful story! Thank you for sharing it with me." Mahree glanced out the window, marveling once more at the massive range of mountains that girdled this world. According to her geological studies, this part of the equatorial range had been formed by the collision of two tectonic plates coming from opposite directions, both meeting at the equator. Other plates on the far side of Ancestor's World had been pushed apart by upwelling magma, causing the rift valley and block upthrusting of the smuggler plateau. But here, where the northern plate overrode the southern one, that meeting had created an Andeslike range.

Mahree had always liked snow-capped mountains, and it seemed they were heading deep into such an alpine embrace. She looked back to Krillen. "Well, our discovery today gives us both something to think about. Is that why you're so quiet?"

Krillen fanned his ears negatively. "Just arranging my questions in my mind. The ones I will ask Ortega, and his human crew boss."

"What do you plan to ask him?" Mahree thought the Na-Dina Investigator was sometimes too tentative when dealing with aliens, including humans. Though his bland manner and methodical pursuit of evidence could solve and had solved many cases, she was used to faster action.

The Investigator blinked slowly. "You are impatient with me, my colleague. Have you lost faith in Krillen of the Law?"

"Oh no!" She'd have to be more careful with her expressions. "I'm just used to . . . to a human approach to crime-solving."

"Perhaps you are used to relying on devices to solve problems for you?" Krillen stared at her, taking the sting from his comment. "The mind is always the best device for solving cases. Don't you agree?"

Mahree nodded. "I do. And you've done wonderfully, tracking down this suspect Nordlund pilot. How can I help?"

"By watching," Krillen said. "When I speak with this human, Ortega's crew chief, a male named Joseph Wozniak, I wish you to observe his expressions. I search for signs of lying, or truth-telling. Or the hiding of something."

She nodded again. "Sure. I'll keep an eye on him." The seat vibrated under her as the belly-jets came on preparatory to landing. "My, that was fast." Mahree looked out the window, catching sight of the lake's blue depths and a landform she thought she recognized.

Krillen leaned over to look out the window. "The jump-jet travels swiftly indeed."

She pointed at a long fissure that ran down the middle of the Mountains of Faith. "Changing subjects, that sure looks like a thrust fault-line to me. See how narrow the fissure valley is? Wonder why Nordlund is drilling on a fault?"

Krillen stood. "I will ask that question of Driller Wozniak." Bending down, the Na-Dina removed a bronze writing slate from his supply bag.

Mahree would have said more, but Captain McAllister opened his drape, looked her up and down again, then smiled that perfect white-toothed smile. "Your carriage has delivered you, Ambassador. Watch your step."

She turned away from the man, tempted to say, "And you watch yours, Captain," but managed to restrain herself. Then she followed after Krillen as her colleague led the way along the aisle, down the stair-ramp, and out into a *freezing* wind that swept up the narrow valley they'd landed in.

A burly, middle-aged man awaited them. He stood beside a six-wheeled, open-topped crawler, wearing a padded jacket, muddy pants, and steel-toed work shoes. A second jacket was stuffed under his arm. The man, who also wore a construction helmet, walked up to her and Krillen. He offered her the padded jacket. "Ambassador Burroughs? I'm Joe Wozniak, and here's a cold-weather coat for you.

Can't do anything for the bare legs, though.''

Mahree shivered in the brisk mountain wind, cursing her stupidity in not changing into pants. But she'd been so rushed!

First, waking up with Gordon this morning, eating a late breakfast together in his tent, and then making slow, passionate love . . .

They'd barely finished when Axum had called them on the com unit, demanding that they come and see her "find." Then Mahree had called Krillen . . .

Still, she should have remembered that traveling to an elevation of four thousand meters meant it would be cold, even on the equator. She accepted the jacket gratefully. "Thanks, Mr. Wozniak. That was very thoughtful of you." Pulling it on, she told herself that her knees were *not* turning blue.

Krillen waited beside her, his only reaction to the freezing wind a lowering of his squat. "You are cold?" His ears showed surprise. "Well, you should have been born with scales. Mother Sky has blessed the People with armor that turns aside this wind."

Wozniak wore a voder earring under his white helmet. The thickly bearded man watched her with pale brown eyes, seeming nervous about something. What? she wondered, making a mental note to mention this to Krillen.

"You're the crew boss for this drilling operation?" Mahree waved at the pile of metal framework rising in the distance behind Wozniak, a pyramid-shaped enclosure of ribbing that sat atop a rust-red steel support base. Inside it pumps pumped, pipes ran in many directions, alien and human workers walked, climbed and ran, and from it echoed a surging *thump, thump, thump* as the whole enterprise drilled.

Their host waited for her to look back, then he nodded. "Sure am. Worked ten years as a mud chemist on a rig in the arctic of Novaya Rossiya, then five years as boss of an oil rig in the jungles of NewAm. Now I'm playing Big Momma to a multispecies crew that misses the bright lights of Jolie." Wozniak grinned wider, then turned serious. "How can I help you, Ambassador?"

She nodded at her colleague. "Actually, you can help Investigator Krillen. He's in charge of the investigation into the murder of the first CLS Interrelator on this world, a former student of mine. Perhaps we can talk while riding down to your drill-site?"

"I don't know anything about the murder," Wozniak said, then turned and bowed to Krillen, one arm slapping his barrel chest. "Investigator Krillen," the man said politely. "My boss the Project Engineer says we are to cooperate with the people of Ancestor's World. If you'll follow me, we'll get this buggy moving and then we can talk."

Krillen rose from his squat. "Excellent. Does this 'buggy' stay affixed to Father Earth, or does it fly through the air?"

Wozniak laughed, a rumbling laugh that Mahree found engaging. "Stays on the ground. Winds are precarious up here. After you, Ambassador?"

She climbed into the rear bench seat of the enclosed crawler, leaving the front to Krillen and the crew boss. The man got in, slapped on the power, grabbed the steering yoke, and wheeled them around toward the gray steel pipes of the drilling rig. "It's a bumpy ride, but not so bad we can't talk," Wozniak said. "Investigator? You had questions?"

Krillen nodded human-style. "Yes. Your personnel record indicates you are a pilot, with a Level Two license. And that you know how to fly jumpjets. Is that true?"

Mahree watched carefully, her position behind Krillen giving her a clear view of the crew boss's facial expressions. Wozniak looked startled, then puzzled. "That's true. Learned to fly a jumpjet on NewAm. The equatorial jungles are tough on ground vehicles. So?"

"Is this unusual?" Krillen asked. "For a crew boss in your position?"

Wozniak pursed his lips. "Not really. The more varied your training, the better your chances for advancement in a big construction company. Nordlund Combine is one of the biggest in this sector of space.''

The crew boss guided the crawler around the embankment of an earthen holding pond, inside of which lay a brown-streaked gray fluid. "So why did you ask me about whether I'm a pilot?''

"Actually," Mahree said, "we're more interested in someone who works for you piloting full time. Mario Gonzales Ortega.''

Wozniak jammed on the brakes and then turned to face them, his face pale beneath the weathering. "You want to know about Mario?'' he asked blankly.

"Yes. We'd like to speak with him, if possible.''

"Madame Ambassador, that's going to be real difficult to arrange," Wozniak said grimly. "Mario was found dead day before yesterday. He got drunk, fell into the lake, and drowned, poor guy.''

Mahree gasped, and then glanced at Krillen. The alien betrayed no surprise, and she wondered if he'd actually expected to hear this.

"Did you report his death to the planetary authorities?'' Krillen asked haughtily, his tail twitching with irritation. "Because I was not informed, and I should have been.''

"Of course we did," Wozniak said indignantly. "Liaison Beloran was up here on a site visit, and we informed him immediately. If he didn't tell you about it, Investigator, that's not Nordlund's fault.''

"I shall have to speak with Beloran," Krillen said. "Very well, then, Crew Boss, you did follow proper procedure.''

This just gets deeper and deeper! Mahree thought. *Was Ortega's death an accident? Or murder? Did Beloran have anything to do with it?*

"Did Pilot Ortega have a habit of drinking too much, Mr. Wozniak?'' Mahree asked, as the man started up the crawler again.

"Unfortunately, he did. Drinking and gambling were Mario's two weaknesses, though he was a good pilot. Never had any trouble with him piloting under the influence, though. He stayed sober when he was working.''

So Ortega's death might have been accidental, Mahree thought.

"So," Wozniak continued, "why'd you want to talk to him?"

"Because," Krillen said bluntly, "Interrelator Waterston was found dead in a jumpjet, which the murderer had to fly after killing him. I have checked the records for all the Nordlund pilots, and only Ortega did not have a solid alibi at the time of the murder. So I wished to question him.''

Wozniak nodded slowly, his tenseness easing. "Well, that makes sense. Anything else?"

Krillen glanced at her, then leaned toward Wozniak. "Yes. Have you ever visited the Blue Pond area? West of the dam site?"

The crew boss thought a moment as he drove the crawler toward the drilling rig. "No," he said finally. "I've traveled around a lot with the mineral surveyors, doing their remote sensing thing, but I haven't been to that part of Ancestor's World. Why?"

Mahree smiled. Krillen was definitely not used to interrogation subjects asking questions in return. The Investigator hissed irritatedly. "Because that is the place where the jumpjet landed!"

"Oh." Wozniak seemed puzzled by Krillen's tone.

"Mr. Wozniak," Mahree said. "We heard that Mario Ortega lost a lot of money gambling here on Ancestor's World. Did he owe you money, by chance?"

A wash of red ran up Wozniak's face, starting from his bull neck. "Hell, no!" he protested. "And I don't like what you're implying, Ambassador!"

"What is she implying, Crew Boss?" Krillen asked, with deceptive mildness. "We have heard a great many things about Pilot Ortega. Which of them are you referring to?"

"Well . . . maybe I spoke out of turn," Wozniak said uneasily. "But you're wrong if you think what I think you're thinking, Ms. Burroughs."

Mahree waited, silent. Krillen had taught her to appreciate the value of silence when trying to obtain information.

And it paid off. After nearly a minute's silence, Wozniak blurted, "Listen . . . all I did was pay Mario a little extra for a couple of bottles of vodka he brought in from Main Camp! It gets cold up here, and a little shot every night warms a fellow up. That's all! I swear!"

Mahree could believe that. Krillen seemed content to let her lead the questioning. "Did Ortega do much contraband smuggling?"

They neared the outskirts of the rig site. Wozniak's shoulders eased their tense set. "Smuggling? It's not like that at all, ma'am. He just did some booze peddling, here and on other supply flights. Though he always seemed to have lots of money on him."

Krillen's ears perked up. "More than you would expect from alcohol importing?"

Wozniak rubbed fingers through his beard. "How the hell should I know? I wasn't his accountant."

Mahree frowned. Could Ortega have had a link with the Sorrow Sector artifact-looters? Money in exchange for information about new archaeological finds? Or could Beloran have been paying him, perhaps for teaching the Liaison to fly a jumpjet? Whatever the connection, it had died with Ortega. Glancing out the crawler's side window, Mahree spotted something strange. "Mr. Wozniak, what are those big tanks for?" She pointed at a group of four giant cylinders that stood on end and were connected to the drilling platform by thick piping. Other pipes connected them with the embankment ponds that flanked one side of the drilling platform.

Wozniak turned tense. "Those tanks are where we mix the chemical 'mud' we use in drilling. It's a fluid that is pumped down the drill hole, to where the diamond-bit drill heads are cutting. It serves to both cool the heads and to draw off the fragments of drilled rock." They pulled up to a red-and-yellow-striped shack, and the crew boss shut down the crawler. "The fluid returns up the drill shaft, flows into the settling ponds where the debris drops out, runs next through a solid particle filter unit, and is then pumped back into the tanks. Our recycling efficiency is very high.''

Krillen seemed bored by her question. Mahree would have been too, except for the man's tense reaction. ''It's pumped back by those pumps over there?'' She pointed to a series of six pumps that were each as large as a jumpjet.

Now Wozniak looked really worried. ''Uh, uh, yes ma'am,'' he said, stuttering somewhat. He licked his lips. ''Uh, inside this shack is where we control the mud mix and monitor the drill head temperatures. Come on inside and I'll show you around.''

Krillen followed the crew boss out of the crawler. Mahree started to do so, realized her knees were half frozen, then forced them to flex. Stumbling after the other two, she entered the mud shack. The thumping racket outside moderated to a dull thud indoors. Four technicians—a human male, a Heeyoon female, and two Drnians—sat before a panel of electronic controls that lined one wall of the shack. At least it was warmer inside. Mahree stepped closer to the crew boss. ''Uh, Mr. Wozniak, aren't those pumps rather large to *just* be pumping fluid up and down the drill hole?''

At the control panel, one of the Drnian technicians overheard and looked back their way. Her large red eyes caught sight of Mahree's collar speaker, part of her CLS-issue voder. ''Oh, they're not, ma'am. They're used primarily for injection fracturing of the ore vein.''

Wozniak cursed, then eyed Mahree nervously when she turned to him. ''Sorry, Ambassador. You get used to hard language working at places like this.''

Krillen had noticed the man's reaction, and now her own response. Mahree fixed the bearded man with an unblinking stare. ''Crew Boss, just *what* is Nordlund drilling for here? What are you mining?''

Wozniak's mood grew distinctly uneasy. ''Uh, we're drilling for core samples. There's a vein of beryllium and cesium a thousand meters down and we're testing its purity.''

On the far side of the room, the Drnian female technician looked surprised, then turned her attention back to her panel when Wozniak glared at her. Mahree had had enough. "Mr. Wozniak, if you do not *tell* me, fully and completely, exactly what this drilling rig is doing here, in the middle of a *thrust fault* fissure, I will demand that the Project Engineer tell me. And I shall tell him that *you* were the one who spilled the beans."

The man shifted from one foot to the other, openly distressed. "Well, yes, ma'am, we are using injection fracturing to open up the ore vein. And we're already doing some side-slant drill-mining of the ore body. Later, we'll send down robot miner cars."

Krillen's ears flared widely. "You will send *unliving* devices down into the chambers of Father Earth?" His tone sounded scandalized.

Wozniak nodded. Mahree pointed at one of the shack's dusty windows, beyond which loomed the rank of giant pumps. "Mr. Wozniak, I studied geology. I've heard of injection fracturing. It was once used on Earth, in old oil and gas fields, to fracture the rock and allow for an easier flow of gas or oil. It extended the life of those fields by decades." She lowered her hand. "But they pumped steam into the rock strata. You're pumping this 'mud' stuff. Why? What are you mining?" She folded her arms across her chest and stared at him.

She counted to ten, silently, then said, "All right, fine," and headed for the door.

"Ambassador Burroughs! Wait! Sheesh, I'm sorry!" Wozniak was openly distressed. "Please. We're not doing anything wrong. The Na-Dina sold us the mining rights, and we're just—"

"One more time, Mr. Wozniak," Mahree interrupted. "And then I go and see Mr. Mohapatra and I call for a team of CLS mining experts to come and investigate your entire operation. Tell me."

Wozniak gulped audibly. "Uhhhhh," he said.

Mahree stared at him, waiting. Wozniak looked so upset that she almost felt sorry for the big man. "We're using mud in the fract job to hold down the radiation flux of an adjacent uranium ore body."

Mahree frowned. "Why is radiation flux damping important?" Again she waited.

The man swallowed. "Because of the radonium."

"What!" Mahree stared at the window above the control panel, where the steel framework of the drilling rig rose up. "You're drilling for *radonium*? Here? On a fault line? And next to a uranium ore body!"

"Yes, Ambassador. But there's no danger of it turning into radonium-two and going hypercritical!" Wozniak wrung his hands, his manner agitated. "The mud chemical mix includes a neutron inhibitor. And the radonium ore vein is separate from the nearby uranium body. Uh, the fault line action has mixed beryllium and cesium in with the radonium. So we *are* mining all three minerals."

Mahree felt faint. No wonder the Nordlund Combine had committed to the massive expense of building the giant earthfill dam on the River of Life! They would more than make back their expenses if the radonium vein in the heart of the Mountains of Faith turned out to be commercially viable. They could kiss off the beryllium and just ship casket after casket of stable radonium-one off-planet, each casket neutron-shielded to avoid a runaway hypercritical reaction.

Stable radonium-one was the fuel that made the transit to metaspace possible. Without it, there would be no Stellar Velocity starships. The ore was very rare, very valuable, and very tricky to mine. If exposed to neutrons, radonium-one mutated into radonium-two—and exploded, more powerfully than any bomb.

Mahree had studied a lot about radonium, especially when they'd had that crisis at StarBridge Academy three years ago. Rob had been sick with worry that the entire asteroid would be blown to smithereens, along with all of his students. Before the crisis had ended, they'd wound up evacuating the whole school.

Mahree had a feeling that she'd just discovered what Bill Waterston and Project Engineer Mohapatra had argued about. And it was a big secret, an important secret. One that the PE might have been willing to keep at all costs . . . including ordering Bill's death.

Krillen was looking at her, his expression puzzled. "Radonium? What substance is this?"

"The power that fuels our Sky ships, and takes us from star to star." Mahree turned to Wozniak. "The inhibitor chemical is regularly recharged? The radiation monitors are checked frequently? They're within noncritical parameters?"

"Yes, yes, yes!" Wozniak glared at the Drnian female technician who'd frowned at his statement. He turned to Mahree, hands held up defensively. "Honest! We're not fools here. The mud holds down the neutron flux of the drilled aggregate, then drops it into the holding ponds, and from here we ship it to a processing plant near the dam site. We have intensive quality controls at every step."

Mahree nodded slowly, accepting the man's reassurance. She would shortly be talking to Project Engineer Mohapatra and would have her own chance to verify his statement. "Fine. Your radonium controls are state of the art. But what about this injection fracture drilling of yours? Liquid injection has been known to free up shear faces in a fault, thus setting off minor earthquakes. Couldn't the same happen here?"

Wozniak's dismay lightened. "No, oh no. Not here. Anyway, feel that?" He pointed to the stone floor, where the ground rumbled in the fifth minor tremor that Mahree had felt since landing in the jumpjet. "This planet is constantly quaking. Part of that's due to subduction diving by the southern tectonic plate under the northern one." He grinned, his black beard spreading wide. "That's how the scalies got the Mountains of Faith in the first place! So what does one more quake matter?"

Mahree doubted the man's glib reassurance. Drilling on fault lines could be done safely, but only with great care. What she hadn't known were the true stakes at play in Nordlund's presence on Ancestor's World. Radonium made a big, big difference. She prayed Sorrow Sector didn't know about this trade secret, then waved to Krillen. "Investigator, if you are done with your questions for Crew Boss Wozniak, I need to consult with the Project Engineer. On the radonium and on this entire drilling operation. This is now a CLS matter, not just a Na-Dina issue.''

Krillen eyed the upset crew boss. ''Driller Wozniak, I do hope you will hire a knowledgeable female to guide you in your explorations of Father Earth. Otherwise, the Lake of Stars might cover you sooner than you think.''

The man nodded nervously, then led the way out of the control shack and into the cold wind.

Damn. Her knees had just defrosted. Hunching her shoulders, Mahree trudged after her Na-Dina colleague, wondering if she would be able to walk up the jumpjet stairs.

Project Engineer Mohapatra welcomed Mahree into his office with a big smile, then bowed low to Krillen when the Investigator walked up to stand at her side. Unable to help themselves, they both stared at the wide window behind the man. It showed a bird's-eye view of the Great Dam.

The dam site lay between buttresslike sandstone walls that soared a hundred eighty meters from river bottom to canyon rim, each wall flanking either end of a wide trench cut deep into the yellow stone that had once underlain the River of Life. For now, a red clay and gravel diversion dam rose just upstream of the kilometers-wide trench, holding back a small lake that had formed when the river was diverted. This smaller dam, itself three kilometers long and thirty meters high, would eventually be part of the footing of the much larger main dam.

Until that bigger structure was built, this one served to divert the River of Life sideways into a tunnel bored into the western canyon face, from which it spurted a half-kilometer later, running back into the original riverbed. In the great space lying between the canyon wall buttresses, people were black specks and earthmovers were brown dots. There were hundreds of specks and dots. The size of the undertaking staggered her.

Project Engineer Narasimhao S. M. Mohapatra was still

smiling when Mahree looked his way. He was a middle-
aged Hindu with coal-black hair, intense brown eyes, and
the manner of a maharajah. "Impressive, is it not?" he said
smoothly. "I suspect that even Emperor Ashoka Vardhana
would have been proud of our efforts."

Krillen did not understand the engineer's reference. Mahree did so only because one of her in-service students on
Shassiszss had been a reclamation engineer from India's
Maharashtra state, who loved to talk about her land's ancient history.

"Perhaps so." Mahree was glad that she'd made Mc-
Allister take her by the Base Camp so she could don her
Interrelator's uniform. Proper attire did help in maintaining
one's dignity. Not to mention that her knees had been red
and chapped after her visit to the Lake of Stars.

Mahree folded her hands in front of her, then dipped her
head. "The emperor's efforts at restoring the great dam and
reservoir of Girnar were indeed a wonder. But this is a
different world, a different people, and I'm wondering why,
again, I see drilling rigs at work." Mahree pointed through
the tinted window to where a caterpillar-tracked rig crawled
across the immense expanse of beige and yellow rock lying
between the canyon wall buttresses. The rig resembled a
beetle lost on a house floor.

Their host's expression froze a moment; then he gestured
to one of the chairs in front of his desk. "Please sit and
relax, Ambassador. All your questions will be answered in
due time." The man faced Krillen, touched his forehead,
then his chest, and bowed respectfully. "Investigator Krillen of the clan Moon Bright, you honor me with your presence. May I offer cool water and share with you the salt of
my home?"

Krillen's ears fluttered with the sign of cautious respect.
"And you, Project Engineer Mohapatra of the clan Human,
are most generous in your offer. Water only, please."

The engineer looked her way. "Your choice of refresh-
ment, my dear?"

"Iced tea with lemon, please," she replied.

"Of course." Still standing, Mohapatra touched a record

slate lying on his desk, and ordered refreshments.

Mahree sank into a thick-cushioned chair placed just a few meters back from the PE's carved teak desk. Their host also sat, his light brown face carefully schooled to an expression of pleasant professionalism. She reminded herself that Nordlund was a legitimate if overly slick corporation, with projects on a dozen CLS worlds. Then she accepted British tea from a male aide who entered, and watched as Krillen took the proffered bowl of water. The bronze vessel bore Hindi script along the rim, and scenes on the side from the story of Rama and his friend Hanuman, the god of good fortune.

She lifted her eyebrows, drawing the engineer's quick notice. "I trust you do not rely on the luck of Hanuman to ensure the safety of the dam you are building."

Mohapatra's thin lips curved slightly. "Of course not. We are a very modern, very sophisticated construction company, Ambassador. We have earned a reputation for reliable work."

"Is that so?" Behind her the aide exited, closing the outer door of this very luxurious office, a place sitting atop a bluff on the east side of the dam.

Mahree decided to be direct with the Project Engineer. "I just returned from your drill-mining site near the Lake of Stars. You're mining radonium there. And perhaps elsewhere." Mohapatra's professional look did not waver. "Why didn't you report this to the CLS Council on Shassiszss? It's a requirement of your commercial license to conduct interworld commerce."

Mohapatra steepled his hands on the teak desk top, his manner calm. "We have. Nordlund has, I mean. Five months ago, when our drill cores confirmed our remote sensing readings, they made a report to the CLS."

That could not be. Mahree had been on Shassiszss at that time and such news would have made its way to her, if only because a human corporation was involved. But the engineer was not a man to be caught in an outright lie. "Perhaps it was sent. But I was on Shassiszss at the time, and heard nothing. Can you explain?"

Mohapatra's dark brown eyes glimmered, as if he knew exactly what she thought. "The presence of radonium on this planet is a commercial trade secret of *great* value to Nordlund. That is why we did not place a holo-tank call to the CLS Ministry concerned with off-world commerce. One of our supply ships left for Shassiszss Station, with a hand-carried copy of the report."

The engineer looked at the clock on his desk, pursed his lips thoughtfully, then smiled coolly at her. "It is a one-month trip from here to Shassiszss, true; however, our ship had to report back home to Earth, have the report approved by management, then made its way to Shassiszss, by way of intervening stops at Hurrreeah, the Apis Worlds, and the Ri homeworld. It's sure to reach Shassiszss very soon now."

Mahree wanted to curse, yell, and stomp her foot. She didn't. Nordlund had assigned a diplomat-engineer to Ancestor's World, one well schooled in the ways of meeting the letter of CLS law while skirting its spirit. "I *do* hope the report holo-cassette has reached Shassiszss by now." She looked out the window behind the man. "Now, what about the drilling rig out there, in the trench you're excavating for the dam axis. What's its purpose?"

Krillen had been quiet during her radonium word-fencing, but now his ears declared his own curiosity. "Yes, Project Engineer, I wondered the same. Do you mine radonium from under the River of Life?"

Mohapatra shook his head, his expression bemused. "No, not at all, Investigator." The man turned in his high-backed chair, waving at the deep trench cut into the rock bed of the river. "Actually, there are *five* drilling rigs doing hydrocutting in the trench. They drill holes into the basement sandstone, down which a separate crew pumps grout." The Engineer turned back around, then explained when he saw Mahree and Krillen's confusion. "I'm sorry. *Grout* is a slurry mixture of concrete and water that is pumped under pressure into the sandstone base under the dam axis. Also into the canyon wall abutments on either side of the riverbed. It's a standard engineering practice," he said casually, reacting to Krillen's agitation.

The Na-Dina stood and whipped his long tail. "You pump liquid rock into the chambers of Father Earth? Whatever for?"

Mohapatra paused, waiting until Krillen calmed. "My Esteemed Krillen, I'm sorry to upset you. I had assumed that because your people were so advanced in constructing stone block, concrete arch, and earthfill dams of your own that you were familiar with this technique."

Krillen scowled. "Our females at the Temple of the River may indeed know of it. I don't. Explain this grouting."

The Project Engineer smiled broadly, as if preparing to impress a second-year engineering student. "Why, the grout is used to seal small cracks and holes in the sandstone. Even though this rock is nicely dense, with a Mohs' scale hardness of three-point-five, still, all sandstone has fracture joints and places where water can penetrate."

Mahree sank lower in her chair, listening to the man's glib explanation, but feeling more and more like something was being hidden from them.

"So we pump grout into the rock, under pressure, to make a vertical grout curtain," the Hindu said. "The grout also spreads out horizontally, following along natural joints. It hardens quickly. The grouted sandstone is now protected from water 'piping' through the joints and eventually undermining the clay core of the dam. Clear?"

Mahree thought it was clear as mud. "Fine. This grout curtain stops water from seeping around to either side of the dam, or underneath it. But, Engineer, what about *faults*? Did your drill cores show any underneath the dam site?"

Mohapatra's expression froze for just an instant. "Of course not, Ambassador. Ultrasound echo mapping of the strata underlying the First Cataract show a seamless block of sandstone, dipping slightly downhill, in the direction of Spirit." The engineer smoothed his perfectly coiffed hair. "Drill cores were taken from either side of the canyon, and in the axis trench. We found no evidence of recent rock slippage."

Krillen's ears showed puzzlement. "Engineer, Father Earth shakes all the time. Thus, the earth moves. What do you mean?"

Their host turned his attention from Mahree to the Investigator. "Krillen of the Law, you are correct. But just because the ground shakes does not mean the stone underneath the diversion dam, or the main dam trench, moves itself. The quaking of Father Earth usually originates some distance away, in the Mountains of Faith and very deep down, in the vicinity of where the southern tectonic plate is subducting under the mountains." The engineer smiled confidently.

Mahree knew just enough geology to follow the man's calm explanation. "I'm sure you're correct about the earthquakes, Mr. Mohapatra. But tell me, why was *this* site chosen? Why not farther south, and farther up the River of Life?"

The calm certainty in the man's face never wavered. "Because this is the last place where the river canyon exists. Beyond this spot, the land downstream flattens out, the canyon disappears, and there is nothing between here and Spirit but a wide valley full of extensively farmed bottomland." Mohapatra smiled again. She was getting sick of that smile. "You see? I promised that all your questions would be answered."

Mahree nodded curtly. "Engineer, that bottomland you mentioned. Its fertility depends on annual flooding by the River of Life, which deposits new silt on old fields. Those fields feed twenty million Na-Dina living along the river, and over a hundred million in the delta." She paused, wishing something she said would shake the man's self-assurance. "Just like the Nile did in Egypt for four and a half millennia—until the Aswan High Dam blocked the silt-carrying waters. Won't this dam cause the same loss of fertile silt to the farms?"

The man's chin trembled, as if he was becoming tired of her negativism. "Ambassador, the art of dam-building has improved in three centuries. The design of the dam's clay core, besides including the standard drain pipes for seepage control, also calls for ten concrete conduits lined with magnetohydrodynamic pulsators. They will lift the silt-laden bottom-waters up and over the crest of the dam.''

''Oh.'' Mahree felt totally embarrassed. Standing up, she gestured to Krillen that they should leave. The Project Engineer also rose, his look solicitous.

The engineer bowed slightly. ''We are professionals, madam. The silt problem is well known, and we warned the Elders of it before the contract was signed. The MHD units will ensure the continued fertility of the Forty-Sixth Dynasty's farming heartland. Plus provide irrigation water for opening up arable depressions lying near the river. Satisfied?''

Mahree wasn't. ''What was your relationship with Pilot Mario Gonzales Ortega?''

Fury showed briefly in Mohapatra's dark eyes. ''He was my employee. Now tragically dead as a result of a fatal character flaw. Nordlund Combine is paying proper death benefits to his family. *Now* are you finished?''

She blinked as if astonished. ''Death benefits? You mean his income from contraband smuggling wasn't sufficient?''

Mohapatra almost said something rash. Instead, his facile face showed hurt innocence. ''I do hope, Ambassador, that the CLS will not try to besmirch the memory of a fine employee.''

Mahree smiled sweetly at the engineer. ''Project Engineer, you have been most helpful. Investigator Krillen and I can find our way out. We will return your jumpjet to you when the Na-Dina Council of Elders has no further use for it. Have a pleasant day.''

Mohapatra did not reply. But his eyes said volumes.

She turned to leave the office. Beside her, Krillen's ears showed him curious to learn why she had just insulted the Project Engineer. Mahree would explain on their way to Spirit. She was overdue on her promised call to Claire and Rob, and the FTL communicator at Bill's old embassy office would do quite nicely. She also planned a separate call to Shassiszss, and for once she wasn't concerned about industrial espionage.

Nordlund was playing too fast and free with their assurances, and the presence of radonium here raised the stakes for the CLS. Her office on Shassiszss should be able to dig up the original survey report of a certain Mizari exploration ship. The one that came here on the heels of Nordlund's bland announcement of an invited First Contact, their contract, and oh, by the way, we just happen to be building the biggest dam in the Known Worlds.

Then maybe the iron face of Narasimhao S. M. Mohapatra would crack.

CHAPTER 14
♦
The Champollion Key

Mahree fidgeted in the uncomfortable chair. She was in a private office of Bill's leased embassy, in downtown Spirit near the Ministry of Dynastic Affairs. The embassy was part of the Temple of Administration. The Ministry's diplomatic office lay outside the Temple itself and just a few hundred meters from her embassy building. The Na-Dina housekeeper had let Mahree and Krillen into the building, explaining that the local Na-Dina trade representatives were downtown meeting with the Minister.

Mahree had then had taken her leave of the Investigator. She needed privacy. Her foray into the plush, scented office of the Project Engineer had left her feeling ill at ease, even angry. Reaching for the desk's holo-tank control pad, she started to code in her call to Shassiszss, but was stopped by a red busy light. She tapped the office intercom.

"Doseen, why is the FTL line blocked?"

"Because," the housekeeper replied, "there is an incoming call on the Horn That Calls The Stars for you, Ambassador. From a Robert Gable of StarBridge. Do you accept?"

In spite of her surprise, she said, "Of course."

Mahree watched the air above the tank shiver, then deep-

ened into a three-dimensional image of Rob's office. He sat
with his cat Bast in his lap, his legs crossed, his manner
casual and friendly. He looked terrific, she thought, and she
realized—for the first time—how much she'd missed him.

"Hi, beautiful!" he said cheerily, even as Bast meowed,
blinking warily at the image they were watching at their
end. "Thought I'd surprise you! You haven't been that easy
to reach lately."

Her face burned. "It's a wonderful surprise, Rob. It's
good to see you."

Some of the cheer left him as he studied her expression.
She felt her color deepen. "I've gotten a brief communique
from Khuharkk', so I've got some idea of the magnitude
of your task there—and I've heard about the attacks on
you." He leaned forward. "Honey, I'm worried. Of course,
you've faced tougher problems than this and walked away
grinning, but"—he shrugged self-deprecatingly—"I can't
help worrying. So I thought I'd give you some moral support, anyway."

That was Rob, always supportive, always there for her.
She felt a flush of guilt and confusion.

"So, how bad is it, Mahree?" he asked solicitously.
"You look really flustered. Did I call at the worst possible
moment?"

"No!" she said too quickly. "No, really. You just surprised me, that's all. I was getting psyched up to call Shassiszss—and that call won't be much fun. My mind was
involved with that—" She took a deep breath and tried to
collect herself. They hadn't spoken in weeks. She *was*
happy to hear from him, happy to see him. She was just
feeling a little . . . conflicted.

"In some ways, things are much better," she told him
in a steadier voice, "now that the smugglers are gone. The
murder investigation is progressing, and Gord—Doctor
Mitchell and the salvage archaeology team are doing wonders despite having to deal with hundreds, maybe thousands
of sites." She grinned and held out her arms. "And I'm
getting a great tan!"

Rob eyed her, his mood thoughtful. Bast grew impatient

and left his lap, disappearing from the hologram. "Things working out okay between you and Mitchell?"

She felt the color returning to her cheeks and opened her mouth, then thought twice about her answer. "What do you mean?"

His eyes never left her face, giving her what she always called his *psychologist's stare.* "The two of you are poles apart philosophically, politically, culturally. About the only thing you might have in common is your work ethics. Gordon can be difficult in the best situation, and you're not in the best situation now. I know you're the quintessential diplomat, but you've never suffered hardheads easily. So, I guess that's what I meant."

It was her turn to give him the stare. She raised an eyebrow. "Is it?"

One corner of his mouth turned up in a sheepish grin. "Maybe not completely. He's a pretty romantic figure. He's there. I'm here. We've been apart a long time."

Without answering his original question, she offered, "When I'm done here, I'll come for a long visit with you and Claire." It hung there between them, unsaid. "Then we can talk."

Rob blinked, then brushed at his dark, wavy hair. "Okay," he agreed, without pushing on the other topic. He flashed her an easy grin. "Claire's adjusting well to StarBridge. But she misses you. We both do."

"I miss you, too. Both of you." She felt confused, frustrated, and upset. *What am I doing? This is awful!*

As if he could read her confusion across the light-years, Rob nodded and said evenly, "Sounds good, Mahree. I'll look forward to that long visit. Stay safe. And always remember—I'm here for you."

"I know that, Rob," she said sincerely. "That's always been my one constant in life."

She waved as the connection ended and his image popped out of existence. As soon as it did, she felt more confused than ever. Tears gathered in her eyes, and she'd never felt lonelier. Over the years and the months and light-years of distance between them, Rob and Mahree had lived separate lives together. They'd both had affairs, and they'd both tolerated those interludes—most of which had occurred during their longest and most painful separations.

But in all that time, Mahree had never before come close to actually falling in love with anyone else. Her heart felt leaden with the choices before her. She loved Rob—seeing him, hearing him had confirmed that in the most graphic way possible. But Gordon fulfilled her in a way she hadn't experienced in a long, long time. Somehow, their affair had passed from a pleasant liaison into something much more serious. And this time, she was afraid that focusing on work—her usual method for dealing with her separations from Rob—wasn't going to make the need in her heart go away.

Clenching her teeth, she turned back to the console and prepared to let work take her mind from her more personal conflicts. She punched in her code for the call to Shassiszss.

Inside the City of White Stone, Etsane followed Beloran and Khuharkk' as they picked their way down a steep stone stairwell. The stairway led beneath the Great Plaza of the city. To either side, white limestone walls rose over her head, enclosing her. They followed the stairs deeper below ground, passing into dark shadows as daylight disappeared. Their hand torches cast cones of yellow light ahead of them.

Khuharkk' had been directing the excavation of a nearby temple building when one of the Na-Dina dig crew called to him. The female digger reported that the ground-penetrating radar probe had detected hollow spaces underneath the Plaza—perhaps a series of tunnels. When they pried up a paving stone half as tall as Etsane, they found the stairwell. With hand torches, record slates, brushes, and pry-bars, the three of them were the first to go down.

Khuharkk' called out, "I'm at the bottom of the stairwell. There's a tunnel ahead."

"Is it blocked by debris?" Beloran hiss-clicked.

"No," said Khuharkk', sounding pleased. "It's just a

long tunnel that leads out toward the center of the Plaza. Come on.''

Etsane wished Mahree were with them. In the week since the diplomat had returned from her conference with the Project Engineer, the two women had spent many hours together going over Mizari Four lexicons, doing comparative analysis of the Royal Tomb ideoglyphs, and making good headway in translating isolated First Dynasty Na-Dina glyphs. The translations, when linked to Etsane's own iconographic analysis of architectural styles and image symbology, were forming an understandable history of this first temple-city of the Na-Dina.

Suddenly, Beloran turned and glared at her, and she realized with horror that she had accidentally stepped on his tail. ''Oh! I'm so sorry!''

The beady black eyes of the alien glowered at her, until he turned away and followed Khuharkk'.

The unfriendly Liaison always made her feel awkward, and Etsane wondered if all Modernist Na-Dina were like him.

They continued after Khuharkk', following the twisting turns of the mazelike tunnel. Finally they turned one last corner; then the three stopped abruptly. They stood in a small rectangular chamber; in it stood the open entrances to eight new tunnels. Etsane thought they must be under the center of the Plaza now. ''Khuharkk', which one do we check first?''

The Simiu's tufted tail lowered. He aimed his light at the dusty floor of white limestone blocks. ''Remember how the steps in the stairwell had that notch in the middle of each riser? That's abrasion from Na-Dina tails. Now, look.''

Etsane stood beside Khuharkk' while Beloran moved to one side. ''I see it.'' Though each of the tunnels had a thin film of dust on the floor, tail scrape-marks showed through the film. The fourth tunnel from the left had a deeper gouge running down the middle of the darkened hall. ''That tunnel's had the most use.''

Khuharkk' laid his pry bar and light to one side. ''Beloran, do you agree that this tunnel was the most active?''

The alien's ears flared in a manner Etsane didn't understand. ''I agree. But that was six millennia ago. I am more curious as to why the Revered Ancestors chose to build with limestone. They had to quarry this stone in the Mountains of Faith, then transport it here by cart and river barge. Why not use the local sandstone?''

That put a talon on the question they'd all wondered about. Perhaps these tunnels held the answer.

The Simiu hefted the pry bar and torch, his vest jangling with its various instruments, then led the way once more.

They passed into the black depths of the well-used tunnel.

Etsane noticed its difference immediately. ''Khuharkk'! There are niches on either side—with bones inside them!''

Beloran hissed, then swung his torch, illuminating the ghostly piles of destructured skeletons. ''A catacomb! This is a burial site for commoners. And''—the alien's torch stopped at one niche, illuminating a rectangular piece of clay—''also for scribes and administrators. That is the recording tablet of a scribe, from when our people pressed styluses against wet clay to record taxes and property transactions.''

Etsane felt thrilled. Maybe these tablets would hold the key to deciphering the ideoglyphs of First Dynasty Na-Dina. ''Beloran, do you recognize the writing style?''

His ears perked up. ''I   yes! That looks like Temple Na-Dina hieroglyphs, but in an archaic form.''

Etsane agreed, judging by what she could see in the reflected light. She looked for Khuharkk'. His torch glowed dimly far down the tunnel.

''I've found something wonderful!'' the Simiu yelled.

Beloran hissed and hurried down the dark tunnel.

When Etsane reached the end of the catacomb tunnel, she followed the others into a small square room. Khuharkk' stood to one side, his torch sweeping back and forth across a white stone wall. On it were carved a series of glyphs.

''Etsane!'' Khuharkk' growled. ''That inscription seems

to be in several different languages. Can you recognize them?''

She stepped closer to the carved bas-relief ideoglyphs. The room's entire back wall was covered by the unpainted glyphs, the text arranged in three blocks, one to the left, one centered, and one to the right. The reading pattern seemed to be from top to bottom within each block.

She peered closely, completely absorbed with this latest discovery. Then she recognized it.

''This middle passage—it's identical to the First Dynasty ideoglyphs covering the wall of the Royal Tomb.'' She squinted in the dim yellow light. ''The section on the right is Temple Na-Dina. It's an archaic form, like that on the tablets we just saw, but definitely the same language used in the Temples today.''

A chill ran up her back as she moved over to the section on the left and touched it ever so lightly with her fingertips. She could barely allow herself to believe what she was seeing. ''This one—this one is—Mizari Four!''

Beside her, Beloran stared in shocked horror.

''Etsane!'' Khuharkk' moved closer, his fur tickling her bare arm. ''Are you certain?''

She clutched his furry shoulder. ''That's the key!'' Wide-eyed, she raised her torch, pointed it at the Mizari Four she had learned from Mahree, and began translating.

''*In the year when Father's Snoring had stilled and the crops—the crops were tall and green, during the reign of—of King A-Um Rakt, Father to his people, Builder of the Great Pond at Shir-Li, Reader of the stars in Mother Sky, and priest to the Ancestors of Faith,—there came—*'' She paused, then nearly danced with joy. ''I can read it! I can read it!'' She scanned the inscription, then pointed at a section. ''There! It talks about the people that came from the sky! From the description, they're unmistakably Mizari!''

Etsane turned to Khuharkk'. ''The Mizari Lost Colony *did* stop here! Finally, we have *proof*!''

''You are mistaken!'' Beloran hissed angrily.

Etsane blinked with shock, then tried to reassure the Na-

Dina. "Beloran, it's clear that your civilization, and your worship of the Revered Ancestors, was well underway before the Mizari arrived. Your people are the ones who created Na-Dina civilization—*not* the Mizari."

Beloran moved back into the shadows of the room. "You are young. Inexperienced. Your translation is incorrect. Our people were never visited by Sky Spirits. Our First Contact came in the Modern Age." Then he walked back the way they'd come, leaving Etsane and Khuharkk' alone.

"I don't understand why he's upset," Etsane said. She used her torch to light up the three blocks of glyphs. "This is just like Jean-Francois Champollion's translation of the Rosetta stone in 1822, or the translation of the Decree of Canopus stones. With this native inscription in Mizari Four, we can link it, glyph for glyph, with the undeciphered First Dynasty Na-Dina, and with the archaic form of Temple Na-Dina." She met Khuharkk's gaze. "For the first time in five thousand years the Na-Dina can translate records from the first seven dynasties!"

Khuharkk' patted her back, his touch reassuring. "I know, Etsane. I know." Her friend glanced after Beloran. "But for some reason, that frightens the Liaison. I don't know why, but he's afraid to learn what really happened at the beginning of Na-Dina civilization. Perhaps he fears cultural ramifications that we cannot understand."

Etsane shook her head, unable to fathom it. She felt only joy and the honor of being the first person to read the earliest records of a great people. That honor came only because she had been in the right place at the right time, with the right knowledge. And that knowledge had been the hard gift of her father, Mefume—and her good friend, Mahree Burroughs.

In the darkness, she thought she heard a ghostly chuckle.

On his way back to the Lab—after showing the catacomb glyph-wall to Dr. Mitchell—Khuharkk' chose the trail between the landing field and the cone-tents of the Guard encampment. Normally, he didn't come this way, preferring to keep his distance from a place overrun with *weapons*.

But after the exhilarating discoveries beneath the Great Plaza, he felt he could magnanimously ignore the metallic gleam of the rifles that stood outside the tents of the Sisters.

What mattered, Khuharkk' had come to realize, was that these females were people of great Honor, who had shown their bravery during many times. Earlier, he'd been saddened to see Bites-Hard burned so badly, so he decided to ask after her.

Pokeel looked up when he stopped in front of her cone-tent. A scroll of papers lay before her, sitting atop her low wooden desk. "Are you Khuharkk', of the clan Red Claw?"

The young Simiu felt honored by the elder female's knowledge of his clan. "Yes, I am the youngest son to the mother of clan Red Claw," he said, speaking slowly in High Na-Dina, determined to show Honor to this commander of forty fighters. "And you are Pokeel, of the clan Sharp Teeth, of the Trade Fighter, Chief Marshal of the Queen's Own Guard." He shifted his stance, feeling somewhat anxious. "Your Sister Bites-Hard was kind to me when the Guard first came here. I wished to ask about her recovery."

Pokeel laid down her flat topographic map and looked directly at him. "You speak the words of the People, rather than relying on the device of the Sky Infidels. Why?"

Khuharkk' sat back on his haunches primly, gazing up at the Na-Dina female. "Because I seek to show Honor to a people I respect."

Pokeel's ears fluttered curiously. She stared at him a long moment and he remembered not to avert his eyes, as his own customs dictated, but to respect hers. Finally, Pokeel glanced at a pot lying in the shade of the tent's awning. "And so you do, Khuharkk'. You show us honor in speaking our language. May I offer you cold tea?"

"Thank you. I am honored to share water with you." He reached into a pocket of his vest and pulled out some pills. "May I offer you some of my salt?"

"Ahhhh." Pokeel's ears fluttered again, this time in pleasure. "My salt is your salt, my water yours." She pulled out two cups from under her table, poured tea into each, and handed him one.

Khuharkk' sipped the bitter liquid and found it refreshing. "This is delicious." His mane rose as he drank. "Is Bites-Hard still in her tent?"

Pokeel sipped her own tea. "She is, but she sleeps now. The doctor from the Temple of Medicine and your own Doctor Strongheart both say she is making a fine recovery. The scales will grow back, though the pattern will be irregular."

"An Honor Scar? Surely, she will be honored by her Sisters, and perhaps the Queen herself."

Pokeel laid down her cup and folded her hands over her chest. "Perhaps. But that is not why the Sisters of the Guard fight so fiercely. We fight to show solidarity with our Sisters, so that the strength of each helps the fierceness of all. And we fight to honor the Revered Ancestors."

"So I've been told," he said in High Na-Dina, even though the hisses and clicks were far different from his language. "But I'm not sure I understand why all that you do must be done for the Ancestors?"

Pokeel looked toward the Base Camp, then to the earthen rampway that led to the Royal Tomb of A-Um Rakt. "We believe there is no separation between the world of the living and that of the dead. When we die, we remain on this world. So, of course, this is Ancestor's World." Her ears fluttered with reverence. "It is hard to see the Revered Ancestors, but they see everything, know everything, and, when we join them, they will weigh our lives on the Balance of Souls. If the Balance is good, then we join the Revered Ancestors in watching over the People. If not—" She glanced down. "If not, then we are reborn into a new egg, fated to repeat the lessons of life all over again. And again. Until they are finally learned."

"I see how our ways of Honor are similar," Khuharkk' said, ignoring the slight ground tremor. "You live before the gaze of the Revered Ancestors, showing them honor by your devotions and your honorable actions. We live our lives with dignity before each other, choosing honorable actions over dishonorable ones.''

Pokeel eyed him. "So *that* is why you fought so fiercely against the smugglers at camp and the slavers at the corrals! And your scars, they are the visible mark of your honor fights?'' Khuharkk's crest ruffled in affirmation. Pokeel wrapped her own tail around her talon-feet. "And your honor scars, this visible sign of honor you show your fellows, you show this to your ancestors as well?''

Khuharkk' answered carefully, not wanting to offend the female. "We do not believe we exist—after death.''

Pokeel looked shocked. "Oh, how tragic!''

Khuharkk' settled his mane. "What we do here and now is what matters to my people. But still, we both believe that others—dead or alive—judge our actions. Yes?''

"Yes,'' Pokeel hissed approvingly. "Tell me more about the way of honor among the Simiu. I am a student of such matters.''

"As am I myself, Chief Marshal. Let us trade stories, and understand our people better.'' Almost slurring his High Na-Dina from eagerness, Khuharkk' began telling the tales of his world, tales of Honor as old as the savannas of Hurrreeah itself.

Gordon relaxed back into his old wooden chair, his boots propped up on the Lab's conference table, listening closely as this week's share-and-compare reporting wound down. It had been two days since Etsane's outstanding discovery of the catacomb glyph-wall in the City of White Stone, and that had given everyone a powerful boost. Forcing himself not to stare at Mahree, he noted that all his colleagues seemed anxious to hear the final two reports. Even Krillen, who had elected to remain in camp while he pursued his investigations, was there, listening quietly.

Gordon nodded at their specialist in the Physical Sapientological Analysis of Na-Dina burial remains.

"Doctor Strongheart, I understand you've finished the first run of gene typing on the body of King A-Um Rakt. Did you find anything interesting?''

"Quite interesting." Her eyes swept around the table. "Using protein probes to investigate PCR-copied DNA that was extracted from the dried blood of the King, I located a number of unusual gene sequences. Though they represent only thirty-three genes out of the one hundred thousand that make up the Na-Dina genome, these genes are not natural to Ancestor's World, or its people." She paused as excitement spread around the table. "They are Mizari genes!"

At the far right, Beloran appeared upset. Etsane, Sumiko, Natual, and Ttalatha seemed overjoyed. The Shadgui Hrashoi ruffled his black fur, clearly at ease. Gordon fixed on the Esteemed Lorezzzs, whose silver and amber scales shone under the lab's fluorescent lights. "My good Lorezzzs, do you agree?"

"Of course! Of course I do!" The Mizari Ceramicist fluttered her fringe of neck tentacles, showing open delight. "Doctor Strongheart compared these gene sequences to ones taken from my own blood, in addition to standard comparisons with the Mizari medical literature. The identification is correct."

Gordon turned back to Strongheart. "Well, madam, tell us what it means to find these genes among the Na-Dina."

"With pleasure," Strongheart said, sounding triumphant. "The presence of Mizari genes among the gene pool of the Na-Dina is *not* an indication of interbreeding. It *is* an indication of their long term presence here, on Ancestor's World, for a period equal to at least one native generation."

Sumiko raised her hand. "Doctor Strongheart, how did the gene transfer occur, if not by breeding?"

The Heeyoon female explained, "Jumping genes, my dear. A feature of cellular biology observed centuries ago on your own Earth, and on the other planets of the CLS, is the occurrence of jumping genes. The chimpanzees, bonobos, and humans of your own world share an overlapping genetic heritage. In fact, all three primate species share more than ninety-eight percent of the same genetic makeup." Her fluffy tail wagged once. "It's the remaining few percent that made the difference, over time, as natural selection and evolution differentiated the three groups.''

"But that reflects *shared* evolution on a common planet,'' Eloiss the Drnian objected.

Strongheart shrugged. ''Yes. And *no*. The Mizari and the Na-Dina do *not* share a common evolution. But they *do* share a common reptilian heritage. Both species are oviparous, bearing their young in eggs. Both species have similar metabolisms and dietary customs, preferring live prey. Both also sneeze, cough, and expel moisture from their lungs. That moisture carries gene sequences within it.''

Eloiss rubbed her bulging forehead. ''Then jumping genes are those genes spread by air or tissue contact?''

"Correct.'' The wolfish alien paused. ''So both species can catch the same illnesses, as witness the Esteemed Lorezzzs' bout with sand fever when she first arrived here.'' The elderly Heeyoon grew serious. ''It's fortunate she in turn went through regular decontamination procedures before slithering out onto the sands of Ancestor's World. It's standard practice on all starships, but in this case it was critical. Otherwise, the Na-Dina could have caught a Mizari disease, one that irritates our friends but might have been deadly to the Na-Dina.'' She eyed Gordon. ''Doctor Mitchell, I recommend this potential for interspecies disease transmission be reported to the CLS Council at the earliest possible time, so all incoming ships can take extra sterilization steps.''

One more thing to worry about. ''Good point, Strongheart. Excellent genetic analysis. Anything more to report?''

"No,'' she said.

Gordon nodded to Etsane. ''Well, Chief Iconographer, what do you have to tell us?''

The girl's smoky brown eyes held barely restrained excitement. ''I've completed a basic vocabulary and grammar of First Dynasty Na-Dina.''

"What!'' Mahree looked amazed at her protégé. ''But—well, that's great! How did you make such fast progress?''

Etsane's narrow, aristocratic face opened up for a moment before she turned serious. ''Actually, Ambassador,

both projects are only partially completed. There are years
of work yet to be done. But, thanks to the Great Plaza
glyph-wall's grouping of Mizari Four, First Dynasty Na-
Dina, and archaic Temple Na-Dina, I quickly reached some
conclusions about this language." Etsane picked up the
slate and pointed it at the wall-screen. "If I may illustrate?"

Gordon folded hands over his belt buckle and nodded
amiably. "I'm really looking forward to this."

The Ethiopian faced the wall-screen. "Ancient Na-Dina
shares much in common with ancient hieroglyphic Egyptian
of the Old Kingdom. As you can see here, both styles of
writing brought together the pictogram, the ideogram, and
the phonogram." On the screen, images flicked on and off
to illustrate her points. "Like Egyptian, First Dynasty Na-
Dina evolved as a true pictorial representation of reality, a
one-for-one symbol. A house symbol for a house, a bird
for a bird, and so forth." The screen flashed again. "Like
Egyptian, the language made use of metonymic methods to
indicate concepts, like a representation of the wind by
showing a billowing sail."

More images flicked past. "With the help of the Mizari
Four panel, I tracked down the homophones in the language, so a symbol that means both 'daughter' and 'bird'
could be differentiated. The difference between the two was
shown by a generic determinative sign added to the phoneme ideoglyph, again as in Egyptian." The attractive
woman looked his way, smiling shyly. "Doctor Mitchell,
your paper on uniliteral signs in archaic Heeyoon Two was
helpful. I found similar signs in the middle text, which in
effect generated a rude alphabet of forty-six letters. Count-
ing all the ideograms, phonograms, and determinatives, I
suspect the language had a range of four thousand signs,
with wide expressive values."

Sumiko frowned, trailing fingers through her short black
hair. "That sounds like Japanese *kanji* ideoglyphs."

Etsane nodded. "Exactly!" She waved her slate at the
screen. "And the archaic Temple Na-Dina of the right-hand
text block is equivalent to the simplified, more cursive *ka-
takana* used in modern Japanese. This is a process whereby

two forms of the same sign mean the same thing.''

Etsane pointed at Pokeel, who, with Axum and the two Historians from the Temple of Records, also sat at the table. ''And, Sisters and Brother, this process is very similar to the evolution of *hieratic* Egyptian from the hieroglyphs used in the temples. Here, as in ancient Egypt, hieratic was an abbreviated form of hieroglyphs. Like Temple Na-Dina, hieratic was used in administrative, accounting, and legal documents. *Demotic* Egyptian was simply a later version of hieratic, the one which evolved by the third century A.D. into a heavily alphabetized language that became Coptic. But the phonemes were still the *same*, going back nearly three thousand years!''

Gordon heard the girl's triumphant conclusion to a long chain of linguistic analysis, something much assisted by the camp's supercomputer and Mahree's Mizari Four lexicon. But the solution was all due to Etsane's dedication. He doubted the girl had slept ten hours in the last couple of days. ''Etsane, that was a fine demonstration of chronolinguistic principles. Seems fitting that it was Champollion's knowledge of Egyptian Coptic that allowed him to recreate the phonetics of ancient Egyptian hieroglyphs, while your own knowledge of Mizari Four, and modern High Na-Dina, allowed you to interpolate the phonemic correlations between the two. Congratulations!''

Mahree raised her hand. ''Etsane, did you find much paleographic variation over time in the glyphs?''

The young woman rubbed her nose. ''Not much, but that part of the analysis is still very, very fresh. I concentrated mostly on matching up the three texts, then using the identified phonemes, uniliteral and determinative signs to translate the ideoglyphs of First Dynasty Na-Dina.'' Etsane grinned sheepishly. ''In the process of doing that, I necessarily developed the raw vocabulary and deduced the grammatical rules that differ from today's Na-Dina.''

Pokeel fluttered her ears questioningly. ''Etsane, I hear your words, but the meaning is as clear as ashfall at sunset. Does this mean you can tell us what the inscription in the Royal Tomb says?''

"Oh, yes!" Etsane thumped her high forehead. "I was so wrapped up in the process of figuring this all out, I almost forgot the most important point." She lowered the slate, folded her hands in front of her, and grinned at Gordon like a kid getting out of school early. "Doctor Mitchell, the Tomb inscription is to be read from left to right, from the top row of the seven down to the bottom row. Just like modern English."

Shaking his head, Gordon said, "Does that mean you've made a full decipherment?"

Etsane's face fell. "Not fully. I've deciphered about sixty percent of the ideoglyphs, but there are some idiomatic glyphs I'm still figuring out." She turned to Pokeel, Axum, and the two Temple Historians. "Perhaps you can look over my glyph list and tell me what you can recognize?"

Axum smiled with her ears. "I'd be happy to come by tonight, Etsane. And—thank you for opening up these hidden pages in the book of our Revered Ancestors. This is a discovery which will make all of the People rejoice."

Gordon agreed. But Beloran, judging by the set of his ears, did not. Why was the Liaison always so sour? It was as if the alien hoped his work would fail.

Fail. Could Beloran have a special reason to be mad at him? More than that common to all the Modernists? He'd always lumped the alien's attitude in with that of the Royal bureaucrats, who loved to protect their turf with bushels of rules. But now—

"Gordon?" Mahree said.

He blinked, turning away from Beloran. Etsane was looking at him expectantly. Ignoring the Liaison, he gestured to the Ethiopian. "Sixty percent translation is still fantastic. Would you read us a segment of what you've done so far?"

Etsane's wide grin returned. "I'd be delighted." Looking down at her record slate, she adjusted it so pictures of the gold foil-coated ideoglyphs appeared on the wall-screen, then started reading. "*In the twenty-sixth year of the reign of Great King A-Um Rakt, the rainbow-scaled Sky Spirits showed the People how to dig a water well deeper than*

*any in the city of Segor A-mun. With stone smelted from
the Mountains of Faith they did devise—''*

Gordon smiled as she read, reliving his own first excitement at the wonder of archaeology, and how it allowed you
to touch the people of long gone. And to share in the great
adventure of any species—the trek across time.

CHAPTER 15

♦

Father's Snores, Mother's Tears

Mahree woke up when she hit the ground, which was shaking fiercely. *Earthquake,* she thought to herself.

Dazed, blinking herself awake, she looked around Gordon's dome-tent, lit only by the flickering strobe of multiple lightning flashes. Giant booms echoed in her ears. The rush of heavy rain pounded on the tent roof. *Gordon?* Where was he? A sudden explosion of light showed him on the other side of the bunk, picking himself up from the sandy ground. "It's a bad one!" he shouted, coming toward her. The ground was lunging back and forth in an uneven, stuttering rhythm. Mahree took his hand, then fell into his arms as a whip-cracking ground shock moved under their feet.

Gordon hugged her reassuringly "We'd better get dressed and get out of here. This is the thunderstorm Krillen said he sensed building last night! We're going to have flash floods on top of this earthquake!"

Mahree sat on the ground and pulled on her shirt. "Floods? Is the Camp safe?"

Gordon had one foot in his shorts, jumping to keep his balance on the other. "Our creek is outfitted with baffles to slow the flood. They should protect us. But no one working out in the valley is safe.''

Mahree felt sudden fear. ''This quake—could it be due to drilling at the Lake of Stars?''

''Maybe.'' Shorts buckled, Gordon was stuffing his foot into a boot when the quake shuddered to a stop.

Queasy, ears ringing, Mahree felt her body thrumming as though from tiny aftershocks. Overhead, the rain beat against the roof even harder. In a moment, they were dressed.

The radio, face down in a corner of the tent, beeped weakly. Gordon caught up the unit and slapped the talk button. ''We've just had a major quake here and—''

''Mitchell! This is McAllister from Nordlund! Our signal is unreliable, so shut up and listen!'' Gordon set the radio on the table and began pulling on his safari shirt. ''We've *also* had a major quake at the dam site. The diversion dam is cracked and we're facing a possible core failure. The impound lake could breach the dam and flood downstream!''

Now dressed, Mahree rushed to the radio. ''McAllister! How could that be? The PE said there were no faults at the site!''

''He lied.'' The pilot's static-warped voice sounded angry. ''To all of us. The dam axis lies above a strike-slip fault. Maybe the grout injection freed it to slip. Maybe it was just time for it to let go. Don't know.''

''Dead people is what lying gets you,'' Gordon said to himself. Then, to the radio, ''Do your folks at the dam need help? We've got the shuttle and two jumpjets.''

''We—'' McAllister's voice died as static surged from a nearby lightning strike. ''—and haven't been able to contact the drilling crew at the Lake of Stars. The quake that just hit you was Force Seven and its epicenter was directly underneath the drilling site. Can you send someone to check on them?''

Mahree grimaced. ''McAllister, they were drilling on a fault line! If they've got contaminated radonium lying around, they could all be dead.''

The radio sputtered and sizzled, but no more words came from it. Gordon looked at her. "Mahree, I'm going to the Lab. People should be gathering there by now. Can you check on the condition of the jets and shuttle?"

"Of course." She grabbed her com unit, stuck it to the belt of her shorts, winced as thunder boomed again, then pointed down at the sodden sand. "Gordon, there's a lot of water coming from somewhere."

"Damn right there is!" He grabbed his pulse-gun holster, threw it over his shoulder. "Bet the water is cascading over the canyon rims by now." He rushed out.

Beyond the flap-door, sheets of rain turned the light of morning pale gray. Bracing herself, Mahree followed.

The rain hit her. A thundering boom bounced back and forth from canyon wall to canyon wall. In an instant her hair was soaked through. She cleared her vision just in time to see Mother's Touch reach down from blue-black clouds and strike the canyon rim, a spiderweb of yellow-white fury.

She heard Gordon shouting something, turned to see Krillen staggering toward them. They ran to meet him, slipping and sliding in the mud. Etsane's tent was the closest, and it was half down, but Mahree saw no sign of the Ethiopian woman.

A moment later, she reached Krillen, just in time to keep him from falling flat on his snout. The Na-Dina investigator was obviously injured, his eyes wide and dazed with pain.

"Krillen?" she cried, supporting him and motioning to Gordon to help. "What happened?"

"Beloran," he gasped, trying to balance on his tail, almost falling over.

"What about him?" Gordon demanded. "I looked for him before we went to bed, but couldn't find him."

"I know how he did it." Krillen sounded incoherent, almost babbling.

"How he did *what*?" Mahree asked.

"How he killed Waterston. The glider . . . it was the glider . . ."

"What? How?" Mahree demanded.

"Beloran hid the glider aboard the jumpjet before he hid

himself," Krillen said, still swaying. "Then, after Waterston was dead, he carried the glider out of the jumpjet, climbed up onto the hull of the craft—leaving the scratches we found—and unfurled the glider. Then he glided away, over the mesa, down to the nearest river port, where he took a barge back to Spirit. He had it all planned." Krillen gasped with pain and held his left leg. "I found him outside Etsane's tent at daybreak."

"Etsane's tent!" Gordon said, looking around worriedly. "Where is she?"

Krillen flinched as lightning struck nearby. "Beloran had her in his grasp, dragging her off toward the landing field. When I tried to stop him, he shot me with a pulse gun. I almost passed out, but then I saw you two."

Mahree felt her stomach grow cold as the rain. "Etsane! Was she injured? Shot?" she yelled at Krillen, her voice rising above the thunder.

"Alive!" he said loudly. "But not fully conscious. As if she'd been struck."

Gordon cursed. "If he's hurt her—"

Krillen fixed them both with a terrified stare. "Beloran is completely mad, Mahree. You and Gordon must rescue Etsane before he kills her. He said he would."

"No he won't!" Mahree said tightly. "If Beloran is heading for the back country, then he'll take his skimmer. To escape on the Royal Road. No one could find them in this storm." *Except me,* she thought fiercely. *I know where the Royal Road goes.*

Gordon nodded. "Head for the landing field! Maybe we can catch him before he reaches the Great Ramp."

"Right," Mahree said, letting go of the Investigator. "Krillen, go to the Lab. Greyshine is in charge until we return. He'll get everyone out in the shuttle if the baffles fail to stop the flash-flood."

"What about you two? The floods could drown you!" Krillen hissed, the boom of thunder battering her ears.

"We'll take that gamble!" Mahree yelled, then started forward. She tripped and barely saved herself from falling. Her boot had caught in something outside Etsane's tent. She picked it up as Krillen limped toward the Lab. Rain-soaked and slick, it was a length of tanned leather. Etsane's sling!

"Bring it," Gordon ordered. "There are times when the old weapons are useful, as Etsane has shown us."

Together, they headed for the landing field at a run.

Gasping for breath, sliding in the wet sand and from the quivering of aftershocks, Mahree nearly fell several times. Gordon reached out to her, giving her his hand, and that helped.

They raced along together, Mahree's heart pounding more in fear for her friend than from the exertion.

When they reached the landing field, they found Beloran's skimmer gone.

Gordon turned to the camp skimmer and jumped in. "Come on! We'll try to head him off!"

She tumbled into the front seat. He gunned the vehicle and they roared ahead, the fans straining, the gyros whining in protest as they fought to keep the craft level. Gordon sent the craft skimming over boulders at a speed Mahree would never have dared.

Surely, she thought, *he's a much better driver than Beloran, who only learned to drive a few months ago. But can we make it across the creek?*

"Can you see them?" Gordon yelled, slewing the skimmer around a huge, house-sized boulder. "We're coming up on Flat Rock and the creek crossing."

See them? In this storm? Mahree thought incredulously. She stood up, gripped the windshield rim, and peered into gray sheets of rain. Gordon piloted the skimmer with precision, but his hands were too tight on the control yoke, knuckles white. It had only taken them a moment to prepare the vehicle and start after the murderous Na-Dina, but the feeling in her heart was that they must already be too late. She hefted the pulse-gun that Gordon had handed her and then reholstered it, wondering if she'd have to use it.

She searched ahead for some sight of Beloran's skimmer. They'd passed Pokeel and the Guards and Khuharkk' coming in as they headed out, and now they'd just crossed over Flat Rock. The formerly tiny creek they'd so casually swum in now raged two meters deep and five meters wide. She'd never seen anything this fiercely primal, this much the image of Nature unleashed. Quake, thunder, lightning, and soon, flood. On Ancestor's World, they were the Four Horsemen of the Apocalypse.

The skimmer shook and rattled as its fans sped them over scattered rock debris of all sizes. The day began to lighten, but rain still pounded them. Mahree scanned the broken landscape unfolding before them again and again, but saw only rock of every shape and degree of erosion.

"Look!" Gordon pointed ahead and to their left, at the side canyon. "There's his skimmer!"

"After him!" Mahree cried, then almost fell as the skimmer bounced off a hidden obstruction.

"We could rip out the fans if we keep on like this!"

Mahree swayed as the skimmer hit again. "We've got to save her!" She would *not* lose another person to this alien lunatic.

Lightning flashed ahead of them, illuminating their quarry. Beloran's skimmer had made it past the first side canyon and now headed for the second and last side canyon, with its arroyo crossing. If he made it across, he'd be home free and able to get up the Great Ramp before they could catch him. Mahree pounded on the windshield. "Faster! Faster!"

Gordon looked at her as if she were crazy, but obediently increased speed.

Mahree was raging, bloodlust filling her mind and heart. *Murderer!* Beloran had killed one of her own students, one of the best Interrelators they'd ever had. If she'd had him in the sights of the pulse-gun, she'd have shot him without a moment's hesitation.

"He's slowing, getting ready to cross the arroyo."

"No!" Mahree pulled out the pulse-gun, leaned her elbows on the top of the windshield and, bracing her feet, aimed the gun's open ring-sight at the shiny silver rectangle of the skimmer.

"Mahree!" Gordon shouted. "It's two hundred meters to them! And you might hit Etsane."

She knew that. But she also knew that if she didn't act,

the alien would get away, would flee up the Great Ramp and disappear into this storm, never to be found again. She squinted, lining up the sight. "I told you . . . I was . . . a good shot . . ." she gasped, and then held her breath. She felt time stretch, felt her ears shut off, felt all her attention focus on the ring-sight and the gleam ahead. For a brief instant, it all lined up.

"*There!*"

She fired.

The blue bolt shot forward like a ball of lightning, moving so fast she could hardly see it, splashing against the rear of the skimmer. Metal shrieked. Black tendrils of smoke rose from the engine compartment. The craft swerved to the left, heading up the last side canyon.

"You got the fans!" Gordon cried out.

Mahree sagged down onto the bench seat. "Oh, God. He's going to crash."

"No, he's not," Gordon said. "He's on the auto-descend landing sequence. We've got them!"

"Watch out!" she yelled to Gordon.

Their skimmer swayed as they crossed over the raging floodwaters of the first side canyon. Briefly, they hovered above five meters of open air. Momentum and fan power carried them over to the other side. The skimmer's rubber skirts squealed as they scraped rocky ground, then went silent as Gordon controlled the bounce, lifting them into half-steady flight. Beloran's skimmer had disappeared around the edge of the canyon wall.

Mahree stood up again, careless of the storm or the wildly swaying skimmer. *Give me just one shot,* she begged the Revered Ancestors. *Just one. Let me get him!*

"There they are!" Gordon pointed as they rounded the brown sandstone wall, coming into a clear view of the side canyon.

"Where?" She looked up the curving canyon, searching the creek bottom, then scanned the boulders piled up against the canyon walls. "Yes! They're down, crashed onto those boulders." She pointed. "Beloran and Etsane are moving. They're alive!"

Gordon nodded grimly. "Alive and . . . watch out!" He swerved the skimmer and reached out to push hard against her chest, forcing her to sit.

Blue light flashed against the front of their own skimmer. She cried out, throwing up her hands. And they went down . . .

Gordon shook his head, half stunned from the auto-descend emergency landing. Their skimmer had crashed perhaps fifty meters downcanyon from the rain-slashed wreckage of Beloran's skimmer. *Mahree!* He turned in his seat.

She looked up at him, a bruise purpling under her right eye. "Gordon!"

"Mahree!" He grabbed her and held her tight. "You okay?"

"I think so," she said shakily. "How about you?"

"Yeah." Turning to look ahead, he spit out the rain that had gathered in his mouth.

Mahree looked ahead. "We've got to save her, Gordon." She made to stand up. The skimmer's crumpled metal floor defeated her efforts. She fell back to the rain-soaked bench seat with a gasp.

Gordon looked around for the pulse-guns, but his holster was empty. He couldn't find Mahree's, either. Lost in the crash, most likely.

Desperate, he grabbed Etsane's sling, then climbed out of the skimmer, his boots slipping on the rain-slick boulders that had piled up against the vertical wall of the side canyon, making a small ramp that reached halfway up to the high rim of the canyon. Gordon shook his head when Mahree tried to follow. "Stay here! Find one of the guns! This is high enough to escape any flash flooding, and with that gun you can prevent Beloran from escaping this way. Please?"

She looked at him rebelliously, her anger and her need filling her face. "Damn it!" Mahree sagged back onto the bench seat. Then she looked upcanyon. He did too, seeing as if through a gray veil. Etsane struggled now in the grasp of Beloran, trying to keep him from dragging her out of the skimmer. Mahree's words came to him clearly, despite the roar of new thunder. "Gordon, are there flood baffles in this canyon?"

He thought of lying to her, then didn't. "No. The old Na-Dina ones were washed away centuries ago." He turned from her, picking his way down the boulder ramp, trying to keep to the side of the canyon.

She called after him, her voice full of pain. "Don't die!"

He didn't plan to.

Keeping to the sheltering safety of boulders washed off the canyon rim, Gordon walked, slipped, stumbled, fell and yet still made progress toward his objective. Through the gray sheets of rain, Etsane saw him coming, a red welt showing through her slashed blouse where Beloran's tail had struck her. Not giving away what she saw, she lifted up her feet and kicked forward at Beloran, catching him in the chest. The alien staggered back, his arms flailing. The pulse-gun fell from his grasp, skittering to a stop on a boulder below the skimmer.

Now!

As Beloran turned to climb down and retrieve his weapon, Gordon rushed over the intervening space between him and Etsane.

Twenty meters.

The rain slashed his face, numbing already chilled flesh.

Fifteen meters.

Lightning flashed high overhead. Thunder instantly deafened his ears. Staggering as another aftershock shook the rocky ground, Gordon crouched, grabbed three small rocks, then rushed on.

Ten meters.

Beloran was out of sight below the skimmer, halfway between the craft's crumpled wreckage and the creek at canyon bottom. Muddy-brown waters surged out of the narrow confines of its sandy bottom, rising upward slowly.

"*Astamari!*" cried Etsane as he reached her.

He stuffed sling and rocks inside his shirt, then grabbed at her bonds, tearing at them with cold-numbed fingers. "Damn!" He turned, grabbed a metal fragment, and sawed at the bindings. The girl's feet were unbound. If he could just free her hands . . .

"Sky Infidel!"

Beloran's scream of fury made him look over the side of the skimmer. Five meters below, the rain streamed off the alien's blue-scaled body. The Liaison's taloned feet were propelling him quickly up the boulder pile on which the skimmer had crashed. The alien raised his pulse-gun, aiming at Gordon. He ducked.

Whap!

The bolt splashed harmlessly against the canyon wall behind him. They were protected by the skimmer—until Beloran reached the middle part of the boulder ramp on which his skimmer, like Gordon's, had crashed, wedging itself in among the rounded boulders.

Suddenly, the skimmer began vibrating. It was a *steady* vibration, a thrumming that was not an aftershock, not thunder, and not anything else. Except for one thing.

The bindings parted. "Etsane! *Run!* Out of the skimmer and up to the top of this boulder pile! There's a flash flood coming!"

The girl looked alarmed, then determined. She reached out to him. "Give me my sling. I will strike down Beloran!"

"No!" Gordon pushed her away and over the side of the skimmer. "You don't study archaeology and not learn how to use ancient tools. I can sling this baby almost as good as you. *Go!* I don't know why, but you're the one he's trying to kill."

Etsane tumbled out onto the boulders, but called back to him even as Gordon loaded a stone into the cup of the sling. "He said I could not live because of my deciphering of the Royal script!" Gordon peered over the edge of the skimmer.

Just three meters away, Beloran lifted up his scaly head. Black eyes fixed on Gordon. "Infidel!"

"Gordon!" Etsane yelled. "He thought if I was dead, the Mizari would leave, the CLS would leave, and his world would be stronger because of the dam and its power."

He didn't care what insanity the alien used to justify murder. Spinning the sling despite the rain and his fear, he rose up suddenly. "Run, Etsane!"

Beloran raised his pulse-gun. "Die!"

Aiming with his chin, Gordon let fly the sling stone with a *snap-thwack* that almost unhinged his shoulder. "Yeah!"

The stone hit Beloran between his eyes. Blue scales parted. Red blood ran freely. The alien clutched his forehead, crying out "Nooooo!" Then he fell backward and tumbled downslope, a rolling ball of blue scales and slashing tail that ended up at the bottom of the boulder pile. One leg wedged between two rocks. The pulse-gun disappeared.

Gordon felt the vibration in the skimmer floor increase. Scrambling out of the craft, he looked up the boulder ramp toward where Etsane had fled. She huddled at the top of the ramp, her back against the canyon wall. But someone else also sat with her. "Mahree!"

His love grinned crazily, waving madly for him to join them. "Get up here!"

The boulders vibrated even more strongly. Looking up the narrow canyon, Gordon froze with horror. A wall of gray water mixed with brown sand and red mud roared around the last curve of the canyon. It rushed at him with the speed of a skimmer.

"*Gordon!*"

He unfroze, looked up the boulder ramp, and climbed for his life.

The ground vibration grew. Rain slashed his face. Climbing, he battled against the cascading water that poured over the canyon rim ten meters above Mahree and Etsane. They were being drenched by the cascade, their clothes plastered to their skin. But they were wedged between the uppermost boulders. The cascading waterfall did not dislodge them.

He climbed.

He slipped.

He slammed knees against the stones.

A shuddering roar filled his ears, a sound like all the demons loosed from some distant hell.

Would the Revered Ancestors claim him for their own?

Gordon had offered water and salt yesterday morning, in company with Pokeel and Axum. He'd treated the sarcophagus and body of King A-Um Rakt with the reverence due all burials. And he'd tried his best to learn what could be learned from a myriad of temple-cities soon to be buried under a giant lake. As his homage to the past, his respect shown for the remarkable civilization of a people whose culture predated that of the pharaohs by two thousand years.

"Gordon!" Mahree grabbed him as he fell into her arms.

"Teacher Mitchell!" Etsane too grabbed him.

He turned in their embrace, settled into the hole between the boulders, and then looked down at the bottom of the canyon.

Beloran the Merchant cried out to them. "Save me!"

Shivering from the wet, the cold, the shock of it all, Gordon sat between his two special women. He watched as the high wall of the flash flood rushed over Beloran's blue scales, burying the murderer under tons and tons of sand, water, and small rocks. He shuddered.

Mahree leaned into him. He looked her way. She sat under a waterfall cascading down from the canyon rim, and yet to him, she looked beautiful. She smiled. "You didn't die."

"No, I didn't." He hugged her close, crying with relief, his cries lost among the shuddering roar of Mother's Tears—the flash flood. The bright flash of Mother's Touch shook them with booming thunder. And a new aftershock hit as Father's Snores reminded them all of how dangerous it is to disturb the chambers of Father Earth.

Etsane pushed against him, shaking. He put his other arm around her and, the three of them holding each other close, he joined his women in silent, thankful homage to Mother Sky and Father Earth.

Two days after the earthquakes and floods, Mahree squatted on the hard stone floor of the meeting chamber of the Council of Elders. She faced the central sand disk and the assembled effigy sticks of the clans of the Na-Dina with a thumping heart. She clenched her hands to keep them from shaking. To either side squatted the sixteen Elders, gathered like her in a ring about the pit as they all faced the red porphyry effigies of the Revered Ancestors. Their manner was subdued, their glances at her wondering, and the pile of salt tablets lying in front of each Elder, and before Mahree, lay unused.

She had come to explain how Nordlund had lied about the safety of the dam site, how a flooding of their upriver villages and cities had been narrowly avoided when the clay core of the diversion dam did *not* breach, and how one of their own, one of the People, had murdered Bill Waterston, her predecessor to this very Council. She felt inadequate to the task. But the presence of Gordon, sitting behind her in the shadows of the round-walled chamber, comforted her.

Elder Salween, from the Temple of Earth Quaking, flared her silvery ears, then fixed dark eyes on Mahree. The woman tossed salt onto the sand. "Ambassador Burroughs, how is your camp? Are your homes safe? Are your people uninjured?"

The woman's voice, speaking firmly in High Na-Dina, sounded sympathetic. Mahree rose, bowed deeply to her questioner, then stood straight. "Elder Salween, the Camp survived intact. The ancient flood baffles prevented damage to my people, to our tents, to the Queen's Own Guard, and to the sarcophagus and body of King A-Um Rakt." A hissing sigh of relief echoed around the chamber as she mentioned the last. "The drilling camp at the Lake of Stars was destroyed, but the workers survived. Sadly, the same could not be said for the person of Beloran, of the clan Flooding Waters, of the Trade Merchant, former Liaison to us."

"Beloran!" hissed Elder Hakeem, representative of the King and the Royal House.

Salween ignored the male's breach of protocol, maintaining her stare at Mahree. Well, at least the senior Traditionalist thought she'd done something right. "Our apologies to your clan, and to all damaged by the actions of this member of clan Flooding Waters." Salween's ears fluttered with anger. "Representatives of his clan have promised thirty years of reparations to the family of Interrelator Waterston. Will this, joined with the completion of your Temple Obligation, be sufficient recompense for their loss?''

Mahree wanted to refuse the financial penalty offer, but refrained. It was the way of the People, and perhaps accepting the reach of their Law in this case would assuage the recriminations she heard had broken out among the two factions. She bowed slightly. ''The offer of reparations is accepted by me, on behalf of Bill's parents. I am sure it will comfort them. Thanks to the final report by Investigator Krillen, this case is now closed. The harm to our clan Human is healed.'' She squatted back down.

Salween's ears showed relief. ''The Law of the Revered Ancestors is satisfied.'' The Elder glanced around the circle of other Na-Dina. ''Do my Brothers and Sisters have questions of this brave female, who brought down the escape craft of the One Who May Not Be Named?''

Mahree's face burned. She didn't feel like a hero. She still felt waterlogged, thunder-deafened, sandblasted, and just thankful that Etsane had escaped death. As had Gordon. She almost reached back to grip his hand, but refrained when the Elder representing the Temple of the River tossed salt into the sand pit.

''Ambassador, what is the status of the Great Dam at the First Cataract?'' The rather young female paused, her ears grimacing, as if the question burned her tongue. ''And is it true that Nordlund lied to the Council about the site's safety?''

Mahree rose from her squat, telling herself not to take advantage of the fact that Renzees' Modernist faction had been shown to have had poor judgment. ''Elder Renzees, the clay core of the diversion dam at the First Cataract, which held back a large lake as it forced the River of Life into a diversion tunnel, is *intact*.'' The young female's ears flared with relief. ''But the gravel layers covering the core *are* cracked, seepage is rising, and piping through and under the core is likely to occur. The dam will hold until the lake can be drawn down, or a controlled breach cut into the core.''

She paused, noticing how closely all the Elders listened as she discussed the life blood of their world. Twenty million Na-Dina had been at risk in the upriver area, where a breach-flood would have inundated many houses and cities. The hundred million living in the delta would have been safe, as would have the tens of millions living elsewhere around the shores of the Northern Sea. But it had been a close thing.

Renzees prodded at her. "And the lie of Nordlund? We understand the Snore of Father Earth that cracked the dam facing came from a strike-slip fault lying underneath the dam axis." The woman, surely a hydrologic engineer like many of her sisters at the Temple of the River, grimaced again. "How did such a fault escape *our* notice? We have barged over the First Cataract for millennia, and yet, none from the Temple ever noticed the fault signs. And we are good at Reading the Ground. Lives depend on us."

Mahree knew that. It was one of the two things that made this whole report a ticklish business. Still standing, she bowed slightly. "Elder Renzees, the fault-quake is *not* the responsibility of your Temple, but of Nordlund, which knew of the fault and lied to you." Reaching back, Mahree accepted the duplicate photo-sheets from Gordon, then passed them out to the Elders on either side. "Your Temple *is* highly trained at Reading the Ground—from ground level. But when the Sky Ship of our Mizari colleagues came here, after Nordlund's announcement of the contract with you, they conducted an orbital survey of the entire land-scape of Ancestor's World, using multispectral scanners."

The Elder from the Temple of Storms, a silvery-scaled male of advanced age, tossed his salt and glared at her. "The Sky Ship flew at length through Mother Sky? We had hoped this was not so."

Mahree cursed the delicacy of diplomatic negotiations. Bowing to the Storms Elder, she explained. "Elder Too-loon, such an orbital survey is standard practice by all CLS survey ships. If there is error here, it lies with our own Council of Elders." Mahree faced back to her first questioner. "But, Elder Renzees, this error of ours now reveals what Nordlund knew, and did not tell you." She gestured at the false-color photoprints. "The strike-slip fault lies directly *underneath* the riverbed, under fifty meters of silt and mud, and *parallel* to it. It is invisible from the surface and does not cross over into a cliff face, where you could Read the Ground and see how the soil speaks of such a break.'' The Temple of the River female hissed her relief. ''The fault extends south to the Second Cataract, where the river turns westerly. Our image was made by a synthetic aperture millimeter-wavelength radar. Like the photographs of Investigator Krillen, it tells us many things.''

Mahree paused. All the Elders had their eyes fixed on the reflected radar photos. ''This image also documents slight elevational differences between the canyon rim on the east side, and that on the west. The eastern rim is lower than the western one. I only discovered this myself when I called my office on Shassiszss and requested a copy of the survey report. It arrived at the embassy yesterday.''

The River Temple Elder peered at the photo. ''I see the line, underneath the silt of the riverbed. This *radar* of yours penetrates through soft soil?''

Mahree nodded. ''Yes, it does. Rock bounces back the signal. With millimeter-wavelength radar, the smallest rock alignments, fractures, and discontinuities may be located. Even those buried under piles of dirt.''

Another Elder tossed out salt. ''So the Great Dam can never be built. That is sad. But the People still need hydroelectric power greater than what we already generate elsewhere, in the Mountains of Faith. Ambassador, can other dams be built along the River of Life?''

Mahree recognized the speaker as the young male from the Temple of A-Um Rakt who, last time, had accused her of wanting to keep the Na-Dina in ignorance. That Temple was the all-male home of the electrical engineers, and those female Honorary Members who shared the Temple's obsession with high technology, including dynamos, generators, and munitions.

Telling herself to be fair, she told the truth. ''Yes, Elder Sashoon, other dams *can* be built on side canyons of the River of Life.'' The Na-Dina beamed, his ears fluttering. ''They could be concrete arch dams, stone block dams, or even earthfill dams. But careful study should be made of the impact on the flow of fertile silt down the River of Life. Your farmlands feed many of the People.''

Elder Salween threw salt into the sand pit, blocking the young man from further questions. ''Ambassador, I am sure *all* future dams will be studied carefully, and the benefits versus risks weighed fully. Power we must have, but not at the cost of infertile fields. And we will ask the CLS for assistance in picking a more truthful contractor next time.''

Mahree tossed in her own salt. ''Does that mean you have decided to cancel Nordlund's contract?''

The old woman from the Temple of Earth Quaking blinked slowly. ''Yes. With penalty claims made against them by our Finders of Fact.'' Behind her, Gordon chuckled. Salween looked to him. ''One good result of this near disaster is that Ancestor's Valley will not be flooded, nor will the thousands of other Ancestral ruins which your people have located. Still, we would ask that Philosopher Mitchell remain among us, and continue his work. There are other Royal Tombs in the Valley, and study of them is recommended by the Temple of Records.''

''Excellent!'' Mahree said, feeling relieved. This was just what she had hoped for. Glancing back, she nodded for Gordon to speak. As he rose, she squatted.

''Thank you, Elder Salween,'' he said in a loud tenor that echoed against the room's domed ceiling. ''My team and I are honored to stay and study the Royal Tomb of A-Um Rakt, the remains of the first seven dynasties, and any other site suggested by the Temple of Records.'' Grinning like a five-year-old, Gordon sat back down.

Mahree felt as happy as Gordon. Soon this part of her job would be over. But not until the last questions were asked, and she made her proposal. She tossed salt into the sand pit, startling Salween, who surrendered the floor. ''Ambassador?''

Rising, Mahree looked around the gathered Na-Dina, then fixed on the middle-aged woman who represented the Queen's Household. ''Elder Alasoo, the last time I was here you made several observations, and focused on the need for the People of Ancestor's World to guard your home, on be-half of the Revered Ancestors. Military options were dis-cussed.'' She paused, waited until she had their full attention, and then made her offer. ''Elders of the People, the Irenics ship called to pick up the slaver captives has arrived. It rests now at the spaceport, beside the S.V. *Emerald Scales*. If the Council makes a formal request to our Council on Shassiszss for protection from outsiders, it will be granted. In fact, I am empowered to offer such protection to you.''

Behind her, Gordon stirred. He hadn't been privy to her last FTL holo-talk at the embassy, when she'd visited it yes-terday to get the report and to meet with Krillen to close out the case. Looking around the suddenly silent circle of Na-Dina, she hoped and hoped. The representatives of both the King and the Queen consulted in low, hissing voices; then Elder Alasoo tossed in salt. ''Explain how this protection would work. Would the craft be always a mark upon the face of Mother Sky?''

''No!'' Mahree calmed her fast-beating heart, and ex-plained the suggestion given her by the Irenics captain. ''Captain Hhortha indicates his ship could monitor local space while parked on the far side of Mother's Daughter. The image of our Sky Ship would not bespoil the robe of Mother Sky. It would fly through Mother Sky, and land on your world, only when absolutely necessary. Advance notice would be given. Permission would be requested of the Coun-cil.''

Alasoo stilled her ears. Mahree nearly swore, unable to read the woman's expression. Then they fluttered with the sign of satisfaction. ''Acceptable. The Queen's Household, and the King, accept your offer of protection, with the con-ditions stated by you.'' The woman's body attitude turned suddenly fierce. ''Be sure to warn your Captain that should he, or any of his people, approach our mountains, our riv-ers, our canyons *without* our permission, they will be fired on by the Queen's Own Guard. Cannon are being emplaced in the proper places. As is the Hand of Mother Sky.''

Mahree felt a chill. Had the Na-Dina truly leaped ahead and developed a pulse-cannon? That's what the words for

"Hand" indicated. Frankly, she did not wish to learn what ancient secrets were still to be discovered on Ancestor's World. Gordon could handle that better than she. "Of course," she said, bowing low. "I will warn the Captain. But contact through our embassy and with the Interrelator will prevent such misunderstandings."

"So we trust." Alasoo squatted down.

Elder Talteen, from the Temple of Records, tossed in salt and fanned her ears excitedly. "Ambassador, it is time to hear pleasant tidings. Would you tell us all the great news? Tell us the Words of our Great King A-Um Rakt. The ones uncovered by the young female, Black Stone?"

Behind her Gordon chuckled again, as pleased as she that Etsane's nickname was known to the Council of Elders. Though her knees hurt from all the standing, Mahree bowed to the old Philosopher-Historian and smiled warmly. "Elder Talteen, Black Stone is also Etsane Mwarka, a woman of the Amharan people of Ethiopia, and descended from a royal line. This last week she found the key to translating First Dynasty Na-Dina. The records of the first seven dynasties are unlocked. The inscription at the Royal Tomb will be fully translated later today, when our camp gathers inside."

Mahree paused, letting the excited hissings of the Elders die down. "But a glyph-wall in the City of White Stone tells the start of this story. It speaks of your Great King, of the Mizari people who visited your world six millennia ago, and of the honor both peoples showed to the Revered Ancestors."

She began, reciting from memory. "*In the year when Father's Snoring had stilled and the crops were tall and green, during the reign of King A-Um Rakt, Father to his people, Builder of the Great Pond at Shir-Li, Reader of the stars in Mother Sky, and priest to the Ancestors of Faith, there came Spirits from Mother Sky . . .*"

CHAPTER 16

♦

The Path of Honor

Khuharkk' stood alone at the edge of the Camp landing field, waiting for Mahree and Doctor Mitchell's jumpjet to finish landing. They'd just returned from meeting with the Council of Elders in Spirit, and he was eager to tell them of his career decision. It had been long in coming, but his talks with Pokeel of the Guard had finally cleared the way to his full understanding of the Path of Honor among the Na-Dina. Of how devotion to the Revered Ancestors guided daily life, and how, as on Hurrreeah, everything one did in the present was a mark of Honor, or dishonor, both for one's people and for one's ancestors. That knowledge had cleansed him of his fear of the dead, of tunnel-tombs, and brought new hope to him.

Unable to hold in his joy, he began dancing. Tail held high, he rocked from foot to foot, hand to hand, then jumped into the air and twisted full circle. His dance honored all he had learned.

With belly jets flaring, the jumpjet settled down onto its rubber pads and the stair-ramp extruded. First out the door was Mahree Burroughs, still dressed in her formal Star-Bridge uniform despite the midday heat. Doctor Mitchell followed after her, wearing less formal clothing of cotton pants, safari shirt, and a bag slung over one shoulder.

Mahree reached the bottom of the ramp and smiled at him. "Khuharkk'!" she said in Simiu. "Isn't that the Dance of Problems Resolved?"

"Yes, oh yes!" he said excitedly, then regained control of himself. He ended the dance, and settled for a shifting from one foot and hand pair to another.

Mitchell raised his eyebrows. "Problems resolved? Didn't realize you had any *big* problems, Khuharkk'. Not since you got yourself those two Honor Scars on your shoulders."

Khuharkk' stood still, feeling total surprise. He'd almost *forgotten* them. What an un-Simiu thing to do! "Yes. No. And, oh! It's just that it's been such a hard thing for me, deciding whether to be a professional Archaeologist like you, Doctor Mitchell, or the Interrelator that I went to StarBridge Academy to become."

Mahree eyed him closely. "You've made your decision, then?"

"Yes!" He stood up, which brought him to shoulder level of the First Interrelator. "Ambassador, I wish to stay here on Ancestor's World to serve my people—and yours—as the Interrelator to the Na-Dina."

The Philosopher looked disappointed. Mahree grinned happily. "Khuharkk', that's just wonderful!" she said, her words changing to a mix of hisses and clicks.

"Oh!" Except for her first words, she'd been speaking to him in High Na-Dina, and he'd been replying the same way, without use of his voder. He'd done the same with Philosopher Mitchell, hardly lisping his English. "I forgot to turn on my voder," he said in surprise, "but it made no difference."

Mitchell nodded. "That's the mark of a fully translingual Interrelator." The older man grinned broadly. "I'm very happy for you, Khuharkk'. My loss is the CLS's gain, and the gain in Honor is Hurrreeah's. It looks like your pair project with Sumiko taught you both good English and some useful flexibility."

"Yes, she helped me a lot." Then he rolled his shoulders, flaring his Honor Scars. "But my talks with Marshall Pokeel of the Guard helped just as much, along with Axum's patience in teaching me Na-Dina."

Mahree stepped closer to him, putting down her own bag on the hot sand. Crouching, she gave him the Simiu greeting salute of respect, bowing her head, then touching forehead, breast, and finally extending her hand, fingers curled, palm up.

The Philosopher rather clumsily copied her. Mahree smiled at the Simiu youth. "Yes, Gordon is right. You show great Honor to your clan, and to all of Hurrreeah by this choice. Your mother and brothers will be proud of you."

Khuharkk' hoped so. But even if this did not match the glory of Arena fights, it felt right to him. It was here that he'd come to value the concept of dead Ancestors who watched over the living, and lost his fear of tombs. Here that he had grown to admire the Na-Dina Path of Honor. He wanted to spend the rest of his life here, on Ancestor's World, no matter the heat, no matter how much his fur matted with sweat, and no matter that it lay close to Sorrow Sector. He again made his plea to Mahree.

"Ambassador, there is need for a new CLS Interrelator to the Na-Dina. I ask for the job. I ask for two reasons. One, to show Honor to the Revered Ancestors of the People. Second, to Honor the memory of Bill Waterston."

Mahree gasped. "That's very special, Khuharkk'." Her expression softened. "Bill was my friend, too. I think he would be pleased."

"I hope so," Khuharkk' said, recalling the young human's easy comradeship. "Now, I think I understand the Path of Honor on Ancestor's World well enough to follow in his dance steps."

Philosopher Mitchell clapped him on the shoulder. "Khuharkk', you do not need to *follow* after Bill. You will dance your own path into the future, shoulder by shoulder with his spirit and his memory."

Mahree blinked quickly, then stood up, putting her arm around Gordon's waist. "Yes," she said, nodding solemn agreement. "Gordon is right. Khuharkk', follow your own Path to Honor. That will be the best memorial you can offer to Bill." She paused, then glanced to the archaeologist. "Gordon, I'm sorry to pull rank on you, but the Na-Dina need an Interrelator *now*, and I can't think of a better choice than Khuharkk'."

"Oh, Mahree, thank you!" Khuharkk' said, struggling to maintain his professional demeanor. "I will work hard for the CLS, for Hurrreeah, and for the Na-Dina!"

Mitchell sighed, then pointed toward the camp. "Mahree, I surrender. But surely he can stay for Etsane's reading of the Royal Tomb ideoglyphs? They were waiting for us to return before proceeding."

She nodded, then picked up her bag. "You're right. Khuharkk' can stay here until tomorrow, when the jumpjet returns to Spirit." Mahree turned to head for camp.

The archaeologist looked thoughtful. Khuharkk' kept silent, sensing that now, after the floods, the quakes, the storms, and the discovery of who had murdered Bill, it was a time for reflection.

For all of them.

He'd made his Dance of Problems Resolved. He'd overcome his fear of the tombs where dead Ancestors were honored. He'd pledged to be Honor-Bound with Etsane. Now, he must live with those decisions. He hoped to return often to assist Doctor Mitchell with his excavations in Ancestor's Valley. And he planned to stay in frequent contact with Etsane. But his first duty would now be to the Na-Dina, and to Hurrreeah. Two peoples, one Path of Honor.

When everyone finished crowding up to peer in at the Royal Tomb of A-Um Rakt, King of the First Dynasty of the People, Etsane moved forward. She sat atop the red porphyry bier on which had rested the dead king's sarcophagus. The main chamber floor had been cleared, but a rope still cordoned off the Treasury side room, off to the right. The king's grave-goods clustered in there. She drank in the yellow gleam of gold, the verdigis of old bronze, and the tarnished brown of silver as scores of items sparkled under the artificial lights. They were the treasure given to the king by his People, to go with him on his journey to meet the Ancestors.

Time. Time to tell the tale. Crossing her legs, and then settling her formal Amharan robes about her, Etsane looked back over her shoulder at the people who watched and waited for her to begin.

Her old mentor Professor Greyshine stood looking on proudly, his thick gray mane brushed to a glossy highlight. He stared at her directly, in the Na-Dina compliment-giving mode. As did his mate, Doctor Strongheart, whose own burial analysis had confirmed the content of her translations at the City of White Stone, and now here in the Royal Tomb.

Standing inside the tomb and close by the Treasury entrance were *astamari* Mitchell and Mahree Burroughs, two people to whom she owed her life, and from whom she had learned much. Without Mahree's initial spotting of those Mizari Four glyphs in the Lab, she might not have hypnostudied that dead language. She would have been unprepared to make full use of the glyph-wall hidden in the catacombs under the Great Plaza of *Segor A-mun*, to use its proper name. They smiled encouragingly at her, looking on like proud parents.

Her heart thumped inside her as she thought again of her father Mefume, of his hopes for her, and of how his hard tasking had led her to knowledge, to hard work, and to the discovery of the century. She would be famous across all the CLS. Now, she must earn that premature notoriety.

She shifted her seating to face the piled-up coils of the single Mizari among her colleagues. The old Ceramicist lay coiled to the left of the tunnel entrance, occupying a place of honor inside the tomb, rather than crowded into the narrow tunnel with most of the others.

"Esteemed Lorezzzs," she hissed in Mizari, then lifted her hands over her head to form a triangle in the traditional greeting gesture. "Your people can be very proud of how one group of them, six thousand years ago, gave help, insight and sharing to the People of Ancestor's World." She smiled. "Yes, there *is* a clue in these glyphs to the fate of the Mizari Lost Colony."

Lorezzzs lifted her triangular head, her neck tentacles fluttering excitedly, her amber and silver scales glittering under the lights. "There is? Wonderful!" She stared at Etsane with glowing emerald eyes. "But I can wait a few moments longer. You must give credit where credit is due, yes?" The Mizari woman tilted her head toward the tunnel entrance, in front of which gathered the Na-Dina contingent.

"Yes, I must acknowledge the critical help of the People." Etsane stared at Axum, dig crew chief extraordinary, at Pokeel of the Guard who stood at formal attention, and at the two representatives of the Temple of Records, an old male and female who, as Philosopher-Historians of their people, had been of critical help to her in translating the idiomatic glyphs. "Thank you, my friends." All four Na-Dina fluttered their fan-ears excitedly and stared back at her. She accepted the compliment, then broke her own stare to look behind them and fix the Drnian male. "Natual," she said. "I'm glad you're going to be staying on, too. I'm looking forward to more dinners."

After all this practice, his version of a smile came quickly. "I am looking forward to that also, Etsane."

Etsane looked forward to the future. Would her friendship and more with Natual actually become a relationship? She did not know . . . but she was going to give it a chance to work, she'd decided that.

After all, she'd have lots of time, spending years in Ancestor's Valley working to record and decipher the thousands of inscriptions and iconographic images of the first seven dynasties. It was too much for one lifetime, but with Natual's help, and that of all the others, she could make a dent in it.

Breaking eye contact, Etsane turned back to face the golden ideoglyphs that covered the entire back wall of the tomb, and reached out to either side. "Ohhh!" The way they gleamed under the lights, the beauty and sweep of the seven rows of glyphs, filling the wall from floor to domed ceiling, from one side of the tunnel entrance around to the opposite side, sobered her. Now, she would reach back six thousand years. Now, she would open the first pages in the Book of the People. Now, she would speak of the glory, the wonder, and the danger of the past.

"My friends," she said, speaking in High Na-Dina, "these glyphs tell a wonderful history, only part of which you have heard. Hear now the entire words of the Revered Ancestors."

Behind her, talon-feet scraped raw stone, boots rubbed the dusty floor, and scaled coils rasped as all leaned forward, eager to hear. Reading from left to right, from top to bottom, Etsane began speaking in a loud, clear voice.

"*The Great King A-Um Rakt, Father to his people, Builder of the Great Pond at Shir-Li, Reader of the stars in Mother Sky, priest to the Ancestors of Faith, and Ruler of Segor A-mun, was the first of the People to speak with the Sky Spirits who descended from Mother Sky. The rainbow-scaled ones were all tail and lacked a talon with which to write in the white stone of the city walls, but they knew how to read the movement of the stars, they knew the ways of dam building, canal digging, well digging, water raising and salt mining, and they knew the hearts of the People. Like the children of the River of Life, the Sky Spirits hungered to know the mind of the Revered Ancestors, whom they said resided somewhere among the folds of the black robe of Mother Sky. They had come to Ancestor's World in search of signs that their own ancestral Spirits had passed this way on the journey to knowledge and the afterlife.*"

Etsane paused as, behind her, her Mizari colleague gasped with excitement at the news of the Mizari Lost Colony. Feeling the chill of the ages upon her skin, Etsane drew closer her robes, placed her faith in the ghostly spirit of her father, and continued.

"*Some signs they found in the Mountains of Faith. Of those signs, none of the People know their nature. But the rainbow-scaled ones felt a debt was owed to the People, and so they stayed among the People, as the guests of the Great King, for forty risings and fallings of the River of*

Life. Much did they teach us. Coming in the eighth year of the reign of the Great King, they spoke to him of how Father's Snores might be observed in a large pond of certain design. The Temple of Earth Quaking had suspected such, but the method of calculating this design was learned from the Sky Spirits. In the fourteenth year of the King's reign, they did observe the male priests of the Temple of Storms flying through the air upon wooden wings that rose when the heated air of Father Earth lifted in homage to Mother Sky. The Sky Spirits warned that such craft might draw the Touch of Mother Sky, especially if made of metal. They gave counsel upon how such flights might be made in safety, speaking of bags containing the essence of Mother's Eye. And from that day forward, only the pilots of the Temple venture forth into the high realms of Mother Sky.

"That's where Beloran learned to build his paraglider!" cried Doctor Mitchell from behind Etsane, interrupting her.

She glanced over her shoulder at the man, who blushed now, as if he'd committed a social error. He hadn't. "Doctor, you may interrupt me any time you wish. But I in turn will feel free to challenge your theories. In the years ahead, as I work with you, that may happen often. Shall we keep count?" She grinned at him, feeling mischievous.

He grinned back, then winked at Mahree. "Well, you got Khuharkk', but at least she's staying here. I think I got the better part of the deal."

Mahree eyed Etsane's new mentor with wry affection. "Gordon, please shut up, and let's listen." The woman faced Etsane and stared. "Etsane Mwarka, of the clan Amhara, please continue."

Etsane faced back to the golden glyphs, picking up where she'd left off. "*In the twenty-sixth year of the reign of Great King A-Um Rakt, the rainbow-scaled Sky Spirits showed the People how to dig a water well deeper than any in the city of Segor A-mun. With stone smelted from the Mountains of Faith, they did devise a water-cooled drill whose bore reached the deepest chambers of Father Earth.*" She paused to accept a cup of water from cream-furred Ttalatha, who had sneaked in to sit at the talon-feet of the Na-Dina representatives. Sumiko did the same, followed by Khuharkk', to whom she was Honor-Bound. His presence pleased her immensely, but she had work to finish.

"Thank you, Ttalatha. Now comes the critical part of the text." She faced back and resumed her reverential translating of the ideoglyphs.

"*In the forty-sixth year of the Great King's reign, the Temples of the People divided into two disputing camps. One camp hailed the Sky Spirits as the Ancestors newly incarnate, returned from the winds of Mother Sky and the chambers of Father Earth, to rule over the People. The other camp, that led by the Great King, warned against such impiety, saying the Sky Spirits were persons like the People, but of greater knowledge and more ancient history. A-Um Rakt pled with his people to be calm, but a challenger arose in the delta, asserting the Sky Spirits favored her. These events sorely tried the rainbow-scaled visitors, and saddened them so much they announced their intention of leaving Ancestor's World. This they did in the forty-eighth year of the Great King's reign, saying that they left to explore further the mind of the Spirits in the Sky, but that some day, when the People had forgotten them, their descendants would return to visit. To such end they gave the King gifts of wonder, by which their descendants would know them. Then they left.*"

Etsane wiped the tears from her eyes. Such a sad way for the meeting of two peoples to end. And yet, while they had visited, the Mizari Lost Colony had helped the nascent civilization of the Na-Dina, a culture based like many from ancient times on the control of rivers and the building of great structures to enshrine their power. On Earth, such cultures were called "hydraulic civilizations," since the control of water was essential to the success of agriculture and feeding the many people who lived in the early cities. As in Dynastic Egypt, so here on Ancestor's World. Behind her, a voice spoke in Mizari, speaking it as a native.

"Does . . . do the glyphs tell where the Lost Colony went?" asked Lorezzzs. "And what happened afterward?"

"Esteemed Lorezzzs, they do not. But listen to the final chapter." She faced the bottom two rows of glyphs with dry eyes and finished a bright and shining story.

"*Great King A-Um Rakt sorrowed at the leaving of the Sky Spirits, but told his People they must work hard, learn the ways of knowledge, and show devotion to Mother Sky and Father Earth, so as to please the Revered Ancestors. Perhaps then, the People could follow where the rainbow scales had gone. All the Temples and most of the People accepted his Words. The delta challenger was defeated. Great cities were raised. Great ponds were built. The annual floods were sent farther afield, to new lands where crops were grown, animals were herded, and wild game was captured, all to feed the Children of the World. Then, in the fiftieth year of his reign, Great King A-Um Rakt, Father to his People, went to join the Revered Ancestors. Here rest his mortal remains, cast loose upon the River of Life for his final journey in the Royal Barge. May he know the Ancestors.*"

"Oh!" cried Sumiko, her voice strained. "What a glorious story."

Etsane turned around, facing her audience. The two Philosopher-Historians from the Temple of Records lay prostrate on the stone floor of the Royal Tomb, overcome with piety as they stared past her at the words she had unlocked.

Pokeel stared at Etsane, her expression satisfied. "It is as the Queen trusted. The Sky Infidels . . . no, the rainbow-scaled ones, they came to show Honor to the People. They were not the parents of the People, but instead, their aunts and uncles. We are grateful."

Astamari Mitchell beamed at her, his eyes wet. "Extraordinary, Etsane! You caught the poetry of their words as well as the key meanings. All the CLS will honor you."

Etsane sighed, feeling exhausted, then spoke somberly to her Teacher, to Mahree, and to all her colleagues. "That is nice. But what matters to me now, at this moment, is how I have honored my people the Amharas, and the memory of my father Mefume." Mahree nodded her understanding.

Blinking fast, Etsane stared a moment at Natual, then

nodded at Hrashoi, Eloiss, Sumiko, Khuharkk', and all the others. "My colleagues, my friends, my Honor partner, you helped me feel accepted here. You gave unstintingly of your professional knowledge whenever I asked. I thank you." Then she faced back to Mahree. "Ambassador Burroughs, I hope you will agree to be my co-author on the *long* paper I must now write about this work."

"Of course I agree." Mahree's expression was as serious as hers. "But only as junior author. It was your work, your insight that cracked this, Etsane."

She turned away from them then, facing back to stare at the golden glyphs. She did not want them to see her crying. Nor did she want them to see how she saw, in the glyphs she had decoded, the ghost of her father Mefume . . . smiling back at her.

At last, there was no longer a need to prove herself to him. She felt free. Free to have a personal life in addition to a great career. Would that life include Natural as a possible life-partner? There was no way to know.

But her career would ever be with her, just as the robes of her people and the gentle touch of her father were never gone from her.

Gordon turned over in bed and looked down at Mahree. Despite the passionate lovemaking they had shared only moments before, despite the joyous release they had shared, she looked lost, almost desolate.

The night air sighed in under the edges of his tent, cooling the sweat on his skin, and even the rumbles of quake aftershocks were muted, as if Father Earth was much pleased with Gordon's work among the Na-Dina. In the night sky, Mother's Daughter hung low on the western horizon, her white glow a pearly gleam that penetrated into his tent, illuminating his work table, the camp radio, his box of dig momentoes, the leather case in which he kept the pictures of his daughters, and the bed on which he and Mahree lay together.

"I love you," he whispered. It was the first time he had

said it straight out, apart from the murmured endearments
while making love.

She turned over to look back at him, her dark eyes full
of sadness. "And I love you, Gordon."

He drew a deep breath. "But . . ." he continued for her,
bracing himself to hear what he didn't think he'd be able
to bear hearing.

"But I can't stay here. You know that," she whispered,
her fingers tracing lightly over his sweaty shoulders, down
across his chest to his flat belly. "I have to leave. Now that
Khuharkk' is taking over as Interrelator, and Bill's murder
is solved, my work here is done. I have to go back to my
real life."

"No," he said softly. He leaned forward to kiss her, a
long, slow, passionate kiss. He felt her immediate response.
"Don't go. We're good together. We could . . ." He swallowed, unable to force the words "get married" out even
when he tried.

She smiled at him. "Gordon. You have your life here, I
have mine elsewhere. I have a daughter, and my work. You
have two daughters, and your work. Our lives just won't
mix, my love."

Pain smote him. Deep inside. Where the scars of the
divorce had begun to heal thanks to Mahree's bright smile,
her caring touch, her quick mind as they worked together
on the mystery of Bill's murder and the glory of the Royal
Tomb. He felt the scars begin to bleed again. "I . . . Mahree, how can you love me, yet leave tomorrow?"

She nuzzled closer to him, her breath warm against his
chest. "How? Because I love Rob also. He is the father of
my child. And . . . I love Claire, and miss her so very
much!" She choked, almost breaking down. "Gordon, I
didn't plan for this to happen. I didn't expect it. But I found
in you something I'd yearned for as a young girl, found
with Rob, then lost. Now, I must try to refind it. I owe that
to my family."

Echoes. The words echoed in his ears, the meaning came
to his mind, but the sense of them, ah, that was too painful
to grasp. "But I . . . I'm afraid I'll go back to drinking hard

again. You were my support. You were the one who made me see I could move away from being bitter about the past. Stay with me. I need you.''

Mahree reached out, hugging him close, so close her lips rested beside his ear. ''I can't be your crutch.'' She held him as he flinched, trying to pull away. Her comforting touch held him close. ''You're a strong man, Gordon. You don't need me, or anyone, to be your crutch. But you do need one other thing, besides the memory of our love.''

Bitterness filled his mouth. She was going. Of that he had no doubt. But . . . at least she cherished the memory of their love. He kissed the top of her head, her forehead, then reached to cup her chin in his hand, pushing her face back enough so he could look deep into her tear-filled eyes. ''For me, our love will never be just a memory.'' She flinched, but he held her chin, keeping their gazes locked. ''What *else* do I need, Mahree, other than you?''

She smiled softly, leaned forward to kiss lightly his lips, then withdrew, though she rested her face in the cup of his hands. ''You need your *daughters* here, Gordon. You need the family you once thought lost to you. Call them! Use the FTL holo-tank at the embassy! Call them, tell them you love them, and I am certain as I am a mother to my own daughter, your Moira and Casey will come to you. They're old enough to travel on their own. Call them, Gordon. Call them!''

The pain in his chest receded a bit. He smiled at Mahree. ''You are so wise. Yes. I'll call them. And perhaps, perhaps they will find their old dad is not such a bore.''

''Never that!'' Mahree said, showing joy through her tears. ''You've taught me so much, too. From you I've learned that I can still fall in love, that romance doesn't have to fade away and die when you grow up. Even though I can never give up what I do, to stay on one planet, you taught me to enjoy the blessings I have now.'' Mahree sighed, lying back down to rest her head in the crook of his shoulder. ''For that alone, I will love you until the day I die.''

Gordon held her for the last time, lying there on his field

cot, their skin bare, their senses attuned to one another and to the night air. And in that holding, he realized this was not another failure. In their joining, in their love shared, he had regained his self-respect.

Yes, the night held many blessings.

Epilogue

Mahree sat alone in the viewing lounge of the S.V. *Emerald Scales*, treasuring a last look at the browns, whites, and rust reds of Ancestor's World. She was leaving behind the ancient Na-Dina, leaving behind Gordon and the love they'd shared, and beginning her journey home. Though the ship was crowded with the freed captives, at the moment she had the entire lounge to herself. By the Ambassador's order.

She stared at space with no one to watch her as she drank it all in. The vid-windows showed her the black, gleaming robe of Mother Sky. They showed the high peaks, valleys, and rivers of Father Earth. And they showed, far across the Arm of Orion, the distant yellow star that was Sol.

She would journey first to StarBridge, to spend a long family vacation with Claire and Rob. And then . . .

And then she would go back to work. She had a duty to herself, and to the CLS. The hydra-monster of slavery, which they had thought dead forever, had returned. Somewhere in the backwaters of Sorrow Sector, slavers were plying their trade, buying and selling intelligent beings. She had to try to stop it, to alert the Security Council to what she had seen and experienced on Ancestor's World. They would need more Irenics, more patrols . . .

It was a daunting task.

Mahree looked out through another viewport, the one facing down the length of Orion Arm. According to Etsane's translations, and the star map painted onto the domed ceiling lying above the sarcophagus of A-Um Rakt, the Mizari Lost Colony had gone in that direction. Which star were they heading for? Had they even known themselves?

But at least it was a clue. After six thousand years of not knowing, it was *something*.

Mahree smiled to herself. Not for nothing had the Great King been named a Reader of the Stars.

Looking down at her feet, she rested her eyes on the squarish box that had been entrusted to her. It held a gift from the People of Ancestor's World to the people of Shassiszss. Inside that box, preserved under a stasis field, rested the Mizari relics that Gordon and Khuharkk' had found lying at the foot of the King's bier. The Star Shrine, the Sacred Shriszz, and the Constellation Globe lay inside. The dark brown box was carved from the scented wood of one of the giant trees that grew tall on the slopes of the Mountains of Faith.

The Council of Elders had sent the box as a gesture to respresent their formal acceptance of the offer of protected status from the Council of the CLS. As the founders of the CLS, the Mizari would surely accept this gift in the spirit in which it had been given.

Reaching down to the travel bag that lay beside her seat, Mahree pulled out the holo-cube of Claire.

Her daughter was tall and slim. Wavy chestnut hair reached to her narrow shoulders. But it was Claire's eyes that held her, that spoke to her in words from memory.

"I don't understand why you have to go! Mom, you could get killed out there!"

She took a deep, cleansing breath, thinking of all that had happened. "Claire, I kept my promise to you. I didn't die. I was smart, and I stayed alive."

That last wasn't completely true. Had she been smart to fall in love with Gordon?

The CLS Ambassador-at-Large didn't know. She just knew that she would never give up the experience, the pain, the joy, even if offered a trip back in time to redo her choices.

Mahree smiled at her daughter's image. "Claire, I'm coming home. Home to you." She cradled the cube in her hands, then, impulsively, hugged it to her breast, thinking that soon she'd be able to hold her child in the flesh.

She sensed that the Revered Ancestors were smiling upon her, and she turned back to the viewport for a last look at Ancestor's World. "Good-bye," she whispered softly.

Afterword

Hello again! It's nice to see you after more than a year away.

I hope you enjoyed this further StarBridge adventure, and I'm glad to tell you that StarBridge #7 is already well underway. Ru Emerson is writing an exciting book that we've entitled *Voices of Chaos*. It tells the story of two young StarBridge graduates who find themselves trapped on a planet on the brink of civil war—and genocide.

Will Prince Khyriz be able to save the Interrelators from the ravages of war? Will Magdalena and Alexis be able to negotiate with the CLS to save the Asha from extermination?

Find out in StarBridge #7, *Voices of Chaos*, which should be out in mid 1997.

And, as always, thanks for reading this series. I still enjoy getting mail from readers c/o Berkley (and I answer all of it, though sometimes I run *very* behind, because my first job, after all, is writing *books*, not answering mail), but I've now entered the electronic age. Readers wishing to send me e-mail can also reach me at: A.CRISPIN@GENIE.COM.

See you next book!

—Ann C. Crispin
March, 1996